The Inner Sea
Ruled by Chaos
Crawling with Dragons

"This Cult of the Dragon. They must be mighty wizards with a profound knowledge of wyrms to warp their lives into undeath and leave their minds intact."

"I suppose."

"You will help me find them, for that is your craft. They will then tell me how to stop the dragons threatening Serôs. I will do so in Umberlee's name, and afterward, the other shalarins will return to her altars in penance and thanksgiving."

Anton shook his head. "You don't understand. There's no reason to assume the cult has what you need, and it wouldn't matter even if they do. They *worship* dragons. They won't help anybody hurt or hinder them."

"If they won't give up their secrets willingly, we will take them."

The Year of Rogue Dragons author Richard Lee Byers crafts a tale of vengeance and deception that can only be felt in the hearts of

The Priests

The Priests

Lady of Poison
BRUCE R. CORDELL

Mistress of the Night
DAVE GROSS & DON BASSINGTHWAITE

Maiden of Pain
KAMERON M. FRANKLIN

Queen of the Depths
RICHARD LEE BYERS

ALSO BY RICHARD LEE BYERS
The Year of Rogue Dragons
The Rage
The Rite
The Ruin
May 2006

R.A. Salvatore's War of the Spider Queen
Dissolution

Sembia
The Halls of Stormweather
The Shattered Mask

The Rogues
The Black Bouquet

FORGOTTEN REALMS®

THE
PRIESTS

QUEEN OF DEPTHS

RICHARD LEE BYERS

Wizards
OF THE COAST™

QUEEN OF THE DEPTHS

©2005 Wizards of the Coast, Inc.

Distributed in the United States by Holtzbrinck Publishing. Distributed in Canada by Fenn Ltd.

Distributed to the hobby, toy, and comic trade in the United States and Canada by regional distributors.

Distributed worldwide by Wizards of the Coast, Inc. and regional distributors.

Cover art by Marc Fishman
First Printing: September 2005
Library of Congress Catalog Card Number: 2004116886

9 8 7 6 5 4 3 2 1

ISBN: 0-7869-3737-8
ISBN-13: 978-0-7869-3737-0
620-88600740-001-EN

U.S., CANADA,
ASIA, PACIFIC, & LATIN AMERICA
Wizards of the Coast, Inc.
P.O. Box 707
Renton, WA 98057-0707
+1-800-324-6496

EUROPEAN HEADQUARTERS
Hasbro UK Ltd
Caswell Way
Newport, Gwent NP9 0YH
GREAT BRITAIN
Save this address for your records.

Visit our web site at **www.wizards.com**

For Eric and Brooke

THE PRIESTS

Hetham studied the murky gap between the dark mounds that were the hills. Nothing there yet, or at least, nothing he could see.

The problem was that despite the enchantment a sea-elf Dukar had cast on him to augment his vision, he couldn't see much. Like all mermen, he was a creature of the upper waters. He wasn't used to these cold, desolate depths. Light as he knew it scarcely existed here, and clouds of particulate matter, a byproduct of the teeming life hundreds of feet higher up, drifted down to obscure any feeble gleam that did arise.

With a flick of his piscine tail, he swam a little closer, squinted, and still saw nothing. He cursed.

Ingvatorc chuckled. "Relax, my friend. They'll be here soon enough."

Hetham's mouth tightened in irritation.

Thus far, the mad dragons had mainly attacked As'arem, the confederated shalarin kingdoms. But the spindly, crested shalarins were part of the Nantarn Alliance, and so troops from all six allied races, and others that merely maintained friendly relations with them, had united to battle the wyrms. Companies of mermen stood with slender sea-elf crossbowmen and goggle-eyed locathah spearmen with jutting fins ringing their faces and lining their limbs. Tritons, beings somewhat resembling mermen, but with scaly legs ending in flippers in place of tails, tended gigantic crabs that served as both mounts and weapons. Morkoths, their forms an ugly blend of fishy heads and octopod bodies, inspected the ranks of their sahuagin and scrag slave soldiers. Dolphins and whales swam about the periphery of the formation.

The battle order put Hetham and his company next to a band of storm giants, towering manlike beings possessed of prodigious strength and potent magic. The merman knew he was lucky to fight in proximity to such formidable comrades. Still, no doubt because he was nervous, he found Ingvatorc's calm and cheerful manner grating.

"What if the wyrms don't come through the gap?" the merman asked. "What if they circle to take us from behind, or from above?"

"They won't," said Ingvatorc, strands of his long, dark hair and beard shifting in the current. "The scouts and diviners agree. You have to remember, the wyrms have gone crazy. They no longer have sense enough to keep an eye out for trouble or use clever tactics. They just swim until they find something to kill, tear into it, then rush onward—" The giant stopped and stared. "They're here. Get ready." He waved his hand, signaling to others that the time for battle was at hand.

Across the formation, other officers did the same, and everyone made his final preparations as silently as possible. The wyrms surely sensed that someone awaited them beyond the gap, but if the warriors of the alliance were quiet—and lucky—the cover afforded by the twin hills might keep the drakes from realizing just how strong a force had ventured forth to engage them.

Hetham heard a rasping screech, a snarl, but still couldn't see anything. Then, at last, the notch between the slopes seemed to churn. Vague, serpentine shapes erupted from the gloom.

For a final moment that seemed to stretch on and on until Hetham wanted to scream, nobody attacked. Then captains and sergeants bellowed their orders. Volleys of crossbow bolts streaked through the water, though Hetham and his company didn't shoot. As yet, they were too far away. Spellcasters pointed wands and staves, or chanted incantations and lashed their hands through mystic passes. Darts of crimson light; glowing, slashing, disembodied blades; and pouncing, seething masses of shadow assailed the wyrms. Glaring at a huge black drake with a withered, leprous mask, Ingvatorc sang more than declaimed his words of power. He ended on a deep, sustained note, and rounds of milky phosphorescence materialized above and below the reptile. They snapped shut on it and engulfed it completely, like an oyster clasping a pearl.

For an instant, it almost seemed as if the allies could batter and harass the wyrms with impunity. One of the mermen cheered. Then, in a surging blur of motion, the reptiles struck back.

A dragon eel, as long as Ingvatorc was tall, with a few crossbow quarrels sticking in its dull scales, lashed its tail and hurtled into the midst of a band of elves. Each snap of its beak obliterated a warrior, nipping him to fragments, or snatching every trace of him from view as the creature swallowed him whole. A haze of blood suffused the space around it.

Wings beating, shimmering water drakes shot through a band of shalarins, wheeled, and streaked at them again. On each pass, they ripped at their prey with fang and claw.

A colossal sea drake, a wyrm somewhat like the dragon eels but even bigger, whipped around a whale, confining and crushing the cetacean in its coils, tearing great chunks of flesh away with its jaws. Dolphins swirled about the duel, hammering the drake with their snouts, but to little effect.

A long-necked dragon turtle, like a living fortress in its massive, bladed shell, opened its beak and spewed its breath weapon. The water in front it bubbled furiously, suddenly boiling hot. The locathahs caught in the effect floundered in agony.

Meanwhile, the dragons capable of casting spells, or possessed of innate magical powers, blasted arcane attacks at the wizards and priests among their foes. The reptiles might be insane, but they still had sufficient wit to use the full range of their abilities and to strive to eliminate their most dangerous adversaries first.

A topaz dragon, eyes glowing like yellow flame, hide reflecting light as if it were a living jewel in truth, stared at a half dozen morkoths. Unlike many of the supernatural effects being conjured on every side, the wyrm's power didn't manifest with a flash, a whine of sound, or anything else perceptible to Hetham's senses. But the morkoth wizards convulsed, their tentacles whipping about. Instantly, the topaz beat its wings and plunged forward to finish them off while they were helpless. The morkoths' bodyguards, sahuagin with round, black eyes; webbed, clawed hands; and maws full of needle fangs, leaped to interpose themselves between their masters and the threat, but the topaz smashed through them in an instant.

A black dragon snarled at a trio of sea-elf Dukars, the enchanted coral bonded to their skeletons now visible to all, jutting from their hands and twining about their limbs to serve as weapons and armor. The water around the mages darkened, curdled. They flailed, evidently unable to breathe, and struggled to flounder clear of the cloud. One of them succeeded, but only to blunder into the dragon's jaws.

The glowing, clamlike prison Ingvatorc had conjured winked out of existence, liberating the black inside. The dragon snarled words of power. To Hetham's horror, Ingvatorc changed, shrinking, his limbs becoming soft, clear, and shapeless as the substance of a jellyfish. Until something, his own magical abilities or sheer strength of spirit perhaps, reversed the transformation. He swelled and solidified back into his true form, then slumped wide-eyed and quaking, striving to collect himself sufficiently to resume the struggle.

Hetham was glad to see his huge companion withstand the curse, but he wondered if it was really going to matter. Nothing else had. The army of the alliance had claimed the ground its commanders had wanted and executed the strategy they'd devised. They'd struck the first blow and struck it hard. Yet as best Hetham could judge, they'd scarcely hurt the wyrms at all. They certainly hadn't slowed them down or dampened their appetite for slaughter. The reptiles were knifing through their ranks as easily as a whale sucked in mouthfuls of plankton.

Heart pounding, Hetham looked over to see if his captain was about to order the company forward into the mayhem. It didn't look like it. Perhaps the officer was afraid, or maybe he simply saw no point in moving. For after all, the dragons were coming to them.

The dragon turtle boiled a squad of tritons with

another puff of its superheated breath. Water drakes and dolphins spun around one another in a combat like intricate dance. The cetaceans fought fearlessly, and their bards sang songs laced with magic, but the reptiles had them overmatched and ripped them to bloody shreds of fin and viscera. A dragon eel caught a giant crab in its beak, bit down, and cracked its adversary's shell. Still alive for the moment, the arthropod groped with its pincers, but the drake kept is scaly coils out of reach.

Two dragons, the colossal black Ingvatorc had tried and failed to imprison and the equally enormous topaz, tore another contingent of morkoths and slave warriors into a gory haze. Hetham saw with a thrill of terror that no one remained between the wyrms and his own company. Sure enough, the reptiles oriented on them and charged, legs stroking and kicking, wings sweeping, and tails lashing.

Some of the mermen turned and bolted. For an instant, Hetham wondered if he was gong to do the same. But evidently he was not, though he wasn't sure why. He was certain he was just as frightened as those who'd fled.

"Aim!" the captain shouted.

The mermen lifted their crossbows. Hetham pointed his weapon of bone and coral and its bolt of blowfish spine at the topaz's radiant yellow eye.

"Shoot!"

The volley flew. Hetham's quarrel missed the eye by a finger's length. For an instant, he thought it might still do some good, but it just glanced off the creature's brow. Many of his comrades' darts did the same. A few lodged in the dragons' scales, but failed to penetrate deeply enough to kill or cripple. It seemed possible that the reptiles didn't even feel the stings.

Some storm giants cast additional spells, but whatever the resulting flashes of green and purple light, sudden chill, carrion stink, and head-spinning moment of dizziness were supposed to accomplish, the reptiles weathered it all without slowing down or veering off. The rest of the band discharged their own crossbows. The oversized missiles might have done the dragons some actual damage, but they dodged the bolts by lashing their serpentine bodies low or from side to side. The black had but a single hole punched in its leathery wing, and the topaz suffered no harm at all.

"Tridents!" the merman officer shouted, reasonably enough. A warrior didn't want to be caught with a missile weapon in his grasp when the foe closed to striking distance, even if said foe's prodigious fangs and talons were such fearsome implements of destruction that Hetham's three-pronged lance seemed a joke by comparison.

The giants dropped their crossbows and unsheathed greatswords of sharp, faceted claw coral. For a sea creature Hetham's size, such a cutting, chopping weapon was all but useless. The resistance of the water kept a merman from swinging it hard enough to do much damage. But beings as strong as Ingvatorc and his kin could wield them to deadly effect. Hetham tried to draw some encouragement from that fact.

Meanwhile, the dragons raced closer, loomed larger, until even the giants seemed puny by comparison. For Hetham, dazed with dread, the moment had a dreamlike quality, and he had the daft thought that if only he'd lived a better life, and so inclined the gods to love him better, it might truly be possible to escape this doom by the simple expedient of waking up.

Just as the drakes were about to close, one of the storm giants bellowed a command or war cry in his own language. He and his fellows lunged to meet the onrushing dragons, essayed a first strike with their long, heavy, gemlike blades, then tried to dodge and spin away from the reptiles' ripostes. Some were such able swordsmen, or had so augmented their natural prowess with enchantment, that they jumped away from that first exchange unscathed. Another, less skillful or less fortunate, sank down to the sea floor with three gaping vertical rents in his torso. Blood streamed out to dirty the water, to taint it with its coppery smell and taste.

"Kill them!" the merman officer cried.

The warrior beside Hetham cried out, "I'm sorry!" dropped his trident, and fled. Everyone else rushed forward.

Hetham had once watched a big shark and eel fighting while smaller fish, ignored, perhaps even unnoticed, whirled around the combatants to feast on drifting morsels of flesh from their wounds. The moments that followed reminded him of that, with his fellow mermen and himself playing the roles of the scavengers.

The dragons were too intent on the giants, by far the more serious of the two threats facing them, to pay much heed to mermen. Unfortunately, the wyrms were so huge and powerful that they could annihilate a smaller creature hovering close at hand without even particularly intending to. The black-scaled "skull dragon," as such reptiles with their shriveled masks were called, raked at a giant, accidentally snagged a merman on the tip of one claw, and crushed him when it set its foot back down. A random swat from a dusky wing shattered the bones in another warrior's body. The topaz pivoted to strike at the towering swordsman on its flank, and its whipping tail smashed the merman officer's head, which tumbled clear of his shoulders.

Even the storm giants posed a hazard. One feinted a cut at the jewel wyrm's leg then whirled his blade high for the true strike at its neck, without seeing the merman obliviously swimming into the arc of the attack. The coral blade sheared off the flukes of his tail.

All but choking on the blood in the water, his eyes smarting and nearly blinded by it, Hetham strained to block out the horror of what was happening, believing his side might actually have a chance. For after all, the giants were fearsome combatants. Their greatswords hacked long, deep gashes in the dragons' hides. At the very least, they were keeping the wyrms busy, and while they managed that, maybe the mermen's desperate little pokes and jabs would actually do some good.

He *wanted* to think so. But despite their wounds, the dragons never faltered, while, one by one, the giants slowly collapsed to the sea floor with crushed, misshapen heads, shredded torsos, and ragged stumps where massive limbs had been. Finally only Ingvatorc remained. The reptiles maneuvered to flank him, and knowing himself overmatched, he started jabbering a spell. Before he could finish, though, the wyrms pounced. He lashed out with a stop cut, and intent on the kill, the topaz didn't even try to avoid it. The blade sliced its flank, but at the same instant, the creature caught Ingvatorc's shoulder in its jaws.

Meanwhile, the skull wyrm plunged its fangs into the giant's lower back. The drakes twisted, wrenching and pulling in opposite directions, and Ingvatorc's torso ripped into two pieces.

With that accomplished, the reptiles rounded on the surviving mermen. The topaz clawed at Hetham. He jerked out of the way and swam backward.

The retreat carried him into water where the drifting blood wasn't quite so thick, permitting a glimpse of the battle as a whole. What he saw came as no surprise but wrung his heart nonetheless.

The army of the alliance was finished, Dukars, high mages, morkoths, mermen, shalarins, sea-elves, and tritons all annihilated, or maybe, in the case of a few lucky folk, put to flight.

We tried, he thought, perhaps addressing the multitude of folk who'd depended on them for their deliverance. I swear by the tides, we tried. But we just couldn't stop them. No one could.

Still, he had a duty to fight on, for these last few moments of life. He aimed his trident at the topaz's mask. If it bit at him, he would try again to put out its luminous yellow eye.

But when he met its gaze, pain exploded through his head, paralyzing him. Before he could recover, its fangs pierced him through.

THE **P**RIESTS

CHAPTER 1

Anton Marivaldi sighed at the aching pleasure as the pert, chattering brunette masseuse thumped and kneaded his muscles. He suspected that after she'd hammered all the stiffness and tension out, she might offer even more intimate services, and if so, he intended to purchase them.

He'd earned his amusements, hadn't he? First had come tendays of imposture, of bearing up under the knowledge that even the tiniest slip could expose him. But he hadn't slipped, and the masquerade had ended successfully in a clatter of flashing blades. His superiors had paid him well for his efforts, and he intended to squander every copper before they ordered him back into the game.

The hot, soapy bath, fragrant with scented oil, did feel truly delicious. The attendant, her thin cotton shift soaked transparent and clinging to her curves, scrubbed his shoulders, and the pressure of her hands slid him down a little deeper into the polished marble tub.

He frowned, suddenly uneasy. Going deeper—for some reason, that was bad, wasn't it? And now that he thought about it, hadn't the bath been a massage just a moment before?

The attendant shoved him down with startling strength, submerging him completely. He thrashed, trying to shake off her grip, and in the process, broke free of the entire dream.

Reality was equally alarming, because he was still underwater. He flailed, kicked, and stroked toward the brightness above. After a moment, his head broke the surface. He coughed and retched out the warm, salty liquid he'd obliviously inhaled and, when he was able, gasped in air instead.

That took the edge off his terror, and he recalled his float, three chunks of broken plank pegged to a crosspiece. He'd encountered the flotsam, adrift as he was adrift, an hour or so into his ordeal. It was the only reason he hadn't drowned long ago.

He cast about for it. The hot summer sun danced on the blue, rippling surface of the Sea of Fallen Stars, making him squint. After a few anxious moments, he spotted the float. It hadn't drifted far. Even in his weakened state—parched, starved, gashed arm feeble—he could probably swim to it and heave himself back on top.

But then again, why bother? Why prolong the misery when it would be easier just to let the float slip out of reach? He doubted drowning was a particularly easy death, but it would be over quickly.

No, curse it, he wouldn't give up! A ship could still happen along, or he might still drift within reach of land. He paddled to the makeshift raft, gripped the splintery wood, and dragged himself back on top of it.

The effort exhausted him. He had to lie panting and trembling for a while before he found the energy to lift his head, peer down into the water, and croak, "You could have woken me when I first slipped off the float. Or helped me get back to it. Or, if you want me dead, it was a perfect opportunity to attack. Just do *something*."

Swimming several yards below the surface, the creature stared back at him.

It was somewhat human in form, but slender as an elf, with dark blue skin and long, webbed fingers and toes. A proud black dorsal fin ran from its hairless brow all the way down to its rump, and some sort of white pendant hung around its neck. Round, dark goggles shielded its eyes. Though Anton had lived his entire life in the environs of the Sea of Fallen Stars, he didn't know much about the various sentient races dwelling beneath the waves. Few of his species did. But if he wasn't mistaken, his unwanted companion was a shalarin.

Whatever it was, he'd apparently attracted its attention at some point during the night, because he'd first noticed it gliding beneath him shortly after sunrise. Initially, given that shalarins didn't have an especially sinister reputation, he'd hoped it would help him. When it failed to do so spontaneously, he'd tried to entreat it via pantomime.

The creature hadn't responded in any way, and he'd wondered if it meant him harm. Though more adept with a sword or dagger, he had a small talent for sorcery, and had considered striking first with one of his spells. Ultimately, though, he'd decided he'd do better to save them for a moment when he knew for a fact he was in peril.

Often, though, the urge to lash out returned, simply because the shalarin's lurking presence was unsettling.

At times, it even felt like mockery of his plight. What did the cursed creature want, anyway? Was it simply curious to see how long it would take him to die? If so ... well, in the course of his duties, Anton had witnessed more than his share of brutality, but this sort of patient, passive cruelty was something new in his experience.

The sun hammered down until he wished it would set, even though once it did, no passing ship could possibly see him. He fought the impulse to drink salt-water and drowsed for a bit. Then he gave a start and cast wildly about.

For a second, he couldn't tell what had jolted him back to full wakefulness. Maybe he'd simply felt himself slipping off the float again.

No. After hours of hovering close, the shalarin was swimming away. That was what had snagged his attention, even in his somnolent state.

Had the creature finally gotten bored with watching him suffer? His instincts warned him no, and they were evidently right, for after the shalarin had gone a ways, it turned and oriented on him once more. It was still interested but had apparently deemed it prudent to put more distance between them.

Was it because something was about to happen to him? He looked around, saw nothing, then dunked his face in the water to better scan the blue-green depths below. A soft, rounded thing resembling a huge sack shot up at him like a stone from a sling. Long tentacles lined with suckers trailed behind it, undulating as if to help propel it along.

After a moment of stunned incomprehension, Anton realized it was an octopus, albeit the biggest specimen he'd ever seen. Indeed, more than big enough to make a meal of a lone man afloat.

Heart pounding, he reviewed his modest store of spells. Some were of no use in combat, while others wouldn't function underwater. But a pulse of pure force might work. He fumbled the necessary talisman—a bit of ram's horn—from his pocket and swept it through the proper arcane figure. Praying that his raw throat and thick tongue could still enunciate the words with the precision required, he recited the incantation.

Power sang like a note from a crystal bell. Visible as a streak of rippling distortion, magic shot through the water. It bashed a momentary dent in the octopus's softness and scraped its hide.

The cephalopod recoiled. You see, Anton thought, I'm dangerous. Go eat something else.

The octopus hesitated for another moment then evidently decided its wound was inconsequential. At any rate, it hurtled onward.

Anton yanked his dagger, the straight, double-edged steel blade coated in gleaming silver, from its sheath. He'd dropped his sword when he'd first gone into the water, lest its weight drag him down. But at least he'd retained this weapon, and it would double as the necessary focus for another spell.

He recited the complex rhyme and sketched the proper sign. The dagger point carved the sigil in scarlet light on the air. A second knife, glowing red like the rune, shimmered into existence in front of the octopus and stabbed into its bulbous body.

Surely now it would turn away or, failing that, linger to try and fight the shining animate knife instead of charging on to close with Anton.

But that was not the case. It veered past the red blade and raced upward. The flying dagger pursued and might get in another jab or two before it winked out of existence, but Anton doubted that would be enough to save him.

The shalarin drifted, kicking and stroking lazily, watching.

All but certain he lacked the time, Anton nonetheless tried to materialize a second blade of force. In his haste, though, he stumbled over the mystical words, botching the spell, and the gathering power dissipated in useless stink and sizzle. Then tentacles came writhing and swirling to grab him.

He struggled to avoid them, but his scrap of timber was too small; he had no space to maneuver or retreat. He managed to drag his entire body up out of the water, to kneel atop the float, for an instant rocking and bobbing precariously. Then a loop of tentacle found his ankle, yanked tight as a garrote, and wrenched him under the surface.

Whether it realized or not, the octopus only needed to hold him under until he ran out of air, and with more of its tentacles whirling to wrap around him, it had an excellent chance of doing so. Floundering, his leg already snared, he had no hope of avoiding them all. He had to concentrate on keeping his dagger arm free.

He twisted and whipped it about to keep it from being entangled. Ringed suckers cut him as they gripped the rest of his body, and he jerked at the pain. The tentacles constricted like pythons, threatening to squeeze the precious, dwindling air from his lungs.

Round, dark little eyes staring, the octopus pulled him toward its jagged, gaping beak. He hacked and sliced at its arms. The dagger's maker had enchanted the edge to a supernatural keenness, and it bit deep, maiming the creature's limbs and severing one entirely.

Still it seemed unlikely to prove sufficient. But as the octopus hauled him within reach of its mouth, its whole body spasmed, and the flailing tentacles loosened. Anton tried to squirm upward out of the coils.

The tentacle wrapped around his ankle still had a grip on him and anchored him in place. He bent over, sawed at it until the tough, dense flesh parted, then swam upward.

Suddenly the need to breathe overpowered him. He expelled the stale contents of his lungs in an explosion of bubbles and helplessly inhaled. At the same instant, though, his head broke the surface.

More luck: the float was still within reach. Wheezing and praying he'd hurt the octopus badly enough to discourage it, he struggled toward the wood. He set the dagger atop the small platform then started to drag himself up.

A tentacle wrapped around his leg and jerked downward. The sudden motion rocked the float. The knife tumbled off the edge and vanished into the sea.

Panic rose, threatening to swamp his reason, and he strained to push it down and think. He didn't have the strength to keep the octopus from dragging him back under water, and he didn't have a weapon anymore, either. How, then, could he save himself?

There was one way, maybe. But it required him to free up a hand.

It was hard enough to hold on with both of them. As soon as he let go with the right, the strain on the left, and the arm attached to it, became all but unbearable, and he cried out at the sudden jerk.

But the pull didn't break his grip, at least not instantly. He must have done the octopus some harm, after all, enough to weaken it a little. Perhaps, then, he had the seconds he needed.

He groaned another incantation and twisted his right hand through an arcane pass. The extremity took on a pale silvery hue, and the fingertips lengthened into talons. A keen ridge, a blade to slash and hack, pushed out from the underside, from the base of the little finger to the wrist.

When the transformation was complete, he drew a deep breath, released the float, and allowed his tormentor to drag him back under the water.

He cut and tore at the octopus, severing two more

of its limbs. It hauled him to its beak, and he slashed that, too, and the soft, pulsing flesh around it. He ripped and sliced, straining for one of the dark little eyes—

The world exploded into blackness. For a moment he didn't understand; then he realized the cephalopod had discharged its ink. Its tentacles released him, and he felt a spurt of pressure. The creature was jetting away. It had had enough.

He struggled back to the surface and, as his hand melted back into its normal shape, back onto the float. The shalarin regarded him for a moment, then turned and swam away.

"That's right," he wheezed, "you see, I am dangerous. You'd better not hang around, or. . . ."

Oh, to Baator with it. Even if the shalarin had been able to hear and understand, he was too spent and in too much pain to finish the threat or do much of anything else. He knew he should examine his new wounds and check to see if the old one had started bleeding again, but it simply wasn't in him. He could only lie still, trying not to cry or whimper too much, with his hands and feet dangling in the water.

Though he somehow avoided sliding or rolling off the float again, he kept drifting in and out of consciousness. Since oblivion washed away misery, he welcomed it. It might well mean the end was near, and during his lucid moments, he supposed that would be merciful. He was too stubborn to put an end to his suffering. He'd proved it twice today already. But the sun and sea might soon do it for him.

He closed his sore eyes. Just for a moment, he thought, but when he opened them, the stars were out and the water was black. He wondered if, without the sunlight baking him, he might last a few more hours and couldn't make up his dazed, wretched mind whether to hope for it or not. Then he noticed a crested, oval-shaped object sticking up, beyond the float but almost within arm's reach.

It was the shalarin's head. The creature had returned and ventured close. Perhaps it reckoned he was finally weak enough to attack without any risk to itself.

The thought stirred the dregs of the resolve he generally felt in the face of danger. He tried to rear up so he could use his hands for self-defense but found he lacked the strength. All he could was flop around a little, like a dying fish in the bottom of a boat.

The shalarin surged up onto the float. The wooden surface rocked, but its new occupant centered its weight before it could overturn.

The creature gripped Anton. He struggled to shake it off but couldn't manage that, either.

The shalarin rolled him onto his back. They were now closer than they'd ever been before, with no distorting layers of water between them, and despite the dark, he picked out details he hadn't discerned hitherto. Slim as it was, it had a certain subtle fullness in the area that would be a woman's bosom, as well as a breadth to its hips, that told him it was a she. Gill slits opened along her collarbone and above her ribs. A round mark—the paucity of light prevented him from making out the color—adorned the center of her brow just below the beginning of the fin. The pendant was a skeletal hand—human, by the looks of it—and she also wore a belt around her narrow waist. Attached were several pouches.

She unlaced one of the bags; extracted something small and roughly cubical in shape; and pressed it to his dry, cracked lips. He found the action mildly reassuring. She probably wouldn't try to poison a man who was already dying, for what would be the point? The action suggested that, inexplicable as it seemed, she'd finally decided to help him.

Unfortunately, she didn't seem to understand that his

most pressing need was water, not food. He wondered if his swollen throat could even swallow anything solid without choking. But he'd try. Maybe the pellet, whatever it was, would help him a little, anyway.

When he sank his teeth into it, it burst into fragments and a copious quantity of oil. The liquid tasted so bitter that in other circumstances, he might have spit it out. But when he swallowed some, it assuaged his thirst like water.

He greedily consumed it and the solid matter—some sort of preserved fish?—too. "Thank you," he gasped.

The shalarin fed him two more cubes then produced a different sort of pellet. It was rounder, tasteless, and as tough to chew as the stalest ship's biscuit he'd ever sampled. Still, hoping it would do him as much good as the other morsels had, he gnawed until it softened and broke apart.

As soon as he swallowed it, the shalarin gripped him with her long, webbed fingers. She half rolled, half shoved him toward the edge of the float.

"No!" he said. "Wait!"

But she wouldn't relent. He struggled to resist and in other circumstances might have succeeded. He was an able wrestler and brawler, and his brawny frame surely outweighed her spindly body. But while the pellets had snatched him back from the brink of death, he was still weak as a baby, and his attempts to grapple and punch were pathetically ineffective.

The float tilted beneath him. Clasping him, the shalarin rolled down the incline, and they tumbled into the sea together. Kicking, she dragged him downward.

He kept struggling but still couldn't break her grip. After a minute the burning in his chest demanded release. He let out the breath he'd clenched in his lungs and gulped in water instead.

It felt different than inhaling air. Water was heavier, more substantial, in his chest. But the sensation wasn't unpleasant, and more important, he wasn't drowning. Something the shalarin had fed him—the round morsel, he suspected—enabled him to breathe. Maybe it helped him to ignore the heightening pressure, too, considering that he didn't need to pop his ears.

But the magic didn't help him see. As he and the shalarin descended, the benighted waters rapidly became impenetrable to human sight. He couldn't even make out his captor hauling him along. It reinforced his sense of utter helplessness—not that it needed reinforcing—and he simply hung limp in the shalarin's grasp and allowed her to do as she would.

It was cold in the depths, though not insupportably so. Perhaps he had the pellets to thank for that as well. He had the feeling he was drifting in and out of awareness, but the unchanging blackness made it difficult to be certain.

Finally, a soft glow flowered in the murk. Below him stood a vast, intricate riot of coral, portions of it shining with its own inner light. Spires rose, or partly rose, from the tangled reefs like trees mired in parasitic vines. Anton might have assumed the city, half buried as it was, was an uninhabited ruin, except that the bluish cryscoral wasn't the only source of illumination. Lamps shined in windows and along the boulevards. Altogether, the lights sufficed to reveal the tiny forms of the residents swimming to and fro.

Fascinated, Anton wished the shalarin would swim faster. He wanted to get closer and see more. But he passed out before he could.

THE PRIESTS

CHAPTER 2

Testing his strength and stamina, Anton swam
back and forth and up and down at the end
of the tether binding his ankle to the marble
couch. The leathery cord reminded him unpleasantly of the octopus's tentacles dragging
him down.

Fortunately, barring a ring-shaped scar or
two to go with all his others, nasty memories
were all he retained from his ordeal. He was
whole again, thanks to the shalarin. When
he'd seen the skeletal hand hanging from
her neck, he'd suspected she was a priestess
of Umberlee, and she had in fact employed a
cleric's healing prayers to mend his damaged
body.

What she hadn't done was talk to him. Not
once, no matter how he entreated her. Such
indifference made him suspect she intended

him for sacrifice or slavery. She was, after all, a servant of the Bitch Queen, goddess of drownings, shipwrecks, and all manner of deaths at sea, a power notoriously malign.

But if she did mean him ill, he didn't intend to meet his fate like a sheep placidly awaiting the butcher's pleasure. He didn't know if he could truly escape, but now that he'd recovered his vigor, maybe he could at least free himself from the rope and find out what lay beyond the nondescript room in which the shalarin had imprisoned him.

Floating in the center of the chamber, he turned his attention to the complex knot securing the cord to his ankle. He'd spent hours picking at it, but it remained as tight as ever. Evidently it bore some enchantment.

With luck, his own magic would counter it. He murmured a charm, marveling once again that he could speak as plainly as if he were on land. In fact, he could function here without much difficulty of any kind. He saw clearly and moved quickly, without the water hindering him. Plainly, the enchantment must have been responsible for that as well, and he wondered if such conditions only prevailed within this one building or if the entire submerged city was equally accommodating.

The knot squirmed and untied itself. He smiled, swam to the doorway, and peeked out into the larger room beyond.

As he'd suspected, it was a temple of Umberlee, dominated by a towering statue of the Queen of the Depths herself. Bigger than a giant, clad in her high-collared cape and seashell ornaments, the deity had risen from the waves to smash a cog with her trident. Sharks cut through the water to seize the mariners toppling overboard.

Smaller sculptures, representations of predatory sea creatures and hideous things that might be aquatic demons, lurked in alcoves. Mosaics depicting Umberlee's battles against Selûne, Chauntea, and other gods adorned the high ceiling and walls. Heaped offerings covered the several altars and overflowed onto the floor.

It was all rather magnificent in a grim sort of way, but somewhat surprisingly, at the moment no one else was here to tend or marvel at the splendor. Anton hesitated then swam to the nearest of the altars to see if some worshiper had given Umberlee a weapon.

A cutlass caught his eye. He pulled the short, curved sword from its scabbard and came on guard, testing the balance and weight. It felt good in his hand, so light and eager that, like his lost dagger, it must have magic bound in the blade. He sheathed it, buckled it onto his belt, turned, and froze.

The shalarin floated in a big arched doorway that likely led outside the temple. In the days she'd tended him, he'd had a chance to observe other details of her appearance. Her dark blue skin wasn't scaly like a fish's, as he initially imagined, but smooth like a dolphin's. The round mark on her brow was red. Here in the depths, she dispensed with her goggles, revealing eyes that were glistening black, all pupil. They gave him a level stare.

"It is death to rob Umberlee," she said in a cold contralto voice. "Fortunately, you have not. It is her will that you take the blade."

"You're talking."

"Yes."

"You wouldn't before."

"I did not understand your language and doubted you understood mine. I had to trade for this." She extended her hand, drawing his attention to a striped tiger-coral ring. "Its magic enables me to speak to you."

"Oh." His ordeal and its bizarre aftermath must

have muddled his wits because that simple explanation for her silence had never occurred to him. "Lady, I'm grateful for your care, and I mean no harm. I only took the cutlass because it alarmed me that you kept me tied and never answered when I spoke." She might at least have given him a reassuring pat on the shoulder or something.

"I kept you secured so you wouldn't wander and come to harm. And because you now belong to Umberlee."

He hesitated. "Exactly what do you mean?"

"What I say. Tell me your name."

"Anton Marivaldi, out of Alaghôn, in Turmish." He wondered if the place names meant anything to her.

"I am Tu'ala'keth, waveservant, member of the Faiths Caste, keeper of Umberlee's house in Myth Nantar."

He assumed Myth Nantar was the name of the city. He'd heard vague reports of such a place, a metropolis where the various undersea races, and even a few expatriates from the surface world, dwelled together. "I understood that you're a divine. Are you saying you laid claim to me somehow, in your goddess's name?"

A glimmering membrane flicked across the blackness of her eyes. Perhaps it was a shalarin's equivalent of a blink. "Yes. What is unclear?"

"Among my folk, you can't just take possession of another person, even if you save his life."

"I did not; Umberlee did." She waved a hand at their surroundings. "What do you see?"

He didn't know what she wanted him to say. "Riches. Sacred things."

"Neglect!" the shalarin snapped. "All the treasures here are old. Who now offers at Umberlee's altars?"

"In my world, every seafarer who wants to come safely back into port."

"But few here, where every creature should adore her. I will tell you the tale, Anton Marivaldi, and you will understand why and how she has chosen you."

"Please." He needed to comprehend what she had in mind so he could talk her out of it.

"How much do you know of shalarins?"

He shrugged. "You live in the Sea of Fallen Stars. You're no great friends to humanity but no foul scourge like the sahuagin, either."

"We did not always live here. Our race was born in the Sea of Corynactis."

"I never heard of it."

"It lies on the far side of the world. Three thousand years ago, some of my folk found their way here. But the mystic gate connecting the two seas closed, trapping them, and so they, and their descendants, were exiled from their home."

"That's unfortunate," he said, but he couldn't imagine what it had to do with him.

"The exiles endured many griefs and misfortunes. One was losing touch with the gods of their forefathers. Those deities apparently had no interest in Faerûn or lacked the ability to project their power into these waters."

Anton waved his hand, indicating the statue of Umberlee. "It looks as if your ancestors adapted. They started worshiping the gods who rule hereabouts."

"Yes," said Tu'ala'keth, "and were surely the better for it, for no deity is greater than Umberlee. Her favor enabled them to prosper. Yet now the faithless idiots turn their backs on her!"

More puzzled than ever, Anton shook his head. "Why?"

"Because two years ago the gate to the Sea of Corynactis opened again—permanently this time." She smiled grimly, or at least he took it for a smile. He wasn't sure her changes of expression always signified the same emotions they would in a human face. "That is a shalarin secret, by the way. It is death for you to know."

"In that case, thanks so much for telling me."

"You must know in order to understand. Since the gate opened, the shalarins of the two realms can communicate, and with that communication has come a great *curiosity*, an *enthusiasm*"—her tone invested the words with bitter scorn—"for the religions of our ancestors, even though those feeble godlings still lack the strength to manifest here. Folk pray to them in preference to Umberlee."

Anton could understand why a worshiper might prefer another deity—most any other deity—to the savage, greedy Bitch Queen, but saw no advantage in saying so. "Maybe they'll return to Umberlee once the novelty of the new cults wears off."

Tu'ala'keth glared at him. "I am a waveservant. I can't simply wait for them to change their foolish minds. It is my duty to *bring* them back."

"With my help?" What in the name of the Red Knight could she possibly be thinking?

"If they weren't blind and deaf, they would have returned already, gashing their flesh and shedding their blood to beg their goddess's forgiveness. At her bidding, a host of dragons has banded together and started ravaging Serôs, to punish those who failed to give her her due. The entire commonwealth is in peril."

Anton frowned. "Lady, with respect, for the past few months, something called a Rage of Dragons has been occurring. All across Faerûn, wyrms are uniting to slaughter and destroy. The shalarins' problem isn't unique."

"It still embodies the wrath of Umberlee. Otherwise, the army of Serôs would have destroyed the drakes, instead of the other way around."

"Well . . . maybe."

"I proclaimed that only Umberlee could save us. I preached it as clearly as I explained it to you. But no one heeded. Finally I forsook Myth Nantar for the wilds of the open sea. It is there one feels closest to the Queen of the Depths, and there, I hoped, I would hear her speak, instructing me on how to achieve her ends."

"That's when you stumbled across me?"

"Yes. I lingered to watch your death as a form of meditation. When the sea takes a life, it is a holy event. Umberlee reveals herself to those with eyes to see."

Anton reckoned he, too, might be starting to "see." "But I didn't die."

"No," said Tu'ala'keth. "Hour after hour, you endured. Even the octopus could not kill you. It became clear that Umberlee wished you to survive, and since she guided me to you, it had to be so you could aid me in my mission. So, quickly as I could, I fetched the items and prepared the spells that enabled me to rescue you."

"I'm grateful, but truly you've made a mistake. I have no idea how to help you. I'm no priest or philosopher or orator, to lure your truant followers back."

"What are you, then? Tell me, and it will become apparent exactly how you are to serve."

"There isn't much to tell. I'm a trader. I took a ship to sell lumber and buy metals. During the voyage, I passed the time throwing dice. I was lucky two days straight, only not really so lucky after all, because a couple of sailors decided I was cheating and attacked me. One knifed me, and I fell overboard. I can only assume that no one but my ill-wishers realized what had happened because the carrack sailed on and left me."

Her black eyes bored into him. "You lie. You use magic. You fight well. You cannot belong to the Providers Caste."

"I don't know how it works among shalarins, but there's nothing to stop a human merchant from learning a little sorcery or training with a blade. Sometimes it comes in handy."

"It may be so. Still you are a liar."

Anton was actually a highly proficient liar. Otherwise, someone would have killed him long ago. Either Tu'ala'keth was suspicious by nature, she had an enchantment in place to tell truth from falsehood, or she possessed an unexpected and inconvenient knack for reading human beings.

However she'd caught him, he had a hunch a second lie would prove no more convincing than the first. It might simply provoke a disciple of cruel Umberlee into trying to torture the truth out of him.

In other circumstances, he might have risked it, and if it came to it, resisted the torment as best he could. But what would a shalarin care about the true nature of his business or the manner in which he'd come to grief? With no stake in the affairs of the surface world, what would she do with the information? Maybe it would do no harm to confide in her.

"All right," he said, "the fact is, I'm a spy in the service of my homeland." He hesitated. "Do you have spies here under the sea?"

She sneered. "Of course."

"Well, my usual chore is to ferret out information concerning pirates and smugglers, so others can catch and punish them as they deserve. But a month ago my superiors set me a new task. Have you ever heard of the Cult of the Dragon?"

"No."

"I guess you sea folk aren't susceptible to their particular kind of madness. Lucky you. They're a secret society of necromancers, priests of Bane, Talos, and similar powers, and common lunatics, laboring to make a certain prophecy come to pass."

"If the prophecy is true, it will come to pass regardless."

"Don't tell me, tell them. The prophecy says that one day, undead dragons will rule the world, and the cult intends to make it sooner rather than later. As near as I can make out, they believe the dracolich kings will favor them and elevate them above the common herd of humankind.

"Anyway, a couple months back, the paladins of Impiltur—a land on the northern shore—discovered that of late, the cultists have been more active and advanced their schemes farther than any sane person could have imagined. They've established a number of hidden strongholds across Faerûn. The purpose of the refuges is to transform dragons into liches, and supposedly, wyrms have been flocking to them and consenting to the change as never before, because they fear losing their minds to frenzy. Evidently undead dragons are immune.

"The Rage has produced destruction and misery enough—you shalarins seem to know all about that—but it's nothing compared to what a horde of dracoliches will do. So the Lords of Impiltur sent out the word: People in every realm need to find and destroy the cult enclaves before they can accomplish their task."

"You were one of the seekers."

Anton grinned. "Yes, and it was just my rotten luck that it turns out the whoresons do have a stronghold somewhere in the region. My guess is on one of the Pirate Isles. If I were pursuing a plan to topple every monarch and ruling council in the world, I'd hide out in a place without governance or law."

"You say you guess. You did not learn for certain?"

"No. I had a lead and tried to follow up. At some point I apparently made a mistake, and some cultist tumbled to the fact that I was sticking my nose where it didn't belong. The maniacs sent abishai—winged demons with a dash of dragon thrown in—to deal with me.

"They caught up with me on a carrack sailing out of Procampur. We fought, and I got the worst of it. Finally they cornered me against the rail, and I jumped overboard. If I hadn't, they would have torn me apart.

"The move worked, after a fashion. For whatever reason, they didn't keep after me. But the ship didn't come back for me either. Maybe the abishai killed all the sailors. Or perhaps the captain decided he didn't need a passenger who lured demons down on his vessel.

"The rest you know. I drifted, and you found me."

Tu'ala'keth floated silently, pondering. Suddenly she grinned. "Of course! It is clear!"

"What is?"

"This Cult of the Dragon. They must be mighty wizards with a profound knowledge of wyrms to warp their lives into undeath and leave their minds intact."

"I suppose."

"You will help me find them, for that is your craft. They will then tell me how to stop the dragons threatening Serôs. I will do so in Umberlee's name, and afterwards, the other shalarins will return to her altars in penance and thanksgiving."

Anton shook his head. "You don't understand. There's no reason to assume the cult has what you need, and it wouldn't matter even if they do. They *worship* dragons. They won't help anybody hurt or hinder them."

"If they won't give up their secrets willingly, we will take them."

He laughed. "Just you and me, you mean, against a dragon or three, a whole coven of spellcasters, and the Grandmaster only knows what else? I know you're a reasonably powerful cleric in your own right, but that's ridiculous."

"You only believe so," she said, "because your lack of faith blinds you. You look at this moment and you see only chance—coincidence. These elements are there, but they make a pattern, and the pattern conveys meaning."

"Look: If we were to march into the cult's fortress and announce ourselves, all it would do is alert them to the fact that people are searching for them, and that they haven't covered their trail well enough to keep from being found. Then, after they killed us, they'd take additional precautions. That would make it all the more difficult for somebody else to locate them, descend on them in force, and wipe them out.

"And that needs to happen, for everyone's sake. A horde of dracoliches will pose a threat to your Serôs and Myth Nantar as much as the surface world."

"What matters is the restoration of Umberlee's worship. Everything else must fall out as it will."

"Lady, I respectfully disagree."

Tu'ala'keth peered at him as if honestly mystified by his intransigence. "You must help. As I explained, your life, like mine, belongs to the Queen of the Depths to spend as she sees fit. If I must punish you to convince you, I will."

"No. You won't. I'm leaving." He swam toward the arch, and she centered herself in the space to bar his way.

Hoping it would persuade her to stand aside, he pulled the cutlass from its scabbard. At the moment, she had no weapon but her spells. Of course, those were formidable enough.

She sneered. "Do you truly believe a blade Umberlee put in your hand will cut a waveservant?"

"I think it might," he said, though her apparent faith in her own invulnerability, crazy as it appeared, was almost enough to make him wonder.

"Think on this, then. Even if you could kill me, what would happen then?"

"Myth Nantar is supposedly full of sea-elves, mermen,

and by your own account shalarins who don't care a snake's toenail about Umberlee anymore. Maybe I can talk one of them into helping me back to dry land."

"After you've killed one of their own? How would your folk treat a stranger who'd done the same? Even if somebody did decide to help you, do you really believe it would do any good? You, the slayer of Umberlee's servant, would still be at the bottom of the sea, where all creatures live only at her sufferance. Rest assured she would avenge me before you could escape."

He hesitated. If it was a bluff, she was selling it well.

Maybe the sensible course was to play along at least until he was back on land. It was possible that with her powers, Tu'ala'keth could even help him locate the cult's lair. Tymora knew, he hadn't had any luck on his own.

He let his shoulders slump as if in resignation. "All right. You win. I'm at your—and your goddess's—service."

For now. But, Lady, you will never see your goal.

THE PRIESTS

CHAPTER 3

When they reached the shallows, Tu'ala'keth stroked the neck of her seahorse, and the animal obediently came to a halt. Anton stopped more awkwardly, nearly slipping from the back of his steed, and the creature tossed its ruddy, black-eyed head in annoyance.

The riders dismounted, Tu'ala'keth waved her hand in dismissal, and the seahorses swam away to roam and forage as they would so long as they didn't stray too far from the island. She wanted them to hear and come if she called.

That accomplished, she and the human swam up the slope of the seabed. They soon reached a point where a person could set his feet down and wade with the upper part of his body out of the water, and Anton chose to do so.

She compelled herself to do likewise, meanwhile striving to conceal her trepidation. Such an emotion was weak and unworthy. She had come on Umberlee's business, and the goddess would protect her.

Still it was one thing to be certain of her deity's power and another to place her confidence in the contrivances of the Arcane Caste. If the talismans they'd provided failed to work properly, she was in for discomfort, even pain.

When she raised her upper body out of water the sun was even brighter, but with her goggles in place, she could see. The air passing through her gill slits felt strange, thin, but sustained her nonetheless. The latter benefit was due to the enchantment woven into her silverweave armor, a fine mesh tunic of worked coral.

Anton made a retching sound and, as she turned to look, finished coughing the water from his lungs. He straightened up, wiped his mouth and shaggy black whiskers, and asked, "Are you doing all right?"

"Of course." She hefted her stone trident. "Onward."

They sloshed toward the white-sand beach. Tu'ala'keth had done a bit of walking in her life, but not much, and it made her feel as clumsy as Anton had looked trying to manage the seahorse. She resolved to master the trick of it as quickly as possible.

She supposed she might have quite a bit to learn, for the landscape before her looked dauntingly un-familiar. In its essence, Dragon Isle—a name of good omen, surely—was a mountain like any other, just one so tall its crest rose high above the surface of the sea. But it had no abundance of fish swarming about its stony crags, just a few gulls swooping and wheeling. The odd-looking vegetation was equally sparse.

Everything seemed muted, too, as if she'd gone partially deaf, and what she could hear was different. Absent was the ambient drone she'd known her entire life, a hum composed of the noises generated by the tides, currents, and countless marine organisms striving to survive. In its place was only the susurrus of the breaking waves and a bit of clamor rising from the town at the end of the strand, where humans and their ilk shouted to one another, scraped barnacles from a beached ship, or pounded pegs into the half-completed hull of a new one.

Bracketed by fortifications where land met water, the settlement was as peculiar as the rest of the scene. Naturally, Serôsian towns had no use for docks or boats floating at anchor, but something else struck her as even odder. All the doors were at ground level, and that was where everyone moved about. Some of the rough coquina structures were several stories high, but even so, it was plain that in a real sense, humans lived their lives in only two dimensions.

The cloth rectangles—fields of black emblazoned with skulls, crossed swords, and similar devices—flapping atop several of the most imposing structures added a final note of strangeness.

Anton shivered and gave her a grin. "It's funny. When I was under water, I never really felt wet. Now that I'm in the air, I can feel I'm soaked."

"What do we do next?" asked Tu'ala'keth.

"The sea turned my clothes to rags. I need new ones. Even more importantly, I need a barber. The cult identified a spy with long hair and a proper Turmian square-cut beard. Accordingly, I mean to turn into a clean-shaven fellow with close-cropped locks.

"So here's the plan. At the end of the beach, there's a path that runs up around the edge of the town. If we take it, we can reach the fellow we need without everybody in town gawking at us."

"But surely some people will see us."

"Oh, yes, the lookouts manning the battlements at the very least."

"What if one of them is a cultist and knows your face?"

"It's unlikely, but should it happen, life may get interesting very quickly. If the prospect frightens you, you can always turn around and jump back into the water."

She scowled. "I would never shrink from anything Umberlee requires of me."

"Of course not. Perish the thought."

As they tramped up the beach, Tu'ala'keth kept a wary eye on her companion. She thought he might try to escape, but so far, he showed no signs of it. She wondered if he'd found the wisdom to embrace his destiny or if he was merely biding his time and reassured herself that it didn't matter either way. Umberlee would make use of him regardless.

Despite the magic woven into Tu'ala'keth's gear, the sun felt unpleasantly hot on her skin, and though she'd used it for years, her long trident suddenly seemed heavy. In time, she hit on the expedient of carrying it tilted over her shoulder, and that made it easier to manage ... until the shaft started galling her skin.

The path climbed as the pirate haven of Immurk's Hold itself ran upward from the harbor to higher ground. The slope made walking all the more difficult, and Tu'ala'keth's calf muscles and the soles of her bare feet ached at the unaccustomed motion. Once she and Anton passed the fortress, she took her mind off her discomfort by peering down the streets and alleys that connected to her route. Her initial impression was that humans shared their habitations with an interesting miscellany of animals: plump, crested, strutting birds that seemed unable to truly fly no matter how frantically they flapped their wings; fat, oinking creatures rooting in muck; a smaller, shaggier, bleating animal with hooves and horns; and by far the most numerous, little brown creatures with short legs and long, hairless tails, digging and scurrying through heaps of refuse.

"Here we are," said Anton. He led Tu'ala'keth down a quiet street so narrow the bright sun overhead left a welcome stripe of cool shade along one side. "I hope Rimardo is still in business."

"Is this someone you trust?"

Anton grinned. "The Red Knight forbid! But the old miser knows how to cut hair and stick leeches on a festering wound, sells clothing pilfered from the dead, and despises everybody too profoundly to go out of his way to help anyone. In the Pirate Isles, that's all you can expect of a barber." He pushed aside the makeshift oilcloth curtain that hung in place of a door.

Rimardo's shop proved to be a filthy one-room shack jammed full of bins, crates, and barrels. The proprietor himself, a scrawny, wrinkled, sour-faced runt of a man, sat the strapping Anton on a tall stool then had to step up on a box to reach his head. Though the spy had warned Tu'ala'keth that folk hereabouts were likely to stare at her, Rimardo showed no interest, nor, after determining what his customer wanted and negotiating a price, did he utter another word. Tu'ala'keth wondered if Anton patronized him partly because of his sullen, incurious nature.

She watched with mingled impatience and interest as the razor scraped away the Turmian's lathery whiskers. To her sensibilities, all body hair was disgusting, and even after the shave, he had his share, just as his muscular frame still had a lumpish thickness. But he didn't look as uncouth as before. The brown hue of his skin was pleasant to look on, and his square features, though coarse compared to those of most any shalarin, nonetheless bespoke resolution, and the green eyes, intelligence.

Rimardo evidently had no mirror a customer might employ to approve or disapprove his handiwork.

Anton ran his fingers over his jaw and scalp to assess the results then said, "Good enough." He rose from the stool and started rummaging through the bins and crates, strewing rejected garments on the floor. Rimardo evidently expected no less of his patrons, for he watched the process without comment.

Anton selected leather sandals; baggy, blue, knee-length breeches; a scarlet sash; and a loose, white, sleeveless shirt that opened all the way down the front. Indifferent to Tu'ala'keth's scrutiny—appropriately so, since her folk regarded nudity as normal, and there was no carnal attraction between their two species in any case—he stripped and pulled them on. "You can keep my old clothes," he said to Rimardo.

The barber spat in their general direction.

Anton grinned. "Yes, well, that's why I wanted new ones." He slipped the cutlass through the sash, tossed Rimardo one of the silver coins they had taken from Umberlee's altars, and led Tu'ala'keth back out into the open air.

"Are we ready now?" she asked.

"Almost. I've been many different men during my years of spying, but none of them had a tattoo of an octopus running down his left arm, and so I hanker for one now. It takes a few minutes. If I can find a secluded spot in which to work...." He cast about. "There." He strode to a neighboring shack, tried the door, and found it warped in its frame. He shoved hard, and it yielded with a squeal.

The little cottage was empty, devoid of furniture and tenants, too. She wondered how he'd been able to tell from the outside.

Anton murmured the same arcane rhyme over and over again, meanwhile drawing on his skin with his fingertip. An image took form beneath the strokes, clear and vivid as if the digit were a needle dipped in ink. She supposed he'd chosen to depict an octopus because of his recent combat and might not even realize the cephalopods were familiars of Umberlee. Still it was fitting that he branded himself with such a sign, whether he understood the significance or not.

When he finished, she said, "Now we begin."

He grinned. "Yes, impatient one. I wanted to be inconspicuous until I achieved the proper appearance, but henceforth, you can attract as much attention as you like. Parade as if you expect people to stare and to make way for you, too. As if you're a personage."

"I am. We both are: agents of the Queen of the Depths."

"That's the spirit."

Now they marched through the center of town, down teeming streets and across bustling marketplaces selling what were evidently plundered goods, cringing or stolid slaves included. Unfamiliar sights, sounds, and stinks came quickly, relentlessly, now. It was almost enough to disorient her, and she watched Anton with special care lest he attempt to lose himself in the crowds.

He didn't, though, and in a few minutes, they arrived at one of the massive coquina structures that appeared to be fortresses as much as houses. A rectangular black cloth, emblazoned with a white grinning skull above and a red axe beneath, flapped from a pole atop the roof.

"Behold the residence of Vurgrom, self-styled 'the Mighty,'" Anton said. "With luck, he and the captains of his faction are still looking for new crewmen. They've suffered losses of late."

"Are you certain?"

"Who do you think informed the Turmian fleet where to intercept Vurgrom's ships before I had to take up the matter of the cult? Shall we?"

Though the house could likely serve as a bastion at need, the wrought-iron gates were unguarded and unlocked. Dozens of air-breathers, human mostly but with a smattering of other races, occupied the courtyard beyond. Some sat at trestle tables gorging, drinking, playing cards, or throwing knucklebones. A few wrestled or fenced with clattering wooden swords. At the far end, though, business was in progress. A knot of folk stood beneath a verandah, where dignitaries slouched in rattan chairs could survey them, should they deign to take notice. Unfortunately, the petitioners had competition for their betters' attention. At the moment, the captains, if that was who they were, seemed more interested in consulting with each other and with the flunkies scurrying in and out of the door behind them.

Tu'ala'keth and Anton headed toward the press. "Captain Vurgrom!" shouted the spy.

One of the petitioners, a squat man with a snout of a nose and two pointed teeth jabbing up from his underbite across his upper lip—an indication, Tu'ala'keth surmised, that his ancestry wasn't pure human— turned and growled, "Wait your turn!" Then he caught sight of her, and his eyes widened in surprise.

"We might do that," Anton said, "if we intended to serve as ordinary reavers. But since we merit something grander, we take priority. Now, I'm sure you recognize my companion for what she is. Shut your hole before she lays Umberlee's curse on you."

The pirate scowled, but he stepped back, too.

"Captain Vurgrom!" Anton called.

A hulking whale of a man with a braided red beard sat in the center of the platform in a high-backed chair that looked in imminent danger of collapsing under his weight. He held a golden, ruby-studded cup in one meaty, copper-furred hand, and a prodigious battle-axe lay at his feet. He looked around in annoyance, evidently, but put away his glower when he spotted Tu'ala'keth.

"I'm Vurgrom the Mighty," he said, "and those who wear the drowned man's hand are always welcome in my palace."

She inclined her head to acknowledge his courtesy. "That is well. I am Tu'ala'keth. I have decided to sail with you for a season. We will take lives together, in sacrifice to Umberlee."

"In other words," said Anton, "we're offering ourselves as officers. Tu'ala'keth is both a waveservant and a shalarin. She wields powers over sea and storm no human, orc, or what have you can hope to match. Whereas I"—he grinned—"have my own talents. I can swing a cutlass as well as any man here and practice sorcery as well. In my time, I've been a navigator and a boatswain, too. I guarantee the ship that brings us aboard will profit."

Someone made a contemptuous, spitting sound.

Surprised, Tu'ala'keth turned to see a burly, sneering, ruddy-faced man clad in dark vestments decorated with dabs and jagged streaks of silver. The hem and the ends of the sleeves were cut in ragged, sawtooth fashion. A patch covered his right eye, and he held a spear in his hand.

It all served to mark him as a priest of Talos the Destroyer, chieftain of the Deities of Fury, and Tu'ala'keth felt a spasm of reflexive dislike. On the surface, Umberlee was Talos's ally, even, in a certain sense, his subordinate, but as a waveservant advanced in the faith, she learned that her goddess and religion strove for the day when they could topple the Storm Lord from his preeminence.

"You sound like very special people," the Talassan jeered. "But you're too late. There was only one captain looking for officers today, and she's already chosen my friend and me for ship's mage and priest."

"Umberlee sent me here," said Tu'ala'keth, "and death upon the sea is her dominion. If you truly revere the powers of Fury's Heart, you will step aside."

"I revere Talos," said the man with the eye patch. "Your patron is merely his whore, and so I caution you to pay him the respect he deserves."

"Theology's always fascinated me," Anton drawled, "but unless I've washed up on the wrong shore, this is an assembly of freebooters, not priests. So I'll simply say this: I don't know you, Patch, or this friend of yours, either. But I'm still sure Tu'ala'keth and I will prove of more use than you to the captain who was considering choosing you—"

"Who *has* chosen us!" said the Talassan, glaring.

"—or to some other with the good sense to recruit us."

Vurgrom grinned. "That's bold talk, stranger."

"Anton Fallone." The spy, who'd warned Tu'ala'keth he meant to give a false name, now turned his gaze on the only female seated among the captains. She was a young human, slim by the standards of her race, with bronze-colored curls. She wore an abundance of glittering, delicate jewelry and a frilly gown that contrasted oddly with her several scars and the dense tattooing crawling on her bare arms, shoulders, and neck. "Captain, I believe you are a person of sense. I see it in your face."

Now that Anton had spoken to her directly, the Talassan's features turned blotchy and even redder. "If you have any sense," he said to the spy, "you and your pet fish won't annoy a priest of the Destroyer any further than you have already."

"I doubt," said Tu'ala'keth, "that anyone here is so foolish as to fear Talos more than Umberlee. It was she who proved her power by smiting these islands only fifteen years ago."

"All the more reason," said the human priest, "to honor the god who holds the Bitch's leash."

It was an obscene image—the mistress of the raging

sea, destruction incarnate, *leashed*—and even had Tu'ala'keth been willing to let the blasphemy pass, she sensed that if she and Anton did, they'd forfeit all hope of winning the pirates' respect and places of authority among them.

Accordingly, she brandished her skeletal amulet on the end of its cord and declaimed a prayer. The folk standing between her and the Talassan realized what she intended and scrambled out of the way. The holy words of the incantation sounded hushed and strange enunciated in air instead of water, but she could feel power massing and knew she was performing the conjuration properly. On the final syllable, a harsh noise blared. People cursed and clapped their hands over their ears. The Talassan staggered a step, and blood dripped from his nostrils.

But to her disappointment, the attack didn't hit hard enough to disrupt his own chanting and gesturing. He thrust out his hand, and a rustling, fan-shaped burst of something yellow and fluid exploded from his fingertips. She tried to jump out of the way, but it brushed her even so, searing her flank despite the silverweave.

She realized the stuff was flame. It was clever of the human priest to strike at her with a force alien to her experience. But she refused to let it spook her or even to take her eyes off him to see if the fire had taken root in her flesh, even though she'd heard it could cling to you and burn and burn and burn.

Meanwhile, another man stepped forth from the crowd. Plainly, he must be the Talassan's comrade.

Tu'ala'keth hadn't taken a good look at him before. Her circumstances were too unfamiliar, too many people were milling about, and things were happening too quickly. She beheld a gaunt, wrinkled man with piercing maroon eyes, a lantern jaw, and a long, tangled mane of graying hair. He wore a russet mantle embroidered with black serpents and carried a long staff of rusty iron, with another snake, carved from carnelian, twining around it.

Tu'ala'keth was no wizard, but she'd mastered her own form of magic, and generally recognized power when she saw it. The man was a conjuror of considerable talents. Fortunately, she didn't have to contend with both him and the Talassan by herself. Cutlass in hand, Anton ran at the warlock, who swept his serpent-girded staff through mystic passes. Strangely, though, he didn't recite any words of power, any more than he'd taken part in the verbal preliminaries to the fight.

She perceived that much in an instant but didn't have the luxury of watching any more. She had to stay focused on the Talassan. Hurrying as quickly as she dared—it would do no good to botch the incantation—she commenced another spell. Had her opponent done the same, she likely would have finished first, but instead, he resorted to a different form of magic. He simply shook his spear at her, and suddenly he seemed huge, fearsome, more vivid and real than anything else in the world. The sheer, naked force of his anger made her want to turn and flee or grovel and beg for mercy.

She understood what was the matter. Most every priest possessed the ability to affright or command the undead, and some clerics exercised such powers against other sorts of beings as well. The Talassan apparently knew how to chasten creatures of the sea.

But mere comprehension didn't negate the effect. She had to deny it. Push it out of her head. She snarled, "I am a waveservant!" and felt the compulsion crumble away.

By that time, though, the Talassan had reached the end of another conjuration. Distortion shimmered around his outstretched hand, and a shrill whine cut through the air. He was attempting a sonic attack of his own, but to Tu'ala'keth's surprise, his effort didn't hammer and tear at her flesh. Instead, the silverweave shivered on her torso as if trying to shred itself to pieces. Her foe somehow recognized that if he destroyed it, she wouldn't be able to breathe.

But the coral mesh held together. She chanted a prayer, and the few stray blades of grass pushing up between the flagstones at the human's feet abruptly multiplied, thickened, and grew tall. For a split second, they undulated like eels then whipped around the human and yanked themselves tight, binding his limbs. They crawled higher still, seeking his head to gag, blind, and smother him.

The Talassan had no choice but to try to dissolve the effect. Otherwise, it would render him helpless. He started jabbering a counterspell, and Tu'ala'keth cried, "Silence!" The charge of magic infusing the word stole his voice only for an instant, but that was enough to spoil the rhythm of his conjuration.

Green strands coiled around his mouth then masked his face completely. He heaved and thrashed, lost his balance, and fell. Tu'ala'keth hefted her trident and ran at him.

"Enough!" Vurgrom bellowed.

Tu'ala'keth felt a pang of frustration and nearly defied the command. But to do so might hinder Umberlee's cause, so she halted short of her target.

An instant later, the coils of grass burned away in a flash of fire. Even bound as he was, the Talassan had somehow managed to destroy them. He sprang to his feet, raised his spear over his head, and shouted rhyming words.

"I said, enough!" Vurgrom said. "The fight's over, Kassur. The shalarin beat you, and her friend beat Chadrezzan." The spectators cheered or groaned and swore, depending on their sympathies.

The man with the eye patch shuddered as if he found the words unbearable, as if the violence of his nature left him no choice but to ignore them. It made Tu'ala'keth feel an odd twinge of sympathy. They might be enemies, but they were also both priests of the Gods of Fury, and understood that by rights, a duel such as theirs should end in death.

But they were also trying to make their way among folk who lacked their sacred insights. So in the end, he broke off his conjuring and gave a curt, grudging nod, and she, too, forbore to strike at him again.

Several paces away, Chadrezzan lay on the ground with blood seeping from a torn lip, while Anton stood over him, cutlass poised to chop. But when the spy saw that the wizard intended to obey Vurgrom's command, he grinned and reached to help him up. Chadrezzan spat, ignored the proffered hand, and rose on his own, moving in a slow, pained manner that suggested that, at some point during the fracas, Anton had kicked or kneed him in the crotch. The spy shrugged and sauntered back to Tu'ala'keth's side.

"Good," Vurgrom said. "Freebooters brawl, if they're any good at their trade. It's natural and gives the rest of us something to bet on. But I don't see any point in letting you butcher one another when you could all be useful to the faction."

"But in what roles?" asked the tattooed woman, her manner that of a protégé seeking guidance of a mentor. "I'd like to bring all four of them aboard *Shark's Bliss*, but I can't lead a company that's all officers and no common hands."

The huge man chuckled. "It's your ship and your decision, honey cake. I can only advise. Though I will say that I would never have taken all the prizes I have, nor won eternal fame, if I hadn't favored men who'd already proved they knew how to win a fight."

"Hmm." "Honey cake" took a second, pretending

to deliberate, though it was plain to Tu'ala'keth that Vurgrom's words had already decided for her. "Waveservant, Anton, my name is Shandri Clayhill. I'd like to bring you aboard *Shark's Bliss* as ship's priest and mage."

"That's outrageous!" Kassur exploded. "You already offered the positions to Chadrezzan and me, and he's a master wizard, able to slay a dozen men or shatter a hull with a single spell. All you've seen this impostor do is cast a couple of petty charms."

"He's right, of course," murmured Anton to Tu'ala'keth. "The mute's a true magician, far more powerful than the likes of me. But I recognized him as an elementalist, and elemental magic isn't dainty. It takes up space. So I hovered close to the crowd as I advanced on him, and he couldn't throw his most potent spells at me for fear of hitting them as well. Vurgrom wouldn't have stood for that."

Captain Clayhill glanced at Vurgrom, evidently making sure Kassur's outburst hadn't swayed him, then said, "My decision stands. But you and your comrade are welcome aboard the *Bliss* as well, on the understanding that, for the time being, anyway, you'll serve as ordinary gentlemen of fortune, receiving one share each, not two."

"We accept," gritted Kassur, "for now." He glared at Anton and Tu'ala'keth, and she answered with a sneer.

THE PRIESTS

Some of the folk in the boisterous crowd staggered or moved with exaggerated care. Others spoke too loudly or slurred their words. Despite the noise and the frequent jostling, a few snored, sprawling back in their chairs with limbs akimbo or with their heads cradled in their arms on wet, scarred tabletops.

Puzzled, Tu'ala'keth turned to Anton. "Is this a sick house?" she asked.

Anton grinned. "A tavern. Don't you have taverns—and intoxicants, and drunks—in Serôs?"

"We have intoxicants, but no establishments like this."

"Well, now that you're a pirate, you'd better get used to them."

Captain Clayhill motioned to them, and

they followed her and the rest of her officers on through the press.

Toward the rear, the common area with its benches, hearth, and hard-packed bare-earth floor broke apart into hodgepodge of smaller rooms, niches, and closets fitted haphazardly together. The captain was evidently familiar with the layout, for she led her officers—save for Tu'ala'keth, a mix of humans and the stooped, brutish, gray-skinned race known as orcs—straight to the private chamber she'd hired for the occasion.

Tu'ala'keth was grateful when the door shut out the noise and stink of the common room. Someone had already brought in pewter goblets and bottles of wine, and several of her companions made haste to pour themselves drinks, but she didn't follow their example. No sea creature drank anything—or else, depending on how one looked at it, one drank constantly, simply by using one's gills—but even if she had been susceptible to thirst, she would have been more interested in the map spread on the table, the curling corners weighted by extra cups.

She saw with relief that she could pick out the place Anton had specified when he'd sketched a far cruder chart in the sand. By her standards, she knew a fair amount about the shape of the world. She could have drawn a map of Serôs in considerable detail. But she'd never had any reason to concern herself with what lay beyond its waters.

"Are you ready?" Captain Clayhill asked. Though still aglitter with jewels and frills, she was no longer the girlish sycophant taking her cues from Vurgrom. Away from him, she put on a harshness, a striding, shoving impatience, which had taken Tu'ala'keth by surprise.

"Yes," the shalarin said.

"Then find us a worthy prize."

"As you wish." Tu'ala'keth seated herself, yet another action that felt clumsy in a medium as lacking in buoyancy as air. "It will be helpful if everyone stays quiet."

The pirates settled to watch her. She gripped her skeletal pendant with one hand, poised the other over the chart, murmured words of praise to Umberlee, and pretended to slip into a trance.

It gave her a vague sense of shame. Her creed taught her to use every weapon and seize every advantage in the pursuit of her ends—to resort to subterfuge whenever she deemed it useful. Still she couldn't help feeling it was one thing to lie about mundane matters, and something else, something akin to blasphemy, to claim she was employing her sacred gifts when, in fact, nothing of the sort was going on. Despite Anton's assertions to the contrary, she had no more talent for divination than any other cleric.

But the spy insisted they needed to exploit her cachet as an exotic shalarin waveservant to further their mission. Since it was manifestly Umberlee's will that the endeavor succeed, Tu'ala'keth swallowed her qualms as best she could.

She let the litany of praise fade into a wordless croon. She'd once known a genuine oracle who made sounds like that. When she felt the first phase of the charade had gone on long enough, she brought her index finger stabbing down.

Everyone leaned to see where she was pointing. "Saerloon," Captain Clayhill said.

"I see docks," droned Tu'ala'keth. The somnolent voice she'd adopted made her sound like the drunken men outside. "Buildings with a wall around them, an enclave accessible from land or sea. People bring bags and chests stuffed with gold to buy what the folk in the compound have to sell."

"It all fitth tho far," said Sealmid. He was the first mate, a human with a broken nose, many missing teeth and, in consequence, a lisp. "A good many rich traderth have a thetup like that. But which—"

Harl the helmsman, an orc whose garments of clashing colors were garish even by freebooters' standards, shushed him.

"I see the men in charge," Tu'ala'keth continued. "They carry staves and wands. They wear red."

Everyone stared at her. Finally the helmsman said, "Are you talking about Thayans?"

"I do not know," Tu'ala'keth said. She wanted them to believe that, as a gifted seer, she could perceive all matter of hidden things, but her instincts told her the ploy would be more convincing if her powers fell short of omniscience. "But Saerloon is not their homeland. They trade talismans and potions for heaps of yellow gold."

"Thayanth," Sealmid sighed. "All honor to the Bitch Queen, but thith doethn't help uth."

"Hear her out," said Anton, his gaze fixed on Captain Clayhill. "Please."

The pirate leader shrugged her tattoo-covered shoulders, where images of blossoms and butterflies mingled with skulls, snarling basilisks, and bloody swords. "I suppose we might as well."

Tu'ala'keth rambled on, laying out the rest of the information in a disjointed sort of way, as if, in her daze, she failed to comprehend its meaning. She reckoned that too would make it seem as if she were plucking it from the spirit world as opposed to repeating facts and rumors Anton had gleaned during his years as a spy.

When she reached the end, she sat quietly for a moment then gave a little jerk as if waking from a doze. "What did I say?" she asked.

Harl gave her a yellow-fanged smile. "You told us

a lot, waveservant. Unfortunately, it was all about Thayans. Nobody raids Thayans. It's bad luck."

"The kind of bad luck where the Red Wizardth turn you into a worm or light you on fire like a candle when you try," Sealmid said.

Tu'ala'keth scowled. "Umberlee has chosen these folk to be her prey, and ours. We will not fail."

Captain Clayhill sat frowning, staring into the depths of her amber wine, then gave her head a shake. "If it worked, we'd make a fortune. But the risk is too great. I waited too long to command *Shark's Bliss* to lose her now."

According to Anton, in theory, pirate crews elected their captains, but the truth was more complex. On Dragon Isle, no one ascended to such a position without the approval of one of the several factions. Tu'ala'keth could readily believe Shandri Clayhill had spent a long, dreary time cultivating Vurgrom before he endorsed her aspirations.

"Try again," the human continued. "Find us another target."

Tu'ala'keth ostentatiously folded her arms. "No. The goddess has already spoken."

Captain Clayhill glared. "I revere Umberlee, and I respect her clerics. But you're one of my officers now, and you'll follow orders."

"Hold on," Anton said. "Let's at least discuss the Thayans before we give up all hope of robbing them. Tu'ala'keth has given us their secrets. That should enable us to discern their weaknesses and put together a plan to exploit them. What if...."

Pretending to devise it on the spot, he laid out his scheme. The notion was that she would prove herself a powerful seer and spellcaster, he would establish himself as a cunning strategist, and as a result, the pirates would come to hold them both in high regard.

After he finished, the reavers sat quietly for a heartbeat or two, pondering. Then Harl said, "It isn't the stupidest plan I ever heard. I can halfway imagine it working."

"Can you halfway imagine the part that cometh after?" Sealmid asked. "Thay we do escape with the loot. Then a bunch of the really powerful Red Wizardth get together and lay a curthe on uth."

"They have an ugly reputation," Anton said, "and deservedly so. But they're not gods. They have their limits."

"Whereas Umberlee is the greatest of gods," said Tu'ala'keth. "Do her bidding, and she will protect you."

"I believe you," Captain Clayhill said. "I do. But to hazard *Shark's Bliss* in the way Anton suggests.... No. It would be too easy for things to go wrong."

Tu'ala'keth stared into the captain's eyes. "You say you believe, but in truth, you have no faith at all, neither in Umberlee nor in yourself. No faith and no courage. Perhaps you had them once, but as you toadied to Vurgrom—and surrendered yourself to his lusts—they withered inside you."

Captain Clayhill sprang to her feet. "Give me your sword," she snarled to Sealmid.

Tu'ala'keth remained seated, as if the human's anger was of no concern to her, thus maintaining the appearance of strength. "Will you strike me, then? To what end? Will the other reavers finally respect you if you kill me sitting in my chair?"

The captain gripped the hilt of Sealmid's broadsword but didn't raise it to threaten Tu'ala'keth—not yet. "The other reavers *do* respect me!"

"No," said Tu'ala'keth, "they do not. To gain their admiration, you strove for your captaincy, but the manner in which you achieved it makes it a lewd jest.

"You know this, and it gnaws your soul. You tell yourself you would do anything to achieve true respect, but you lie. The trouble with the mask of servility is that, worn too long, it starts to impress its shape on the face beneath. Without realizing it, the pretender opens himself to genuine meekness and uncertainty.

"So it is that you fear to wager what little you have already gained. Even though no pirate wins glory except through daring and ferocity.

"Umberlee wishes to wake these sleeping virtues in you. Because you have the potential to be the greatest of reavers and stain the waters red with the blood of your prey. I see it now. It is why she sent me to you.

"But to achieve your destiny, you must pay heed when she speaks through me. It begins here. Do what other captains fear to do. Plunder the Thayans. Win the respect of Dragon Isle, so that one day, you may rule it. Vurgrom and his rivals aspire for supremacy, like Immurk in his day, but the prize will be yours if you find the strength to take it."

Captain Clayhill stared at Tu'ala'keth in manifest astonishment. Finally the human's lips quirked upward. "It's tricky to know how to respond when somebody insults you with one breath and praises you with the next."

"I did neither. I spoke the truth as the Queen of the Depths revealed it to me. Hear or ignore it as you please."

Captain Clayhill turned to Anton. "Tell me your idiot plan again," she said, "from the beginning."

When she'd set sail, *Shark's Bliss* had been a sleek, handsome, two-masted caravel. As Anton considered her now, he supposed she was still handsome, but it was harder to see. The primary impression was one of calamity. The ship wallowed low in the waves, as if she were sinking. The sails hung in tatters.

The crippled state of the vessel made the pirates grumble. Just as tense, Captain Clayhill stood beside Anton on the aft castle gazing out over the heaving, gray-green expanse of the sea. Her fingers with their gleaming rings kneaded the rail. Even on the brink of battle, she still wore a frilly, impractical gown, like a lady attending a banquet or ball.

"Where is she?" the captain asked.

"She'll be back soon," said Anton, hoping it was so. Tu'ala'keth could take care of herself, and was inconspicuous when she swam primarily beneath the sea. Yet even so, it was chancy to go looking for a Red Wizard's vessel. She couldn't know what enchantments he had in place to detect sentient creatures, or spellcasting, in his vicinity.

Finally Durth, the orc in the crow's next, called, "I see her!" In another moment, Anton did, too, as she parted company with her seahorse and swam to the ship. He tossed the rope ladder over the side, and blue skin and black fin wet and gleaming, the shalarin climbed upward with a facility that demonstrated she'd finally mastered the knack of moving nimbly even out of the water.

"Did you find them?" Captain Clayhill asked.

"Yes," said Tu'ala'keth. She adjusted the strap securing her tinted goggles to her head. "I spoke to the wind and current, and they shifted their courses. As a result, the Thayans will come close enough to sight us."

"Good." The captain turned and shouted down the length of the ship: "It's time! Go below if you're supposed to. If you're staying on deck, look tired, thirsty, and helpless. If you're carrying a weapon bigger than a knife, get rid of it."

"Prejudice against orcs, that's what this is," Harl said. All the members of his warlike race had to hide in the cramped, half-flooded hold. Otherwise, the *Bliss* wouldn't look as they needed her to look. He gave Anton a wink and headed for the companionway.

Kassur and Chadrezzan had to go below as well, but did so with an ill grace. Tu'ala'keth dived back over the side to conceal herself beneath the waves.

Then, once again, there was nothing to do but wait. Anton had spent much of his life on one ship or another, and knew how long it took for two vessels to rendezvous on the open sea. Still time crawled.

At last, squinting, he glimpsed the Thayan caravel, a speck far to the northeast. He was sure the Thayans' lookout had spotted *Shark's Bliss* as well. But would they change course to meet her?

He thought so. She flew the flag of Aglarond, Thay's bitter enemy, and looked defenseless. Were Anton a Red Wizard, he'd certainly take the time to plunder the foundering ship, capture those on board to ransom or enslave, and salvage the vessel itself if possible. It was too juicy an opportunity to pass up.

Yet he sweated until he could tell the Thayans had in fact turned southwest.

He supposed he still had reason to be anxious. The Thayans could conceivably maintain a certain distance and batter *Shark's Bliss* with magic, volleys of arrows, and bolts from their ballista. If they did, the pirate vessel, unable to maneuver or run, had no hope of surviving. His ruse had seen to that.

But the Thayans wouldn't take that tack, not if convinced they had nothing to fear. Such a barrage could only diminish the value of their prize.

The Thayan caravel was larger than the *Bliss*. Her hull, sails, and streaming banners were all varying shades of crimson, and she maneuvered so smartly that enchantment was surely involved.

"Prepare to be boarded!" someone shouted. Grappling hooks flew, and crunched into the pirate vessel's timbers. The Thayans heaved on the lines, drawing the ships together. With *Shark's Bliss* riding low in the water, the red caravel's deck was a few feet higher, but even so, it would be possible to clamber from one to the other.

The Thayans proceeded to do so. Clad in leather armor and armed with javelins, boarding pikes, and short swords, the shouting warriors herded their new prisoners into a single clump. Anton tried to look scared and submissive while studying the newcomers. He needed to identify the spellcasters.

He could see only one magician, a short, tubby Red Wizard with a rosy-cheeked, incongruously jolly face. Like all members of his fraternity, the Thayan had shaved every hair from his head, eyebrows included. Vermilion tattooing showed on his neck and wrists. He was likely marked over much of his body, but the scarlet robe hid most of it.

It was lucky the Thayans had only one warlock, and that he'd elected to come aboard *Shark's Bliss*, where his foes could reach him more easily. Armed with a spiked ball and chain, clad in flame-yellow vestments, a priest of Kossuth the Firelord still stood in the forecastle of the crimson ship. He could be trouble.

"Now then," said the Red Wizard in a cheerful tenor voice, "who's the skipper of this unfortunate vessel?"

"I am," Shandri Clayhill said.

The Thayan's eyes opened wide in surprise. "Are you indeed? How charming. May I ask, how did the ship come to grief?"

"A squall. Look, I have coin and land back in Velprintalar. I can reward you for rescuing us."

The Red Wizard chuckled and fingered one of the gold-and-diamond necklaces dangling on her bosom. "You already have rewarded me, dear girl, and will again later, more intimately. If you're enthusiastic, perhaps you can avoid—"

Still bound together, the two ships fell.

As planned, Tu'ala'keth had cast a spell to scoop the water from beneath their hulls. They dropped several feet, down a hole in the gray-green sea. Everyone slammed down hard when the vessels hit bottom, but at least the pirates had known what to expect, whereas the sudden plummet caught the Thayans entirely by surprise. Some surely suffered sprains and broken bones. All looked stupid with astonishment.

The spell effect ended as abruptly as it began. Saltwater crashed across the deck, engulfing everything, and Anton was suddenly afraid they'd remain submerged, that they lacked the buoyancy to rise. But then they bobbed up into air and sunlight.

Screaming crazily, pirates erupted from every hatch that led down into the hold. Despite their lack of weapons, the freebooters who'd remained on deck also sprang at the stunned and disoriented Thayans.

Anton looked for the Red Wizard. Though the reavers currently had the advantage, a powerful mage might alter that with a single spell. But not if he was denied the time to cast it.

There! The plump wizard had placed his back to the rail, and some of his bodyguards had positioned themselves in front of him. The man in red intoned a chant as sonorous as a dirge and swept his hands in slow passes. Cool, whispering gloom drifted across the deck, as if the sun had passed behind a cloud.

Anton knew he'd never fight his way through the bodyguards in time to stop the spell, but fortunately, that wasn't his only option. Another Thayan—swept overboard or killed by a pirate, the spy neither knew nor cared—had dropped his javelin on the deck. Anton snatched it up and threw it.

It was a difficult throw because the spear had to pass between two of the guards to reach its mark, but he managed it. The point drove deep into the Red

Wizard's chest. Looking bewildered, he stumbled backward to slam into the rail. It cracked in two, and he tumbled into the sea. Sunlight scoured the shadow from the air.

Anton instantly pivoted to find the priest of Kossuth. Curse it! Nobody else had neutralized the divine, and he was conjuring, too, bellowing and swinging his chain weapon over his head. The spiked ball at the end had ignited and left an arc of flame behind it like a tame shooting star.

Anton would never reach the brazier, as such folk were called, in time to stop him. He peered about for another missile, even a makeshift one, but nothing came to hand. He wondered just how horrific the fire magic was going to be.

Then the brazier lurched forward, and blood gushed from his mouth. His knees buckled, and when he collapsed, he revealed Tu'ala'keth standing behind him. She yanked her stone trident from his back and raised it in salutation.

Anton grinned and nodded back. Then they each turned to find another foe.

The fight lasted only another minute before the Thayans started throwing down their arms. They were able warriors, but without leadership or magic of their own, they couldn't stand up to the pirates' fury or the flares of flame, lightning, and withering darkness with which Kassur and Chadrezzan assailed them.

The freebooters cheered, and Anton smiled and shook his head. All things considered, the first phase had gone easier than expected.

Tu'ala'keth declaimed the sacred words and with the aid of her helpers, shoved the surviving Thayans over the side, one at a time. Some of the naked prisoners merely wept or advanced to the sacrifice as if sleepwalking. Others begged for mercy, screamed curses, or struggled to break free of their captors' grips.

Their resistance didn't bother her. It was appropriate that the sacrifice should fight to survive if it could. Umberlee even spared a few of them, as she'd spared Anton. What vexed Tu'ala'keth was the attitude of many of the pirates, who mocked and jeered at the doomed Thayans, behaving as if the ritual was an entertainment.

"Silence!" she cried at last. The spectators gaped in surprise. "This is a holy occasion. Do you wish to anger Umberlee, who gave you victory? She is quick to anger, I assure you. You can easily turn her against you."

"Glory to the Bitch Queen," said Harl. The orc was one of the pirates who'd volunteered to assist in the rite. Other freebooters repeated the phrase in a ragged chorus.

The deference pleased Tu'ala'keth—until she thought to contrast it with the apostasy of her own people. Then it took an effort of will for her to maintain a worshipful frame of mind until the conclusion of the ceremony.

After that, she turned her attention to the hold. Her magic could help the squeaking, gurgling hand pumps draw the water out. But before she could begin the prayer, a joyous whoop aboard the red caravel snagged her attention.

"Look at this!" called Durth. He threw back the lid of a brass-bound leather chest and lifted out a fistful of pewter vials, displaying them for all to see. No doubt they contained magical elixirs. A second box yielded gleaming, finely crafted broadswords and rapiers, surely bearing enchantments bound in the steel.

"The hold ith full of magic!" Sealmid cried.

Everyone cheered, and when the clamor subsided,

Kassur and Chadrezzan were standing with Durth, Sealmid, and the other folk who'd gone to explore the Thayan vessel. Tu'ala'keth blinked, for she hadn't seen the Talassans make their approach. All at once, they were simply there, at the center of attention.

"It is a rich prize," said Kassur. Tu'ala'keth had yet to hear Chadrezzan utter a word. Either he truly was a mute or he'd sworn a vow of silence. "I say we take it back to Dragon Isle and enjoy it."

"As I recall," said Anton, "we've only completed the first part of our plan. Stripped to the waist, a rope in hand, he stood at the base of the *Bliss*'s aft mast, where he'd been helping to replace the tattered sails with serviceable ones. "We have the talismans that were going to Saerloon, but not the gold the Thayans expect to send home. I say we steal everything."

"That's foolish," the man with the eye patch answered. "We were lucky once. Our prize had only one Red Wizard and a single priest aboard, and we caught them by surprise."

"As we expect," Anton said, "to take their counterparts in Saerloon by surprise."

"That may not happen," Kassur said. "Even if it does, I guarantee you, we'll find several Red Wizards on hand, some far advanced in the mysteries of their craft. We'll find defenses in place, and whatever the shalarin claims, I doubt her scrying discovered all of them. It isn't worth the risk. Let's pass the dice while Lady Luck's still smiling."

Tu'ala'keth understood what was truly in the Talassan's mind. He still coveted her position for himself, and Anton's rank for Chadrezzan. He wanted the crew of *Shark's Bliss* to sacrifice primarily to Talos, not Umberlee. But none of that would come to pass so long as she and the Turmian kept guiding their comrades to notable victories. Thus, the storm priest counseled turning back not because he expected the raid on Saerloon to fail, but because he feared it might succeed.

"Are you scared?" Anton asked him.

"If so," said Tu'ala'keth, "how dare you wear the Destroyer's vestments? Does he not command his followers to be fierce and bold?"

Kassur hesitated. He evidently hadn't expected anyone to accuse him of being lax in the observance of his own savage creed. Perceiving that he didn't know how to respond, the pirates muttered to one another.

"Talos doesn't command us to seek our own destruction!" Kassur managed at last. "He tells us to destroy our enemies!"

"Then let's destroy them," Anton said.

Tu'ala'keth turned to the aft castle, where Captain Clayhill had positioned herself to watch the sacrifice and supervise the ongoing repairs. Some of her jewelry still glittered dazzling bright in the sunlight. Other pieces were dull with spatters of Thayan gore.

"You began this voyage with courage and faith," said Tu'ala'keth. "I urge you to continue in the same spirit."

"If you want to come home with as grand a haul as any pirate's ever stolen," Anton said, "and a tale people will tell not just for a tenday or two, but for the rest of our lives."

Harl laughed. "That sounds good to me, Captain. Especially the part about the loot."

Shandri Clayhill drew a deep breath then gave a nod. "So be it. We sail to Saerloon, and may the gods pity any Thayan bastard who wanders within reach of our blades."

The reavers cheered. Kassur and Chadrezzan glared at Anton and Tu'ala'keth with balked, bitter anger in their eyes.

Even late at night, Saerloon was a bustling port, and the land adjacent to the water was accordingly too valuable for any of it to go waste. Still, as Anton surveyed the Thayan compound at the northern end of the harbor, it seemed to him that it stood a little apart from its neighbors, as if shunned. Maybe it was just his imagination.

Or maybe it wasn't. Everybody hated Thayans, and rightfully so. The whoresons wanted to conquer all of Faerûn. People being people, though, they tolerated the Red Wizards and their minions because they sold magic cheaply. They bought it even though the coin went back to Thay to finance the zulkirs' schemes to undermine and ultimately subjugate their neighbors.

But the coin these particular Thayans were sitting on would not be going back to Thay. If Anton had his way, it was bound for Dragon Isle.

The scarlet caravel glided toward to the dock. Clad in the armor and clothing of the former crew, most of the pirates were aboard. They'd left a few hands on *Shark's Bliss*, the minimum required to see her safely home.

Harl turned the helm a notch. "If we haven't fooled them," he said, "I guess we'll find out when the thunderbolts start flying."

"We flashed the proper signal with the lantern," Anton said. Of course, that was only if the Thayans hadn't changed the code and if the information he'd picked up in a thieves' den in Selgaunt had been accurate to begin with. "This is the caravel they're expecting. The dark should keep them from seeing the ship is crawling with orcs." He shrugged. "I'm optimistic."

Harl snorted. "'Crawling with orcs.' Nice talk."

A breeze wafted the stink of a great city in their direction, a smell compounded of garbage and smoke.

The caravel glided closer to the dock, where a pair of bald, robed Red Wizards and their bodyguards waited to greet her, and workers scurried about lighting torches to facilitate the process of mooring and unloading her. The flickering yellow illumination revealed the hulking statue at the water's edge. Twice as tall as a man, it was nearly as wide as it was high, with enormous clenched fists and a face that was all snarling mouth and a single glaring eye.

Anton studied the Thayans. As best he could judge—the night hampered his vision, too—none of them looked alarmed or even particularly wary. It wasn't until the pirates started tossing lines to the dockhands that one of the latter abruptly goggled in shock. Maybe he'd noticed the flat-nosed countenance of an orc or Tu'ala'keth's narrow inhuman features and black dorsal fin.

Given a chance, the dockhand surely would have cried a warning. But Tu'ala'keth, in the stern castle, and Kassur, in the forward one, each cast the same spell, and all the ambient sounds—the creak of ropes and timbers, the splash and hiss of the water, the conversation on the dock, and the muddled drone of the city beyond—cut off abruptly, supplanted by utter silence.

Weapons in hand, the first pirates sprang from the caravel to the dock like a wave sweeping onto the shore. In so doing, they slammed some of the Thayans off the platform into the water, and perhaps those were the lucky ones. They might survive if they could swim away.

A warrior thrust his spear at Anton. The spy parried—thanks to the magic bound in the massive cutlass, the quick, precise defensive action was easy enough—and hacked open the Thayan's belly. The soldier reeled and toppled off the pier.

Anton pivoted, seeking the Red Wizards. He had no doubt the magicians were still dangerous, even bereft of the ability to recite incantations. Some spells, and a good many sorcerous weapons, didn't require the wielder to jabber words of power.

At first he couldn't tell anything. The pier was too narrow. The combatants were jammed together, obscuring the view. Then he caught a glimpse of a Red Wizard leveling a wand. Captain Clayhill slashed his neck with a boarding pike. Half severed, his head flopped back on his shoulders, blood spurted, and the arcane weapon dropped from his twitching fingers.

Good, one down, but where was the other? There! Anton pushed toward him. Before he could reach him, though, the Red Wizard brushed back his voluminous sleeve and ran his fingertip down the curved length of a tattooed sigil. He vanished in a flash of light—

—and reappeared beside the monstrous statue. His mouth worked as he screamed the command that would bring it to life then snarled in frustration as he realized the zone of silence enshrouded the image, too.

He still needed killing, however, as soon as possible. Anton looked for a way past the frenzied fighters blocking his path, but it was hopeless. He snatched a sling from his belt, loaded it with a lead bullet—and the Red Wizard stroked his tattooed forearm. Once again, he disappeared.

His departure left Anton with nothing to do but slaughter his share of the remaining Thayans as rapidly as he could. To his relief, he and his comrades needed only a few more heartbeats to clear the pier. Afterward, he grabbed Captain Clayhill by the arm and dragged her onto dry land, beyond the statue. The hum of the city popped back into his ears.

"One of the Red Wizards got away," Anton panted. "He'll warn the others. We have to keep moving." Every moment they delayed gave warriors time to wake, grab their weapons, assemble into squads, and take up defensive positions. Every second was another chance for a wizard or priest to weave a spell.

"I know," the captain said. She beckoned urgently, yelling curses even though she must have known her crew couldn't hear her, and the pirates came scrambling onto the shore. She barked a few orders, and they charged up the slope toward the buildings ahead, dividing into teams as they went to envelop the entire complex quickly.

Anton and his companions smashed open doors and killed whomever they found beyond. Some of the pirates tried to linger and search for loot, but he bellowed at them to stay with the squad.

In the center of a small garden with gravel paths, a marble fountain abruptly emitted an eye-watering stink. "Run!" he cried, an instant before the marble basin spewed acid like a geyser. Most of the freebooters reacted quickly enough to avoid all but the diffuse, merely blistering fringe of the discharge. But one man toppled, clothing and skin dissolving. His body was covered in bubbling, sizzling burns, and his eyes melted in their sockets.

A wisp of spider web enlarged without warning, snaring the men it engulfed in sticky cable. The arachnid at the center grew as well and, when it was as big as a cat, scuttled to bite the first of its prisoners. Straining, Anton managed to slip the cutlass through some of the mesh restraining him, and the preternaturally keen edge severed the gluey strands. He slashed himself free, cut once more, and split the spider's eight-eyed mask just as it started to pounce at him.

It was all grueling, frantic, desperate work, and from a certain perspective, it was all inconsequential. Where were the rest of the enemy spellcasters? They were the chief threat, the adversaries the pirates truly needed to confront.

They reached the end of the lane running between

two rows of low sheds and buildings, peeked out into the open space beyond, and at last Anton saw the Red Wizards.

The surviving Thayans were making a stand in a two-story limestone building like a small but well-fortified manor house. Soldiers shot crossbow bolts through arrow loops or, kneeling, from behind the battlements on the slate roof. The magicians lurked behind windows, popping into view just long enough to hurl bursts of fire and hammering hailstones at the corsairs laying siege to the place then ducking back out of sight.

The quarrels and flares of magic were taking a toll on the pirates. It was obvious they needed to break into the house and fight the Thayans at close quarters. But it was difficult when their enemies concentrated their attacks on anyone who sought to approach. Even when some daring soul did reach the side of the house, he found it impossible to kick in a door or pry open a shutter. Some charm evidently prevented it.

Tu'ala'keth, Kassur, and a couple of others had taken cover behind a big, forked-trunk tree at one corner of the battlefield. Chadrezzan wasn't with them, though. Apparently, like Anton himself, he was late reaching the heart of the battle.

The priest and priestess of Fury chanted and swept their arms in mystic passes to no particular effect, as far as Anton could tell. Either they were attempting something subtle, or the enemy spellcasters were neutralizing their efforts.

Perhaps he and Tu'ala'keth together could think of an effective tactic. Crouching low, he ran toward her and the others, and the air ahead of him crackled and burned blue.

The shining haze coalesced into a trio of dark, long-legged creatures with streaming tails and manes. For an instant, Anton wondered if the Red Wizards had wasted a summoning spell on something as mundane and relatively harmless as horses. Then he noticed the pale, curved horns and glowing crimson eyes. The beasts were black unicorns, corrupted with a taint of demon blood, a prime example of the many abominations bred in Thay.

Plainly heeding an order to kill the clerics, the unicorns charged the group behind the tree. Anton sprinted after them, but wasn't exceptionally concerned. Black unicorns were dangerous foes, but Tu'ala'keth's magic, and Kassur's, should suffice to fend the creatures off.

Then, however, wind howled. Anton could barely feel the disturbance in the air where he was, but it staggered the pirates behind the forked tree and ripped leaves spinning upward off the branches. Tu'ala'keth's goggles jerked off her head and hurtled into the air as well.

It shouldn't have mattered. The sunlight of the surface world couldn't blind her in the middle of the night. But in the same instant the whirlwind died, as abruptly as it began, her face lit up like an ember fresh from a blazing fire. She pawed at her features as if she could wipe the glow away, but to no avail.

The black unicorns thundered nearer.

Help her! Anton thought. But as Kassur, brandishing his flickering spear, started to conjure, he backed away from her. No doubt he wanted to ensure that the defense he meant to create would shield only himself.

Tu'ala'keth must have mastered her panic, must have heard her attacker's pounding approach, for at the last instant, she tried to spring out of the way. Even so, the black unicorn's horn gored her side, spun her, and dropped her to the ground. The creature turned and reared to pulp her beneath its battering hooves.

Still Kassur made no attempt to aid her. It was Harl who rushed in, scimitar raised, interposing himself between the unicorn and its intended prey. He started to strike a blow, but the creature was faster, and the orc dropped with his head bashed to gory, lopsided ruin.

At least he'd distracted the unicorn long enough for Anton to close with it. He hoped to take the beast from behind and cut a leg out from under it before it knew he was there, but it must have heard or smelled him coming because it whirled to meet him.

He cut; gashed the equine's flank; then twisted to the right when the pale, whorled horn drove at him. That put him in position for a chop at the unicorn's neck, and he raised the cutlass to try. The beast's horn suddenly glowed like crystal filled with tainted moonlight. It whipped its head sideways and bashed him in the chest with the luminous spike.

But it didn't hit with the point, just the side of the shaft. It should have been a solid, bruising clout, but nothing worse. Alas, the supernatural force the unicorn had invoked amplified the power of the blow. It knocked Anton into the air and threw him several feet. He slammed down hard.

His chest burned, and he felt as if he couldn't draw a breath. He had no idea how badly the attack had wounded him and had no time to worry about it either. The unicorn sprang after him and reared to hammer him with its hooves.

Anton tried to roll out of the way. For an instant that seemed to stretch out endlessly, he thought his abused body wouldn't answer to his will, but then he broke through the paralysis that came with shock and flung himself to the side. The unicorn's hooves slammed down mere inches away, pounding dents into the ground and flinging up bits of dirt.

He had to roll again before he could attempt to

scramble to his feet. He was still straightening up when the black unicorn leaped at him, crimson eyes blazing, horn shining with another infusion of malefic power.

He needed another moment to settle into a balanced fighting stance, but he didn't have it. He'd simply have to manage as best he could. He tried to sidestep and cut at the same time.

The unicorn crashed into him. Flung him reeling backward and down on the ground. He was sure he'd taken a mortal wound, but when he ran his hand over his torso, he couldn't find a puncture. Some part of the beast's body had struck him, but he'd dodged the horn.

Something screamed an inhuman scream. Anton forced himself to sit up and look around. His foe lay on its side several feet away, the cutlass buried in the base of its neck. It gave a final cry, and its head thudded down onto the ground. Blood oozed from its mouth and nostrils.

Anton smiled then glimpsed a surge of motion from the corner of his eye. He turned his head, and another black unicorn charged him.

Tu'ala'keth's steely contralto voice cried words of power. The grass beneath the unicorn's hooves grew long and whipped around its lower legs. The beast's momentum kept it plunging forward anyway. Bones snapped, and it crashed to the ground to shriek until the shalarin drove her stone trident between its ribs.

She then hobbled to Anton. The blinding luminescence on her face had disappeared—she'd probably extinguished it with a counterspell—but blood poured from the rent in her side.

"Are you badly hurt?" she asked.

"I've been knocked around," he said, "and taken a little jolt of magical virulence, but I can still fight.

You're the one who's really wounded. Fix it before you bleed to death."

"Yes, now that I have time." She declaimed a prayer and pressed her hand against the gaping cut. Her webbed fingers glowed blue-green, and the gash closed. Meanwhile, Anton yanked his cutlass from the first unicorn's carcass and looked to see what else was happening.

Kassur and Chadrezzan stood near the body of the third unicorn, which burned as if someone had dipped it in oil and set a torch to it. Sour-faced, the Talassans were glaring at him and Tu'ala'keth, but they turned away as soon as they noticed him looking back.

Anton realized it hadn't been a Red Wizard who'd blinded Tu'ala'keth. It had been Chadrezzan, hiding in the shadows.

The knowledge infuriated him, but retribution would have to wait. The attack was faltering. The pirates were game, fighting hard, but as long as the Thayans' bastion remained unable to be breached, they held an insurmountable advantage.

He turned to Tu'ala'keth. "Are you fit to keep fighting?" he asked.

She sneered. "Of course. Umberlee's power sustains me, just as it does you."

"Right. How could I forget? Look, I need to get to the side of the house to try my charm of opening."

The glimmering membrane flicked across her obsidian eyes. "Do you think it will overcome the enchantment the Red Wizards used to seal the place?"

"It untied your magic tether, didn't it? I'm lucky with that particular spell. But maybe not lucky enough to run across the clear space without taking a few quarrels in the vitals, or a lightning bolt up the arse."

"I will shield you." She raised the bloody trident over her head and chanted words in her own tongue. A grayness thickened in the air. In a moment, most of the world vanished beneath a blanket of mist. The vapor smelled of the sea.

"The enemy will banish the fog quickly," said Tu'ala'keth. "We must run."

"Wait! I've lost track of where the doors and windows are."

"I remember." She gripped his hand. "Come on."

They rushed the house. A quarrel whizzed down out of the fog and past his head. Evidently some of the Thayan warriors were shooting blind.

But that was the only missile that came anywhere near him, and the façade of the enemy fortress swam out of the murk. As Tu'ala'keth had promised, she'd led him straight to a door.

Just as they reached it, though, a pulse of magic that made his head throb scoured the fog from the air. They pressed themselves against the side of the house to make it awkward for anyone inside or on top to target them, and he began the spell. Knowing he had sufficient power to attempt it only a couple of times, and that the articulation needed to be perfect to overcome Thayan wizardry, he resisted the urge to hurry, even when quarrels thumped into the ground behind him.

As he reached the final word, silvery sparks danced on the surface of the heavy four-paneled door. He tried to twist the wrought-iron handle. It wouldn't budge, nor would the door shiver even minutely in its frame. It seemed of a piece with the wall around it.

Footsteps shuffled overhead, and Tu'ala'keth rattled off a prayer. Anton glanced up just as the warriors on the roof overturned a cauldron. Boiling water poured down, but the stream divided as it dropped. It splashed, steamed, hissed all around him and the shalarin, but left them untouched.

"Next time," said Tu'ala'keth, "they will drop

something besides boiling water. I will find that more difficult to deflect."

"Point taken." He resumed his conjuring.

In response, the entire surface of the door glowed silver. He twisted the handle, and the latch released. He and Tu'ala'keth scrambled inside, and blazing coals rained, thumping and rattling down on the spot they'd just vacated.

Anton cast about for defenders waiting just inside the entry. Feet were pounding above his head, but as yet, no one had appeared to bar the way. He turned and bellowed to the pirates: "Come on! Come on! We've got a way in!"

The freebooters dashed forward. The Thayans might have decimated them as they emerged from cover, except that Chadrezzan, shrouded from head to toe in vermilion flame, his serpent-staff held high above his head, hurled burst after burst of fire over their heads. While the barrage lasted, the Red Wizards and their minions had no choice but to hide behind their casements and merlons.

The first pirates reached the doorway. Anton and Tu'ala'keth led them deeper into the house.

It was a different fight now, through rooms, along hallways, and up stairs. With walls in the way, no leader could hope to oversee or direct more than a small part of it. Warriors lacked the space to stand in proper formation. Wizards and crossbowmen couldn't harass their enemies safely at long range.

Which was to say, it was brutal, howling chaos, and in such a melee, the sheer viciousness of the pirates gave them the upper hand.

Or at least Anton thought it did. In truth, he too had only the haziest impression of what was occurring beyond the reach of his blade, and didn't dare divert his attention from the enemies in his immediate vicinity to look around.

Finally, though, he killed another Thayan, cast about, and couldn't find any more to fight. Durth yelled, "I saw a mage run up this way!" He scrambled up a staircase with a door at the top, and two of his fellow orcs scrambled after him. The lookout grabbed the handle.

"Stop!" cried Tu'ala'keth.

The word was charged with magic. Durth froze for a heartbeat then turned to her in anger and confusion.

"It is warded," the waveservant said. "I will deal with it." She hurried up the steps, and Anton followed.

Tu'ala'keth gripped her dead man's hand and recited an incantation. Power tinged the air green and made it feel damp. She thrust the tines of her trident into the door, and for an instant, a complex design, inscribed in lines and loops of scarlet light, flared and sizzled into being but without doing anybody any harm.

"Now," said Tu'ala'keth, "we may pass." She threw open the door.

Beyond the threshold was a richly appointed suite, surely the private quarters of the ranking Red Wizard in Saerloon. His leg torn, leaving bloody spatters and footprints on a gorgeous carpet as he limped about, the mage was stuffing various possessions in a haversack seemingly too small to hold them. It must be one of those enchanted containers that was larger inside than out.

The mage cursed and pointed an ebony wand with a milky crystal on the end. The attackers ducked for cover as best they could in the confined area of the top risers and the small landing.

With a roar, force exploded through the doorway and smashed the sections of wall on either side into hurtling scraps. Time seemed to skip, and Anton found himself lying amid a litter of wood and plaster on the floor at the base of the steps.

His ears rang, his whole body felt as if it were

vibrating from the impact, but he didn't seem to be dead or maimed. He looked around for his companions. One of the orcs had both legs twisted at unnatural angles with a jagged bit of broken bone sticking out of one, but other than that, it looked as if everyone might be all right. They were just battered and dazed.

The concussion had blasted away the top of the staircase, but a bit of the supporting structure remained, affixed to the wall. Anton used it to clamber high enough to peek into the Red Wizard's quarters.

The wretch was gone.

Anton dropped back down to the floor, where Tu'ala'keth awaited him. "He escaped," the spy admitted. "Used magic to whisk himself away with his most valuable treasures."

"Will he return with more warriors?" asked Tu'ala'keth.

Anton grinned. "That's the funny part. Thayan trading enclaves count as Thayan soil. They insist on it. That means the local watch and what-have-you carry no authority within these walls, and most likely they resent it. They won't be in any hurry to come accost us even if a Red Wizard begs them."

His slate-colored cheeks and forehead bristling with splinters, Durth shook his head. "Still when I think of the swag the dog just snatched away from us...."

"Don't worry," Anton said. "We still have the gold."

And, as they discovered when they broke into the strong room, it was a lot of gold. It was as much as he'd ever seen in one place—enough to take everyone's breath away.

Captain Clayhill turned to Chadrezzan. "It will be heavy," she said. "Can you conjure some of those floating disks to carry it to the ship?"

The magician inclined his head.

"Then let's move. The Sembians could still bestir themselves to chase us."

"If they do," said Tu'ala'keth, "the wind and currents will not favor them."

❧ ❧ ❧ ❧ ❧

Tu'ala'keth knew Anton had taken a late watch. She found him alone in the forecastle, gazing over the black, silver-dappled expanse of the moonlit sea. Knowing how humans depended on the glare of the sun, candles, and the like, she wondered if he could actually see much of anything.

She joined him at the rail and pointed to starboard. "Do you see the school of mackerel," she asked, "swimming just below the surface? If the others were awake, we could net ourselves a good breakfast."

"No," he said, "I can't make them out. You should sleep, too, if you want your side to finish healing."

Beneath the silverweave she'd painstakingly mended, her wound gave her a twinge, as if agreeing with him.

"I wished to talk to you," she said. "You seem troubled."

He snorted. "I'm trying to act triumphant. I must not be the dissembler I hoped I was if a creature who doesn't even know humans can see through me."

"You and I are the hands of Umberlee, sealed to a single purpose. That is why I ken your feelings."

"Or you're just shrewd."

"Tell me what bothers you. Do you fear our charade is taking too long? It has occurred to me that while we play games above the sea, the dragon flight may already have laid waste to all As'arem . . . perhaps even all Serôs."

He lifted an eyebrow. "I'd just about decided you never felt doubt or worry about anything."

"I am mortal and thus incapable of perfect serenity. Besides, Umberlee is demanding. It may be that she has chosen us as her agents but is testing us, too. Or testing me, anyway, as an exemplar of the shalarins. She has set me a challenge, which I must quickly overcome, or she will give the wyrms leave to obliterate my race."

"That's a cheery thought. For what it's worth, I'm told dragon flights run around erratically. They don't always race from one big collection of victims straight to the next. So chances are pretty fair they haven't chewed up all of Serôs yet. I was actually pondering something else."

A fish jumped, making a soft splash off the port bow. The deck rose and fell beneath their feet. "What were you brooding over?" asked Tu'ala'keth.

"Just that we've done, and instigated, a lot of killing."

His tone was somber, though she had no idea why. Slaughter was a holy act when the slayer dedicated the kill to Umberlee. "And so?" she asked.

"So nothing, I suppose. The Grandmaster knows, after all this time, it shouldn't bother me. I've stood and watched murders, rapes, and acts of torture, because to intervene would unmask me, thwart my mission, and so, theoretically, allow even more suffering elsewhere in the world. But it still does trouble me sometimes. Of late, maybe more than it used to."

She groped for comprehension. "But the pirates and Thayans are both enemies of your people, are they not? Was that not part of the reason you bade me point Shandri Clayhill at Saerloon? So that whoever died in the course of the raid, Turmish would be the better for it?"

He nodded. "I wasn't sure you understood that, but yes. Still, no doubt, the zulkirs are scum, and so are Red Wizards. You couldn't rise in, or even stomach, the crimson order if you weren't. But do you think every warrior, sailor, and dockhand we killed was a fiend incarnate? Or were they just ordinary folk doing their jobs and trying to get by? Checkmate's edge, it's not their fault they were born Thayan. Some may even have been slaves."

"They certainly were not fiends. Demons are magnificent entities. Viewed clearly, they afford us a glimpse of the divine."

Her observation failed to divert Anton from his own chain of thought: "But really, I don't mind Thayan blood on my knife. It's the deaths of our shipmates that weigh on me because we knew one another." He sighed. "When I first took up this line of work, one of my mentors warned me the hard part was befriending the enemy. Not the doing of it, but the consequences. Because when you betray them, you bear the guilt."

"Your true loyalty is to Umberlee, and in any case, you have not betrayed the reavers."

"We lied to them."

The remark reminded her of her own misgivings, but she pushed them aside. "For a sacred purpose! And if that is not enough, the ruse gave them the courage to win glory and wealth."

"But Harl won't get a chance to spend his share. He died protecting you."

"For that reason, Umberlee has taken his spirit into her keeping, as she will one day welcome us if we do not fail her." She peered at him, saw her words had given him no comfort, and felt a pang of frustration. "Why did you become a spy in the first place, if you are too squeamish for the work?"

Where wise counsel had failed, the exasperated question surprised a smile out of him. "'Squeamish?' I haven't heard that before! In truth, I didn't start out to be a spy. When I was a boy, I loved tales about paladins. I wanted to grow up to be one and begged my parents for permission to train with the Fellowship of the True Deity."

"But they refused?"

"Oh, no. They were pious folk and approved of my aspirations. But it turned out that, while I took to swordplay and the rest of the combat training, I had no real patience for the constant prayer, fasting, meditation, and general asceticism an apprentice paladin had to endure, and discipline and self-denial only became more difficult when I started noticing girls. Perhaps because I chafed at them, I couldn't establish the special bond with Torm his knights must have, nor learn to work even the simplest bit of divine magic. By trying, I discovered a small knack for the arcane, but that was beside the point.

"When it became clear I was hopeless, my masters discharged me, and I enlisted in the Turmian army. If I couldn't be a mystical hero, I'd at least be a chivalrous one. I imagined myself dubbed a knight on the battlefield, fighting single combats with champions from enemy armies, devising brilliant strategies to turn certain defeat into total victory ... suffice it to say, if it was a piece of rubbish from a heroic saga, it was rattling around in my head."

"I take it that the army, too, was not as you envisioned it?"

Anton chuckled. "Sad but true. My superiors showed a strange reluctance to place a raw recruit in command of his own company, or otherwise reward my manifest talents as they deserved. I grew bored with regimentation and routine and disliked taking orders from fellows I deemed less clever than myself, and certainly less worthy than the paladins back in the cloister. In short order, I turned into a shirker and a troublemaker. Once my impudence even earned me a flogging.

"But occasionally I earned my keep. I always volunteered for scouting, carrying dispatches cross-country, any task I could undertake alone, guided solely by my own wits. Then I did well. In time my checkered career caught the notice of one of Turmish's spymasters, who convinced me I was better suited for his trade than a life in the ranks."

He shrugged. "And that's the tale. I've been playing this game ever since. Lies and low blows may look shabby compared to paladin's miracles and valor, but they, too, serve a purpose. At least when some clerk doesn't just take my report and stuff it in a cubbyhole unread."

"You yearned to serve a deity," said Tu'ala'keth. "Yet now that the greatest of all has claimed you, you find no joy in it. What makes you so perverse?"

He hesitated. "I promised to help you—and Umberlee—and I will. But your deity stands for cruelty, greed, and destruction. Torm is virtue, honor, and loyalty. It's scarcely the same thing."

"You must open your eyes," said Tu'ala'keth. "You see sharks devouring prey, tempests destroying ships and drowning mariners, victors slaying the vanquished—Umberlee's reflections in the mundane world—and you cringe. As well you might, for these events are terrible. But so, too, are they sacred and beautiful. They are life expressing and refining itself. Without the urge to feed and to have and to master, what creature would discover its strengths, or do anything whatsoever?"

Anton shook his head. "You may be right, but I can't feel what you feel. If it's any consolation, I don't spend much time contemplating the glories of Torm anymore, either. Of course I still believe in him, and all the gods. I'm not insane. But it's hard to imagine them stooping to take an interest in the small, grubby lives of people like Harl and me. I suspect that by and large, we mortals are on our own."

"No," she said. "The gods may sometimes hate us, chastise, slay, and damn us, but they are never remote or indifferent. I believe that if you are true to our purpose, Umberlee will reveal herself to you, and you will know better."

"Well, maybe so." He glanced up at the moon and the trailing haze of glittering motes people called her tears. "Hmm. It's past time for Williven to relieve me. Let's go wake the lazy bastard."

THE **P**RIESTS

Someday, when Shandri Clayhill had taken enough prizes, when other captains sailed aboard vessels she'd provided in exchange for a cut of the plunder, when she was as a grandee by the standards of Dragon Isle, she'd have her own coquina mansion, swarming with flunkies, slaves, and sycophants. For now, though, when she had business to conduct ashore, it was necessary either to hire a room in a tavern or borrow space in Vurgrom's mansion.

The latter was plainly more suitable for divvying up the spoils from the red caravel and the Thayan enclave, even if she disliked having her blustering chieftain sitting to one side, cup in hand, overseeing the proceedings. It would be too easy for him to countermand one of her decisions or offer "advice" that would effectively preclude her making one in the first place.

But really, how likely was that, in the wake of her triumph? So let the fat fool watch and reflect on the fact that, for all his boasting, it had been a long while since he'd taken such a prize. Maybe then he'd stop patronizing her and treat as he did the other—the male—captains who'd pledged him their fealty.

She resolved to stop chafing at his presence and focus on the task at hand. To whit, supervising her crew, who for the most part looked happy enough as they pawed through the bags and coffers heaped in the middle of the floor, raking out gleaming gold coins and other treasure. Some playfully donned oddments of sparkling jewelry. For an instant, she scowled, wondering if they were doing so in mockery of the way she customarily adorned herself, but then decided they probably meant no harm.

An orc unstoppered a pewter vial, took a sip, then jumped so high he slammed his head against a rafter. His friends laughed as he dropped back down to the floor. Sealmid fingered the edge of a broadsword. The enchanted blades the Thayans manufactured in quantity were inferior compared to truly splendid arms such as Kassur's spear or Anton's cutlass, but wickedly sharp nonetheless. The minimal contact sufficed to slice the first mate's skin, and grinning, he raised his hand to display the welling blood.

Of course, it was fairly easy to divide specie or even minor potions and talismans seized by the dozen. If anyone chose to quarrel, it would be over the more potent magic the Red Wizards and their chief lieutenants had reserved for their own use. But after stuffing their pouches and sea bags with silver, gold, and gems, the ordinary gentlemen of fortune had no claim on the more precious enchanted articles, and surely the voyage had yielded enough of the latter to satisfy even a complement of officers as acquisitive as those who served aboard *Shark's Bliss.*

As captain, Shandri got first pick. She advanced to the table, took up a greatsword, and pulled it from its scabbard. She didn't actually need to since she and her lieutenants had already examined all of the items, but she felt a certain theatricality was appropriate to the occasion.

She spoke the word—Mask only knew what it meant—graven on the blade just above the leather ricasso. Darkness swirled inside the steel, and she sensed the sentient weapon's eagerness to kill, a gleeful malevolence directed at all the world but her.

It was a magnificent sword, and a big one, too, nearly as long as she was tall. If she fought with it, no one could possibly think of her as a fat old man's dainty concubine. She brandished it, and everyone gave a cheer.

She also chose an onyx ring that would enable her to see in the dark like an owl, and she reckoned, she was through. She beckoned for Sealmid to take his turn.

The first mate chose a bow—seemingly made of polished amethyst though it flexed like yew—and the purple quiver of arrows that went with it. Durth, who fancied himself the finest archer in all the Pirate Isles, cursed, and the human gave him a mocking toothless grin. The lookout strode forward, clenching his gray-skinned fists.

"No!" Shandri snapped. "I called him; he chose; that's the end of it."

The orc took a deep breath and let it out slowly. "Yes, Captain," he muttered.

"You can pick last, to remind you to keep a grip on your temper." She cast about. "Anton."

Anton sauntered to the table, made a show of inspecting the remaining articles, then grinned, selected a cape, and spun it around his shoulders. The garment was a vivid scarlet, a fitting wrap for a Red Wizard, but shot though with threads gleaming gray like steel. The magic in the weave could absorb the force of a cut or blow as if the cloth were a piece of plate armor.

He then picked up three red-bound books and a wand.

A deafening boom thundered through the room. The floor shook, and Shandri staggered a step. Taking advantage of its new mistress's sudden lack of balance, trying to reach for the nearest potential victim, the greatsword shifted in her grasp. No! she thought, and it abandoned the effort. She sensed the mind inside the blade, half sheepish, but likewise half amused.

There was no time to think about that now. She pivoted to see what had caused the bang. Chadrezzan stood glaring, gripping his serpent-girded staff with both gaunt hands. From his stance, she surmised the mute had disrupted the proceedings by striking the butt of the rusty rod on the floor.

"What are you doing?" Shandri demanded.

Chadrezzan jabbed a long, skinny finger at Anton.

"What he means," Kassur said, "is that the wand and grimoires should rightfully go to him."

"Nonsense," Anton said. "He's not an officer. He doesn't get a double share."

Chadrezzan gestured to himself, then to the priest of Talos.

"He's pointing out," said Kassur, "that neither one of us is weighted down with gold. In fact, we haven't pocketed a single copper. That was so we could fairly claim the spellbooks and wand."

"That's too bad," Anton said, "because it still doesn't give you the right to choose ahead of me."

"Be rational!" snapped the priest. "Thanks to a fluke, you can call yourself ship's mage, but your handful of paltry spells doesn't derive from the learning of a true wizard. They're just a bit of freakishness, like an extra toe."

"It makes no difference," Anton said.

"It does!" At the most peaceful of times, Kassur stamped about glowering, seemingly full of anger he could barely contain. Now his face was brick red, and as he shouted, spittle flew from his lips. "You can't profit from the lore in those volumes or use the wand either!"

"I can profit from it all if I sell it."

"Chadrezzan will use it to augment his abilities." Kassur pivoted toward Shandri. "Captain, you saw the magic he threw at the Thayans and how potent it was. We never could have won without him."

"We never would have won," said Anton, "if I hadn't opened up the house."

"That was one spell," said Kassur, without diverting his monocular gaze from Shandri. "Chadrezzan cast more than a dozen. Imagine what he'll be able to accomplish for us all once he masters the secrets of the Red Wizards. It's stupid—and selfish—to deny him the chance."

Some of the company clamored in agreement, but as many appeared to favor Anton. Durth said, "If I had to give up the bow, then your friend can do without the stinking books."

"As well as the wand," Kassur retorted, "and the cape? If you can't see anything else, it should at least be clear to you that the greedy bastard's laying claim to too much."

Shandri thought he might well be right, but with the disparate items involved, it was difficult to be sure.

She was certain she didn't want to lose Chadrezzan or Anton from the ship's company or appear less than fair and impartial in the eyes of her crew. She also did not want to do anything Vurgrom would view as a mistake. Feeling overwhelmed, she hesitated.

The tiny image of one of the oil lamps reflecting in each black lens of her goggles, Tu'ala'keth stepped forth from the crowd. "This squabble is foolish."

Anton grinned. "That's what I'm trying to tell them."

The shalarin gave him a stare. "I mean it is you who are the fool. I told you at the start, we have come to Dragon Isle to craft an instrument of sacrifice. To spill blood upon the waters for the glory of Umberlee. Anything that strengthens *Shark's Bliss* serves our purpose. Accordingly, Chadrezzan shall have his tools."

The declaration resolved Shandri's doubts. If Anton's closest ally, who was likewise the voice of a goddess and the harbinger of Shandri's destiny, said he was in the wrong, then wrong he must surely be.

"Yes," Shandri said. "The spellbooks and wand go to Chadrezzan and Kassur, as their entire shares. Anton, you'll have to content yourself with the cape. Or put it back and take something else."

Anton looked back and forth between her and Tu'ala'keth as if astonished they hadn't supported him. "I planned the raid. We wouldn't have any of this swag, not one particle of gold, if it wasn't for me."

It sounded as if he were claiming to be the leader, and Shandri's belly tightened in anger. "Everyone contributed to our success—under my direction. If you want to keep your position, remember that."

"Otherwise," said Tu'ala'keth, "the Queen of the Depths will discard you and find a weapon more to her liking."

"To Baator with the both of you." Anton turned toward Vurgrom, who lounged smirking as if the argument were a play staged for his amusement. "Sir, we all know you're the one who's really in charge. You tell us: Who's in the right?"

Vurgrom stroked his chin. "Well, after my famous raid on Yhaunn—"

Velvet skirt flapping around her legs, Shandri dashed the few paces separating her from Anton. The greatsword shot up over her head. She didn't feel she was lifting it, but rather that it flew and pulled her hands along. Yet it was nonetheless expressing her ire, and the sensation was exhilarating.

It was only when the dark blade flashed down at her lieutenant's head that a measure of clarity returned, and she realized she didn't truly want to slay him. She strained to cut wide of the mark, and Anton, though startled, managed a scrambling step backward. The sword missed.

"All right!" Anton cried, raising his hands. "If you're willing to chop me to pieces over it, Chadrezzan can have what he wants!"

"I—" Shandri faltered. She'd started to say she hadn't intended to strike at him, but realized blaming it on the influence of the sword would make her seem weak. "Good. Then we can put this squabble behind us."

"As you say. I have my share of the loot, and I'm tired. I believe I'll find a place to lay my head." He turned and stalked toward the door.

Shandri disliked seeing him depart in such a bitter mood, but knew she couldn't call or scurry after him. That too would create the wrong impression.

"Some of the crew," said Anton, "wanted to burn the compound to the ground." He emptied his mug of grog, and one of his admiring listeners refilled it, slopping a bit of the clear, pungent liquor onto his hand. "Shandri Clayhill was willing to go along with it. But I convinced everyone it would be wiser to sail out before anybody else showed up to hinder us. Besides, leave the Thayans a cozy nest to come home to, and we'd know right where to find them when we want to rob them again next year."

His audience laughed then fell silent as they noticed the newcomer at the fringe of the circle. Anton, too, felt a pang of surprise. Upon entering the tavern, a stuffy, murky, candlelit shack of a place stinking of spilled beer, he had, with a spy's reflexive caution, taken inventory of the folk inside, and afterward tried to keep track of departures and new arrivals. Still, up until this moment, he hadn't spotted the tall, lean, grizzled man fastidiously clad in blacks and grays. Either the old fellow had an exceptional talent for creeping about unobtrusively, or he employed magic to accomplish it.

Or in all likelihood, both, for the newcomer with his wry, shred, weather-beaten face was Teldar, chieftain of the largest faction on Dragon Isle. On previous missions, Anton had seen the legendary freebooter from a distance but never up close.

Like everyone else lucky enough to have a seat, he rose in respect. With a murmur of vague apology to the hairy, amber-eyed hobgoblin he was dispossessing, Teldar appropriated a chair and motioned for everyone else to take his ease. Peg leg thumping the floor, the tavernmaster came rushing with a straw-wrapped bottle of wine and a silver goblet. Apparently he knew from past visits what the great man liked to drink.

The tavernmaster was no sommelier. The shaking he'd given the bottle while conveying it to the table demonstrated that. Still he evidently thought that for Teldar, with his gentlemanly airs, he ought to make an effort. He ceremoniously poured a small measure of red wine into the cup and waited for the old pirate to sip and give approval. Teldar played along with some blather about the bouquet, the aftertaste, and grapes growing on the sunny side of the hill, meanwhile giving Anton a wink. The tavernmaster limped away, beaming.

"Aelthias sailed with me," Teldar said, "before his injury. A mage aboard a Cormyrean Freesail pretty much burned his leg out from under him, and the healer had to cut off what was left. I helped set him up here."

"It's an honor to meet you, Captain," Anton said.

Teldar waved a dismissive hand. "Nonsense. You're the hero of the hour, conducting a successful raid on a Thayan outpost. Or I suppose I should say, one of the heroes. I'm surprised to find you drinking with this lot, fine fellows though they are, instead of celebrating with your shipmates up in Vurgrom's house."

Anton frowned as if reluctant to explain. "I had a . . . disagreement with Captain Clayhill."

Teldar nodded. "Ah. Well, of course, she's only just assumed command of *Shark's Bliss*. I suspect you're a more experienced freebooter than she is. Though I don't believe you and I have met before."

"Until recently, I sailed out of Mirg Isle. It's just where I happened to wash up when I decided to try my hand as a gentleman of fortune."

"That explains it. Is Mirg Isle where you met the shalarin priestess?"

Anton grinned. "Just how long did you lurk about listening to my tale before deciding to reveal yourself?"

Teldar smiled in return. "You must think me a sorcerer like yourself. Not long at all, actually. But all Immurk's Hold has at least heard rumors of the raid on the Red Wizards. It's a shame you and your captain fell out after achieving such a coup."

"I didn't want to quarrel with the bitch. I simply wanted my due." He told the tale of his supposed grudge. "We were just talking, and she tried to cleave me in two! When what I'd asked was only the hundredth part of what I deserve!"

Teldar sipped his wine. "What is it you think you deserve?"

"The red caravel. Or, at any rate, some ship of my own. Naturally, Shandri Clayhill and Vurgrom would thereafter receive a share of the prizes I took."

"You came to Dragon Isle only a few tendays ago. Do you think anyone rises to a captaincy so quickly?"

"I don't see why not, if he can plan a successful foray against folk as dangerous as the Red Wizards. I'll wager these lads would sail under my flag."

Tipsy with the rounds he'd bought them, a number of the pirates cried out in agreement.

Teldar rubbed his shoulders as if trying to work out an ache. Perhaps, spry as he still seemed, arthritis had begun to trouble him. "I suppose that's my cue to declare that if you'll join my faction, I'll give you a ship."

"I don't know about that, but I doubt we met here by chance. I believe you have some reason for talking to me."

"You're right. But it was to take your measure, nothing more."

"Well, then: Do I pass muster?"

"You have courage and intelligence, qualities I hold in esteem, and ambition, one I regard with a degree of ambivalence."

"You must have been ambitious yourself to become the most powerful man in the Pirate Isles."

"But I've never tried to eliminate the other factions here in the Hold. Well, except for when some fool attempted to murder me. I've never proclaimed myself 'pirate lord.' I've never endeavored to bring the corsairs on the other islands under my sway and forge us all into one great brotherhood, a fleet to rival that of Impiltur, Sembia, or any kingdom on the Sea of Fallen Stars.

"I could do it even now, and some days I still feel the temptation. But I remember what happened to Urdogen the Red and his ilk. Provoke the lands we plunder, or other proud, ambitious reavers, beyond a certain point, and they'll go to any lengths to butcher you and all who follow you. Whereas I've lived a lengthy, prosperous life."

Anton spread his hands. "I just want to be a captain like any other."

"The average captain avoids annoying Red Wizards. It was a splendid accomplishment, and I admire you for it, but we of Dragon Isle may yet pay a toll in blood and misery because of it."

"I don't see how. We came under cover of night, aboard one of the Thayans' own vessels, wearing their own clothes, and killed nearly everyone we found. It would be a good trick to trace us back here." He paused a beat. "May I speak frankly?"

Teldar chuckled. "I thought you were already."

"Maybe I am ambitious. I see opportunities. Of late, the gods have blessed the Pirate Isles. Dragon flights have attacked the coastal realms but left us alone. They've weakened our prey while we remain strong. Of course I want a ship, now, not months or years hence, to make my fortune while the pickings are easy. More than that, I want to follow a leader with the boldness and vision to commit all his strength to raid whole cities or any target a lone ship couldn't overwhelm."

Now Teldar laughed outright. "Are you saying you wouldn't condescend to accept a ship from me even if I offered?"

"No, sir. I know you're a great man, the most respected in these isles. Anyone would be proud to join your faction. I'm just saying I mean to look out for myself. To catch the freshest wind that blows my way and snatch every coin that rolls within reach."

"My house is your house," said Teldar, "whenever

you feel inclined to visit. We'll talk further. But for now ... well, I'm afraid I've grown too old and dyspeptic to drink the night away as a pirate should. But you young cutthroats enjoy yourselves." He rose and dropped a handful of clattering silver on the table.

A cool breeze blew, bearing the damp, salty tang of the sea. Lathander, god of the dawn, had just begun silvering the eastern horizon. Soon Tu'ala'keth would need her goggles. At the moment, though, they dangled from her neck beneath the hooded cloak she'd found in Vurgrom's house. She hoped that with her face shadowed by her cowl and her crest of fin squashed down, she looked unremarkable in the the itchy, confining mantle.

She prowled from one tavern, brothel, and gambling den to the next, most still roaring despite the hour. Anton was supposed to be in one of them, but she couldn't go inside to find out which. Her rudimentary disguise was unlikely to deceive even the most inebriated observer at close range.

Finally, up ahead, a big, black-haired man stumbled from a torch-lit doorway. His cape was red with strands of gleaming gray in the weave, and an octopus tattoo writhed its tentacles down his arm. He wandered into the nearest alley and relieved himself against a wall.

Tu'ala'keth strode toward him. "Anton!" she whispered.

His head jerked around. "Oh, it's you. I truly must be drunk. I didn't spot you muffled up in all that black." He fastened up his breeches, turned, and blinked at her. "What in the name of the Lanceboard are you doing here? You and I are supposed to be quarreling, remember?"

Anton had needed a dispute with his shipmates to

create the impression he was dissatisfied. Now the other factions would seek to recruit him. In the process, they'd boast of their enterprises, and give him the opportunity to pry into their secrets. Meanwhile, Tu'ala'keth, still a prized and trusted member of Vurgrom's organization, would find chances to investigate his activities. At some point during the course of it all, she or the Turmian would uncover information that pointed to the Cult of the Dragon's secret lair.

That was the plan, anyway. But it wasn't what mattered at the moment.

"Listen to me," said Tu'ala'keth. "After you left, I made a point of keeping an eye on Kassur and Chadrezzan."

"Why?"

"Because they're our enemies, and because, unlike everyone else—unlike you, obviously—they only drank a cup or two of liquor."

"I had to buy drinks and keep pace with everyone else. That's how you give the impression of good fellowship. I know a charm to sober up, and I cast it from time to time. But I used up the power then still couldn't get away." He belched then eyed her quizzically. "You said something about Cha . . . Chadrezzdandan?"

She gripped her skeletal amulet, recited a prayer, and planted her other hand in the center of his chest with its repulsive bristling hairs. The spell would purge poison from a shalarin's system, and she hoped it would wash alcohol out of a human's veins as well.

Her fingers tingled and glowed blue-green, and he jerked back from her touch as if she'd struck him, banging up against the wall. "Ouch!" he said. "Thanks. That helped. Now what about the Talassans?"

"They stayed sober and eventually slipped away from the celebration. I believe they mean to kill you."

"You could be right. I never spotted them peeking in at me or stalking me, but that means little. Curse it, anyway. I knew they'd try to murder one or both of us eventually, but why did it have to be so soon?"

"Because you offended them anew, and like me, they worship a deity of Fury. Whenever possible, we act on our anger without delay."

"But they'll have to delay if we can make it back to Vurgrom's house. They can't strike us down in front of our shipmates. The question is how to sneak there? I think, skirt the edge of town, the way we did our first day here, then come downhill."

"I can fill the streets with an early-morning fog."

He frowned, pondering, then shook his head. "No. It worked in Saerloon, but in this situation, I'm not willing to blind Kassur and Chadrezzan if it means blinding us as well. We'll keep to the shadows and hope for the best."

"As you wish."

They skulked forward. Her pulse ticking in her neck, Tu'ala'keth peered back and forth and up and down, checking doorways, windows, the mouths of alleys, and rooftops. She told herself it was no different than playing hide-and-seek with an enemy amid the maze-like twists and cavities of a coral reef. She was not at a disadvantage in this alien environment, nor was she frightened.

"Thanks for coming to warn me," Anton murmured.

"You are my partner in Umberlee's sacred work."

"Right. But thank you, anyway."

A shadow shifted at the edge of her vision, where the stifling wool hood cut it off. She jerked around, and Anton pivoted with her. Reacting to the sudden motion, a small four-legged animal bounded away.

"Just a cat," Anton said.

"I see that now," she said stiffly.

They crept onward. Somewhere in the ramshackle settlement, a chicken—no, the proper term, she had learned, was rooster—crowed. Up ahead, where the narrow lane intersected another, a man in rags lay motionless on the ground. Perhaps he was a reveler stupefied by drink. Or maybe someone had murdered him. In theory, Immurk's Hold was a haven where all pirates, even the bitterest rivals, observed a truce, but as Tu'ala'keth's own situation demonstrated, the reality was otherwise. If a reaver wished to slay an enemy, the town simply asked that he pursue the vendetta with a modicum of discretion.

In any event, the important thing was that the human sprawled in the intersection wasn't Kassur or Chadrezzan. He was too short and pudgy and dressed in grubby, nondescript clothing, not vestments decorated with jagged stripes and spangles or a cloak adorned with serpents. She was just about to turn her attention elsewhere when he heaved himself up into a sitting position.

She saw then that the thing wasn't plump but rather bloated with the progress of decay. Sores, the marks of the sickness that had ended its life, mottled the puffy, discolored face. The mouth hung open, and dark fluid had oozed forth to stain the chin. The glazed eyes were empty.

It was a corpse, surely reanimated by Kassur's magic. He probably hadn't even needed to kill it or dig it up. The inhabitants of Immurk's Hold could be lackadaisical when it came to disposing of their dead.

The cadaver gripped a dented tin pot in one swollen hand and a black iron skillet in the other. It fumbled them over its lolling head and banged them together. The clanking seemed preternaturally loud in the empty predawn streets.

Anton snatched his cutlass from its scabbard. No doubt he meant to silence Kassur's sentinel by cutting it to pieces, but Tu'ala'keth had a faster way. She gripped her amulet and willed forth a blaze of spiritual power. The corpse finished rotting in a heartbeat, corrupt flesh eroding away in strips, bones crumbling to powder.

Still the dead thing's sudden action had taken her by surprise, and she knew she hadn't acted quickly enough. She turned to Anton and said, "Kassur and Chadrezzan surely heard that."

"I know. We need to get under cover." He cast about.

By making for the edge of town, they'd distanced themselves from coquina mansions, solidly constructed warehouses, barracoons, chandleries, and the like. The structures on the perimeter were a motley collection of shacks pieced together from driftwood, logs harvested from the interior of the island, and whatever other materials came to hand. Tu'ala'keth saw little reason to prefer one to another.

"There," Anton said and led her to the flimsiest of all. It looked as if the builder, though initially intending to erect a proper cottage, had grown slothful partway through the process. The façade and one other wall were made of wood, but the remaining two and the roof were simply flapping canvas stretched over a frame, thus creating a structure half house and half tent.

Anton tried the door and found it fastened. He whispered his spell of opening—Tu'ala'keth found it marginally encouraging that he hadn't squandered all his magic resisting the effects of dissipation—and on the other side of the panel, a bar squeaked as it slid in its brackets. That noise sounded jarringly loud as well, but she knew it was just because of her nerves.

She and Anton scrambled into the house—all one sparsely furnished room, with rushes strewn on the dirt floor—and he shot the bar behind them. A human mother and two small, snaggletoothed boys of mixed blood sat up from their pallets to goggle at the intruders. Perhaps the children's orc father was away at sea.

Anton pointed his cutlass at the family. "Stay where you are, and don't make a sound," he said.

White-faced, the woman gave a nod.

The windows facing the street were made of canvas as well, so as to admit a little light. Anton cut a peephole in one then knelt behind it. Tu'ala'keth crouched beside him.

"You must realize," she whispered, "this structure is no refuge. Chadrezzan can blast it apart with a flick of his fingers."

"I know," he said, "but first he and Kassur have to find us, and that's the point. With luck, they'll need to get close, and we'll have a better chance than we would with them lobbing flame and lightning from a hundred paces away."

"I understand."

"Then hush and use your ears. We may well hear them coming before we're able to see them."

He was right. After a few moments, something hissed out on the street. At first she couldn't see it, but then Anton tore the peephole larger, expanding their field of vision.

It was fire making the sibilant sound. Shrouded in yellow flame, turning his head from side to side, Chadrezzan stalked along with a look of intense concentration on his face. Kassur followed behind, spear at the ready. He too had cast some sort of defensive enchantment, revealing itself as an outline of scarlet phosphorescence around his body.

"They are not peering into doors or windows," whispered Tu'ala'keth. "They must be seeking us with magic. My guess is Chadrezzan has given himself the ability to read minds. He is sifting through all the thoughts in the area, trying to pick out ours, while

Kassur labors to sense the enchantments in your cutlass and my silverweave."

"That's how it looks to me, too. Here's what we'll do: I'm going to go out the back and circle around. Give me a few seconds then start thinking, Umberlee, help me, over and over again. If Chadrezzan is listening to thoughts, that should point him at you. You should cast spells, too, to snag Kassur's attention—defensive magic, if you've got some prepared. The Grandmaster knows, you're likely to need it."

"I am to distract the Talassans while you take them from behind."

"Right. As soon as I do, you hit them, too." He turned toward the rear of the home.

"Wait." She murmured a prayer and wrote a glyph on his brow with her fingertip. It glowed blue for a moment then faded. "A ward against flame . . . I've had them ready for the casting ever since we first quarreled with the Talassans."

"Thanks." He scuttled to the rear of the cottage, slashed through the canvas wall, and disappeared.

She counted to ten then started doing as he'd instructed her, invoking the goddess and shielding herself in a structure of interlocking enchantments like the components of a suit of plate. Before long, it had the desired effect. Kassur whirled in her direction and pointed with his spear.

"Yes, storm priest," she called, "we see you, too, and we are ready for you. Flee before I call the wrath of Umberlee down on your heads."

Kassur laughed. "Such threats might be more intimidating if you weren't cowering behind a wall. As if that could save you." Declaiming rhymes in some grating, infernal language, he raised his lance over his head, and the weapon flashed bright as lightning. Chadrezzan planted the butt of his iron staff on the ground, and the soil writhed at its touch. Power pulsed from the two humans, blurring Tu'ala'keth's vision and cramping her guts. Gripping her drowned man's hand, she commenced her own spell.

Then a shaft of force, visible as rippling distortion in the air, shot from the shadows behind the Talassans. It slammed into the center of Chadrezzan's back and knocked him stumbling forward, spoiling—Tu'ala'keth hoped—his silent conjuration. Anton instantly charged out into the open to continue the work his spell had begun.

Kassur surely realized what was happening, but didn't permit it to distract him from continuing his own conjuring. He and Tu'ala'keth finished simultaneously.

Glare and heat blazed at her. The stained, torn cloth in the window frame burned to ash in an instant, but that was the second she needed to save her sensitive deepwater vision. She frantically twisted away from the flash, and though the magic seared and blistered her skin, afterward, she could still see. She pulled her goggles back on—stupid not to have replaced them before—and peered out the opening.

The flying trident of luminous force she'd conjured jabbed at Kassur. He had two bloody grazes on his arm where it had gored him already. He parried with the lance and shouted words of power at it, trying to dispel it.

Meanwhile, Anton rushed Chadrezzan. But the wizard didn't rely solely on his burning aura to protect him. Instead, he sneered and soared up into the air. Tu'ala'keth had wondered how the Talassans had arrived on the scene so quickly, and now she knew at least a part of the answer. Chadrezzan had empowered himself with the ability to fly.

She chanted a counterspell to strip the enchantment away, but before she could reach the end, a wave of sickening terror assailed her. She faltered in her recitation, and the botched magic wasted itself in a feeble flickering.

Kassur had exerted his power to chastise the denizens of the sea. Shuddering, Tu'ala'keth silently cried out to Umberlee, praying for the strength to shake off the crippling fear. A measure of the deity's own inexhaustible wrath surged into her and washed the dread away.

In her fury, she yearned to kill Kassur up close, with her hands. Unfortunately, on Dragon Isle, her stone trident was too conspicuous a weapon to carry if she hoped to walk abroad incognito, so she'd left it behind in Vurgrom's mansion. But her magic could arm her. She whispered a prayer, the air seethed green, and sharp, bony spines extruded themselves from her skin. It hurt for a moment, but the pain didn't balk her. It only served to heighten her rage.

She strode to the door, unbarred it, threw it open, and found herself facing Kassur, now rid of the harassment of the disembodied trident. Judging from the way he held his spear, he'd planned to use it to force his way in. He gaped at Tu'ala'keth in surprise, no doubt because he'd expected to find her still crippled with fear.

She shouted a shalarin battle cry and sprang at him.

Her first blow ripped open his face to the bone, snatched away the patch that was a part of his regalia, and revealed what appeared to be a normal, functional eye underneath. She drove in again, trying to grapple, so dozens of the spines jutting from her body could pierce him all at once.

He scrambled back and swung the spear into line to threaten her. She struck at it and knocked it away from her heart, but the point still slid into her biceps. The lance flashed and sizzled, and her body shook. The odor of her burning flesh mingled with the smell of ozone.

The spear went dark, its power expended until the

next thrust. Kassur yanked it back out of her arm. Her knees buckled, dumping her on the ground. Blooding streaming from his shredded profile, the storm priest lifted his weapon for a killing stroke.

Tu'ala'keth kicked at his lower leg, the only part of him she could reach. Thanks to the paralyzing effect of the lightning pent in the spear, it was a spastic, floundering attack. But she still had her goddess-granted fury to lend her strength, and the thorns on her foot sliced deep into the limb. Kassur gasped and toppled down beside her.

Now she had her chance to wrestle, to pull and grind him against her and let the blades cut. She clambered on top of him.

The spear, though deadly, was too long to wield at such close quarters. He dropped it and snatched a dagger from somewhere. The point banged against her silverweave, surely bruising her ribs but as yet, not piercing the coral armor.

He was all bloody gashes and punctures now, yet fought on with a ferocity akin to her own. He gasped out the opening syllables of a spell.

She resolved to silence him short of the conclusion, cut the tongue from his mouth or mangle the larynx in his throat if necessary. But then, as they thrashed and rolled, she caught a glimpse of Anton and Chadrezzan.

Still suspended in the air, the mute pointed the wand stolen from the Red Wizards at the foe below his feet. Jagged flares of shadow exploded from the tip of the arcane weapon, while Anton lunged back and forth, trying to dodge. When a discharge caught him anyway, he convulsed.

It was plain he had no chance, not while Chadrezzan hovered above his reach. Tu'ala'keth gathered her spiritual strength and screamed, "Fall!"

The magical command smashed through the wizard's psychic defenses, and momentarily helpless to disobey, he allowed himself to plummet. He slammed down hard enough to snap bone but evidently not to kill or even stun him, for he immediately rose once more. Supported solely by his gift of levitation and not his flopping, shattered legs, he resembled a marionette hauled upward by its strings.

Despite the punishment he'd taken, Anton somehow found the strength to charge and, when Chadrezzan soared above his head, to leap. He caught hold of the burning wizard's garments with his free hand, and his foe carried him aloft as well. He slashed and stabbed with his cutlass, and Chadrezzan—who must have lost the wand when he'd fallen—jabbed and battered with the butt of the serpent-wrapped staff.

At which point, agony ripped through Tu'ala'keth's body. By diverting her attention to Anton and Chadrezzan, she'd given Kassur the chance to complete his spell, a blast of malignancy that savaged her from the inside out.

For a moment, the pain made her spastic. Kassur broke free of her spiked embrace and scrambled to his feet, nearly fell again when the torn leg threatened to give way, but shifted his weight to compensate. He snarled an incantation, and a fan of flame exploded from his outthrust hands.

Flame. Thanks to her wards, she was in some measure immune to it. But Kassur presumably didn't know that.

Though she might have tried to roll aside, she let the hot, hungry flare wash right over her. Its kiss seared her, but it was bearable. She screamed and flailed as if it weren't then lay shaking, to all appearances incapacitated, or so she hoped.

Kassur scrutinized her then looked about for his spear. He surely didn't mean to take his eyes off her, and only did so for an instant. Still it was the opening she needed.

She reared up onto her knees, flung herself forward, tackled him, and carried him back to the ground. He banged his head, and perhaps that finally jolted some of the fight out of him, for she landed a slice across the throat, ripped his eyes away, and hammered her fists on his chest, driving her spikes between the ribs and into the heart and lungs.

Some time after that, her fury abated sufficiently for her to comprehend it was impossible to hurt him any further. She looked around for Anton and Chadrezzan then froze in dismay.

The spy and the wizard, his corona of flame now extinguished, lay tangled together on the ground. Neither was moving, and it was impossible to tell if either was alive.

She tried to stand. The world seemed to tilt, and she flopped back down. She was on the verge of passing out and would have to help herself before she could aid another.

She chanted, and vigor surged through her limbs. It wasn't enough to silence all her pains, but that could wait. She rose and hurried to Anton.

He was still breathing. Indeed, except for the contusions where the butt of the iron staff had caught him, he was unmarked. Yet even so, his skin was icy and his pulse raced, making it plain he was sorely wounded. Chadrezzan's wand was surely as lethal a weapon as any crossbow or trident, despite the fact that its shadowy discharge didn't break the skin.

Gripping the bony symbol of Umberlee's power, Tu'ala'keth declaimed the most potent charm of healing at her disposal. Anton thrashed, and his eyes flew open. He coughed hard several times as if he had a bone caught in his throat.

When the fit passed, he wiped his teary eyes and said, "Why is it that whenever you heal me, it hurts? The priests of Ilmater are gentle as doves."

Ilmater, martyr god of the weak and helpless—she sneered at the mention of his name.

"Never mind," Anton continued. "I'm grateful anyway."

"What now?"

"It's convenient that we made for the edge of town. If we can just drag the corpses on into the hills a little ways, we'll come to a cliff where we can dump them into the sea."

"As an offering to Umberlee?"

"If you like. But mainly to make life easier for me. People will assume I killed the Talassans, and I want them to. It will help convince the other factions I'd make a valuable recruit. But I don't want Shandri Clayhill to try to punish me for slaughtering members of her crew. Without any dead bodies to prove Chadrezzan and Kassur didn't just run off, she probably won't make an issue of it."

"What of the woman on whom we intruded? She witnessed what happened, or enough of it."

"Good point. I'll threaten her again, and give her some Thayan gold, too. I imagine the combination will keep her mouth shut."

THE **P**RIESTS

Pondering how best to broach the matter at hand, Tu'ala'keth shadowed Captain Clayhill through the benighted house. Long skirt whispering against the floor, jaw clenched, and body stiff, the human strode rapidly, oblivious to the fact that someone was trailing along behind her.

The pirate's path ended in the deserted, moonlit courtyard, where she took up a boarding pike with a blunted point and edge and squared off against a straw practice dummy. Slashing and stabbing furiously, she grunted and snarled. Her jewelry lashed and clattered about her body, and the muscles in her bare, tattooed arms and shoulders bunched and flexed.

Tu'ala'keth watched from the verandah for a time then asked, "What troubles you, Captain?"

Shandri Clayhill jerked around. "Waveservant. I didn't know you were there. Nothing's wrong. I'm just practicing."

Tu'ala'keth descended the steps into the yard. "You cannot deceive me. I am your shadow. Your destiny, by Umberlee's command."

"Well...." The human wiped sweat from her eyes. More of it plastered her bronze-colored hair to her brow. "It galls me to lose Kassur and Chadrezzan."

"We will have better fortune with *Shark's Bliss*, and all who sail aboard her, devoted solely to Umberlee."

"So you say, but their magic served us well in the fights with the Thayans. It will vex me if we lose Anton, too. It's his right to seek a place on another ship, but you're supposed to be his comrade. Can't you convince him to stay?"

"Perhaps I can. Perhaps I will. But why are you, to whom the Queen of the Depths has given her favor, so concerned? Can you not see that *you* are the luck and strength of *Shark's Bliss*?"

The human's mouth twisted. "That has a brave sound to it, but I can't take prizes without good men at my back."

"You will find many reavers eager to sail with a captain who bested Red Wizards, and were you not distraught, you would know it. Let us speak, then, of that which oppresses you and clouds your visions: of the man you dream of killing when you batter this mannequin. It is plain you have just come from his chamber. I smell him on you."

Shandri Clayhill glared, and for a moment, Tu'ala'keth wondered if the human would tell her to mind her own affairs. But then she sighed and said, "I thought that after Saerloon, things would be different."

"Yet Vurgrom still treats you as his harlot."

"Maybe I should have expected it. The Lord of

Shadows knows, I'm not his only woman, but for the past couple years, I've been his favorite."

"As you sought to be."

"I don't deny it! I meant to use him, and it got me what I wanted. But I didn't know what I was getting into. He's fat, getting old, and drinks too much. He's grown jaded bedding hundreds of women and even females of other races. He often needs ... perversity to stir his desire."

"Daughter, you need feel no shame. You stalked and claimed a victim to satisfy your wants. That is the dance of predator and prey, blessed in the sight of Umberlee, though in this guise a far lesser thing than the bloodshed and slaughter for which she intends you. But if you continue to humble yourself when it is no longer necessary, when your fate beckons you onward, then you truly will be at fault."

"Can I refuse him when he's still the chief of our faction? When he could demand that I give back *Shark's Bliss*?"

"Yes! Because he lusts for the plunder you will bring him more than he aches for your flesh. Because he knows that if you forsake him, some rival faction will be overjoyed to recruit such a successful captain. You have power now, the power to command respect. You simply have to muster the courage to use it."

Shandri Clayhill drew a deep breath, as if preparing for some great exertion. "You're right."

❧ ❧ ❧ ❧ ❧

Vurgrom and Shandri whirled to the rhythm of the reel, while the yarting, longhorn, and songhorn wailed, the double-headed hand drum clattered, and the spectators clapped and stamped out the beat. He tried to press against her as he was accustomed to. She shoved him away, maintaining a bit of space between them.

At the end of the dance, he sought to cling to her for another. But she'd fulfilled the requirements of courtesy, done what was required to maintain the impression that she and her superior were on amiable terms, and she twisted away from him and snatched hold of Durth's hand. She and the grinning, gray-skinned orc pranced away, stepping high and kicking on the final beat of every other measure.

Sweaty, breathing heavily—when had he grown so old and fat that a single dance winded him?—Vurgrom turned and headed for his customary seat overlooking the torch-lit courtyard. One of the serving wenches gave him a lascivious smile as if offering herself in Shandri's place. But he'd had the girl—he'd had them all—and as he dimly recalled, she was nothing special. He sneered, and she hastily lowered her eyes.

He lumbered up onto the verandah and flopped down in his chair, which creaked under his weight. He picked up the wineskin he'd left beside his battle-axe and squeezed a spray of a tart Sembian white into his mouth.

"Captain Clayhill," murmured a contralto voice, "is disrespectful."

Vurgrom turned. It was Tu'ala'keth who'd crept up behind him. But she looked different—even stranger and less human, maybe, because of her spindly frame, dorsal fin, and lustrous black eyes.

Vurgrom realized he was staring and shifted his gaze a little. "It's good for morale," he said, "when the captain celebrates with the crew. Shandri's shrewd to dance with the orc."

The shalarin smiled. "You are generous, and she is ungrateful."

"Well ... maybe a bit." It was poor leadership to discuss Shandri with someone of lesser rank, particularly an officer under her command. But Tu'ala'keth had expressed his own opinion so succinctly it was difficult not to agree with her.

Besides, he now recognized that she didn't seem different so much as more ... pleasant to look on, maybe, or at least sympathetic. Her frame wasn't gaunt, as he'd always imagined, but rather slim and graceful, like the body of an elf, and her dark, narrow features conveyed warmth and empathy despite the impediment of the goggles.

"I marvel at her arrogance," the shalarin said. "By Umberlee's grace, she has conducted one successful raid, and now she deems herself better than the benefactor who made it possible, who has taken more plunder than she can even imagine, whose dread name is spoken even in Serôs beneath the waves."

Tickled by the flattery, Vurgrom grinned. "It's because of my victories that I can afford to indulge her foolishness." He supposed it was truer than not. He'd taken his share of ships and sacked his share of hamlets, even if his adventures hadn't been quite as glorious or profitable as he liked to claim.

"Your forbearance does you credit. Unless it reaches a point where others believe you weak. Then the lesser men who have always feared your strength will swarm on you."

"I didn't need that bit of advice, but thank you, anyway." For a newcomer and a member of an exotic species, she betrayed an admirable comprehension of the realities of life on Dragon Isle. "I wonder, though, why you gave it to me. I thought you'd decided Shandri is the Bitch Queen's pet and, therefore, entitled to your loyalty."

"Umberlee inspires," said Tu'ala'keth. "When it pleases her, she grants strength and luck to her petitioners. But she owes no loyalty to small, limited beings like ourselves. She has no compunction about abandoning us if ever we fall short of her requirements."

Glistening membranes flicked across Tu'ala'keth's eyes. The silvery flicker fascinated Vurgrom, and for a moment, he almost lost the thread of the conversation.

"Has Shandri fallen short?" he managed.

"It may be so. I came to your house that first day because the goddess whispered that herein, I might discover a spirit like a shark's tooth. But if it belonged to Captain Clayhill, would I constantly need to coax and urge her onward?"

"Maybe," Vurgrom said, "you found the right house, but the wrong soul."

"That possibility," said Tu'ala'keth, "has occurred to me."

"Let's speak plainly, then. Sail with me, not one of my underlings. I can use your counsel and magic, and I promise Umberlee blood aplenty." It would be a joy to see Shandri's face when she found out he'd lured her prized ship's cleric away.

But to his chagrin, Tu'ala'keth seemed in no hurry to agree to his proposal. Instead, she studied him thoughtfully. "You may be the one," she said. "I would like it to be so. But my preferences are irrelevant. What matters is that this time I see clearly and waste no more of my mistress's grace."

"You must have heard tales of my exploits."

"How could I avoid it, abiding in this house?" He wasn't sure if she was mocking him or not. If so, it didn't anger him the way it usually did. "More importantly, I have seen you, and the strength in your limbs." She ran a fingertip along his forearm.

Her webbed hand of midnight blue made his flesh look bone-white by contrast. Her skin was cool and silky smooth, almost slippery, as though still wet from the sea. The light, gliding contact afforded him a wholly unexpected thrill of sensual pleasure.

"I can well believe," she continued, "this arm has slain a thousand men and could slaughter a thousand more."

"Well, then," he said, his voice thick in his throat.

She took her hand away. "But when folk speak of the greatest corsairs on the Sea of Fallen Stars, they name Teldar first and Vurgrom the Mighty second. You have sought to supplant him for years and never accomplished your purpose. I wonder then, can you truly be brave and merciless enough to serve as Umberlee's blade?"

"Yes! If you—and she—will only help me, I'll master all the Pirate Isles and plunder every prize my ships can reach."

The shalarin smiled. "Well said. I will ponder the matter, and we will speak again." She turned and walked back into the mansion. In a moment, the shadows swallowed her.

❖ ❖ ❖ ❖ ❖

Tu'ala'keth had quarters in Vurgrom's mansion, but preferred to rest in the sea. Anton knew the route she took from the sprawling coquina house down to the water and thus could intercept her along the way when they wanted to confer unobserved.

Even though it was summer, the night air carried a chill. He hunkered down in the usual shadowy notch between two buildings; wrapped himself in his scarlet cape; and reflecting sourly on just how much of his life had been spent in uncomfortable circumstances, and settled himself to wait.

For a long while, he had nothing but scurrying, chittering rats and the rhythmic boom and hiss of the surf to keep him company. Finally, though, when the stars were fading and the eastern sky was lightening to gray, the shalarin came striding down the street, head held high, trident canted over her shoulder.

Anton rose and stepped out into the open. "I expected you sooner," he said.

"Have you learned something?" she asked.

"Unfortunately, no. I just wanted to find out if you've had any luck."

"Not yet. That is why I am attempting a new ploy."

Anton frowned. "I don't like the sound of that. I know the pirates. You don't. You need to check with me before you make a move."

"You could not have dissuaded me, for the need to try something different is obvious. We won a place among the reavers and killed the foes who resented us for it. It was a good beginning, but since then we have accomplished nothing at all.

"Indeed," she continued, "I do not know how you expected to. The affairs of Immurk's Hold are too complicated. Ships constantly set sail for undisclosed destinations, and every captain keeps his particular secrets. To make it even worse, Dragon Isle is only one of several pirate strongholds. We must rely on hearsay to assess what's happening on Alphar Isle and Mirg Isle, and most of the time, we can't even ask directly for news of the Cult of the Dragon, lest our curiosity arouse suspicion. I do not understand how spies ever discover anything about anything."

"You have to be patient," Anton said. "We poke about and poke about, and it seems nothing's happening. Then, if we're lucky, we peek in the right window, and suddenly we have the answer. Trust me, that's the way it works."

"The wyrms ravage Serôs," she replied. "Umberlee's altars stand neglected. I cannot afford patience beyond a certain point."

He sighed. "You'd better tell me what you did."

"I prompted Shandri Clayhill to refuse when Vurgrom calls her to his bed. Once she was out of the way, I began the process of fixing his interest on me."

"I don't understand. Our two peoples aren't drawn to one another in that way."

"Normally, no. But I know spells to enhance my personal magnetism to such an extent that it will not matter what is natural and what is not. At least, not to Vurgrom. Captain Clayhill says he often makes loves to females of other races, and if that is not enough, I mean to persuade him I am the key to realizing his aspirations. Desire and ambition will twine together in his mind, each deepening the other. Then, as I tease him and lead him on, I will cozen his secrets out of him."

Anton shook his head. "It's a bad idea, for all sorts of reasons. For one, you don't know Vurgrom's sitting on the information we need, so you can't justify the added risk."

"He is one of the two most important men on Dragon Isle, and the one to whom Umberlee led me."

"*I* led you to Vurgrom simply because it was likely his faction was recruiting."

"But you are Umberlee's agent, and even were you not, she reveals herself through chance."

"I can't be sure about that, but I do know enough about divine magic to understand that when you cast a spell to increase your force of personality, everybody's going to feel the pull. Some other priest or wizard is likely to realize you're trying to enthrall Vurgrom and give him a warning."

"I will approach Vurgrom at quiet moments, and fade into the shadows when our discourse is through. Other folk will have little opportunity to scrutinize me while the magic lends me grace."

"What about Captain Clayhill? It doesn't matter that she's rejected him. I guarantee you, given what they've shared together, she's still keeping an eye on him. She'll notice what's going on and realize you convinced her to end the affair, not for her benefit, but to open up opportunities for yourself."

"That," said Tu'ala'keth, "is where you come in.

Shandri Clayhill is worried about keeping you aboard *Shark's Bliss*, and as her history attests, she is willing to use her charms to secure her ends. Encourage her to seduce you; then keep her out of my way."

"What if I'm not the sort of man who lights her candle?"

"She gave herself to Vurgrom. How particular can she be?"

He laughed. "There is that. I'm going to be busy, playing jump-in-the-daisies with her and palavering with the other factions, too. But since I see I can't talk you out of this, we'll try it. Just be wary. Maybe you look at Vurgrom and see a fat, randy sot, but he's dangerous. He's murdered dozens in his time, and if he suspects you of tampering with his mind, a carnal itch won't stop him from adding you to the tally."

A caravel such as *Shark's Bliss* could never go unattended, even in port. She always needed a hand or two to guard and maintain her. But while her crew had loot to squander in the stews and taverns of Immurk's Hold, they had no interest in staying aboard a minute longer than necessary.

Such being the case, Anton wasn't particularly surprised to see Captain Clayhill alone on deck. Someone else was surely aboard, but maybe he was working below.

The absence of her underlings gave the pirate a reasonable amount of room to practice with her new greatsword. Grunting, face intent, she stamped back and forth, circled, blocked, and cut. Her ridiculous skirts swirled about her legs, and her jewels sparkled in the hot afternoon sunshine. The enormous blade, however, didn't gleam even when bathed in brightness. A murky dullness oozed inside the steel.

Anton rowed straight on toward the ship floating at anchor in the harbor. The breakrocks, a system of artificial reefs, lurked beneath the waves to rend the hull of any large vessel whose pilot hadn't learned to thread the maze, but his little boat didn't draw enough water for it to matter. He shipped the oars, tied his craft to *Shark's Bliss*, and swarmed up a rope onto the larger vessel.

By that time, of course, Shandri Clayhill had long since seen him coming. Still, as he swung himself over the rail, she took a lurching step toward him. The greatsword twitched an inch or two upward, as if she were contemplating a head cut, and her jittery nerves had given away her intent.

Anton grinned. "Easy, Captain! It's not the Sembian navy paying a call, only your ship's mage."

"I see that!" she snapped. She grabbed the greatsword's scabbard, shoved the weapon in hard enough to clank the guard against the silver mouth of the sheath, and set it down on the deck. "I'm simply surprised. I haven't seen much of you lately."

"I know," he said, putting on a rueful expression. "The truth is, after the way I acted when we divvied up the swag, I was ashamed to face you. I was greedy and arrogant, and I'm sorry."

Her eyes widened in surprise. She plainly hadn't expected an attempt at conciliation and wasn't certain what to make of it. "If you're so sorry," she said, "tell me what became of Kassur and Chadrezzan. I know they didn't simply run off. The mute wouldn't leave his grimoires behind."

Anton had already decided to give her a version of the truth. In his experience, such confidences opened the way for other forms of intimacy.

He made a show of hesitation then said, "I killed them. I killed them in self-defense. They came after me. But after offending you, I feared to tell you."

"So why do it now?"

"To regain your trust, if it isn't too late."

"You're more likely to make me angry all over again. If you hadn't stormed out that night, it needn't have come to slaughter."

"I truly regret quarreling with you but not because it would have averted trouble with the Talassans. We were going to fight eventually. I think you knew that."

"Well, maybe the wrong party survived. I've lost two valuable officers, each a more powerful spellcaster than you."

"But neither as wily a tactician nor as sprightly a dancer." He smiled. "Besides, Tu'ala'keth says you don't need Kassur or anyone else in particular. The Queen of the Depths has marked you for greatness. Why, then, would you worry about attracting followers? We lesser mortals must vie to convince you we're worthy to sail under your command."

Her lips quirked upward. He could tell she liked the flattery but doubted its sincerity. "If you're eager to remain aboard *Shark's Bliss*, then why spend your time reveling with the chieftains of the other factions?"

He shrugged. "I told you: I felt sheepish hanging around Vurgrom's mansion after making a jackass of myself. Besides, if folk want to stand me drinks and praise me as if I were Immurk come again, why would I say no? It's a pleasant way to pass the time. But it means nothing. In fact, it's beginning to bore me.

"We should go back to work. This is the height of the raiding season. Even with dragon flights wreaking havoc, the sea lanes are fat with trading vessels. Yet *Shark's Bliss* sits in the harbor."

She pulled a sour face. "I want to go out again. We can't build a lasting reputation on one venture, no matter how bold or successful. But the crew still has plenty of gold to spend."

"It doesn't matter. They'll go if you tell them to. They believe in you."

Yet she, for whatever buried reason, found it difficult to believe in herself. She wanted to be strong, and in reality, she was. Yet she sported the impractical gown and the rest of her regalia to conjure the image of a colorful, eccentric pirate captain out of legend, because she feared the underlying reality would impress no one. More important, she hungered for avowals of admiration and fidelity.

It was all Anton needed to discern to worm his way into her affections. The rest was simply a matter of glibness.

"Then we'll sail," she said. "We'll buy provisions and lay our plans."

"I'm glad. But I should go now. I interrupted your weapons practice and you're probably eager to get back to it." He looked for a twist of disappointment in her face and found it readily enough. "Unless you'd like to spar?"

She grinned. "I would. I have wooden swords in my cabin."

"Why not use live blades? We're skillful enough to avoid cutting each other, and with a new sword to learn, you ought to practice some parries against a real weapon."

He'd watched her dogged training—her near-obsessive labor to make herself as formidable a combatant as any in the Pirate Isles—enough to notice she only practiced with the greatsword while isolated aboard *Shark's Bliss*. Since he'd handled the weapon itself before she'd claimed it, he reckoned he knew why.

She averted her gaze a little, as though abashed, and he was certain of it. "That's not a good idea," she said.

"Why not? Because of the spirit inside the blade?"

"Yes. It's . . . bloodthirsty. I've decided it's dangerous to draw it except when I'm alone or have foes to kill."

"But Shandri," he said, "you're the mistress of the sword as surely as you're the mistress of this ship. It can't do anything you don't permit. But I imagine it's like a dog. It will keep testing you and trying to get its own way until you prove you're in control."

"Do you truly think so?"

"Yes, so let's fence." He picked up the greatsword and tossed it to her then drew his cutlass. "Just take it slow at first."

"All right." She took hold of the leather-wrapped hilt and pulled the long weapon from the scabbard. As she came on guard, it quivered, and darkness billowed up the blade like blood dispersing through water. Anton felt a pang of unease and wondered if what he'd suggested was as stupid as it suddenly seemed. But even if so, it was too late to back out now.

She slowly cut at his flank, and he brought the cutlass across in a leisurely parry. The greatsword leaped high, above the defense, and hacked at his head. He sprang backward, and the vicious stroke hurtled down, missing by a matter of inches. Shandri started to rush after him then jerked herself to a halt. The dark blade shuddered in her grasp.

"You see?" she gasped, shame in her voice.

"I see the hound slipped the leash for a second, but then you regained control. Let's try some more."

For a few slow exchanges, everything was all right. Then, when they sped up a little, the greatsword spun downward, trying to sever his foot at the ankle. This time, though, the muscles in her bare, tattooed arms bunching, Shandri stopped it in mid-stroke.

"No!" she screamed. She wrenched herself around, marched to the mast, and hammered the flat of the sword against the wood. "Bad dog! Bad dog!"

In response to its punishment, evidently, the blade

turned pitch black. When she finished beating it, the pirate glared at the weapon. Anton surmised that she and the sword were speaking mind to mind.

After a minute, she turned back around. "Once more," she said.

From that point forward, the greatsword refrained from trying to kill him, even when sparring at full speed. At the end, eyes shining, face exultant, Shandri set the weapon aside and gripped his forearms. It was almost a hug, the implication of an embrace from a woman who wasn't certain he'd welcome the familiarity.

She needn't have held back. He was now sure they'd be lovers by the end of the evening. But with that certainty came a sudden, unexpected spasm of self-disgust.

Maybe it was because, in a vague way, her lack of self-worth reminded him of the boy he'd been, hating himself when the other novices prattled of mystical communion with Torm and he had nothing to say, when they started conjuring wisps of light or healing sores and scratches with a glowing touch while he tried repeatedly and failed. Or maybe it was because he'd seduced too many trusting women over the years. Whatever the reason, he didn't want to use and ultimately betray Shandri in the same way.

But it was his work, and if the means were shabby, the ends were important, or so he had always striven to believe. He smiled back at her and brushed a lock of sweaty bronze hair away from her eye.

A slender, gleaming shadow in the moonlight, coral tunic glinting, Tu'ala'keth picked at her plate of raw, spiced shrimp and perch. Born in a world without fire, she had no taste for cooked food and preferred a seat without a back so as to avoid compressing the sweeping fin running down her spine. Vurgrom had learned these details and dozens of others over the course of the past few days, yet in the ways that mattered most, she remained a mystery. Maybe that was why she fascinated him.

It wasn't an entirely comfortable fascination. He wasn't used to lying sleepless, imagining the pleasures a wench had withheld in actuality. He'd always taken what he wanted when he wanted it.

But Tu'ala'keth was different: a shalarin waveservant, the partner he needed to topple Teldar at last. He had to treat to her with circumspection.

Or so it had seemed at first. But she'd made it plain she was judging him, assessing his fitness to champion her savage, relentless goddess, and in the middle of a tossing, feverish night, it had finally dawned on him just what sort of test it might actually be.

Still, when her long, dark fingers reached for a certain dark green morsel, he almost stopped her. Because what if his understanding was deficient? He took a drink of brandy to drown his doubts, and as he swallowed, she did, too. Now it was too late for second thoughts.

"Did you like that?" he asked.

"Yes," she said, black eyes reflecting the teardrop glow of the candle in the center of the table. "We pickle seaweed in As'arem, also. Tell me more of the smugglers on Kelthann. Do they dispose of all the plundered goods our faction seizes?"

Vurgrom snorted. "Don't you ever get bored, talking about raiding and the like? It's a beautiful night." Perched on a balcony at the top of the house, they had a fine view of bright Selûne and her tears shining in a cloudless sky, the wavering yellow lights of Immurk's Hold running down to the harbor, the dark, heaving vastness of the sea, and the waves crumbling to pearly froth near the shore. Far out on the water, a ship's lanterns glowed at the bow and stern. "Too beautiful for my list of gripes about greedy, thieving, gutless go-betweens." He covered her cool, silken hand with his own, and experienced the usual pang of excitement.

She must feel it, too, for her flesh quivered. But her voice remained steady and cool: "I wish to know about your dealings so I can give you whatever help you require."

"If you and Umberlee deem me worthy," he said dryly.

"Yes."

"Maybe you should tell me again what the goddess expects, so I'll know what to do to measure up."

She eyed him quizzically, but he was sure she'd accede to his request. She never tired of talking about Umberlee. Even he, who doted on her—much as he'd struggled against such a needy, mawkish emotion—grew weary of it sometimes.

Sure enough, she rose, and clasping his hand, drew him to the balustrade. "Behold the sea," she said.

"All right."

"On the—" She hesitated then frowned.

He had to suppress a smirk of anticipation. "Are you all right?"

"Perhaps your cook has not yet learned how to prepare food that agrees with me. My stomach ... never mind. I am well. On the surface of the waves and beneath them, every moment, a thousand thousand predators kill and devour their victims. Most people understand this, even if they rarely bother to think about it."

"I follow you."

"Now recognize ... recognize—" she paused to massage the round mark on her forehead—"recognize all those separate deaths as aspects of a higher unity. Comprehend that the sea itself, acting through its creatures, is the killer. Per ... perceive it for what it is, a gigantic set of eternally gnashing, tearing jaws."

"Umberlee's jaws," he said.

"Yes, and to find favor in her sight, you must embody the same qualities. You must be fearless and ruthless. You must take—" She swayed and grabbed the balustrade to keep from falling. "Something is wrong with me."

Vurgrom let the leer stretch across his face. No need to hold it in anymore. "I drugged you, dear one. It will wear off by morning."

Or at least it would if she were human. The apothecary couldn't guarantee it would affect a shalarin in precisely the same way. But Vurgrom had decided it was worth the risk to bring an end to his frustrations. As it would, one way or another.

To his surprise, Tu'ala'keth still had the strength to tear her hand from his and stumble a couple of paces backward. Of course, she had nowhere to run in the confined space of the balcony. "You ... are a blasphemer."

"How do you figure?" Vurgrom replied. "Weren't you just now telling me the Bitch Queen wants me to be bold and merciless and take what I want? All right, then, I'm taking you. That's the test, isn't it, to see if I dare. Well, watch me."

Tottering, she gripped the skeletal hand dangling on her breast and gasped the opening words of an incantation.

He lunged and punched her in the jaw, snapping her head to the side and spoiling the cadence of the spell. He wrested the sacred pendant out of her fingers then yanked it from around her neck.

"No magic," he told her and hit her again. Her legs buckled, and her arms flopped to her sides. He grabbed her before she could collapse and hauled her to the table. He swept the dirty dishes crashing to the floor to make a space then thrust her down.

The coral tunic—silverweave, she called it—should have come off easily. She wasn't fighting anymore, and the armor was split all the way down the back to accommodate her fin. But it clung to her somehow, perhaps by virtue of an enchantment.

The more he struggled with it, the angrier he became, while desire burned hotter and hotter inside him. For an instant, he felt like a stranger to himself, as if his urgency was unnatural, or some sort of malady, but he pushed the reflection aside. If his need was a sickness, then satisfaction would provide the cure.

Finally, with a soft clinking, the silverweave pulled apart. In his frantic yanking and fumbling, he'd evidently released some sort of hidden catch. He didn't know how or where, but neither did he care. He only had eyes for Tu'ala'keth's narrow torso with its subtly inhuman contours and gill slits on the collar bones and ribs. In that moment, it seemed both the strangest and most desirable thing he'd ever seen, and he stretched out a trembling hand to caress it. As if his excitement had kindled a comparable ardor in her, she shuddered violently.

Tu'ala'keth and Anton stood arguing in the narrow side street. He offered his objections to her scheme, and she refuted them. Yet when he finished, she felt obscurely disappointed.

"You didn't," she said, "make the one point that might almost have deterred me." She'd thought that by now, he understood her well enough to think of it.

"What point is that?" he asked.

"I intend to cloud Vurgrom's mind, not my own, and to beguile him properly, I must allow him to touch me from time to time. It will be repulsive and unnatural for me."

"Can you bear it?" Anton asked. "Act as if you enjoy it?"

"Yes." Within limits, she thought. "As I told Shandri Clayhill, I will be a hunter stalking her prey, and that is a sacred act."

"Good," said Anton, except that he wasn't Anton anymore. Somehow, between one heartbeat and next, he'd swelled into hulking, blubbery, leering Vurgrom. The pirate chieftain flung his arms wide, pulled her into a crushing embrace, and planted his lips on hers.

His mouth stank—and tasted—of wine and gluttony. Viler still were the mustache and whiskers, the bristling hairs jabbing into her skin. She suffered it while she silently counted to three then squirmed be free of him.

He lumbered after her, and the chase was like a dance, flickering from one day and location to the next. On the verandah, in the solar, in his suite and aboard the small sailboat he kept as a toy, she lured him in and pushed him back again.

"It's a matter of balance," she told him, "of pitting one emotion against another. As long as you fear to offend me as much as you yearn for my touch, you won't demand too much, and I can tolerate you."

"Can you tolerate this?" He was Kassur now, complete with eye patch, and he thrust out his hands at her. Yellow flame leaped from his fingertips, inspiring a jolt of terror that shocked her from her delirium.

Unfortunately, reality was equally nightmarish. Confused, for the first moment she understood only that the "balance" she intended to keep her safe had somehow tilted precipitously. She was on her back with Vurgrom leaning over her, mauling her. His ruddy face with its broken capillaries was contorted with passion, and it was plain he meant to use her as brutally as he'd treat a slave.

When she tried to clench her fists and pummel him, her limbs flailed uselessly, and she felt a burning throughout her frame. For a moment, she imagined the fire from her delirium had somehow accompanied her into the waking world to sear her in truth. Then, however, she realized the feeling wasn't really heat but rather a kind of starved frenzy—the panic of a body no longer able to breathe.

Vurgrom had divested her of her silverweave. Most likely he didn't understand she needed it to survive out of water, for she naturally hadn't told him of her vulnerability. Now if she couldn't recover the coral mesh quickly, that sensible reticence would be the death of her.

"Armor," she croaked. "Dying."

He slapped her and resumed his pawing, as if he had no more comprehension than a beast. Perhaps he didn't. Maybe that was what her magic had made of him.

It was certain only magic could save her now. She struggled to compose her thoughts for conjuring. It was difficult when her body hurt so badly, Vurgrom's caresses were so loathsome, and she could feel life itself withering inside her. She reached out to Umberlee, and the goddess granted her a wave of frigid anger, sweeping through her mind to scour weaker, useless emotions away.

Tu'ala'keth wheezed the opening words of the invocation. Straining to control her spastic hand, she attempted a mystic pass. Vurgrom realized what was happening and reached for her throat to silence her.

She flailed her other arm across her body, blocking the human's clutching hands. It gave her time to complete the spell. Despite the fumbling execution, power seethed through the air. Vurgrom shrieked, scrambled off her, and floundered backward, fetching up against the door that led to his apartments. Shaking and whimpering, he gawked at her.

The magically induced terror would only last a few heartbeats. She had that much time to save herself from asphyxiation. She heaved herself up off the tabletop, tried to catch her balance, but her legs gave way beneath her. She collapsed to her knees, banging the left one hard, a sharp stab of pain to punctuate the ongoing, all-encompassing excruciation.

She cast about for the silverweave, and failed to discern it or much of anything else. Even when its dazzling sun forsook the sky, the world above the waves had always been bright by her standards, but now darkness seethed and swam through the air, obscuring everything. A fresh cramp in her guts suggested the cause might be the poison Vurgrom had fed her.

Still the armor had to be here, didn't it? Well, no, actually, it didn't. Not if, wild with passion, Vurgrom had flung it off the balcony.

But if that were true, she was as good as dead, and Umberlee's cause, as good as lost, and so she refused to believe it. Instead, she crawled, praying that, her near blindness notwithstanding, she'd spot the tunic when she dragged herself close enough.

She didn't. But eventually, when she set her hand down, something clinked beneath her palm, and she felt the familiar mesh of sculpted coral. She scooped up the silverweave and examined it by touch as much as sight, searching for the sleeves. She located one and fumbled an arm in, and Vurgrom bellowed, a roar of rage, not panic. His footsteps shook the balcony as he charged.

Until she had the silverweave on properly, she couldn't fully benefit from its enchantments. She was like a beached fish with the edge of the surf washing and receding over its body. Her gills worked one moment and not the next. It wasn't enough to quell her spasms or restore her depleted strength, but she had no time for anything more.

She groped about—she still could only barely see—found the heavy golden goblet from which he'd swilled his brandy lying within reach, and grabbed it. As he bent over her kneeling body and poised his thumbs to gouge her eyes, she rammed the cup into his groin.

It was a puny blow, but it caught him where he was sensitive. His mouth fell open, and he groaned. She bashed him in the knee, and he fell beside her, which enabled her to pummel him about the head.

He howled and tried to shield himself with his arms. She rolled away beyond his reach and back onto her knees then hastily drew the silverweave on as it was meant to be worn.

At last she could breathe as easily as if she were under water. It didn't end her spasms or restore more than a frail shadow of her former strength—no hope of that with the drug still ripping at her guts—but it helped.

Vurgrom scrambled to his feet and charged. "Trip!" she gasped. He caught one foot behind the other and fell headlong, bashing his face against the floor. She reared over him and pounded his skull with the goblet, which bonged and crumpled under the force of the blows. Blood streamed from his split scalp to stain his coppery hair a darker hue, and he stopped moving.

Tu'ala'keth yearned to keep hitting him until she was certain he'd never stir again, but that would preclude him serving Umberlee's purpose. Besides, she was nearly as avid to end her own distress.

She set the cup aside and retrieved the drowned man's hand from the floor of the balcony where Vurgrom had tossed it. She cast restorative charms on herself and, clasping the hand, she purged the poison from her system. The clenching pains in her belly eased, and the veils of darkness shrouding the world dropped away.

Next, she prayed for enhanced vitality. The magic flowed through her in a cool tide, easing her aches and replenishing her strength. She then found one of the sharp knives she and Vurgrom had used to slice their food, crouched over him, and chanted a healing prayer.

It was only a minor one. She didn't want him fit enough for further fighting. He moaned, and his blood-shot eyes fluttered open. She set the knife against the throbbing artery at the side of his neck.

"Struggle or cry out," she said, "and I will kill you."

"Bitch," he said, his voice low. "If you were a proper woman and not some ugly fish, the drug would have kept you helpless."

"I perceive," she said, "you have shaken off the glamour I cast upon you. No matter. Your attempt at molestation has taken us beyond such tricks. Now I will ask questions. You will answer truthfully or die."

He stared at her. "'Questions?' You bewitched me just to get some sort of information?"

"Yes."

He snorted. "All right. I'll tell you anything. But you have to swear by your goddess to let me live if I give you what you want."

Tu'ala'keth scowled. "Very well. I swear it on the wrath of Umberlee. Now what do you know of the Cult of the Dragon?"

He peered at her quizzically. "Just what everyone knows. They're wizards and lunatics who like wyrms. What kind of fool question is that?"

Anton had warned her Vurgrom might know nothing helpful. Was it possible the spy was correct?

No. It wasn't. Umberlee had surely brought her to this moment for a reason.

"You have no dealings with the cult?" she persisted.

"No! Never."

"Then who among the pirates does?"

"As far as I know, no one."

"Where in these islands is the cult's stronghold?"

"I don't know that they have one. If they did, they'd keep it a secret, wouldn't they?"

She pressed the knife against his neck, reminding him of its proximity. "Thus far, Captain, you have given me no help. You must do better, or my oath will not constrain me from cutting your throat."

"I can't tell you what I don't know!"

"Let us try again. Somewhere in the Pirate Isles, a group of recluses has established a community. They do not raid as the rest of you do, and their purpose is a mystery. They would prefer to go unremarked, but you have discerned their presence because you strive to know all that occurs hereabouts. Point me to them."

He frowned. "Well, if you put it that way . . . Tan?"

Her pulse quickened. "Tell me."

"They've been there for a few years now. Someplace, whatever shelter they've built, you can't see it from offshore. They trade for some of the plunder passing through Mirg Isle, necessities like food and cloth, but stranger and more valuable items, too, like alchemical supplies and fine gems."

"What account do they give of themselves?"

"Mostly, they don't. The rumor is, they're monks, the last followers of some dead god trying to pray and magic him back to life, but nobody really knows. They could be wyrm worshipers."

They were. Tu'ala'keth was certain of it, and flawless jewels and alchemist's equipment were the proof. According to Anton, the cultists required such things to transform living dragons into dracoliches.

"So," growled Vurgrom, "have I earned the right to go on living?"

"I promised," she said, "in the name of Umberlee.

Now consider the choice before you. You can seek revenge on me, but only by making this humiliation public. Forever after, folk will laugh over the tale of how an 'ugly fish' besotted Vurgrom the Mighty. Or you can do nothing, in which case no one will ever know."

He glared at her. "Curse you—"

"Just think about it." She snatched up the battered cup and bashed him with it. His eyes rolled up in his head.

She reckoned he'd remain unconscious for a while, but that was no reason to dawdle. She strode into Vurgrom's suite, retrieved her trident and goggles, and hurried on to the door leading to the remainder of the house. She opened it to behold one of the pirate chieftain's followers, a tall, thin man with a sallow face and drooping mustachios, peering directly at her.

"Yes?" she said.

"I thought I heard noises," he replied. "Somebody yelling, maybe."

"Everything is all right. You can go about your business."

It was possible he'd obey. She still had the enchantment in place to enhance her force of personality. It wouldn't rouse his amorous inclinations—it had taken guile to make Vurgrom react in that fashion—but it might incline him to believe whatever she told him.

"Oh," he said. "Well, then. . . ." His dark eyes squinted at her. "Waveservant, is your face bleeding?"

She realized Vurgrom had marked her, and that despite her efforts to heal herself, she must still bear visible scrapes and bruises. After the ordeal she'd suffered, the sting of such petty injuries simply hadn't registered.

"I had an accident," she said. "It is nothing."

"I think," the thin man said, "I should talk to Captain Vurgrom. For a second, anyway."

"He is sleeping and will be angry if you wake him."

"Then he'll swear and yell at me, I suppose. But I still need to do it."

"As you wish." She withdrew a pace into the suite, giving him room to pass. Then, as he strode through the opening, she drove her trident into his stomach.

He stared at her and doubled over. She pulled the weapon from his body, and he toppled. She stuck him five more times until the writhing stopped and he lay motionless in a pool of blood.

His death, though necessary, was unfortunate, for suppose someone else came looking for him? Even if Vurgrom remained unconscious, or woke but chose to heed her advice, Tu'ala'keth's situation was still precarious. She swept her skeletal amulet through a sinuous pass and murmured the opening phrase of another spell.

Anton ushered Shandri into the private room he'd hired on the top floor of the settlement's least objectionable inn. Candlelight gleamed on crystal and white porcelain trimmed with gold leaf. Red roses perfumed the air, and the sweet, breathy notes of a longhorn trilled from an alcove. The casement stood open, providing a view of the harbor below and the myriad stars above.

Shandri exclaimed in pleasure, as well she might. With all the plunder moving though Immurk's Hold, a good many luxuries were available, yet in most respects, it remained as crude and raucous a place as any outlaw haven. Accordingly, it took some doing to collect the elements of an elegant, romantic supper for two and assemble them to create the proper effect.

Not that Anton had any authentic claim to breeding or refinement, but as he'd hoped, the trace that had rubbed off on him during his contacts with wealthy merchants and aristocrats was sufficient to impress his companion.

"Vurgrom's banquets are splendid," she said. "But this is . . . lovely."

"Shall we?" He seated her then poured them each a cup of a ruby-colored Impilturan wine. He toasted her. "To Shandri Clayhill, fiercest and most ravishing corsair on the Sea of Fallen Stars."

"To Anton, her gallant ship's mage."

They drank. To his undiscriminating palate, the red was too sour, with a hint of bitter aftertaste, but he pretended to savor it so as not to spoil the mood. "The cook said the first course will be up in a minute or two."

"I'm in no hurry," Shandri said. "I could sit here all night."

"I'm glad you like it. Someday, maybe we'll sup like this every evening."

She smiled. "I doubt the Hold is up to the task of providing such elegance on a regular basis."

"Who says we'll always live on Dragon Isle?"

"We'll always live on one of the Pirate Isles. Where else is there for reavers to go?"

He shrugged. "We wouldn't be the first raiders to strike it rich at sea then use a piece to the loot to bribe their way to a pardon, or even patents of nobility, on land. Mind you, I'm in no hurry, but it's something to bear in mind."

"Something to dream of, at least." Bracelets glittering in the candlelight, tattoos crawling on her slim but muscular arm, she reached across the stainless linen tablecloth and laid her hand on his. "I do like it that you imagine us together years hence."

"Of course," he said and felt as if he meant it, for a spy deceived others by splitting himself into two people. The one who revealed himself to his dupes truly became the role, the lie, at odd moments even forgetting he was simply a mask. But behind the semblance lurked the true personality, loyal only to Turmish, ready to burst through the shell as soon as circumstances warranted.

"Where, exactly, would you wish to live," Shandri asked, "once we're ready to put our cutthroat ways behind us?"

He grinned. "Saerloon seems to be lucky for us, but it's a nasty sort of place. I wouldn't want to raise a family there."

She laughed. "Oh, you've decided on children as well."

"Naturally. Fifteen or twenty stout sons, and maybe a daughter or two to help with your embroidery."

"If I have to learn to embroider, forget the whole thing."

"Fair enough. You needn't touch thread or needles of any kind. I see us spending the bulk of our time on a country estate. Someplace with sheep, hedges, and—"

Something pale and luminous stirred at the edge of his vision. Startled, he looked around. A shape was oozing through the crack between the door and the jamb. Once clear, it hovered in the air, thickened, and wriggled until it shaped itself into a spectral hand. It crooked its index finger in Anton's direction.

"What's the matter?" Shandri asked.

She was looking where he was, but plainly perceived nothing out of the ordinary. Tu'ala'keth had explained that if she used this particular spell, only he would be able to see the disembodied messenger.

"It's nothing," he said. "I thought I heard the server on the stairs. But I've just now remembered something. I have to go."

She frowned. "Why? I'm your captain. What urgent obligation can you have if I didn't impose it on you?"

"It's Tu'ala'keth. I promised to assist with a

ceremony. Something she must do tonight, before the tide goes out."

"Curse it, the waveservant is under my authority as well. Her wishes don't take precedence over mine. You—" Shandri caught herself. "No. I'm just being bitchy because I'm disappointed. I don't really want you to break a promise to Tu'ala'keth. We'll both attend her and worship as she instructs. She tells me I need to pay homage to the goddess, and here's an opportunity."

"I'm sorry. I wish you could accompany me, but Tu'ala'keth said I need to come alone."

Shandri frowned. "That's odd. Usually, she wants as many people as possible to pray and offer to Umberlee. She hates it if anyone holds back."

"I guess it's a special ritual. Please, stay here. Eat. The meal should be grand, so don't let it go to waste. I'll return as soon as I can."

"Yes, you will. I order you to."

He rose, she followed suit, and they embraced. She gave him a deep, passionate kiss, and it stirred him. It saddened him a little to reflect that in all likelihood, he'd never see her again.

He extricated himself from her arms, turned his back on her, and followed the floating hand: out of the room, down the stairs, and into the street.

Hanging several paces in front of him at head level, the construct led him through crowds of roistering pirates and finally into the quiet side street where he and Tu'ala'keth sometimes met. She stood waiting in the niche between the shanties. Two sea bags lay amid the litter at her feet, another indication things were happening fast.

The phantom hand blinked out of existence the instant he laid eyes on its maker. "I have our share of the Thayan treasure," she said. "It may prove useful."

"What's going on?" he asked. "Did Vurgrom know

where the cultists are? Did he finally give up the secret?"

"In essence, yes."

Anton shook his head. "I can't believe your luck."

"Our 'luck' is the grace of Umberlee."

"Then, not to quibble, but it's too bad she didn't give you even more of it. If everything had gone as planned, we wouldn't be absconding so hastily."

"Now that we have what we came for, it is time to go. But I confess, you are right. Vurgrom responded to my enchantments in a way I failed to anticipate, and he assaulted me."

"You mean—"

"I stopped him before it went very far then extorted information from him at knife point. After we parted company, I found it necessary to kill one of his underlings. Thus, it is possible Vurgrom's folk are already hunting me. We will need to exercise caution as we make our departure."

"Apparently so. How many of those pellets do you have left? The ones that let me breathe under water."

"Only one."

"Enough to let me swim or ride one of the seahorses a goodly distance from Dragon Isle—and drown between islands when the magic wears off. We need to steal a small, fast boat."

"It will be fast when I call the wind to fill the sails."

"Good." He stepped forward to pick up one of the sea bags, and a cry rang out.

"Men of *Shark's Bliss*! Of Vurgrom's faction! I've found the traitors! Follow me!"

Anton pivoted to see Shandri standing on guard several yards away, glaring, dark sword shivering in her hands.

"I followed you," she said. "I cared for you, but I'm not an imbecile, even though you played me for one, and what you were babbling just didn't make sense."

Anton reflected bitterly that he was the imbecile. Normally, he took care that no one shadowed him, but tonight, he'd been too busy keeping track of the ghostly hand. Whereas Shandri, with the ring that let her see in the dark, had had little difficulty keeping him in view.

"And I was wise to be suspicious," the pirate continued. "Because, if I'm not mistaken, people worship Umberlee at the water's edge, not in filthy little alleys."

"All right," he said, "I did mislead you. But I can explain."

"Don't bother. I heard some of what you and Tu'ala'keth had to say to one another. Enough to understand the two of you are spies. You came here to steal a secret, and now that you've got it, you hope to vanish in the night. Well, it won't be that easy." Once again, she shouted: "*Shark's Bliss!* Vurgrom's men! I need you!"

"Be silent," said Tu'ala'keth. "We have done no harm to you or your ship, and we intend none. But if you continue to shout, we will kill you."

"'No harm?' What about your lies?"

"I said you can be strong, and so you can. The choice is up to you."

Shandri sneered at Anton. "You told other lies besides that one."

"Love is pleasant," said Tu'ala'keth, "but it is a petty thing compared to the mastery and slaughter which are your birthright. You demean yourself by making much of it. Now sheathe your sword and trouble us no more. Otherwise, I will kill you."

Shandri smiled. "Try."

"As you wish," said Tu'ala'keth. She gripped her bony pendant, started to conjure, and several men and orcs came dashing around the corner and down the street. Umberlee, it seemed, was even stingier with her "grace" than Anton had imagined. Folk were actually combing the streets for the shalarin, and they'd heard the pirate captain yell.

Sealmid was at the head of the pack, amethyst bow in hand. "You found them," he said to Shandri. "I didn't know you'd even joined the hunt."

"Thus far," said Tu'ala'keth, "you are all faithful worshipers of Umberlee. Do not offend her, lest she curse you."

"We thaw what you did to Yuiredd," said the first mate. "We'll take our chantheth." He pulled an arrow from the quiver hanging at his hip.

Retreating, Tu'ala'keth resumed her chant. Pirates drew their blades and stalked after her.

Shandri said, "Anton is mine." She charged.

He snatched his cutlass from the scabbard, barely in time to parry a head cut. The clanging impact jolted down his arm.

"Don't do this," he said. "I don't want to kill you, and you don't really want to kill me."

"Yes," she said, "I do." The dark blade leaped at him.

As they circled, he caught glimpses of Tu'ala'keth's part of the battle. Now outlined in some sort of protective blue-green aura, she conjured a howl of sound. It staggered her foes but didn't stop them. The next time he saw her, pirates were hacking at her, while Sealmid loosed an arrow. The shaft veered like a bird on the wing to swing wide of the archer's comrades, turned, and struck the shalarin in the back. From his vantage point, Anton couldn't tell whether it pierced her silverweave or not, but it knocked her lurching forward, and a broadsword slashed at her torso. Snarling, she caught the blow on the haft of her trident.

Her eyes seething with shadow like the greatsword, Shandri struck blow after furious blow, until Anton's arm felt half-numb from the stress of parrying. It seemed impossible that anyone could hit so hard with such a ponderous blade and recover quickly enough to attack again just an instant later. He realized he'd never seen the pirate wield the living sword in actual combat, when she and it were united in their avidity for the kill. He hadn't understood what a fearsome weapon it truly was.

She was pressing him so hard that already, it was difficult to attack or riposte, and if anything, she kept striking faster and harder, as if battle-rage were making her steadily stronger when by all rights, she should be tiring.

To make matters even worse, she was using the superior length of her weapon to good effect, keeping a measure that allowed her to attack him but not the other way around. He needed to adjust, to slip inside the critical space where his cutlass could cut and stab but a greatsword was unwieldy.

He parried repeatedly, looking for the opening he needed—until a sweep of the dark blade snapped his own in two, leaving just a jagged stub protruding from the bell guard.

Shandri laughed and sprang at him, swinging the greatsword at his neck. He blocked with the shattered cutlass—until the bell crumpled or broke beneath her hammering blows, it could still serve as a makeshift buckler—and snatched a dagger from his sash.

It was a pathetic weapon compared to the greatsword, especially considering that, by pushing him so relentlessly, Shandri wasn't even permitting him to shift it to his right hand. But it was all he had left.

"I love you," he said and, hoping the words might make her hesitate for a split second, lunged. Shandri instantly took a retreat, opening up the distance again, and the greatsword leaped at his belly. Somehow he stopped short, and the stroke whizzed harmlessly by. He blocked the next one with the broken cutlass.

Such good fortune couldn't last. She was going to

penetrate his guard eventually, most likely within the next few heartbeats. He risked another glance at Tu'ala'keth, and saw she was still in no position to help him. A couple of her opponents sprawled on the ground, dead or incapacitated, but the rest were still assailing her, and one of Sealmid's arrows was sticking through her bloody calf.

Anton would have to save himself, and it was plain his combat skills were insufficient. He supposed that left sorcery.

The problem was magic would require him to focus his attention on the intricate business of conjuring, which was all too likely to slow his reactions as he tried to parry and dodge the greatsword. But still, it seemed his only chance.

He threw the knife at Shandri's head, but it flew wide of the mark, and she didn't even bother ducking. He told himself it didn't matter. The real point had been to free up a hand. He reached into his pocket, fumbled out his bit of ram's horn, and she feinted high and cut low. He recognized the true attack just in time to leap backward and avoid a fatal chop to the guts. Still, the dark blade sliced his arm. His fingers flew open, and he dropped the spell trigger.

The greatsword pounced at him. It was a blur now. It was like dark lightning flickering in an infernal sky. He realized he had no more time to grope for and manipulate another talisman, even if she'd permit him to hold on to it, nor could he possibly stand still long enough to execute any sort of cabalistic pass without her burying the sentient blade in his body. His only hope was a spell purely verbal in nature.

He couldn't believe it would actually save him, but he gasped out the rhyming words. The greatsword leaped at him, and as he'd feared, with his attention divided, he failed to defend as nimbly as before. He caught the blow on the ruined cutlass, but the dark blade smashed through the battered guard and sheared deep into his arm just below the wrist.

Perhaps because of the virulence in the living sword, the shock of the blow, harbinger of pain to come, was nearly enough to arrest thought. Nearly, but he wouldn't let it ruin the spell. He fought to maintain the cadence, to enunciate precisely, to grit the remaining syllables out.

Magic sighed through the air, and responding to the charm of opening, each of Shandri's many bracelets and necklaces unfastened itself to drop clinking and glittering to the ground. The diamonds even fell away from her earlobes.

Anton had suspected that even if he managed to complete the spell, it wouldn't matter. Furious as she was, she wouldn't care when the baubles dropped off. She might not even notice.

Yet she did. Maybe it was because she so loved the jewelry or simply because she was so surprised, but she stopped attacking. She took her eyes off her adversary to glance down at the treasure strewn around her feet.

Anton rushed her.

The greatsword cut at him but too late. At last he was too close for it to threaten him. He drove the broken cutlass at Shandri's face, half slashing with the jagged stump of blade and half bashing with what remained of the bell. He grabbed her, hooked his leg behind her, and threw her down. The back of her head cracked against the ground. He cut at her neck, and his ruined sword made a ragged cut. Blood gushed. The pirate thrashed for a moment, and she was gone.

Panting, Anton looked around. Tu'ala'keth was still fighting, the outcome of the battle still in doubt. He twisted the greatsword's hilt from Shandri's death grip.

As soon as he grasped it himself, a surge of gleeful

viciousness washed away his weariness and the throbbing in his wounded arms. For a moment, the influx of the greatsword's savagery sickened him, but he accepted the contamination anyway because he suspected that, in his spent and injured condition, it was only by surrendering himself to the weapon's bloodlust that he could prevail.

He jumped to his feet and charged Sealmid. The bowman was aiming another shaft at Tu'ala'keth but must have glimpsed Anton from the corner of his eye, because he pivoted and sent the arrow streaking directly at him.

Anton should have died then, pierced through the heart. But the greatsword, of its own volition, shifted across his body and knocked the arrow off course. Anton struck Sealmid down, and felt an exultation as the blade bit deep. He jerked it free and turned to find the next foe.

After that, he lost himself in the dizzying joy of slaughter. Until only one target remained within reach. He raised the sword to cut it down.

"Enough!" said Tu'ala'keth. "I am your comrade. The fight is won."

With that, he recognized her but yearned to kill her even so. Fortunately, though, revulsion at the cruelty welled up from deep inside him, a sort of counterweight that enabled him to push the alien passions back into the sword. He threw the weapon down, sensing a twinge of its irritation just as it left his hand.

"Umberlee has blessed us," the shalarin continued. She knelt, gripped the arrow transfixing her leg beneath the point, and drew the fletchings through the wound. "We were outnumbered. I had not wholly recovered from my mistreatment at Vurgrom's hands. Yet we are victorious."

"For now," whispered Sealmid, still lying where he'd fallen. Anton was surprised the first mate was alive, but it was plain he wouldn't be much longer. Blood soaked his clothes from neck to crotch, and more of it bubbled on his lips.

"What do you mean?" asked Tu'ala'keth.

"Vurgrom'th thending everybody to kill you bath-tardth, not ... jutht uth. Had to round everyone up, haul them out ... of the tavernth, but...." The dark froth stopped swelling and popping in his mouth.

Anton found it easy enough to complete the dead man's thought. "But by now, Vurgrom's got men patrolling the waterfront to cut off our escape. Curse it, anyway!" He gripped the more serious of his gashes in an effort to stanch the bleeding.

"After I heal my leg," said Tu'ala'keth, "I will help you with that."

"Do it fast. We need to move away from here. Somebody else may have heard Shandri yelling, or all the commotion afterwards."

"Where shall we move to?"

"Good question, considering that the whole island hates a spy." But wherever they went, he meant to go well armed. He stepped over the greatsword to examine one of the pirate's cutlasses.

Tu'ala'keth rose stiffly to her feet. "Take Shandri Clayhill's sword."

"It clouds my mind."

"It purifies you. When you hold it, you are truly fit to serve Umberlee. It would not surprise me to learn that some of her worshipers here on land had a hand in the forging of it."

"Then they can have it back."

"It is the finest weapon here. You are too shrewd to spurn such an instrument."

He realized with a pang of resentment that she was right. He survived by his wits and shrank from using any magic that could muddle them, but in the present desperate circumstances, the greatsword might prove more useful than any lie or ruse. He still chose a cut-lass, but when he and Tu'ala'keth skulked onward, he carried the living blade, drowsing in its scabbard once more, as well.

Teldar gazed out over the entertainments his lar-gess had provided, at his followers guzzling grog and ale, gnawing chicken legs and slabs of pork and beef, ogling and pawing the dancing girls, and flinging clattering dice or slapping cards down on a tabletop in a game of trap-the-badger. As the clamor attested, everyone was having a good time, and he reckoned he'd lingered long enough to play the part of a proper pirate chieftain. Now he was free to retire to diversions more in keeping with his own humor, a volume of old Chon-dathan verse and a dram of cinnamon liqueur.

He pushed back his chair, nodded goodnight to anyone who might be looking in his direction, and exited the hall. Outside in the lamp-lit gloom of the corridor, the relative quiet and fresh air, untainted by the odor of dozens of sweaty, grubby reavers packed in too small a space, came as an immediate relief.

He took a deep breath, savoring the moment. Then Anton Fallone—if that was his real name—stepped from a doorway farther up the passageway. Teldar reached for the hilts of his short sword and poniard, drew them, and came on guard. He accomplished it all in one quick, smooth motion, as a master-of-arms had taught him in another life, more years ago than he generally cared to recall.

"You don't need your weapons," Anton said.

"What are you doing here?" Teldar asked.

The younger man grinned. "Well, you did tell me I'm welcome anytime."

"That was before Vurgrom put out the word that

you and the shalarin are spies. Where is she, by the way?"

"Hiding outside. I reckoned that even if one of your people spotted me sneaking in, he might not take any notice if I just kept these hidden." He pushed back his scarlet cape and lifted his arms, displaying torn, bloodstained sleeves and the scabby gashes inside. "But Tu'ala'keth's harder to overlook."

"What do you want?"

"Could we talk about it in here?" Anton nodded toward the doorway through which he'd just emerged. "It's a nice room and more private than a corridor in a busy house."

Teldar frowned, pondering. All he had to do was shout, and his men would come running to take Anton prisoner. Then he could question the spy in complete safety. Yet his instincts told him the intruder meant no harm, and even if he did, the pirate was confident of his ability to handle a lone assassin. So, as Anton had piqued his curiosity, why not grant him a private conversation? At the very least, it promised to be interesting.

"After you," Teldar said.

As Anton had said, it was a pleasant room, with shelves of fragrant leather-bound logs and rudders taken from scores of prizes, framed charts from places as far away as Lantan decorating the walls, and a lanceboard with its sixty-four squares of alternating red and white. The chessmen sat neatly centered in their starting positions, ivory on one side, carnelian on the other.

"All right," the pirate said. "You're a spy. For Impiltur, Cormyr, or whomever. I suppose you and your accomplice have gleaned the most about Vurgrom's business, but you've had ample opportunity to pry into my affairs, and the dealings of all Immurk's Hold, as well. Should you escape to report your findings, you could do all us reavers incalculable harm. Perhaps you even know the disposition of the breakrocks, and the rest of our defenses. Maybe you've stolen all the secrets your masters need to launch a full-scale assault on Dragon Isle. What, then, can you possibly expect from me?"

"You're a shrewd, careful man, and you built this fortress. Accordingly, I suspect it has an escape tunnel, with a well-provisioned sailboat at the end. If you saw fit, you could help Tu'ala'keth and me get away, and even your own followers—who, I realize, might take exception—would know nothing about it."

Teldar snorted. "I could also stick feathers in my ears and squawk like a gull. But it's unlikely."

"Look," Anton said, "you're right: I am a spy. I'd deny it if I thought it would help, but I can tell the game is up. I've worked against you pirates for a while now. The intelligence I've gathered has sent your ships to the bottom and their crews to the gallows.

"But I swear on the Red Knight's sword, this summer, I have a different target: the Cult of the Dragon."

"Then why trouble Dragon Isle?"

"Because it was a way to pick up their trail."

"And did you?"

"As a matter of fact, yes. My next move is to make my report. Then my superiors will send a fleet to wipe the madmen out."

"Interesting, but I'm still unclear as to why I should help you. You're a dangerous man, and have, by your own admission, injured me in the past. It would be sensible to ensure you won't do so again."

"Ordinarily, I'd agree with you. But this is a unique time. Do you understand the cult's ultimate goal?"

"To turn live dragons into undead ones?"

"Yes, and this is their moment. As I understand it, wyrms who haven't yet contracted frenzy are scared of getting it, and changing into dracoliches renders them immune. So they're seeking out the cult in record numbers, and the necromancers and such are making a supreme effort to transform them as quickly as possible. By the end of the year, we could have a dozen dracoliches bedeviling the Sea of Fallen Stars. Maybe more. Imagine what that would do to your business."

"I've never seen a dracolich," Teldar replied, "but from what I've heard, it wouldn't be a pleasant prospect."

"Then help me prevent it. I'm not asking you to send your own ships to fight wyrms and sorcerers. Just let me fetch the folk who are willing to take on the job."

Teldar sheathed his weapons and doffed his slate-gray cape. "We'll wrap the shalarin in this to bring her inside. That fin on her back will keep it from fitting properly, but it has a virtue in it that will make her inconspicuous even so."

"Before we fetch her, I have to ask one more thing of you: Tu'ala'keth's intentions aren't the same as mine, and she doesn't know what I intend to do with the information we've gathered. Please, don't tell her."

"All right, but in that case, why am I helping you, if not to visit destruction on the cultists?"

"Because we're bribing you with a story that will make Vurgrom a laughingstock, and with all the jewelry Shandri Clayhill used to wear."

Teldar smiled. "Well, that will be a nice bonus." He gestured toward the door. "Shall we?"

THE **PRIESTS**

CHAPTER 7

Arms aching, one hand resting on the tiller, Anton peered back along the sailboat's wake. He still couldn't see any sign of pursuit, nor, for that matter, could he see much of Dragon Isle itself anymore, though the towering promontory called the Earthspur still blocked out a section of the stars.

As the island was fading from view, so, too, was it time to put it from his thoughts, as he'd put so many comparable episodes behind him. But as yet, he hadn't managed to close the door on the memories.

Tu'ala'keth sat in the bow. "You are troubled," she said, "even though we have now accomplished the first portion of our task. Do you regret killing Shandri Clayhill?"

He didn't feel like talking about it. But by confiding in Tu'ala'keth, he would inspire her trust in turn, and that was what he wanted. So, as was so often the case, his honest inclinations didn't matter. "I shouldn't. She was an enemy of my homeland, and anyway, you gave her a chance to save herself. But I do."

"You and I should not have attachments. Not now. Nothing should distract us while we are blades in Umberlee's hands."

His lips quirked upward in a bitter smile. "That's the way I always live: Only the task matters."

"It is the best way to live. You should rejoice in possessing such a spirit. But I see you do not. Not tonight."

Off to starboard, something splashed. He wondered if it was one of the seahorses keeping pace with them. "No, not tonight."

"I do not blame you. We must strive to emulate Umberlee, but we cannot be as fierce and dauntless as a goddess, no matter how we try. I, too, have my weaknesses and doubts."

"You hide them well."

"Nevertheless. I misjudged Vurgrom twice. I never dreamed he'd assault me, no matter how I teased him, and I imagined the threat of humiliation would deter him from sending his underlings to kill us."

He shrugged. "It's understandable you made mistakes. Humans are strange to you."

She hesitated. "But I also lied to you, Umberlee's champion, my comrade in a sacred venture, and for that I am truly sorry."

He squinted at her, but even though she wasn't wearing her goggles, he couldn't read her narrow, fine-boned face in the dark. "What are you talking about?"

"I said that when we shalarins reestablished contact with our kindred in the Sea of Corynactis, the vast majority of us forsook Umberlee for the gods of our ancestors, and that much is true. That was the impetus. But this is what I did not tell you: The others did not abandon all the deities of Faerûn. Though they pay homage to the old powers, they also still gather at the altars of Trishina, Persana, and Eldath. It is *only* the Queen of the Depths whom they have scorned."

He shook his head. "I don't understand why you bothered to lie about that. For our purposes, what's the difference?"

"None. But it reflects poorly on me, does it not? Were I as able a priestess as the clerics of Trishina and the other deities, I too could convey the glory of my patron and inspire her worshipers. Or so it seems to me when I grow discouraged. I misrepresented the situation to hide my shame."

"You're too hard on yourself. You talk about the beauty and grandeur manifest in Umberlee's cruelty, but surely you understand that no matter how eloquently you describe it, most people will never understand." The Grandmaster knew, he didn't. "They'll keep praying to her solely out of fear, and look for excuses to turn away."

"Hmm. It may be so."

"Anyway, don't fret over what you told me. It was just one tiny, insignificant deception in a whole life of lies, hearing and telling them both." He sighed.

"Plainly, I do not understand humans. I hoped conversation would brighten your mood, but thus far, I have failed at that as well. Does it help to reflect that you only knew Shandri Clayhill briefly and that she never really knew you at all?"

"No, because that's true every time I take a lover. I'm always playing a part, and I always slip away when my job in that port is finished. But I'll tell you what does cheer and frighten me at the same time: I may be done with it now. Out of the game."

"Spying, you mean?"

He nodded. "I know two ways to go about it. The first is to be as inconspicuous as a mouse—or rat—and sniff around the edges of secrets. It's safer, and because nobody really notices you, you can come back and spy on the same rogues another day.

"So that's the way I've always preferred, but it won't always yield the information you need in time to do anybody any good. When it won't serve, you have to hobnob with the chief scoundrels. You have to establish yourself as a friend, an important accomplice ... or a lover."

"But then," said Tu'ala'keth, "it is more likely your foes will recognize you for what you truly are and remember you thereafter."

"Yes, and that's what's happened to me. I can't spy on pirates and smugglers anymore, not with Teldar and Vurgrom themselves knowing my identity. Of course, Turmish has other enemies. My masters could reassign me somewhere removed from the sea. But I don't know if I want that. Maybe this turn of events is a sign it's time to try something else."

"My friend," said Tu'ala'keth, her cool contralto voice unusually gentle, "you must remember: Your life is not your own to use as you wish. You belong to Umberlee. Someday, if we are victorious, she may release you from her service. But for now, perhaps it is unwise to anticipate, lest it make you discontent."

"Right." He realized he had more to say to her, and even though he knew it would be futile and counterproductive, the sudden urge was too strong to resist. "Tu'ala'keth, our errand ... I warned you before, the Cult of the Dragon will never help you kill wyrms. It's contrary to everything they believe."

"They pay homage to the dark powers. They will bow to the will of Umberlee."

"No, they won't. They may have priests among them, but even so, their truest gods are dragons and their own delusions. You need an impressive achievement to convince the other shalarins to return to your faith, I understand that, but helping me fight the cult will do it. I explained they're a threat to your world as much as mine."

"Even if that is true," said Tu'ala'keth, "no one in Serôs knows of the menace, so no one would notice its elimination. What people do perceive is the dragon flight, slaughtering everything in its path. That is the doom we must avert."

"All right, I'll concede that. But after the Turmian navy takes the cult enclave, you and I can pore over the papers, spellbooks, and what have you. Maybe the answer's in there."

"What if they destroy the records when they see their cause is lost? What if the only man who could help us dies in the assault? What if it takes so long to summon your fleet that Serôs perishes in the meantime? No. We will do it my way."

"Let's at least approach the cultists like spies as opposed to rapping on their front gate like peddlers."

"Impossible. They are members of a secret fellowship ensconced in a remote and hidden stronghold. How could we, or any strangers, pass among them without attracting notice? Oh, we could scout their fortress from a distance, perhaps even sneak in and out in the middle of the night, but that will not further our purpose."

"It might. Somehow."

She smiled, her teeth a gleam of white in the gloom. "I realize you think I am reckless, foolish—"

"Suicidal."

"But you must have faith. Never forget you are Umberlee's knight, now graced with her sacred sword, a mark of greater favor even than the blade she permitted you to take from her altar."

Enough of this, he thought. I tried, but you wouldn't listen. What happens next is your own fault.

They talked a little more then fell into a weary, companionable silence. Sail distended, propelled by the wind Tu'ala'keth had conjured, the boat rose and fell as it cut through the swell. The motion was soothing, and he hoped it might soon rock her to sleep.

Tu'ala'keth marveled as Anton, face cold and intent, cut down the pirates. He'd always been a formidable fighter, but at this moment, with the greatsword in hand, he was magnificent. She'd never been more certain that Umberlee had appointed him to be her comrade.

Then, unexpectedly, her pride in him gave way to a twinge of apprehension then to full-blown dread. Her emotions changed for no reason she could comprehend—until the filthy street transformed into Captain Teldar's sailboat, with the mast rising above her recumbent form like a finger pointing at the stars.

The slumber of her people differed somewhat from that of mermen, or, she assumed, humans, because of the membrane that veiled a shalarin's eyes. Unlike those flaps of opaque flesh called eyelids, it was translucent enough to allow unconscious recognition of prominent shapes, which often then figured in the sleeper's dreams.

Thus, she'd registered Anton's proximity. The spy had risen from the bow, drawn the greatsword, and crept to within reach of her. Now he was poising the blade for a death stroke. The mast and triangular sail were in the way, hampering the sort of cut for which the weapon was designed, but he'd evidently decided a thrust would do.

She tried to spring to her feet, but her wounded leg throbbed and made the action slow and awkward. She realized she had no chance of avoiding the blade.

In desperation, she silently called to the wind. She'd conjured it sometime ago, long enough that it might no longer heed her, but it seemed her only chance.

The wind howled, gusting from a different quadrant than before, and the boat bucked violently. Anton lurched off balance and flailed, fighting to avoid toppling overboard. In such a condition, he couldn't complete the attack, and Tu'ala'keth dived over the side.

As always, she felt a thrill of relief as the sea embraced her. She belonged in the water, and no silverweave or goggles, no matter how artfully crafted, could make it seem otherwise. But she didn't pause to savor the familiar sensations of her natural environment, the caress of the currents and the perpetual background drone. She was too angry.

After all they'd endured together, she'd believed Anton accepted his role in Umberlee's plan. She'd certainly done everything in her power to teach, inspire, and reassure him. Yet evidently her efforts had gone for naught. The human had betrayed her—and, far more important, the goddess—as soon as he discovered an opportunity.

He could have known glory as Umberlee's faithful champion. Now, by his own choosing, he was only a tool for Tu'ala'keth to use, of no more intrinsic worth or significance than Vurgrom or Shandri Clayhill.

He was a tool, moreover, that had evidently outlived its function when they escaped from Dragon Isle. Now the intelligent course of action was to kill him, just to ensure he never found another chance to hinder her schemes.

She sneered to think how easy it would be. She was safe below the waves where he couldn't reach or even see her, and he was afloat on a vast expanse of water that would answer to her whims. Her battles in Immurk's Hold had depleted both her magic and her stamina, but she had enough of both remaining to obliterate a single apostate air-breather.

She gripped the drowned man's hand, reviewed the deadliest spells she had left for the casting, chose one ... and hesitated.

She'd leaped to the conclusion that Anton had nothing more to contribute. Such was her disgust that she was eager to believe it. But perhaps she was being too hasty, for after all, Umberlee had taken care to place this particular instrument in her hands. The signs had been unmistakable.

Tu'ala'keth thought for a moment then smiled anew. She understood what role the traitor had yet to play, and in all likelihood, it would involve a more painful demise than a quick death at sea.

Her objective, then, was to subdue rather than slay. It would require more finesse, but still should prove easy enough.

One of the seahorses came flitting inquisitively around her. She shoo'd it away and swam to the surface. Anton crouched in the boat gazing out over the swells. He'd exchanged the greatsword for the crossbow they'd found packed away with the other supplies, but it didn't matter. He didn't notice the top of her head sticking up into the air.

Well, if he didn't see her now, he'd missed his chance. She whispered an incantation, and fog came steaming up from the water, hiding the boat in billowing masses of vapor.

Or at least, the fog hid it from anyone above the waves. She could make out the tapered shape of the hull perfectly well when she dived back under the surface, and thus had no difficulty aiming her next spell.

The water immediately beneath the boat heaved itself up into a towering crest. The vessel hung at the top for a moment then plummeted down into the trough beside it. She allowed a heartbeat or two for the sea to come smashing over the sides then lifted the boat and dropped it again.

Though she kept it up until the spell expended all its power, Anton never did tumble into the sea. He must have been hanging on tight. Still he was surely soaked and battered, half drowned, and blind in the mist as well.

She reached out with her mind, meshed her thoughts with the simpler, nonverbal ones of the seahorses, and visualized what she wanted them to do. Obedient as ever, they swam astern of the sailboat, ascended to the surface, and splashed about, raising a commotion to hold Anton's attention.

Tu'ala'keth glided to the bow and pulled herself up. Her wounded leg gave her a twinge, but she still managed to clamber quietly aboard.

The fog veiled everything. The mast and sail were blurred and ghostly. Anton appeared as the vaguest shadow at the far end of the boat. But she'd pinpointed his location, and that was enough.

She stooped and picked up her trident, still lying where she'd left it in her haste to escape. She reversed it to use the heavy stone shaft as a cudgel then crept toward the stern. She picked her way around the sail and continued.

She aimed the butt of the trident at his head, and at the last possible moment, he sensed her presence. He jerked around, lifted a fold of his cape to guard himself, and discharged his crossbow, one-handed, in a single flurry of motion.

Her thrust glanced off the enchanted garment as if it were a sturdy turtle-shell shield. Fortunately, haste, or the soaking his weapon had received, spoiled his attack as well. The bolt flew wild.

He raised the crossbow to use it as a bludgeon, but she was quicker. She smashed the blunt end of the trident into his solar plexus, where, at this moment, the cape didn't cover. That froze him in place, and she bashed him over the head. He collapsed. She kept beating him until he stopped moving.

THE **PRIESTS**

CHAPTER 8

Like the rest of the Pirate Isles, Tan was in its essence a huge rock sticking up out of the sea, with some greenery on the lower slopes but little on the heights. But unlike Dragon Isle, it was volcanic, its flanks sculpted by ancient lava flows.

As Vurgrom had warned, Tu'ala'keth could see no sign of habitation beyond a few abandoned-looking cottages and shanties, and the beached, decaying husks of a couple of fishing boats. Yet the cove where the empty village rotted appeared to be the only safe or convenient place to land. Should she put in there?

No, she decided, definitely not. If the cultists were as jealous of their privacy as their reputation indicated, they might well have set a trap. It would be awkward if she had to fight her way clear, perhaps hurting or killing someone, before she even had a chance to explain her purpose.

She rummaged through her sea bag, found the pellet that would enable Anton to breathe underwater, and crouched down beside him. His face bruised, cut, and bloody from the thrashing she'd given him, he lay bound and gagged—and thus unable to conjure—in the bottom of the boat.

She pulled the cloth from his mouth and showed him the spherule. "Eat this," she said.

"No," he said. "Tu'ala'keth, don't do this."

"Refuse if you wish," she said, "but you are going beneath the waves either way. I may still have a use for you, but I no longer *need* you, and it would please me to watch you drown."

Glaring, he opened his mouth, and she gave him the pellet. After he chewed and swallowed, she replaced the gag.

She had no further use for the sailboat, so didn't bother lowering the sail, dropping anchor, or otherwise securing it. Let the sea have it for a toy, to toss about and finally sink or shatter. She bound Anton and her other possessions to the seahorses, who disliked it but suffered it at her behest. Then they swam for shore.

As when approaching Dragon Isle, she and her unwilling companion parted company with the mounts in the shallows and waded onward. They had to clamber over a jumble of rocks, with waves crashing to spray all around them and an undertow dragging them backward, to exit the water. She'd loaded Anton with the baggage. Denied the use of his hands, he couldn't manage by himself. She grabbed his forearm and heaved him up, then waited for him to retch the water from his lungs. With the gag in place, it mostly came out his nose.

"I intend," she said, "to circle around and approach

the village from higher up the slope. You will move quietly, or I will kill you."

He jerked his chin at one of the sea bags she'd tied to him then gave her a sardonic look. She understood: His bonds and burdens were scarcely conducive to stealth.

"You must do the best you can." She jerked the length of rope she'd knotted around his neck. "Onward."

Once they climbed above the settlement, it was easy enough to discern that which had been imperceptible from the water. A cog, entirely seaworthy by the look of it, though the crew had taken down the two masts to facilitate concealment, listed on one side behind a screen of brush. Voices muttered from one of the dilapidated shacks.

Brandishing her skeletal pendant, Tu'ala'keth whispered a prayer to augment her force of personality. Then, gripping her trident in one hand and Anton's leash in the other, she stepped out into the open. "Men of the Cult of the Dragon," she called, "come forth!"

But the startled creatures who emerged from the shanties weren't "men," but rather, to all appearances, hybrids of human and wyrm. They walked on two legs and carried spears but stood half again as tall as a man—or shalarin. Their hides were scaly, and bat-like wings sprouted from their shoulder blades. Tails lashed behind them, and they had the faces of lizards, framed by jagged bony ruffs and manes of coarse black hair.

Before their falling out, Anton had told Tu'ala'keth of such brutes. They were called dragonkin and some-times served the cult. She'd already been sure—well, nearly—that the wyrm worshipers had established themselves on Tan, but it was nonetheless gratifying to behold incontrovertible proof.

But the reptiles gave her scant time to savor the moment. They glowered at her and Anton for a second, and one hissed and hefted his lance for throwing.

"Stop!" she cried, and the magic locked his limbs in position. Before he could recover, or any of the others could decide to attack, she advanced on them, glaring. She wanted them to think her fearless, and to assume she had good reason to be. She wanted them to imagine her powerful enough to strike them all dead in an instant.

"Do you not see my amulet?" she demanded. "I am a waveservant, a priestess of Umberlee, who holds you all in the palm of her hand so long as you dwell in the midst of the sea. Now, who else wants to strike at me?"

None of them did, apparently.

"Good," she said. "Which of you is in charge?"

The largest of the dragonkin snapped its leathery wings and sprang forward. Its hide was ocher with brownish spots and bands, and in addition to its spear, it wore a scimitar—a symbol of rank, perhaps. Its flesh had a dry, musky smell. She sensed it was leery of her but, even so, averse to appearing meek in front of its underlings.

"How you get here?" it growled.

"We swam."

"Why?"

"I must see the master of this place. To deliver a message from the Queen of the Depths."

The dragonkin grunted. "Not supposed to take strangers up mountain. Supposed to kill."

"You cannot thwart the will of the greatest of all goddesses, but you are welcome to try. If I have to walk over your corpses to reach my destination, so be it."

"Uh, no. We go up. No fish-woman come here before. Maybe Eshcaz or wearer of purple will want to see. Or maybe Eshcaz want to eat." The creature waved its clawed hand at the trail snaking up the mountainside.

❖ ❖ ❖ ❖ ❖

The cult enclave was larger than Anton had imagined it could be. He started to realize it during the hike up the mountain. In certain hollows, where no one out at sea could spot them, slaves toiled, tending crops, and dragonkin lashed them with whips and bastinadoes when they faltered. Perhaps some of the thralls had dwelled in the empty village on the beach before the wyrm worshipers staked their claim to Tan. Others must be captives purchased from the pirates of Mirg Isle. All were gaunt and haggard from hunger, ill treatment, and despair.

The actual stronghold was equally grim, and even more impressive. Anton had suspected a honeycomb of caverns inside the cone of the volcano but hadn't dreamed they'd prove so extensive, so well populated, or so a-bustle with activity. Goldsmiths labored over glittering gems and precious metals, crafting intricate medallions too large for a human to wear. Sweating alchemists squinted into fiery kilns or supervised heated liquids as they bubbled, steamed, and streamed through twisting, forking mazes of glass pipe. Black-robed priests of Velsharoon, god of liches and necromancy, chanted before a sarcophagus—or an altar carved in the shape of one—in a chapel reeking of carrion. Wizards declaimed their own spells, invoking spirits Anton could glimpse at the periphery of his vision, but which vanished when he looked at them directly. Seers tossed bones and examined the patterns or stared into churning mirrors. The discharge of so much magic in a single place made the eyes water and the stomach squirm.

A smell somewhat like the body odor of their dragonkin escort—the reek of actual wyrms, Anton assumed—lingered everywhere, and he spotted at least three of the colossal creatures, prowling restlessly through gloomy passageways or napping in unused galleries. As most dragons were powerful spellcasters, he assumed it was pride that kept them from pitching in to help with the arcane chores their worshipers had undertaken on their behalf.

He'd never seen a dragon before, not even from a distance, and the immense creatures were as frightening as he'd heard. But his predicament had already been about as dire as could be. Dragons only worsened it in a notional sort of way. Perhaps that was why he managed to cling to his composure until he and Tu'ala'keth reached what was evidently the end of their journey.

The dragonkin led them to a huge chamber near the apex of the volcano, where gaps in the walls admitted shafts of sunlight from the summer sky outside. Another breach in the rock, this one a chasm in the granite floor, quite possibly plunged all the way down to a reservoir of still-smoldering magma. Yet plenty of space remained for more slaves to pursue the prodigious, backbreaking task of chiseling a huge, complex geometric design and array of glyphs.

All this Anton observed in a moment, before movement at the far end of the cavern, atop a ledge midway up the wall, arrested his attention. He'd already noticed a shape hunkered there in the gloom, but had interpreted it as a protruding swell of rock. For surely it was too immense to be alive.

Alas, no. A gigantic wedge-shaped head, studded with horns on the beak and chin and larger ones sweeping backward from the brow, shot forward at the end of a serpentine neck. The striking motion carried it into a patch of sunlight, revealing the deep, glossy vermilion of the scales. The titan opened its jaws and roared. The echoing bellow shook the cave, brought bits of stone showering from the ceiling, and suffused the air with a stink of smoke and sulfur.

Everyone cowered, slaves and dragonkin overseers alike. Anton recoiled, somehow tangled his leg with one of the sea bags, and fell hard enough to evoke a jab of pain from his cuts and bruises. But he barely noticed the discomfort. He was too afraid.

Reds were the most terrible of all malevolent wyrms, and he hadn't realized any dragon could grow so huge. It looked ancient—and thus, powerful—as the volcano in which it made its lair.

He waited, petrified, for the red to annihilate him and everyone else, for at the moment he took it for death incarnate. Accordingly, it never occurred to him that it would do anything but kill.

But evidently the roar had served to take the edge off its ire for a little while, anyway, for it didn't follow up with a burst of sorcery or a flare of fiery breath. It simply swiveled its head to glare down at the man beside it. Compactly built, clean shaven, and white haired, clad in a dark—likely purple—robe, the cultist looked tiny as a beetle next to the object of his adoration.

"Why are they not finished?" the dragon snarled.

"It's exacting work," the cultist replied in a prim, well-educated baritone voice—the voice of a tutor or clerk. Some trick of the acoustics in the chamber enabled Anton to make out his softer tones even from dozens of yards away. "They have to cut the symbols precisely."

"Sammaster promised that by now, I would already be a dracolich!"

"The First-Speaker said many things then wandered off and left me to perform the actual work. I'm doing the best I can. It's partly a question of manpower. We need more slaves." He hesitated. "Your hoard is greater than the wealth of many a prince. If you could spare just a small fraction, purely to help us bring about the consummation you desire—"

"You dare," the wyrm thundered, the noise so loud it made Anton feel as if someone had slammed him in the head with a club, "ask for *my* treasure? You *dare?*"

The cultist abased himself. "I'm a donkey. I beg forgiveness."

"Know this," said the red. "Should you fail me, you won't die easily, not even if frenzy has me in its claws. I swear it by the thousand fangs of Tiamat."

Anton realized his terror had ebbed to a degree. He'd stopped shaking, and his heart was slowing.

Maybe the example of the snowy-headed cultist, who was able to stand up to the colossal wyrm to a point, anyway, had shamed him. Maybe he'd found some encouragement in the fact that the madmen had yet to create a single dracolich, for surely the impatient red was first in line. Or perhaps it was simply his manhood reasserting itself. But in any case, he resolved that whatever happened next, he'd meet it with a fortitude worthy of even a paladin of Torm.

As he struggled to his feet—no easy task with his hands tied behind him and the sea bags weighing him down—he looked over at Tu'ala'keth then sighed in grudging admiration. To all appearances, she was the one person who hadn't flinched from the red's display of temper. Her features composed behind the goggles, she still stood straight and tall.

Of course, like the cultists, she was crazy in her fashion. In certain circumstances, it was evidently an advantage.

She turned to their escort. "You will present me to the wyrm," she said.

The dragonkin stared at her. "To Eshcaz?" it asked, plainly astonished that anyone would seek to approach the red when he was in such a vile humor.

"If that is his name," she said. "It is why you brought us here, is it not?"

The hulking dragonkin shrugged, a gesture that

tossed its wings and made them rustle. "Come, then."

They all tramped deeper into the chamber. Anton noticed he was starting to hyperventilate, and forced himself to breathe slowly and deeply.

❧ ❧ ❧ ❧ ❧

As they approached Eshcaz, wending their way through the kneeling, toiling slaves, Tu'ala'keth realized the air was growing warmer. The dragon's body radiated heat like a bed of coals, and his blank golden eyes glowed like twin suns. He was so gigantic—

She scowled and ordered herself not to feel the dread and awe that gnawed at her composure. The emissary of Umberlee mustn't quail before any creature, even this one.

Soon enough, Eshcaz twisted his head around to glare at her. The white-haired man studied her with curiosity and calculation in his narrowed eyes. She could see now that his dark robe was in fact wine-red, and reckoned he must be the "wearer of purple," human master of the enclave, but subservient to the "sacred" dragons nonetheless.

"I brought a waveservant," the dragonkin called, "and . . . uh . . . some prisoner."

"Greetings, Lord Eshcaz," said Tu'ala'keth. "I am indeed a waveservant, the keeper of Umberlee's temple in Myth Nantar, in Serôs beneath the sea. I bring gifts and a message from the goddess."

The red made a rumbling sound. It might have been a chuckle. "Give me the gifts first."

"As you wish." She relieved Anton of his burdens then emptied the sea bags to make a glittering, clinking pile of coin and gems, topped with Anton's red cape. The greatsword, however, she set aside. She remained convinced it partook of Fury's essence. Thus, it belonged on Umberlee's altar, or in the hands of a warrior devoted to her service.

Eshcaz stared at the gold and jewels like a starving creature regarding food. His eyes shined brighter, and his forked tongue flickered forth as if to taste the treasure.

"This too is a gift," said Tu'ala'keth. She shoved Anton stumbling forward. "He is one of your enemies, a Turmian spy. He discovered your whereabouts and planned to muster a host to attack you. By the grace of Umberlee, I made him captive before he could report to his superiors. Accordingly, you are safe."

"I'm always 'safe,'" growled Eshcaz. "Do you think any fleet or army could challenge me?"

"Now that she's seen you in all your majesty," said the wearer of purple, "I'm sure she doesn't. Still, if things happened as she claims, she's at least spared us some inconvenience. Now, I suspect, she's going to ask for something in return."

"It is not what I ask," she said. "It is what the Queen of the Depths commands." She began to tell them of the dragon flight menacing Serôs and of their role in its obliteration. The slaves' chisels clanked and scraped in the background.

It didn't take her long to realize that, despite the enchantment still in place to heighten her powers of persuasion, her declaration wasn't having the desired effect. Eshcaz, the wearer of purple, and the dragonkin officer all peered at her as if she were babbling nonsense. Anton gave her a sardonic look that said, I warned you.

Refusing to let it rattle her, she kept her tone cool and matter-of-fact as she pressed on to the end. For after all, she hadn't expected them to accede immediately. It would take some palaver back and forth.

"Waveservant," said the wearer of purple. "I regret the devastation of your home, but you must understand...." He spread his hands. "To put it bluntly, we're on the side of the dragons. All of them."

"Nonsense," she said. "You have no way of reaching out to dragon eels, dragon turtles, and their ilk. They don't figure in your plans and prophecies."

"They may," the human replied. "Even we don't know the full extent of the First-Speaker's designs. He may indeed shepherd some of the undersea wyrms to us before we're through. Indeed, I have good reason to anticipate it. But even if he doesn't, we could never conspire to harm any dragon. We venerate them."

Eshcaz snorted, suffusing the air with a sulfurous haze. "Compared to me, Diero, such fishy things are vermin, as is every lesser wyrm slithering about these caves. Your true purpose is to serve and 'venerate' *me*, and I suggest you keep it ever in your mind."

Diero bowed. "I do, Sacred One."

Tu'ala'keth felt a thrill of hope. "Do I understand, Lord Eshcaz, that you have no objection to helping Serôs?"

"None . . . in principle." The red leered, and she realized he was toying with her. "But I see no advantage in it, either. My servants have more important work to do."

"I have called upon you in the name of the greatest of the powers of darkness, whom we both serve in our fashions."

"You aren't listening. I bow to no one and nothing. Others serve me or perish."

"You are proud," she said, "and given your strength, it is proper that you should be. But surely your long life has made you wise as well. Wise enough to understand that even the mightiest of dragons ought not to offend the cruelest, most implacable goddess of Fury."

"I see no goddess hereabouts."

"Then open your eyes. She stands here with me."

"I don't care if she does. She has no dominion over

me. I'm a creature of air, stone, and most of all, flame. Let her appear, and I'll boil her to steam."

"As long as you live on an island, you sit in her hand. She need only close it to crush you."

"I'm bored with this," said Eshcaz. "Someone, take that trident away from her and tie her up. I've never eaten a shalarin. I believe I'll have her for supper."

Tu'ala'keth could scarcely comprehend that matters had gone so disastrously wrong. But when her escort lifted its spear to club her with the shaft, the threat jarred her into action.

"Stop!" she cried. The reptile froze in place long enough for her to drive the trident into its guts. She yanked the weapon free. The dragonkin toppled.

She pivoted, seeking the next threat, and didn't have to look far. Half a dozen other dragonkin were advancing on her, whips and batons at the ready. Braided leather struck at her. She jumped to the side, and cracking, the lash missed.

Anton ran toward the greatsword where it lay on the floor. Perhaps he had some desperate hope of using the preternaturally keen edge to cut his bonds. A dragonkin diverted its attention from Tu'ala'keth for the moment necessary to bash him over the head. Anton collapsed and lay motionless, blood flowing from his scalp.

Tu'ala'keth cast about, seeking a way out of the circle of dragonkin closing in on her, and beyond that, a way of escaping the entire situation. Thus far, she could see neither.

She brandished her trident above her head and bellowed words of power in as theatrical a manner as possible. Maybe the aura of grandeur in which she'd previously cloaked herself made the display intimidating, for the reptiles balked for a moment, giving her precious time to conjure.

Then, however, they scuttled forward once more.

Whips surged through the air, too many for her to keep to the precise, demanding measures of the spell and dodge them all as well. Lashes slammed her, staggered her, split her skin.

Ignore the pain. Articulate the prayer.

Magic rustled through the cave with a sound like a breaking wave, and darkness followed in its wake. Even she, with her sensitive deepwater eyes, couldn't see through the heightened gloom, nor, she was certain, could the dragonkin.

The difference was that, knowing the shadow was coming, she'd fixed the precise location of one of her foes in her mind. She immediately charged, and when instinct told her she was close enough, thrust with the trident. The attack crunched through the dragonkin's scaly hide and into its broad body. It grunted and fell, dragging the weapon along as it went down.

The slap of rushing footsteps and swish of a dragging tail sounded to her left. She freed the trident, pivoted, ducked, and thrust. Though she was still fighting blind, her luck held. The three-pointed lance punched into another target. The reptile floundered backward, dragging itself clear of the tines, and kept on reeling away.

By now, she could hear the wearer of purple declaiming the tongue-twisting rhymes of a counterspell. Violet phosphorescence seethed through the air, scouring the darkness away.

That at least enabled her to see the two dragonkin she'd just speared. As she'd hoped, both were hurt too badly to continue fighting, and by neutralizing them, she'd cut a gap in the noose that had been tightening around her. Beyond lay one of the tunnels, admitting shafts of sunlight.

In all probability, running out onto the mountainside would only delay the inevitable. Still she bolted in that direction.

At that point, Eshcaz reared and cocked his head back. His throat swelled, and Tu'ala'keth realized that even a few more seconds were too great a boon for a blundering fool like her to ask. The red was going to incinerate her here and now.

But the wearer of purple screamed, "No! Please! You'll burn the slaves, too, and we need them!"

Eshcaz spat a plume of dazzling flame. But it was directed at the ceiling, not the floor. Perhaps he was venting his wrath at being balked.

Tu'ala'keth sprinted onward, around cowering thralls, until another dragonkin, one she hadn't noticed hitherto, jumped in front of her. Ruddy with yellow markings and a scarred, truncated tail, this one was armed like a warrior, with shield and sword. It cut at her head, she tried to block with the trident, and it deceived the parry to slash at her flank. The stroke hurt her ribs and knocked her lurching off balance. But it didn't cleave her flesh; her silverweave had spared her any lasting harm. She thrust low; the trident crunched into the reptile's knee; and it went down. It tried to heave itself around into position to threaten her anew, and she finished it off with a stab to the torso.

At that moment, something snapped, a sound like the crack of the whips, or the noise the sails on *Shark's Bliss* made when a sudden gust of wind swelled them, but vaster. The cave darkened as something cut off much of the light spilling in through the gaps in the upper walls. Slaves screamed and scrambled. Tu'ala'keth realized Eshcaz had spread his prodigious wings and was jumping off the ledge, intending to kill her with fang and claw instead of fire.

Heart hammering, she sprinted. As the dragon slammed down behind her, jolting the floor, she reached the opening, saw it was only a few more strides to the other end, and pounded onward.

She felt heat and sensed immensity at her back. She plunged out of the passage and wrenched herself to the side. Flame boomed out of the tunnel, blistering her skin even though it didn't actually touch her.

Now what? she wondered wildly. She was no safer than before. In another instant, the wyrm would lunge from the hole—

But no. If it was going to do that, she'd already hear it coming. She took another look at the opening and registered what, in the course of her frenzied flight, she'd failed to realize before. This particular passage was too narrow for a creature as huge as Eshcaz to negotiate.

But of course he had other ways to go in and out. She'd only increased her lead by a matter of moments. That was how long she had to find a way to save herself.

She cast about and saw a chance.

She clambered along the steep slope. She thought she'd grown used to this strange world where people had to worry about slipping and falling but suddenly she felt slow and clumsy again. The bloody trident was merely an encumbrance now, and she dropped it to slide and bounce down the escarpment.

She resisted the temptation to glance about. It would only slow her down, and anyway, she was sure she'd still know when her pursuer burst out into the open.

At last she reached her goal, a spot beneath which the face of the island became a sheer vertical cliff. The green sea crashed to white foam against the jutting rocks far below.

Someone had once told her air-breathers had an instinctive fear of falling. She doubted sea-dwellers did, but nonetheless, the prospect daunted her. Could anything plummet such a distance without dashing itself to pulp?

Maybe it was possible, with the aid of magic, and

certainly she had no option but to try. She gripped the drowned man's hand and chanted, and Eshcaz exploded from a breach farther up the mountain. He unfurled his crimson wings with their purple edges, obscuring much of the sky, and the bright sunlight shining through the membrane made them glow like stained glass.

Tu'ala'keth rattled off the final syllables and hurled herself over the edge, endeavoring, as best she could in her unpracticed way, to imitate the divers she'd observed among the pirates. She tried to fall head down, with her body straight, so she'd enter the water like a knife stabbing into flesh ... if she didn't crash down on one of the rocks.

She silently spoke to the wind she'd summoned, bidding it to blast up at her from below. Afterward, she couldn't feel any difference, but perhaps it was slowing her down a little.

Gloom engulfed her. She glanced upward. Wings folded, foreclaws poised to catch and impale, Eshcaz was plunging toward her and looming larger by the instant. Because of the braking power of the wind she'd summoned or through some trick accomplished flyers mastered, he was dropping faster than his prey.

Tu'ala'keth reversed her instructions to the wind. Her only hope now was that it could blow her down even faster than she would naturally fall.

The heaving surface of the sea was dull and gray with the dragon's shadow. She smashed into it with stunning force, missing one of the fanglike rocks by less than the length of her arm, and plunged deeper. The stone swelled wider toward the base, and she had to shake off the shock of impact to stick out her hands and push off, lest she batter and scrape herself against it.

Above her, Eshcaz leveled out of his dive and hurtled along just above the waves. Had he tried to follow her into the water, he would have slammed his huge body into one or another of the rocks, but perhaps he would have turned aside regardless. As he'd said himself, he was a creature of earth and sky, not the sea.

That didn't mean he wasn't still dangerous. She stroked and kicked, swimming deeper, looking for a refuge.

Overhead, a sudden brightness bloomed. Water seethed and bubbled as the wyrm's breath boiled it. But Tu'ala'keth had already descended far enough that the worst of the heat failed to reach her.

She found a hollow space in the roots of the island and hastened inside. A blaze of jagged shadow stabbed down through the water. But it was yards away, and she realized Eshcaz had aimed the magic by guesswork. He'd lost track of her, which meant that, much to her own amazement, she was quite possibly going to survive.

THE **P**RIESTS

CHAPTER 9

What," Diero Agosto asked, "will the shalarin do now?"

"I don't know," the spy answered through gritted teeth, his bruised, scabby, bloodstained face glistening with sweat. He lay spread-eagled on the long, splintery table that was the rack, wrists and ankles wrapped in sturdy leather cuffs.

"Will she return here?"

"I doubt it. You made it clear you won't help her. But I don't know."

From the corner of his eye, Diero saw the dragonkin take hold of the windlass. From his stance, it was plain he meant to give it a vigorous turn or two.

The wearer of purple rounded on the hulking reptile. Annoyance made his voice shrill: "No! I didn't tell you to do that."

The creature grunted. "Want truth, right?"

Diero sighed. "He's telling the truth. He did from the start."

As far as the wizard was concerned, his fellow Turmian had behaved with admirable good sense. He had nothing to reveal that would cause additional problems for his superiors or his people, so why not speak and spare himself unnecessary pain? It was simply his misfortune that candor couldn't forestall all of it. Diero had still needed to torture him for a while, just to make sure his story didn't change as the agony tore away at him.

The dragonkin shook its head. "Lying, I think."

It verged on being comical, in an irritating sort of way. "You just want to cripple him, so he's of no use except as food."

"Well ... hungry! Can't eat beans, peas, and other muck humans grow. Can't hardly fish, or somebody sailing by sees us. Don't hardly get any of slaves, when they die—dragons always take."

Diero sighed in grudging sympathy. "I know it's difficult, being on short rations. I assure you, I have my own problems and frustrations." Such as the constant need to pander to Eshcaz's vanity, demeaning work for one of the ablest magicians for hundreds of miles around. "But it will all be worth it when we rule Faerûn as the dracoliches' deputies."

"Hope so," the dragonkin grumbled.

"Well, to reach that joyful tomorrow, we must observe some discipline today. Look at the arms and shoulders on this one. He can do a lot of carving before the work breaks him down." Diero studied the reptile's lizardlike features. It was tricky to interpret dragonkin expressions, but he was finally picking up the knack. "So I can count on you to give him to the overseers with his limbs still in their sockets?"

The torturer bared its fangs, but in such a way as to convey disappointment, not defiance. "Yes."

Tu'ala'keth lingered in the niche in the bedrock long after Eshcaz wearied of fishing for her and flew away, and she was still there when night darkened the waters. For she felt she had nowhere else to go.

Her burns, whip cuts, and bruised ribs smarted. She could have eased the discomfort with a prayer, but chose to endure it instead. It seemed a fitting if insufficient rebuke for her misplaced self-assurance and general ineptitude.

The worst of it was that Anton had readily predicted the fiasco, and she'd ignored him. She'd only been able to see one path to her goal, and assumed her constricted vision equated to revelation.

But perhaps Umberlee had never revealed anything. Maybe it was merely Tu'ala'keth's deluded self-importance that made her believe the goddess had charged her with a vital task or provided aid and guidance along the way.

Perhaps Anton was right, and the powers didn't care about anything mortals attempted during their brief little lives.

Suddenly, after a lifetime of certitude, Tu'ala'keth was sure of only one thing: She'd failed and survived to rue it. It would be better, perhaps, if Eshcaz had burned her to ash, or torn her apart.

But he hadn't, and in time, when the emptiness in her belly made her feel weak and ill, the same brute instinct for survival that had made her flee the dragon drove her forth from her hiding place. She glided with the current until she spied a perch large enough to satisfy her hunger then veered in its direction.

Recognizing the threat, the fish fled, but she put on

a burst of speed and closed with it anyway. If she'd still had her trident, she would have speared it, but as it was, she had to kill it as one wild thing killed another. She seized it with her hands, sank her teeth into its scaly back, and biting and rending, tore the thrashing creature apart.

Fine bones crunched between her teeth. Blood billowed, tingeing and perfuming the water. Despite her bleak mood, the perch's raw flesh was sweet, and she knew a sudden exultation at the success of the hunt, at extinguishing another's life to perpetuate her own vitality.

With that unexpected ecstasy came a renewed comprehension of what every creature ought to understand, but which even priestesses sometimes failed to appreciate. This act of predation was sacred. It *was* Umberlee.

In grasping anew the essential nature of the goddess, Tu'ala'keth discerned that even if her schemes had been flawed, her intentions had not. If the Queen of the Depths manifested herself whenever one creature devoured another, then plainly, the worship of sentient beings wasn't too small a matter to engage her interest. She craved it, demanded it, and punished those who denied it, just as her creed declared.

Accordingly, it actually had been Tu'ala'keth's duty to reinvigorate such worship. She needn't doubt when the pattern implicit in all that had happened—the coming of the dragon flight, her discovery of Anton, the convenient vulnerabilities of needy Shandri Clayhill and vain, lecherous Vurgrom—proved it.

The problem was that she'd ultimately lost her way. She'd misunderstood what was necessary. But that didn't mean she'd failed, not yet, not while she could still fight, kill, and embrace her goddess in the holy act of shedding blood. She simply had to see more clearly.

Though they hadn't in fact confirmed it, she remained convinced the cultists had the answer she needed. The flow of events had borne her to Tan for a reason. But the wyrm worshipers refused to help her. How, then, was she to proceed?

It was plain enough: She'd have to wrest their secrets from them. Anton had even told her so, and she now realized he'd still been speaking as Umberlee's champion, even if he didn't know it himself.

But obviously, she couldn't do it alone and had no idea where to turn for assistance. Serôs had lost one army to the dragon flight and was frantically piecing together another. In such dire circumstances, it was inconceivable that the Nantarn Council would give her any troops for what they'd view as a purely speculative venture in the strange, irrelevant world above the waves. Nor would Anton's folk be any quicker to heed a stranger, a member of an unfamiliar race and the cleric of a deity they dreaded rather than loved.

Still, she abruptly realized, that left one possibility. Flicking bits of perch from her fingers—tiny fish came rushing and swarming to vie for the scraps—she silently summoned her seahorses.

Anton's hands were raw and cramped, his knees sore, his shoulders on fire. He was accustomed to swinging a sword and sailing a ship. He'd performed many sorts of manual labor as he played one role or another. But none of it had prepared him for the grueling work of chiseling unholy symbols in a granite floor.

Part of the problem was the residual ache in his joints. At the wearer of purple's insistence, the torturer had stopped short of mangling him for good and all, but that didn't mean he'd escaped unscathed. Maybe, in time, he'd find the toil easier to bear.

Or maybe he'd gradually wear out, starve, and die, as the other slaves did. All things considered, he'd rather not remain a prisoner long enough to find out.

Accordingly, weary and wretched as he felt, it was time to start acting like a spy again. He lifted his head to survey his fellow thralls.

Checkmate's edge, what a dismal lot they were, slumped in the malodorous little cave that served as their pen. It wasn't their emaciation or festering whip marks that dismayed him, those were unavoidable. It was the fact that they weren't even whispering to one another, just sitting or sprawling in silence. Misery and hopelessness had hollowed them out inside.

Still they were the only allies he was likely to find. He pondered whom to approach first, and how, and the wrought-iron grate rasped open. Dragonkin emptied wooden pails of vegetables and hardtack onto the floor.

As the grille clanked shut again and the key twisted in the lock, the slaves lunged for their daily meal. Though desperate to grab as much they could, most stopped short of actually laying hands on their fellows. But a tall man, with a broken nose and a livid ridge of scar on his jaw that even shaggy whiskers couldn't hide, seized two of the frailest-looking captives by the shoulders and flung them backward, in effect usurping their shares for himself. Maybe it was such merciless theft that had kept him looking vital and strong, and his movements, quick and sure.

At any rate, sore and spent as he was, Anton felt little enthusiasm for the prospect of accosting the resident bully. But it was an opportunity to claim a leadership role for himself. So, joints aching, he clambered to his feet. "Leave those fellows alone. Everybody eats."

The tall man sneered. "You're new, so I'll explain how things work in here. My name is Jamark, and I decide what happens and what doesn't. So you sit back down, shut up, and you can go without your supper tonight to teach you respect."

"If you want me to respect you," Anton said, "you'll have to beat it into me."

Jamark shrugged. "We can do it that way, too." He raised his fists and shuffled forward.

When Anton tried to close his own hands, they throbbed. He wasn't sure he could make a good, tight fist, or grip and hold an adversary with his accustomed strength. But he'd just have to cope.

Suddenly Jamark abandoned his mincing boxer's advance for a bellow and a headlong charge. Caught by surprise, Anton tried to twist out of the way but didn't make it. His adversary slammed him back into the granite wall, jolting pain through his ill-treated body. Some of the other slaves exclaimed at the impact. Well, at least he'd succeeded in getting them to make some noise.

Jamark reached for this throat. Anton jammed his arms up between those of the other man, breaking the chokehold, then hammered his opponent's face with the bottoms of his fists. The blows stabbed pain through his hands.

But they didn't balk Jamark, who hooked a punch into his temple. Anton faltered for a split second, time enough for the other man to bull him back into the wall. It bounced his skull against the stone, splashing sparks across his vision, and drove the wind from his lungs. Jamark caught him, threw him to the floor, and heaved a leg high to stamp on him.

Anton couldn't avoid the attack. Caught between his foe and the wall, he had nowhere to go. His only hope was to stop it. He grabbed just in time to catch the descending foot and yank and twist it viciously. The ruffian lost his balance and fell.

Anton threw himself on top of Jamark and pounded

elbow strikes into his kidneys and any other vulnerable spot he could reach. The ruffian reared up and cocked his arm back for a particularly brutal punch. But it was a mistake to wind up that way; it afforded Anton a good opening to smash him in the teeth. Jamark's head snapped backward, and blood flowing from his gashed lips, he collapsed. Maybe he was still conscious—his eyes were open—but that final blow had knocked the fight out of him.

Anton turned to the other slaves. "After all that," he panted, "I hope you bastards saved some food for me."

They had, and once he caught his breath, he settled down to eat it. Alas, it only took a few bites. As he finished, Jamark sat up and gave him a glower.

"You were lucky," the bully said, "and you're stupid, too. Those men I pulled back are dying anyway. That little bit of food won't do them any good. It could make all the difference to the rest of us."

Anton smiled. "Somehow, I had the impression you didn't mean to share it with anyone else."

Jamark wiped his bloody lips then spat. "So what if I didn't? I was loyal to my shipmates in my time, but in here, it's every man for himself. It's your only hope of stretching your life out as long as possible. Though it's up to you whether you'd rather do that or die fast and end the pain."

"I'd rather escape, return with the Turmian fleet, and kill Eshcaz, the wearer of purple, and all their flunkies. Maybe we can if we all hang together."

Jamark smiled sadly. "I thought that, too, when I first got here. But it's hopeless."

"Even for a sorcerer?"

The other man eyed him dubiously. "I haven't met many mages who could brawl like you."

"Still, I know a few tricks, and the cultists aren't aware of it." Tu'ala'keth hadn't mentioned it, and since Diero hadn't known to ask about it, Anton had experienced no difficulty withholding the secret, even when the torment was at its most excruciating.

"Then ... you can whisk us all away from here?"

It pained Anton to dowse the other man's sudden flicker of hope. "No. I'm nowhere near that powerful. But I can at least get out of this cage. I assume a guard comes by from time to time?"

"Yes."

"Does he—or it—take a head count?"

"Not as I've noticed." Jamark grinned. "Dragonkin aren't all that clever. I doubt it could count unless it did it out loud, pointing with its finger."

"That's all right, then." Anton rose, and everyone pivoted to look at him. He explained that he planned to find some food and that they needed to stay put. One could leave, but if they all disappeared, it would be noticed. He pressed a finger to his lips then turned his attention to the iron grille sealing the chamber.

He whispered the charm of opening, and the lock clacked as it disengaged. The difficult part was easing the door open. In dire need of oil, the hinges squealed as they had before, and he winced at the noise. But no one came rushing to investigate.

He pushed the grate almost back to its starting position, but left it unlatched. With luck, no casual observer would notice the difference. Then he skulked down the passage.

To his relief, creeping through the benighted caverns wasn't quite as difficult as he'd feared. The reptiles might be able to see in the dark, but the humans couldn't and had mounted flickering oil lamps at intervals along the walls. A good many creatures and people were still up and moving about—probably necromancers slept by day, like vampires—but the acoustics were such that he could hear them coming, and the complex was so maze-like that it was usually possible to duck into a niche or side gallery until they passed.

Finally he found what he was seeking, a nook the cultists had converted into a makeshift larder. With a frown of regret, he passed by the freshest and most appealing food—a smoked ham, cherries—in favor of dried and preserved stuff the madmen had presumably laid in to eat when everything else ran out ... or to grudgingly feed to their captives. One box yielded ship's biscuits, hard as oak and crawling with mites. Another contained leathery venison jerky and a burlap sack full of dried apples.

He gobbled some of each then stuffed more inside his shirt. As he was finishing up, he heard noise in the passage outside: trudging footsteps and the swish of a dragging tail.

Most of the crates and barrels were flush with the wall, and he had no time to shift them. He hastily crouched down behind one of the few boxes someone had left in the center of the chamber.

The cursed thing just wasn't big enough. If the dragonkin glanced in his direction, it was almost inevitably going to spot him. The Red Knight knew, he was in no shape for another fight, but he whispered an incantation and sprouted a sharp, bony ridge from the bottom of his hand.

The footsteps halted, and he heard the rasp of the dragonkin's respiration. It was standing in the doorway, peering in, without a doubt.

Could he kill such a formidable creature with a single strike, before it raised an alarm? To say the least, it seemed unlikely. Still he gathered himself to jump up and charge, and the dragonkin grunted and slouched on its way. It hadn't noticed him.

Miraculous. It occurred to him that Tu'ala'keth would attribute the luck to Umberlee. Or she would have, before he tried to murder her.

He gave the dragonkin time to move off then slipped back to the cell, closed the door behind him, and divvied up the pilfered food. The other captives wolfed it down as voraciously as before.

"This was dangerous," said Jamark through a mouthful of jerky. "If the cultists find out, they'll punish us."

"I notice the risk didn't stop you from grabbing a portion. I didn't take too much, and only the stuff they're least likely to miss. If they do, they may well assume one of their own has been pilfering since I gather even they're a little hungry."

"Well ... yes. They haven't been to Mirg Isle to reprovision in a while. Too busy preparing for their hellish rituals."

"Right, and on top of that, we're locked up, so how could we possibly steal? But I will. Enough food to keep us strong, and weapons, too. That may be trickier. But I'll wager I can at least find a knife or two no one will worry about and a place to hide them until we're ready."

"For what?"

"Here's one possibility. The cultists have a cog. You and I know how to sail her."

"So we steal her and put out to sea. Then Eshcaz and the other wyrms fly after us and kill us."

Anton smiled. "All right, maybe it isn't a perfect scheme. But we'll keep thinking ... and watch for an opportunity."

THE PRIESTS

CHAPTER 10

The realm called the Xedran Reefs was not, in fact, all coral reef. Most of it was open seabed lying under shallow, sunlit water aglitter with a multitude of flitting multicolored fish.

Tu'ala'keth had plotted a course through the region so as to skirt all the reefs but the one that was her destination then proceeded warily. It was the only way to avoid sentries and patrols who would otherwise attack her on sight. But now that her goal was within reach, she guided her seahorse, and its riderless counterpart swimming along behind, through clear, open water some distance above the sea floor. She wanted Yzil's guards to spot her, and with luck, recognize her.

Where were they? It had been years since she'd visited Exzethlix, but it was hard to believe the xenophobic inhabitants had grown so lax. As the minutes passed without incident, a ghastly thought occurred to her: The dragon flight had passed this way and destroyed the city, denying her the aid she so desperately needed.

But finally, as the suspicion was taking hold of her in earnest, a patrol peered out from the cover of a floating, tangled mass of dark green sargasso weed. She halted the seahorses and waved her hand.

Locathahs, thrall warriors with piscine faces and jutting ridges of fin on their arms and legs, aimed their crossbows at her. Curse it! This, too, came as a surprise. She'd been prepared for an initially hostile response, but not a murderous one. Ixitxachitls were inveterate slave takers, and would normally try to capture a lone and unarmed traveler alive.

She urged her mount into motion, it dodged, and the first quarrels hurtled harmlessly past. She called out to the leader of the patrol and didn't need the magic of her ring to translate. She'd mastered the language of the 'chitls on previous visits.

"I am Tu'ala'keth, a waveservant known to your devitan. He has given me leave to come and go as I please."

The locathahs reached into their arrow sacks for fresh bolts. A voice said, "Reload, but don't shoot unless I order it." With that, their officer emerged from the hanging mass of weed.

At first glance, a human might have mistaken the ixitxachitl for a common ray, a flat, soft, rippling thing, dark on top and pale on the underside, with a long, thin tail snaking out behind. But a predatory intelligence lurked in its blood-colored eyes, and fangs like needles ringed its maw.

"I remember you," it said.

"Good. What ails this place? Why are there no sentries posted farther out?" For that matter, how was it this particular patrol only had a single 'chitl leading it, and that one of low rank? She could tell it hadn't yet achieved the vampiric condition to which they all aspired by the condition of its teeth. It lacked the pair of elongated upper fangs.

"I won't harm you," it said. "I don't think the devitan would wish it. But you must go away."

"Impossible," she said. "Umberlee sent me here."

"Whatever you're talking about," the demon ray said, "now is not the time."

"I ask again: What is amiss? I am willing to help you mend it so long as you promise to aid me in return."

The 'chitl hesitated. "It's not my place to tell outsiders what goes on Exzethlix."

"Then take me to Yzil, and let him do it."

"I—"

"Unless the devitan has rescinded the order granting me safe passage, it still stands. You can obey it as is your duty, bring help to your city, and earn your ascension to vampirism in the process. Or you can discover how the Queen of the Depths chastises those who seek to hinder her servants. In the unlikely event you survive, Yzil will no doubt have further punishments to inflict on what is left of you."

With a flutter of its body and a lash of its tail, the demon ray turned toward its minions. "You'll stay here and obey your orders until I return." It wheeled back toward Tu'ala'keth. "Follow me."

Exzethlix came into view a few minutes later. To Tu'ala'keth's eyes, it rather resembled the decaying corpse of a coral reef, largely denuded of the life that generally flourished about such sprawling growths and carved into grotesque and uncouth shapes. But it looked the same as it always had. Whatever misfortune had overtaken it, the maze of chambers and tunnels remained intact.

As she'd anticipated, her guide led her toward the

primary temple, likewise the seat of government, for in the Xedran Reefs, the clerics of Ilxendren—in her view, a mere demon, albeit a powerful one, posing as a deity—were preeminent in everything. Gliding 'chitls and toiling thralls watched as she passed. Misliking the place, her seahorse tossed its head, and she gentled it with the touch of her hand and mind.

Constrained by magic, the mermaid lay motionless atop Ilxendren's green marble altar. Despite her paralysis, she managed to roll her eyes wildly and shoot Yzil a look of mute appeal.

Did she actually imagine her master might spare her? Perhaps so, for she'd proved to be a particularly useful slave. But unfortunately for her, that was the point of the ceremony, to offer up someone of actual value.

The devitan wrapped the tip of his tail around the greenish claw-coral knife, recited the concluding prayer, and opened the thrall from throat to waist. Even in her agony, the spell held her immobile. Blood billowed up from the gash.

Blood was blood—the warmth, coppery scent, and taste, always delectable—and even at such a solemn moment, Yzil felt a greedy urge to bury his lips in the wound and drink his fill rather than let it diffuse into the water. He quashed the impulse and stared intently, looking for images or, failing those, patterns in the swirling stain.

There! It ... but no. The ixitxachitl realized that in his desperation, he'd perceived the suggestion of a runic form where, in fact, it simply didn't exist. This augury was as useless as all the others, and he twisted away from it in frustration.

But that only brought him face to face with Shex,

looking on with an expression of concern that, Yzil very much suspected, masked an underlying satisfaction.

"I fear," said Shex, "that I saw nothing."

For a moment, Yzil was tempted to say he had. But it would be blasphemy to claim Ilxendren had communicated with him when it was untrue, and besides, the lie probably wouldn't hold up.

"Nor I," he admitted.

"A pity," said Shex. He pursed his lips, sucking at his fangs in a display of deep thought that made Yzil want to smite him with one of his most virulent spells. "Devitan, I hesitate to propose this again—"

"Then don't."

"—but since all your efforts have proved unavailing, and the life of the city itself is at stake, I suggest you journey to Xedras to consult with His Holiness. Surely he can provide an answer."

No doubt, Yzil thought bitterly. The problem was that the Vitanar had long suspected him—correctly—of embracing the Qyxasian heresy, of believing that commerce and dialogue with lesser races would facilitate their ultimate subjugation. If he entered the capital as an abject failure, unable to defend his own domain, His Holiness would surely take it as an opportunity to strip him of his rank, his liberty, and quite possibly his life.

But how much longer could he refuse? In theory, Shex was a mere vitan, chief priest of a single temple, unable to compel a devitan, the primate of an entire city, to do anything. But in actuality, he'd come as the Vitanar's representative, and a time was rapidly approaching when Yzil would be able to deny him no longer, lest continued resistance make matters even worse—assuming such a thing was possible.

"I'm reluctant," Yzil said, "to trouble His Holiness when I'm certain that, with more study and prayer, Exzethlix can solve its own problems."

"He wouldn't consider it 'trouble,'" Shex replied. "Like the god who speaks with his voice, he cares for the strength and vitality of all our race."

"Still," said a new voice, managing the ixitxachitl tongue with facility despite the handicap of a tongue and voice box never intended for the purpose, "it would be unnecessary. I will help you, for a price."

Baring their fangs, tails lashing, all the vampire rays in the shadowy coral hall with its dozens of irregular arched doorways turned toward the shalarin. Yzil understood their startled outrage. No one but ixitxachitls and sacrifices ever entered this holy place. Tu'ala'keth had not only intruded, but presumed to speak unbidden. Her escort, a common warrior, looked as if he couldn't decide whether to attack her or grovel in apology for her insolence.

Yzil felt a pang of anger himself, though it was more out of concern for his own well-being that the sanctity of the shrine. Years ago, Tu'ala'keth had approached him with a bargain. Like all spellcasters, the two of them were eager to acquire esoteric lore and the power that came with it, and it was certain that, pursuing their separate paths, each had discovered secrets unknown to the other. Such being the case, they'd share as much as they could, without, of course, forsaking or betraying their respective faiths.

It had actually worked out quite well. The tricks Tu'ala'keth had taught Yzil helped him ascend and cling to his high rank while scores of ambitious wretches such as Shex strove to usurp it. In the end, Yzil might even have grown a bit "fond" of the shalarin, if he understood what that alien concept truly meant.

Still after an absence of a decade, why did Tu'ala'keth have to turn up now? If one cared to take it that way—and Shex undoubtedly would—her intrusion here was further evidence that Yzil had lost control. Worse, his collaboration with her could itself be construed as proof that he'd embraced Qyxas's forbidden views.

Yet she'd spoken of providing help, and really, now that she'd already interrupted the proceedings, could she make things much worse? Perhaps it would be sensible to hear her out.

The other ixitxachitls had all pointed themselves in her direction. In another moment, they'd swarm on her, and she hadn't made a move to protect herself. She simply gave Yzil a cool, level stare.

He'd often thought her arrogant self-assurance would someday be the death of her. It still might, but not just yet. "Stop," he said. "For the moment, the shalarin is under my protection."

She inclined her head as if acknowledging a simple courtesy.

"Who is this thrall?" Shex demanded.

She answered before Yzil could. "Tu'ala'keth, waveservant and keeper of Umberlee's shrine in Myth Nantar."

"And envoy for the Nantarn Council," Yzil added, knowing she was quick-witted enough to go along with the lie. Despite their general disdain for inferior races, as a practical matter, ixitxachitls sometimes had to negotiate with them. He reckoned it was safer to present Tu'ala'keth as an emissary than to admit the two of them had traded conjuring techniques and lists of the true names of netherspirits and elementals.

Still the explanation elicited a dubious stare from Shex. "Does His Holiness know you're treating with the allied peoples?"

"About matters of consequence only to my own city," Yzil said. "That lies within in my authority, as you presumably know. Waveservant, you . . . claim you can help us?"

"I do," said Tu'ala'keth. "But I must know the details of your plight."

"No!" snarled Shex. "Say nothing."

"You're not in charge here," Yzil said. "I am. Don't presume to give me another order, or I'll kill you before you finish speaking."

Shex folded himself small in apology but for only a moment. It was a token gesture, not a show of true respect. "Please, forgive me, devitan. I expressed myself poorly. But surely you see you can't confide weakness to a shalarin. She'll tell our enemies. We already need to kill her just for overhearing the little bit she has."

Tu'ala'keth smiled. "If you mean to kill me, it cannot hurt to tell me everything."

That startled a chuckle out of Yzil, who couldn't recall the last time that anything had amused him even slightly. "She has you there, Shex." He faced Tu'ala'keth. "Do you understand how ixitxachitls reproduce?"

It took her a moment to respond. Plainly, whatever she'd expected him to say, it wasn't that, which meant her claim that she could end the crisis derived from nothing more than her confidence in her own abilities and the power of her goddess.

"I do not know a great deal about it," she said at length, "but I have always assumed the females lay eggs."

"You're right," Yzil said, "and something is coming in the night and smashing them."

"'Something?'"

"No one's seen it, even though I've pulled nearly all my troops back into the city to stand watch. I've also performed divinations, but some opposing power prevents them from revealing anything helpful."

Or conceivably, the difficulty could be that he'd fallen from favor with Ilxendren, and accordingly, the god declined to communicate with him. He didn't believe it himself, but knew his minions had begun to wonder, and that Shex would unquestionably suggest it to the Vitanar as soon as he had the opportunity.

"I assume," said Tu'ala'keth, "you gathered all the eggs in one repository, then sealed and shielded it with magic."

"Yes, but it didn't keep the . . . entity out."

"How many eggs does it destroy?"

"A dozen or so each night. One such loss is of little consequence, but over time, the sum will become catastrophic."

"Does it eat the embryos?"

"No. It simply kills them."

"Hmm." The shalarin frowned, pondering.

After a few seconds, Yzil could contain himself no longer. "Can you help us?"

"I already told you, yes."

"Then you understand what's attacking us, and how to deal with it?"

"Not yet. But Umberlee does, and she will aid me."

"This is preposterous!" said Shex. "The shalarin is a slave creature and the priestess of a lesser power. It's blasphemy for her to claim she can do what priests of the one true god cannot, and sin for us to hear it without striking her down."

"Then strike me down," said Tu'ala'keth, "if you can."

"Done." Shex declaimed the opening phrases of a prayer intended to riddle her body with wounds, as if she'd been stabbed by a dozen spears at once.

But Tu'ala'keth simply gripped the skeletal hand dangling around her neck and cast forth a flare of raw spiritual power. Her goddess had a measure of dominion over all sea creatures, even ixitxachitls, and because she had no need to recite an incantation, she was able to strike first.

Still Yzil reckoned she'd made an error. Shex was a cleric, too, strong of will and spirit. This, moreover, was a shrine of Ilxendren, where the influence of the god of vampirism, vengeance, and cruelty was exalted, and other forces, muted.

Yet even so, power, the strength of her faith made manifest, hammered and burned from her pendant. Every ray in the shadowy hall flinched, and Shex, the target of the attack, simply couldn't bear it. Abandoning his spell halfway through, he wheeled and bolted into a corner, where he cowered helplessly.

Yzil supposed he should be outraged to see the servant of an inferior power best a vitan, but despite his honest devotion to Ilxendren, it just wasn't in him. It was too gratifying to see Shex humiliated.

Tu'ala'keth pivoted back toward Yzil. "Now," she said, "I will tell you Umberlee's price. Above the waves, on one of the islands to the southeast, stands a stronghold. You will help me take it. It will be a difficult battle, perhaps the costliest one Exzethlix has ever fought, but profitable as well. The caves are full of treasure, and you can keep most of it."

Though still shuddering uncontrollably, Shex managed to turn around, face his tormentor, and swim back out into the center of the chamber. "You can't go to war," he said, "without the Vitanar's permission."

"I couldn't launch a major campaign against another part of Serôs," Yzil said. "I can lead a raid against airbreathers. Devitans do it all the time."

Shex glared. He looked as if he were about to blurt out something unforgivable, punishable, but to Yzil's disappointment, mastered his temper in time. "Devitan . . . with all respect . . . it signifies nothing if, by a fluke, this creature momentarily afflicted me. It's still wrong for you to defer to her and look to her to protect Exzethlix. You know it, I know it, and your people know it."

Unfortunately, according to an orthodox interpretation of Ilxendren's creed, he was right. Yzil struggled to think of a convincing rebuttal.

But Tu'ala'keth spoke first: "Vitan, it is no wonder that, even in your deity's holy place, you could not stand before me, for you are a wretched excuse for a priest. Like mine, your god embodies the chaos that underlies all things, yet you are deaf to the dark powers when they speak through chance events—like the fortunate chance that brought me here when you need me."

Yzil bared his fangs. "Don't you dare presume to preach to a servant of Ilxendren."

"Then perhaps I can bargain with you. Give me a single night to solve your problem. If I fail, you may indeed kill me, and the devitan will accede to your judgment in all matters pertaining to the defense of the city."

Shex turned to Yzil. "Will you?" the emissary demanded.

Yzil started to say no, absolutely not, then hesitated. As matters stood, he couldn't hold on to his position much longer, and the sad truth was he had no idea how to resolve the crisis by himself. Perhaps Ilxendren truly had sent Tu'ala'keth to help him. The ways of the Great Ray were strange and unfathomable, maybe even strange and unfathomable enough to manipulate the priestess of another faith into doing his bidding. In any case, Tu'ala'keth was cunning, and perhaps that made her worth gambling on.

"If the shalarin fails," he said, "you and I will set forth for Xedras in the morning. I swear it in Ilxendren's name."

Shex leered. "Then I'll see you when the waters brighten."

The vault was another spacious chamber hacked from the living coral. As was the case in most sections of Exzethlix, the curves, angles, and vague implications of big sculpted glyphs had an indefinable wrongness to them. Tu'ala'keth's head started to ache and her belly, to squirm if she let her gaze linger on certain details for very long.

Like the rest of the 'chitls' works, the place had no doors. Though their prehensile tails afforded them a limited capacity to manipulate objects, the rays would have found such contrivances inconvenient, and didn't even use them to safeguard their most precious possessions. But the symbols incised around the arched entryway should have done the job just as well. When someone spoke the trigger word, they'd generate a barrier of magical force.

But that had proved useless. So, floating at the threshold, Tu'ala'keth scrutinized the inscription, looking for some deficiency that would enable an intruder to breach the ward. Everything appeared to be all right.

Yzil flipped the winglike edges of his body in a gesture denoting impatience, derision, or both. "Every priest in the temple has already inspected that."

"But I had not." Gripping the new trident the devitan had given her, an enchanted green claw-coral weapon keener, lighter, and sturdier than the one she'd lost, she swam on into the vault. The devitan followed. The sentries curled themselves smaller and bobbed lower in the water, saluting him.

Small, pale, and soft-looking, in some cases gummed together with slime, the eggs lay heaped in glistening mounds as high as Tu'ala'keth was tall. "I did not realize," she said, "your race was so prolific."

"When they hatch," he said, "the newborns strive to eat one another. The majority die to feed the fiercest and most deserving of life."

She nodded, pleased to see Umberlee's spirit manifest in the process, even if the foolish rays didn't recognize it. "As far as I can tell, you have made no effort to differentiate one egg from another. I take it the parents have no desire to reclaim and rear their particular offspring."

Yzil scowled. "I don't even know what it is you're babbling about. Do you know how to protect the eggs or not?"

"Umberlee will guide me."

"Then let's get on with it."

"As you wish. Send the guards away."

Yzil hesitated. "Is that wise?"

"They have accomplished nothing so far and could prove a hindrance tonight. You and I will eliminate the threat."

"Go," the devitan said. Bodies rippling, the 'chitls glided from the vault. "Shall I activate the ward?"

"Why? It has proved to be of no use, either."

"All right, then what are we going to do?"

"I am going to meditate. You will remain quiet, so as not to disturb me, and keep watch."

"What's the point of meditating now? I've already done that, too, in this very spot, without gaining any insight."

Tu'ala'keth smiled. "Now you are the one wasting time with needless questions."

"I'm the ruler here, and I've staked everything I possess on your assertions. I demand to know what you think you're doing."

"Very well. Consider this: Whatever unseen agent is destroying the eggs, it has to move through the water which surrounds them, and my goddess is empress of the sea. It lies within my power to attune myself to the water in this chamber, to feel through it as if it were an extension of my own skin. If I succeed, I should sense the intruder, no matter what its nature or how stealthily it skulks about."

"Have you ever attempted this trick before?"

"No. It will require a deeper trance than I have ever entered."

"Then . . . never mind. It's still a good idea. I should have thought of it."

"You could not do it. Your Ilxendren rules over sea-dwellers, but he is not a deity *of* the sea, and therein lies the difference. Now be still and let me concentrate."

When it was clear he meant to hold his tongue, she began. She studied the water around her, trying to perceive the salty fluid itself, not the objects it contained. She tried to hear it murmur over surfaces, and feel its warmth and sliding pressure against her skin.

Once she'd fixed her mind on her impressions, she brought the membranes slipping across her eyes, blinding her to all but the brightest lights and most prominent shapes. Simply by focusing her attention inward, she dulled her remaining senses. Yet at the same time, she kept her preexisting sensations as vivid as before. Now, however, they rose primarily from memory and imagination. They were a concept of water, a mental construct to manipulate as she saw fit.

With a clear sky high overhead, and tamed by the countless barriers comprising Exzethlix, the waters therein were placid and so, too, was the simulacrum Tu'ala'keth had conjured for herself. That was the first element she had to change. She imagined insistent currents shoving her, increasing their strength by degrees until she would have had to swim vigorously to hold herself in the same position. She understood she wasn't truly moving. The sensation was an illusion, a trick she was playing on herself. Yet in a mystical sense, it was altogether real.

Next, she purged everything except the raw, elemental sea from her imaginings. The reef, carved into grotesqueries pleasing to the ixitxachitls' alien aesthetic, flowed into a form entirely natural but no less threatening, with coral spikes and edges to sting and tear, and countless crannies with moray eels lurking in their murky depths. Beyond, in a limitless ocean, krakens, sharks, squids, and demons pursued their prey, seizing and rending eternally, insatiable no matter how many victims they devoured.

She made the sky above scab over with inky storm clouds. Lightning flared, thunder roared, and rain hammered down. The wind screamed.

A corresponding violence erupted within the sea. The currents, strong and treacherous before, surged and became irresistible. They tumbled Tu'ala'keth from one impact to the next, slamming and scraping her against the coral.

A spell might have quelled the water, but it would also have defeated her purpose. She had to submit to the turmoil. She went limp and allowed the ocean to abuse her however it wished. The coral slashed and ground away her skin. Bones snapped in her foot and arm. Her right profile plunged toward a stony, branching growth, and even then, clenching herself, she managed not to flinch. The coral stabbed out her eye.

It was agony, but gradually, it became something greater as well, a transcendent state in which she was both the victim and the malevolent ocean smashing the life from its toy. The sea's vast joy so eclipsed her pain that the latter became insignificant, and as her blood streamed away, and her heart stuttered out its final beats, she became aware of something greater still, a splendid dance of slaughter that was everything . . . and silence and peace at the core of the frenzy.

The fierce current bashed her once more then whirled her lifeless, flopping body beyond the reef. Small fish came to feed on her then fled when a colossal shadow engulfed them all.

Though dead, Tu'ala'keth could still see the prodigious octopuses and weresharks when they writhed and glided across her field of vision. What she couldn't do was turn her head to behold the far huger entity whose familiars they were. She both yearned to see and was glad she couldn't. Her instincts warned that the sight would be too much to bear, that ecstasy or terror might extinguish her utterly.

But she could pray, if only silently, and it seemed appropriate that she do so: I am trying to do my duty, great queen, as best as I understand it. It has taken me to strange places. Places where I am clumsy and ignorant. Places where I lose my way. Still I persist.

The answer came back as a wordless surge of passion as nuanced and intelligible as speech. At its core was malevolence. Umberlee hungered to destroy any creature who engaged her attention, her own priestesses included. But cruelty wasn't the dominant note in the complex harmony that was her thought, but rather, subordinate to exhortation and a sort of cold, conditional approval.

The message, reduced to its essence, was this: You are on course, but the time grows short. Kill for me. Kill everything that stands in the way of your goal.

With that, the goddess and her retinue moved on, disappearing as quickly as they'd arrived. Tu'ala'keth's heart thumped and kept on beating thereafter. The water flowing into her gills washed the blighted immobility from her limbs. Her broken bones knit, and new skin flowed over her wounds.

It was time to reconstruct physical reality. She quelled the currents then added the contours of the vault, the heaps of eggs, and Yzil to her visualization.

In so doing, she shifted her awareness back to the mundane world, but remained deep in trance even so. Though free of pain, her body was exquisitely sensitive, as if from the battering her spirit had endured. It enabled her to feel water flowing and yielding all the way across the chamber.

She was reluctant to move or unveil her eyes for fear it might dull her newfound powers of perception. Still, Yzil, an acute observer in his own right, discerned a change in her.

"Can you speak?" he asked.

She decided she could. "Yes."

"You traveled a long time."

"I journeyed all the way to the Blood Sea, in Fury's Heart." It was there Umberlee herself had deigned to recognize her. She felt a pang of wonder and wished she could speak of it, but it was too holy and private an experience to share with an unbeliever.

"Did it do what it was supposed to?"

"Yes, but this is new to me. I did well to send the guards away. As I suspected, their movements might have confused my perceptions and blinded me to the emergence of our foe."

"I hope it does emerge. While your spirit was away, it occurred to me that the enemy, if it understands our situation, need only take a night off. Then we won't be able to vanquish it and will have to endure the consequences of our failure."

"Nonsense. If the entity does not destroy any eggs, we will claim victory, and how can Shex refute us?

The 'chitl chuckled. "When you put it that way, I don't suppose he can. I've missed that shrewd mind of yours. I'm lucky you returned just when I could make use of you."

"As I am fortunate your situation is desperate enough that you were willing to promise aid in return."

Except that it wasn't truly a matter of luck. It was possibility, pattern, and energy rising from the boil of coincidence that was the universe to guide and empower those who embraced the furor. But she knew she didn't need to explain it. Yzil, himself a cleric of chaos, albeit vowed to a lesser deity, already understood.

"You never really told me who it is you want to attack," he said.

"Dragons and the coven of necromancers who worship them."

He eyed her askance. "I'm not sure I ever heard you joke before."

"Nor have you now. I told you it would be difficult, but—"

She sensed surreptitious motion and pivoted in that direction. Something was there, hovering above a pale mound of eggs, but she couldn't make out what. It clutched one of the soft orbs in its jaws, fingers, or claws and squished it to jelly then it was gone.

"Do you see it?" Yzil said.

"Almost," she said. Trailing strands of slime, an egg bobbed up from another pile and ruptured into goo and drifting specks.

"We need better than 'almost,'" the ixitxachitl snarled. Flat, flexible body writhing, lashing tail defining mystic figures, he rattled off a prayer. A virulent darkness billowed across the chamber like an octopus's ink, but lacking a clear target, failed to achieve an effect. As it faded from existence, a third egg crumpled and burst.

Tu'ala'keth focused ... focused ... gradually discerned intermittent flurries of motion ... then suddenly saw the creatures clearly.

They weren't invisible in the technical sense, but might as well have been, for they were made of the same saltwater that surrounded them, congealing from it to break the eggs then dissolving back into it. It was the reason no ward could keep them out. They could manifest wherever water was, and in Serôs, that was everyplace.

Their forms were flowing, inconstant, swelling

and dwindling from one second to the next. A double-headed eel became a crab then passed from existence into lurking potentiality. A dolphin-thing abandoned any semblance of a fixed shape for the oozing bell-shaped body and trailing tendrils of a jellyfish. The constant transformations made them difficult to count, but there were at least half a dozen.

That was too many, but Tu'ala'keth reassured herself that at least she had a fix on them now, and they were some breed of water elemental, subject to the innate authority of a waveservant no less than fish and ixitxachitls. She gripped the drowned man's hand and evoked a flare of Umberlee's majesty.

The intangible blast hurled them backward, and their presence on the physical plane became more definite. Though still twisting from one shape to the next, they were no longer bleeding in and out of the world entirely, and Yzil exclaimed as he spotted them at last. Tu'ala'keth's display of faith hadn't destroyed or cowed them, but it had, for the moment, frozen them in a condition that would enable her and the 'chitl to come to grips with them.

If Yzil's eyes could make out the elementals, so could hers, and the profound relaxation of a trance could slow her in battle. With a pang of regret at sundering her mystical communion with the waters, she unveiled her eyes and embraced her normal state of consciousness. A thrill sang along her nerves as her physical senses regained their former immediacy.

The elementals charged, agitating the water around them and blowing apart two of the egg mounds. The gleaming ovoids tumbled and rolled.

Yzil snarled an incantation. The spirit in the lead, currently clad in the form of a hammerhead shark, frayed apart and crumpled in on itself at the same time as the magic cast it back to the otherworld of limitless water that was its natural home.

The others kept rushing forward.

Trident leveled, Tu'ala'keth declaimed a prayer of her own, to exert a momentary mastery over the watery substance of the remaining spirits' bodies. When she felt the elements of the spell lock into place, she bade the creatures rip apart. Two of them faltered, flailed, and when the spasm passed, continued the advance as if afflicted with palsy.

But they kept racing in as best they could, and their comrades with them. A murky thing shaped like an enormous angler fish opened its jaws wide to seize Tu'ala'keth in jagged fangs.

She drove the coral trident into its face. Its substance writhed, and she hoped she'd struck it a mortal blow. But it started to resolve itself in the guise of a squid, its long, fleshy lure becoming one of the tentacles. The limb lashed her across the face.

The blow snapped her head back and mashed and cut her lips against her teeth. But she refused to let it stun her, and when the elemental reached to enfold her in its arms, she dived beneath the writhing tangle, rolled, and speared it in the body. It gave a cry like a wave shattering on a rock then burst into a thousand droplets, which at once lost cohesion in their turn.

Two more elementals were maneuvering to close with Tu'ala'keth but weren't in position quite yet. She had time to begin another incantation and to look about and check on Yzil.

Despite his needle fangs and toxic vampire bite, the devitan, like most members of his race, had no liking for close combat. Accordingly, he'd fallen back into a corner and sealed it with a curtain of seething, whispering gloom. Elementals probed it and battered it but hadn't yet managed to break through. He proclaimed another banishment and shoved a spirit in the form of a sea snake back to its proper level of reality. In so doing, he punched a hole in the wall between the worlds that, in the instant before it healed, made Tu'ala'keth's entire body ache like a rotten tooth.

She retreated, dodging attacks, giving herself time to complete her conjuration. Fangs locked on her shoulder. The pressure was excruciating, but the bite didn't pierce her silverweave or spoil her prayer either. A second blue-green trident sprang into existence and launched itself at her attacker, a malformed, translucent mockery of a tiger shark. The elemental recoiled from the stabs, releasing her in the process.

Just in time: her other adversary lunged at her. Presently in mid-shift from lobster to fish, it was pincers, eye stalks, and segmented shell in front, fins and undulating piscine tail behind. Alas, the ongoing metamorphosis didn't make it awkward or unsteady.

Tu'ala'keth faked a dodge in one direction then kicked in the other, flummoxing the spirit for an instant. She rattled off a spell, and an earsplitting howl roiled the creature's liquid body. It didn't kill it, though.

Pincers stabbed and snapped, trying to shear her to pieces, then flowed together and became a set of gaping jaws big enough to swallow her whole. She cried Umberlee's name, praying for rage and the power it brought, and lashed out with all her strength. The green coral tines of her weapon plunged deep into the roof of the elemental's mouth. She reached inside herself, evoked another measure of the pure raw essence of soul and faith, and sent it blazing up the shaft. The spirit exploded into harmless water.

Once the threat disappeared, she realized Yzil was declaiming the rhyming words of a spell. His shadowy shield was gone. An elemental in the guise of a moray had him in its gnashing jaws and was chewing him to bloody shreds but without disrupting his concentration.

The eel-thing wavered. Holes burst open at various

points along its form as though several unseen blades had stabbed it all at once. It screamed and flew apart, and across the vault, its kindred suffered the same fate.

All but one. Wearing the guise of a porpoise, it fled for the exit. Yzil called the trigger word, activating the magic pent in the arch. Seething with a hint of gnashing jaws, darkness bloomed in the opening.

Trapped, the elemental wheeled to face its foes. Yzil rattled off the opening words of another banishment. His body was a patchwork of gory wounds, but thanks to his vampirism, they'd already started to close.

"No!" said Tu'ala'keth. "Do not!"

Yzil abandoned the spell uncompleted. The spirit rushed him. Fortunately, the disembodied trident Tu'ala'keth had conjured remained in existence and, at her silent command, hurtled through the water to interpose itself between the porpoise-thing and its target. The elemental veered off to avoid being impaled.

"Why shouldn't I kill it?" Yzil demanded.

"Because," she replied, "it is unlikely the elementals found their way from their world to ours by themselves or would have cared about smashing the eggs even if they had. Someone conjured them, and if we break this one to our will, it can tell us who."

"You have a point,' said Yzil. "What about the V'greshtan binding?"

"If you carry it ready for the casting, I can supply the responses."

They began the intricate contrapuntal incantation. The gathering magic turned the water hot one moment, chill the next. The elemental lunged at them repeatedly but couldn't slip past the darting trident of force.

As Tu'ala'keth declaimed the final syllable, a complex symmetrical structure of glowing red lines and angles sizzled into existence around the elemental. It looked like a geometer's model of an essential three-dimensional form rendered in light. Additional strands of power passed through the center of the cage, connecting the vertices defining one face with corresponding points elsewhere. Suddenly transfixed by dozens of the needle-thin scarlet beams, the spirit howled and thrashed.

"Submit," said Yzil, "and I will lessen the pain."

"I submit," groaned the elemental, its voice like the hiss and rumble of the surf. Its porpoise body melted into shapelessness.

"Who sent you?" the devitan asked.

The spirit hesitated. "Master, you bound me, I acknowledge it, but I still bear another's yoke as well. I cannot—" Tu'ala'keth felt Yzil assert his will, bidding the magical cage to hurt its prisoner. The elemental broke off speaking to scream and flail anew.

When the paroxysm passed, Yzil said, "I control you now. I have the power to torture and kill you. I and no one else. Answer my question."

The spirit shuddered as incompatible compulsions fought for dominance. Finally, it whispered, "Wraxzala." Its liquid substance churned with agony.

"Wraxzala," Yzil echoed, surprise in his voice.

"Who is that?" asked Tu'ala'keth. Her torn lips throbbed, and she evoked a small pulse of healing energy to blunt the discomfort.

"The vitan of one of the temples here in the city," Yzil said. "She's ambitious, like all of them, so it makes perfect sense that she'd try to discredit me. If His Holiness strips me of my offices, it makes room in the hierarchy for her to move up. I'm only surprised because I imagined Shex responsible for this particular treachery."

"Because, being the Vitanar's envoy, he seemed by far the greater threat."

"Yes."

"Well, then," said Tu'ala'keth, "let us consider our options."

❖ ❖ ❖ ❖ ❖

Shex glided back and forth in the comfortable suite of chambers Yzil had—no doubt grudgingly—assigned him, while a half-grown locathah male cowered in a cranny in the coral. Shex had sent for the slave to be his supper then realized he felt too restless to eat.

His creed taught that self-possession was a fundamental virtue, for without it, calculation and guile were impossible. But he supposed that in his present circumstances, even a vitan could forgive himself a measure of excitement. For in a few hours, the Vitanar's enemy would capitulate to him then His Holiness would reward Shex with Yzil's offices and chattels.

Unless Yzil managed to end the threat to the eggs.

But that was impossible, surely. The devitan had tried repeatedly and failed. He wouldn't fare any better now just because a shalarin, of all things, had pounced out of nowhere to assist him. At first, Tu'ala'keth's intrusion had rattled Shex, but only because it was so unexpected. She was just a slave creature and the servant of an inferior power. It was preposterous to imagine her playing any sort of decisive role in the affairs of ixitxachitls.

Shex's belly gurgled, and he wondered if perhaps he could bring himself to drink something after all. He rounded on the locathah, advanced on it in leisurely fashion, and savored its wide-eyed, cringing dread.

Maybe after he slaked his thirst, he should give some thought to what might be causing the city's problem and what a more resourceful devitan might do to solve it. For after all, it would be his puzzle to unravel soon enough.

He opened his jaws. The locathah whimpered and shuddered but offered no resistance. It understood its only chance of survival lay in capitulation. In the hope that its master, if not annoyed with it, might stop short of draining all its blood.

Then, outside the apartments, voices sounded. Shex pivoted toward the doorway.

A water elemental in the wavering, translucent semblance of a porpoise raced through the opening. Alarmed, the vitan retreated and rattled off the first line of a prayer of protection.

But the spirit made no effort to attack. Instead, it sank lower in the water, abasing itself before him. "Save me, Master!" it cried.

Plainly in furious pursuit of the elemental, Tu'ala'keth, Yzil, and a dozen of the latter's guards burst into the suite. "By the Great Ray!" the devitan cried. "I should have suspected you, Shex, but I never guessed."

Shex felt a flutter of incipient fear in his belly and struggled to quash the emotion before it could shake his composure. "Suspected me of what, Devitan? I don't understand what's happening here, but I know I've done nothing wrong."

"You can't lie your way out of it," Yzil said, "not with your familiar groveling before you. I'm pleased to report the waveservant and I exterminated all the others, before they could destroy more of the eggs, but this one escaped and fled to its master for protection. That worked out nicely, for it led us right to you."

"This is some sort of misunderstanding," said Shex. Or, more likely, it was a trick! "I didn't conjure this elemental or any other."

His body riddled with half-healed puncture wounds, Yzil swam closer. "Give it up, Vitan. Everyone understands you had abundant reason to make a covert attack on Exzethlix. You coveted my domain for yourself and believed that if you made me appear incapable of defending it, the Vitanar would award it to you."

"I'm glad," said Shex, "you recall my relationship with His Holiness. As his envoy, I'm untouchable."

"In most circumstances, yes." Yzil glided nearer. "After committing treason of this magnitude, no."

"The allegation is absurd. But if you believe otherwise, I demand a trial."

"All right, but pay attention, or you'll miss it. As devitan of Exzethlix, I find you guilty and sentence you to death."

"A trial before His Holiness, in Xedras! He'll punish you if I don't get it."

Yzil laughed. "Don't be ridiculous. Do you truly believe the Vitanar cares about you? You're a pawn, worth protecting, but only to a point. He won't object to the expeditious execution of a traitor caught committing atrocities. Doing so would tarnish his reputation, and even the great must pay some heed to how their vassals view them. You likely would have discovered that yourself in time, but alas, you've run out of it."

"Give me a trial by combat! Fight me yourself! Let Ilxendren judge between us." Under normal circumstances, a vitan could hardly expect to defeat a devitan. But Yzil had just fought a battle and still bore the wounds. Shex was fresh. He reckoned he had a chance.

Yzil sneered. "I deny you *trial* by combat. I've already judged and sentenced you. But I do mean to fight you, simply for the pleasure of killing you myself. Understand, though, that if, by some extraordinary fluke, you beat me, these others will still destroy you."

We'll see about that, thought Shex. Once he slew Yzil, he'd be the highest-ranking ixitxachitl in the chamber, indeed, possessed of authority equal to that of any vitan in the city. It was possible no one else would prove bold enough to carry out Yzil's sentence.

He retreated and started murmuring a prayer. Yzil simply bared his fangs and rushed him. He hoped to end the fight immediately, with one savage assault.

Shex dodged. Yzil shot past him and started to wheel.

The vitan glimpsed motion at the periphery of his vision. The elemental was darting at Yzil's flank, commencing an attack in aid of the ixitxachitl it had inexplicably identified as its master. Shex had a split second to wonder if that was a good thing or not, and Tu'ala'keth lunged, interposing herself between the semitransparent porpoise-thing and its target. The spirit veered off to avoid the tines of her trident.

Shex reached the final word of his incantation. The water immediately in front of Yzil's snarling countenance swirled with a dark malignancy. The power was meant to sear his eyes blind, but when the stain came in contact with his body, a bluish light gleamed briefly from his hide. He had charms in place to counter hostile magic, and when he charged, it was obvious he could still see.

Shex started to evade then realized he was moving precisely as Yzil wanted him to. The devitan was trying to maneuver him into a nook in the coral and trap him.

Stroking desperately, Shex changed direction and launched himself up and over his onrushing foe. Yzil reacted in time to lash him with his tail. The blow flicked him on his ventral side and should have produced a sting and a welt, no more. But it burned and kept on burning, the pain sinking into his vitals like acid eating away at him.

Clearly, he'd fallen prey to another spell his adversary had cast beforehand, and he'd just have to block out the torment for now. He had to concentrate on fighting. He snarled the opening line of another prayer, and Yzil whirled around to face him.

Meanwhile, the water elemental tried ineffectually to get by Tu'ala'keth's trident, and she declaimed a banishment to return it to its native plane. It was obvious to Shex that the porpoise-thing wasn't really trying to help him. It and the shalarin were merely putting on a show to substantiate the lie that the creature was his thrall. He wondered if anyone else could tell. Then Yzil charged, and he forgot all about it.

Shex faked another dodge over the top then dived beneath the devitan, succeeding in slipping past without even suffering another tail strike. He was clearly more nimble than his adversary. Perhaps Yzil's wounds were to blame.

Shex reached the conclusion of his spell. Grayness flowered in the water then clotted into a shark with pale, luminous eyes and jagged black teeth. With a thought, he nudged it at its intended prey, and it instantly surged into motion.

Now it was Yzil's turn to evade and retreat before an opponent he was reluctant to face in close combat. But if the demon-shark didn't get him, Shex would by hammering him with one attack spell after another while he was too hard pressed to retaliate. Even a devitan's defensive enchantments wouldn't stop them all.

Shex sought to afflict Yzil with uncontrollable panic. With a snarl, the devitan resisted the curse. But it froze him in place for an instant, and the demon shark snagged the left edge of his body in its ebon teeth and started to gobble him down.

Yzil tore himself free but left a substantial portion of his left side behind. Blood billowed from the tattered remnants. Shex cried out in pleasure because no one, not even a devitan, could endure such a hurt and go on fighting.

Except that Yzil did. He swung himself around and

buried his fangs in his attacker's flank, just behind the gill slits. Evidently as susceptible to the malignant effect of the bite as any mundane creature, the spirit-shark convulsed and kept on thrashing. Yzil sucked at its wounds for a second then rushed Shex, emerging from a cloud of dark, pungent gore and leaving a trail of it behind himself.

But it didn't matter. Yzil hadn't been able to catch Shex when his body was intact, and the ragged, lop-sided cripple he'd become obviously wouldn't swim as well. The vitan stroked almost lazily backward and commenced another spell.

Yzil said, "Stop."

No! thought Shex, and obeyed anyway. He stopped retreating and conjuring both. He strained to resume moving, and his body flailed, breaking free of the enchantment. Then Yzil struck, driving his fangs into his opponent's spine.

Ghastly pain ripped through Shex's entire body. He struggled to pull free and bring his own fangs to bear, just as Yzil had done with the shark. But the devitan wrapped his tail around him, crumpling and binding him together, and gnawed the bite wound deeper. Then he began to drink in earnest.

Shex's blood, strength, and will all flowed out of him together, and he dangled quiescent in Yzil's grip. He noticed his erstwhile supper smirking at the spec-tacle of his demise and wondered if the idiotic locathah believed it had truly escaped anything, if it imagined the rest of the ixitxachitls would use it more gently.

Then it became too much effort to wonder that or anything at all.

❦ ❦ ❦ ❦ ❦

It was morning when a flunky conducted Tu'ala'keth to Yzil's suite. The coral chambers were large and accordingly luxurious by the standards of a 'chitl, but to her eye, rather bare of furniture, utensils, and similar amenities.

Body rippling lazily, Yzil floated among a litter of drifting corpses. A trace of blood, the little he hadn't consumed, clouded, scented, and flavored the water. When he'd sent Tu'ala'keth away, he'd claimed she wouldn't be safe in his presence, and beholding the slaughter, she rather believed it.

"I know it looks like gluttony," he said, "but I fear the truth is even sadder: I'm getting old, and after an injury like that, it takes a lot of blood to restore me."

"You did not have to fight Shex," she said.

"No, but it was satisfying and a good way for a devitan to conduct himself now and again. It reminds the underlings why they're afraid of you."

"Are you well now?"

"Oh, yes." He curled the edges of his flat body so she could better inspect them. "The scars are impressive and still smart a little, but even those will fade in time."

"Have I fulfilled my pledge?"

"Yes, brilliantly. Shex is gone. It reflects poorly on His Holiness that his emissary was denounced as a traitor, so he's likely to leave me in peace for a while. Wraxzala won't dare destroy any more eggs now that we know how she was accomplishing it, and as soon as I contrive an adequate excuse, I'll rid myself of her as well. Happily, she's not the Vitanar's pet, so it shouldn't be particularly difficult."

"Then I assume you are ready to repay me."

Yzil curled himself slightly smaller, a gesture conveying embarrassment or apology and surely one to which a ferocious, imperious devitan was unaccustomed. "I truly appreciate your help, waveservant. But you must ask a different boon. I don't care how much plunder we could take. I won't send my troops to fight dragons and wizards. Not on land. The risk is unacceptable."

"What about the hazards of doing nothing? I explained to you, I have to conquer the wyrms on Tan in order to defeat the dragons running amok here in Serôs. If no one stops them, they could ravage Exzethlix."

"Or they may go elsewhere. My comrade, we're both initiate in the ways of blood and chaos. If you say you know these cultists hold a solution to your problems, I believe it. But sometimes the dark powers provide answers to our questions that, while true, don't really help us because we lack the strength to turn the revelations to practical advantage."

"Yesterday, I lacked the strength. Today, I have it. Exzethlix is the sturdy spear in my hand."

"No, it isn't."

"You have always desired the free run of Myth Nantar, to trade in her markets and speak in her councils."

The 'chitl laughed bitterly. "As if the allied peoples would ever tolerate ixitxachitls."

"They accept morkoths, who hold as many slaves as your folk. A morkoth even sits on the Council of Twelve. When I destroy the dragon flight and restore the worship of Umberlee, I will become an influential figure in Myth Nantar. I will exert that influence on your behalf."

"At which point, His Holiness indicts me for heresy."

"Naturally, the matter will require circumspection, but I trust you have not forgotten how to scheme. Nor to gamble."

Yzil pursed his lips and sucked at his fangs, pondering. At last he said, "No. Tempting though it is. I'm sorry."

"As am I," said Tu'ala'keth. "I had hoped to do this amiably."

The ray glared at her. "Meaning what?"

"Today, you are the savior of Exzethlix. Such a hero that, for a while, even the Vitanar will hesitate to interfere with you. But your situation would deteriorate quickly if folk found out you deliberately condemned the wrong person for the destruction of the eggs and left the actual culprit swimming free."

"I did it that way because you suggested it!"

She shrugged. "Who will care? You still bear responsibility for your own decisions."

"You realize," he said, "that if I kill a shalarin, a slave creature, here and now, no one will question or care about that either."

"Are you entirely healed? As you gorged on blood, did you take the time to replenish the spells you expended last night? Are you positive you're a better fighter than I am, and that you could strike me dead so efficiently I wouldn't even be able to escape these apartments and confide my secrets to someone before I expired?"

He bared his fangs. "There had better be a lot of treasure."

THE **P**RIESTS

The locathah spread the mouth of the net bag, and the fish swam sluggishly forth. They were already dying, poisoned by the enchantments the spellcasters had poured into their veins, and that was fine. It made them easier to catch.

Wraxzala kicked forward, converging on the cloud of fish with the other ixitxachitls, and sank her teeth into her share of the bounty. The blood was vile, bitter with power, and she had to clench herself to keep from retching it back up. Pain burned through her guts and blurred her vision then waned.

Afterward, she didn't feel any different, and wondered if the magic had truly prepared her for the venture to come. Then she sneered at the very notion, for obviously, nothing could do that.

She peered back and forth, at the other warriors, ixitxachitl and slave, waiting here in the shallows with the surface of the benighted sea rippling just a few yards above their heads. Yzil—curse him!—had promised the surviving thralls soft treatment, and his fellow 'chitls, advancement, and some of the stupider folk in each category looked eager to get started. Most, however, appeared so tense and morose, it was plain they shared Wraxzala's trepidation.

By the Five Great Deeds of Vengeance, how she wished she'd never threatened the eggs! When Yzil killed His Holiness's envoy instead of her, she'd believed she'd enjoyed a miraculous escape but now understood the devitan actually had identified her as the guilty party. He'd just opted to punish her in a different fashion.

But this way at least she had a chance. She was, after all, an ixitxachitl and a vitan, blessed by Ilxendren and superior to all lesser creatures. Logically, that ought to mean she and her allies could defeat them, even under adverse circumstances.

She resolved to keep telling herself that until she believed it.

The vitan in charge—she wondered sourly what he'd done to anger Yzil—gave the command, and the company advanced. Soon the seabed sloped high enough that the locathahs, koalinths, and their ilk had to plant their feet and wade with their upper portions sticking up out of the water. At that point, stealth became impossible, and Wraxzala decided she, too, might as well experience the world above the waves. With luck, she might even have a few heartbeats to get used to it before she had to start fighting for her life.

She swam upward, through the heaving interface between sea and air, and onward. Once she exited the water, the medium supporting her felt thin and insubstantial, yet she didn't fall. In fact, precisely because it offered less resistance, she had a giddy feeling she might even be able to swim faster above the waves than below.

She zigzagged awkwardly, seeing how much effort it took and how it felt. Other ixitxachitls rose from the waves to either side. Then, on land, among the dilapidated huts, some creature started yelling. She couldn't understand the words, but it was obvious what was going on. A sentry had spotted the invaders coming ashore.

Hulking bipedal shapes with folded wings, serpent heads, and dragging, writhing tails shambled forth from the shacks. Wraxzala had never seen such brutes before, but according to the wretched, meddling waveservant, they were called "dragonkin." In these first confused moments, the reptiles failed to understand just how many ixitxachitls and thralls had risen from the depths to threaten them. They evidently thought they could make a stand on the beach and push the intruders back.

The ixitxachitl commander shouted an order. Dozens of locathahs with their goggle-eyed piscine faces, and brawny koalinths with big, scalloped ears and shaggy manes now plastered to their skulls, shouldered and discharged their crossbows. Many of the bolts flew wild. Like Wraxzala herself, the missiles moved differently in air. But some found their marks, and dragonkin fell.

Most of the surviving reptiles scrambled for cover, from which they would likely seek to harry and slow the advance. The invaders would need to root them out before they could pass in safety, but though they'd pay a toll in blood, they could certainly manage it. The real problem was that two other dragonkin turned, spread their leathery pinions, and flew inland ... to fetch reinforcements, without a doubt.

Though Yzil had been too cagey to say it in so many

words, Wraxzala understood that, according to his strategy, that was more or less what was supposed to happen. As she and her companions fought their way up the mountainside, they were supposed to lure the enemy forth to engage them.

But by the poison tides of the Abyss, please, not yet! If the wyrms and all their minions descended on the invaders before they even established a beachhead, they'd have little trouble wiping them out.

Wraxzala had absolutely no inclination to imperil herself by chasing the fleeing dragonkin. But unfortunately, only ixitxachitls had any hope of overtaking them, because only they could swim in air. The thralls had partaken of a simpler, less costly enchantment, which merely enabled their gills to function out of water. For they, after all, had legs to provide mobility on land, and their masters had assumed that would prove sufficient.

"No more shooting!" Wraxzala cried. She waited for other voices to echo the order then charged forward. Several other 'chitls did the same. At least she wasn't entirely alone.

She raced over the ruined village. The rocky ground rose steeply just behind it. Patches of vegetation clung to the lower slopes.

She still felt clumsy speeding through the air. Every slight flick or tilt of her body achieved too much, and she veered crazily from one overcompensation to the next. But she couldn't worry about that now.

She peered, trying to pick out a dragonkin, and spied a rhythmic flicker of mottled wings. Unfortunately, the reptile had a considerable lead, in distance and elevation, too.

Only magic could hinder it now. Still pursuing, she rattled off an intricate sequence of rhyming palindromes. The power, as it gathered and poised itself to strike, made a sound like bright, wicked laughter.

A set of shadowy, disembodied jaws appeared directly in front of the dragonkin. The reptile tried to veer off, but the construct leaped at it and caught it anyway. The shadow creature plunged its fangs repeatedly into the dragonkin's body.

The dragonkin wrenched free and riposted with its spear. The lance plunged right through the shadow-stuff without doing it any harm.

Once the reptile realized it couldn't strike back, it started veering and dodging, trying to distance itself from its attacker. The flying jaws, however, matched it move for move.

Wraxzala was reasonably certain the construct couldn't kill the enormous brute, but that wasn't the point. The harassment was just supposed to keep it in place while she beat her way closer. She was trying to steal up on it, but in this strange environment where all sound seemed muffled, couldn't tell if she was being quiet or not.

Finally she judged she'd sneaked close enough for a different and perhaps truly devastating curse. She whispered the opening words, and the jaws faded away as the spell that had birthed them exhausted the last of its force.

She hoped the dragonkin would simply attempt to continue on its way. But despite its uncouth appearance, it had brains enough to realize a spellcaster had afflicted it. Now free of the punishment, wounds bleeding, it tilted its wings and wheeled in the air, seeking its tormentor. It spied Wraxzala, snarled, and threw its spear.

Underwater, it was impossible to fling a lance for any distance, and so the attack caught her by surprise. Reflex jolted her into motion, though, and she dived. The spear streaked over her.

She declaimed the final syllable of her invocation. The dragonkin grunted as its body went rigid. Unable to move its wings, it plummeted and crashed down amid some big, sturdy plants—Wraxzala thought they were called "trees"—on a ledge.

She swam warily downward, peering to see what had become of her foe. If she had to use another spell to finish it off, she would, but hoped the fall had killed it. With a long night of battle ahead of her, she needed to conserve her power as much as possible.

Unfortunately, on first inspection, the thick, tangled limbs and their shroud of leaves confused her eyes. She was used to picking lurking enemies out of a mass of kelp or coral, but here the shapes were different.

Hoping it would help, she swam lower still. With a sudden rattle and snap of branches, the dragonkin exploded out at her. Its talons slashed at her face.

She spun herself out of the way and onto the reptile's back, between the roots of its wings. She drove her fangs into its neck.

It convulsed, and they fell together. Twigs jabbed and gouged at her as they crunched and bounced through the foliage, finally jolting to a stop at the crossing of two substantial branches midway down.

The dragonkin was hearty. The virulence in her initial bite hadn't shocked it into helplessness. It fumbled at her with its claws, trying to grab her and tear her loose. But the angle was awkward for it, and it couldn't manage a solid grip. She ripped open a throbbing artery in the side of its neck, and its life quickly pumped away.

She drank some of it then swam back up above the trees, where other 'chitls were wheeling and swooping about. "I killed one of them," she called.

"We got the other," replied a warrior. He was one of the stupid ones: He sounded gleeful, as if the raid were a game.

Wraxzala wondered just how playful he'd feel when the wyrms emerged from the apex of the volcano. It would happen by and by. She and her comrades had merely delayed the inevitable.

❖ ❖ ❖ ❖ ❖

Tu'ala'keth cautiously raised her head halfway out of the water, ducked back down, and turned to Yzil, who was hovering beside her. "The way is clear," she said.

"Good." He and the other 'chitls in the vanguard swam up into the air to see for themselves.

She rather wished she were able to do likewise, but the 'chitls hadn't offered her this particular magic. They claimed they barely had enough for themselves. She suspected they were simply unwilling to share the precious resource with someone they regarded as a "slave creature," but she hadn't made an issue of it. During her time with the pirates, she'd had plenty of practice walking and assumed she'd manage well enough.

Trident in hand, her new satchel dangling at her hip, she waded up onto a shelf of granite and took another look around the sea cave. The air was damp and salty, alive with the echoing boom and murmur of the surf. Shells, starfishes, and clumps of weed littered the floor where it sloped down to meet the water. An oil lamp, unlit at the moment, reposed in a niche in the wall, and bits of broken stone lay about the entrance to a passage slanting upward. Someone had smashed away rock to make the path more accessible.

"You were right," said Yzil. "There is a way up."

Tu'ala'keth shrugged. "It was not difficult to deduce. The wearer of purple mentioned that in time, he and his fellow lunatics might provide undeath to the dragons of the sea. How could humans accomplish that without workrooms where land and water come together?"

"Well, don't feel too smug. It's a *narrow* way up. I was hoping we could sneak up on them quickly."

"If we make haste, we still can."

"Let's hope so." Yzil turned toward the other hovering, flitting ixitxachitls, and the locathahs and koalinths still sloshing up out of the depths, and started barking orders.

It took him a few minutes to get everyone organized, and he and Tu'ala'keth led the ascent. The 'chitl's broad, flat body all but filled the passage, the rippling edges nearly swiping the walls.

He hesitated at a point where the smoothly sloping floor gave way to a succession of chiseled edges and right angles. "What's this?"

She smiled for an instant. "Stairs. No inconvenience to you, but I suffered stumbles and stubbed toes before I learned the trick of them. I suspect your slaves will, too."

Yzil showed his fangs. "If that's the worst they suffer tonight, they can count themselves blessed."

❧   ❧   ❧   ❧   ❧

Anton had pilfered a few small knives without his captors noticing, but now that he'd figured out where to hide it, he wanted a sword. It didn't need magical virtues like Tu'ala'keth's cutlass or Shandri's huge and thirsty blade. Any hilt weapon that extended his reach by more than a finger-length would do.

Surely somewhere in the caverns lay a dull, notched, rusty, poorly balanced sword nobody wanted or would miss. But he'd crept about for a long while without finding it and wandered dangerously far from his cage in the process. He supposed it was time to give up, for tonight anyway, and to steal some more food and make his way back to his fellow prisoners.

He turned, and a quavering roar shook the tunnel.

It sounded as if it might actually have words in it, but since he didn't speak the language of dragons, he couldn't be sure.

Whether it did or not, it roused the entire complex. Echoing voices babbled on every side. Footsteps scurried. Trumpets bleated, repeating the alarm the wyrm had sounded. A sickly blue shimmer and whiff of rot washed through the air as, somewhere, one of the necromancers cast an initial spell.

Intent on covering at least some of the distance back to the prison before the tunnels filled up with cultists dashing in all directions, trying to balance the conflicting imperatives of haste and stealth, Anton trotted as quickly as he dared until red light shined from an irregular opening just ahead.

The spy felt a pang of fear and self-disgust. He'd known a fire drake had claimed that particular side gallery for its lair, but the cursed thing had been asleep ever since he'd first discovered it, and so he'd come to consider this particular passageway as safe as any.

But it wasn't anymore. The commotion had roused the reptile and drawn it forth. Anton cast about for a hiding place. There was nowhere within reach.

The fire drake crawled out into the corridor. A runt compared to Eshcaz or any of the magnificent horrors proclaiming themselves "true dragons," it was nonetheless bigger than a horse and wagon, and its crimson scales radiated heat and light like metal fresh from the forge. Its blazing yellow eyes fixed on Anton.

He bowed to it deeply but quickly, like a lackey in a frantic hurry. "Someone is attacking the enclave!" he cried. "The other wyrms need you, milord!"

The drake showed its fangs. "I'm a female, fool!" Wings flattened against her back so as not to scrape on the ceiling, she lunged.

For one ghastly instant, Anton thought she was

charging *him*; then he perceived that her true intent was simply to traverse the passage as fast as possible. He flattened himself against the wall.

The dragon's scaly flank nearly brushed him, and he flinched from the searing heat. Then the excited wyrm hurtled on by and around a bend, without ever registering that the human groveling before her had worn the rags and sported the shaggy whiskers, grime, and lash marks of a slave.

Anton hurried onward, hiding and backtracking repeatedly as the tunnels filled up. At least it gave him a chance to eavesdrop on snatches of conversation:

"—attacking up the mountain—"

Anton smiled; he'd guessed right about that much, anyway.

"—crazy to challenge the Sacred Ones."

"They're crazy just to challenge us! I know a spell—"

"—some kind of bats, or demons that look and fly like them."

"No, it's gill-men. They crawled up out of the sea."

He frowned, puzzled. Was it possible Tu'ala'keth had returned at the head of an undersea army? He couldn't imagine how. She had no influence over her fellow shalarins. That was the galling realization that had launched her on her demented mission. He was still mulling it over when he finally managed to skulk back to the cage.

His fellow captives were all pressed up against the grille and raised a clamor when he appeared. On another night, he would have berated them for it, but it didn't matter anymore.

"What's happening?" demanded Jamark. "We heard all the noise and asked a cultist when he ran by, but he didn't stop."

Anton explained what little he knew. "So it's time," he concluded and, heedless of the squeal and bang, threw open the door. "Dig out the knives."

They didn't move; they just regarded him uncertainly. Eventually Stedd, a scrawny, homely, balding fellow who'd owned a dozen tanneries until pirates captured him and his beautiful young wife refused to pay his ransom, said, "Maybe that's not the wisest thing to do."

"Of course it is," Anton said.

"Why?" Stedd retorted. "We've only got knives, and most of us aren't trained warriors. Where's the sense in taking on well-armed dragonkin, magicians, and wyrms? If somebody else has come to wipe out the cult and rescue us, wonderful. Let's stay here where it's safe and pray they succeed. We can thank them when the fighting's over."

"That might not be a bad plan," Anton said, "except for a reason you already mentioned yourself: The cultists are powerful and have the advantage of a highly defensible stronghold. We can't count on the newcomers, whoever they are, to win without our help. But if we sneak through the caves, stabbing maniacs in the back while they're intent on the threat outside, maybe we can make a difference."

"Or die for nothing," the tanner said.

"Damn you all," Anton said. "Half of you would be dead already if not for me. But forget that and ponder this instead: This is our one chance. The opportunity we yearned and prayed for, never believing it would ever really come. I plan to make the most of it, even if I have to fight alone. If anyone wants to help, I'll be glad of the company. If others are so cowardly they can't bear to leave the cage, that's all right, too. Just stand aside while I pull out the knives."

Jamark made a spitting sound. "Ah, to Baator with it. I don't care if I die, as long as I kill a dragonkin first." Some of the others muttered in agreement.

In the end, almost everyone followed Anton away from the cage, even Stedd, sweaty, eyes darting, one of the knives clutched tight in an overhand grip. For his part, Anton still lacked a blade. Since they didn't have enough to go around, he'd decided to trust his sorcery to protect him for the time being.

"Where are we headed?" Jamark whispered.

"An armory," Anton answered, "not too far away. It was never practical to steal from it before, but now the cultists are in the middle of an emergency. They may have left it unlocked and unattended. There may be some weapons left inside. We'll find out."

❧ ❧ ❧ ❧ ❧

In his time, Diero had been a military man, serving as a war mage and officer in baronial armies and mercenary companies around the Sea of Fallen Stars. Drawing on his hard-won expertise, he had, despite the constant press of his other duties, made time to plan the mountain's defense, and to explain everyone's assigned duties in the event of an attack.

Accordingly, it exasperated him to see the dolts all running around in confusion instead of proceeding briskly to their proper stations.

Part of the difficulty was that most of the others lacked military training. Even the dragonkin were barbarian raiders, not veterans of a civilized army. Their human counterparts tended to be spellcasters with an unhealthy attraction to the forces of shadow, outlaws, and a motley assortment of malcontents, some every bit as deranged as dragons cultists were commonly held to be.

The real problem, however, was that the wyrms they served were ordering them out onto the mountain just any old way. Eshcaz was a case in point. Crouched in the center of the half-finished pentacle in the center of the great hall, shrouded in a haze of acrid smoke leaking from his mouth and nostrils, he bellowed commands, and lesser beings scurried to obey, more terrified of displeasing him than of any possible threat awaiting them outside the caverns.

Diero murmured an incantation. The world seemed to blink like an eye, he experienced a sensation of hurtling like an arrow loosed from a bow, and he was standing at Eshcaz's immense and scaly feet. The smoke stung his eyes, and the heat was unpleasant.

But he didn't permit his discomfort—or his annoyance—to show in his expression. He might be the most accomplished human spellcaster on Tan, but even so, he wouldn't wager a copper on his chances if the red opted to chastise him for what he interpreted as a show of disrespect.

"Sacred One," the wearer of purple said, "may I ask what you're doing?"

Eshcaz twisted his neck to sneer down at him. "What does it look like?"

"It looks as if you're rallying your troops for battle. But I wonder if you've considered that you're sending them forth from a strong defensive position into the open."

"I'm sending them where the enemy is."

"If that's the strategy you've chosen, so be it. But it might work all the better if you conducted a proper reconnaissance first. Or at least gave your servants time to form up properly."

"To what end?" Eshcaz replied. "Odds are they won't even have to do any real fighting. The other wyrms and I will annihilate the intruders all by ourselves. I just want you worthless mites to witness our wrath and to kill any nits on the other side who might otherwise scatter and hide well enough to escape our notice."

With that, he wheeled toward an exit large enough to admit his colossal frame. Diero had to scramble to avoid being pulped by his swinging tail. The red rushed forward, occluding the stars framed in the natural arch as he passed through, then leaped up into the sky.

Diero took a long breath, struggling to quell his irritation.

It wasn't that Eshcaz was stupid. That might actually have made his attitude less irksome, but in fact, like all mature dragons, he was cunning. Yet he was also impatient, reckless, and possessed of a fundamental wildness that made him favor boldness, instinct, and improvisation over caution, system, and analysis.

Olna sauntered up to Diero. Her straw-colored hair gathered in an intricate braid, the witch was slim and rather pretty, with bright eyes and a generous mouth made for laughter and frivolity. When he'd first met her, it had rather surprised Diero to learn she'd committed a magical atrocity so heinous she'd had to flee hundreds of miles from her native Damara to escape retribution.

"Well, this is a mess," she said.

Over the course of the past few months, they'd learned they could speak candidly to one another, for neither suffered from an inability to distinguish wyrms from gods, or the delusion that Sammaster's interpretation of a cryptic prophecy necessarily constituted the final word on the destiny of the world. Rather, they'd each reasoned their way to the conviction that dracoliches, if produced in sufficient numbers, might well conquer a significant portion of Faerûn, and when it happened, their supporters would reap rich rewards.

"It's ridiculous," Diero agreed. "The dragons see no need for strategy or tactics. They assume their sheer might will suffice to obliterate any threat."

"Well," said Olna, "to be fair, they're almost certainly right."

He felt his lips quirk into a grudging smile. "I suppose you have a point."

"So, do we go outside, too?"

"Mist and stars, no. There are still dragonkin and such in the tunnels. Perhaps enough to defend the key entry points, and if things go wrong outside, the dragons will be glad we stayed inside. Let's get to it."

❧ ❧ ❧ ❧ ❧

Sharkskin satchel bouncing at her hip, Tu'ala'keth drove her trident into a human's chest. Another man fell with a ixitxachitl covering him like a rippling mantle, fangs buried in his throat.

That finished clearing the way . . . to a granite wall. Yzil scowled in irritation and started to turn away from the carnage.

"Wait," said Tu'ala'keth.

"Why? It's a dead end."

"Perhaps not. This passage is large enough for one of the smaller wyrms to negotiate, and it appears to me that the stone at the end displays a less intricate grain and texture than the granite to either side."

She walked forward and probed with the trident. The coral tines sank into the rock without the slightest resistance. She stuck her face into the illusion and found it to be no thicker than a fish scale. Beyond it stars gleamed, surf boomed and hissed at the base of the island, and the deep, rough voices of koalinths shouted and shrieked somewhere closer at hand.

She turned back around. "It is an entrance. Someone has simply concealed it with a phantasm."

"You have a keen eye." Yzil turned to one of his fellow 'chitls. "You and your company will defend this place. If any humans or dragonkin happen along, you'll need to kill them, but your primary concern is to destroy any wyrm that tries to pass through in either direction.

Hide as best you can, and hit it hard the instant you see it, before it senses you. Use your most damaging spells, and some of you, get your teeth in it. With Ilxendren's help, your bites may cripple even a dragon."

The 'chitl curled itself smaller. "Yes, Devitan," it said glumly.

"Buck up," Yzil snapped. "You drew the desirable chore. Some of us are venturing onward to kill the *big* dragon."

❖   ❖   ❖   ❖   ❖

"It's just a little farther," Anton said.

But up ahead, in the lamp-lit darkness, the passage forked, and dragonkin abruptly shambled out of the right-hand branch. The caves were so noisy now, the stone bouncing echoes to and fro, that he hadn't heard them coming.

The ogre-sized reptiles gawked at the humans. They were rushing to fight invaders, not slaves who'd escaped their confinement, and the unexpected sight made them hesitate.

It gave Anton time to rattle off an incantation and brandish the three gray pebbles he'd found and painstakingly polished after Tu'ala'keth took his original set of talismans away from him. Power whined, and vapor billowed into being around the dragonkin. They staggered, retching.

The fumes faded as quickly as they'd appeared. "Get the bastards!" Anton cried. "Now! While they're off balance!"

Some screaming with fury, fear, or a mixture of the two, his fellow captives charged. He jabbered the charm that made his hand into a blade then sprinted after them.

Jamark rammed his knife into a dragonkin's groin, and the creature's knees buckled.

Stabbing madly, two humans swarmed on a second reptile and drove it reeling backward.

But otherwise, the enemy quickly took back the advantage. A dragonkin aimed and braced its spear. An onrushing captive failed to react quickly enough to evade the threat. The point punched all the way through his body and, covered in gore, popped out his back. Unwilling to take the time to pull the corpse from the end of the weapon, the reptile simply dropped it and shredded another victim with its claws. Meanwhile, hissing and snarling, its comrades speared and slashed the puny creatures who'd dared to challenge them.

Anton wondered grimly if he and his allies could possibly prevail. Then he spied the dragonkin leader, and the long, straight sword it was just starting to draw from its scabbard. Shadow swirled inside the forte of the blade.

Unfortunately, the reptile stood toward the rear of its squad. Anton veered away from the warrior he'd intended to attack and plunged into the mass of frenzied combatants.

Some of the dragonkin struck at him as he raced by, and he dodged as best he could without slowing down. Another inch of dark blade cleared the sheath, and eager to start killing, the sword itself jumped, assisting the process and emerging fast.

Anton dived under a jabbing spear then leaped into the air. His first blow had to kill. Otherwise, the greatsword's fury was likely to prop up the leader long enough for it to retaliate, and to say the least, he doubted his ability to withstand the assault.

The dragonkin saw him coming, and took a hasty retreat that didn't quite carry it out of reach. It lifted the sword and scabbard to block but not quickly enough. He chopped at its neck with all his strength.

Blood gushed, and partially severed, its head flopped. It toppled backward.

He dropped to the floor, scrambled forward, and finished drawing the greatsword. No doubt the weapon had been eager to butcher him only a moment before, but now it welcomed him with a thrill of delight. For one set of hands on the hilt was as good as another.

As before, he loathed the touch of its mind, its bloodlust and gloating cruelty oozing in to contaminate his own thoughts. But he opened himself up to them anyway, and the sword rewarded him. It washed aches, weakness, and fatigue away, as if his hours on the rack and all the subsequent abuse had never happened.

Grinning, he pivoted and hacked a dragonkin's legs out from under it then split its skull as it went down. He turned again and buried the greatsword in a reptile's spine.

At that point, the other dragonkin realized a significant threat had materialized behind them. Several moved to encircle him.

Even with the greatsword, he might not have withstood that tactic for any length of time. But by riveting the reptiles' attention on himself, he'd taken the pressure off his surviving comrades. They seized the opportunity to snatch the spears of fallen enemies from the floor and, adequately armed for the first time, assailed the dragonkin once more.

Somehow, it proved enough. The last dragonkin fell, and the greatsword jerked Anton around toward Stedd. "No!" he told it, just as Shandri had, silently adding, be patient. I have plenty of foes left to kill.

The blade quieted, humoring his quaint, irrational notion that some people ought not to be slaughtered.

Oblivious to his argument with the weapon, Jamark shot him a grin. "Nice sword," the scarred man said.

So it was, in its repellent way. Anton had assumed it lay amid Eshcaz's hoard but now reckoned he understood why it didn't. Tu'ala'keth hadn't presented the weapon to the red with the rest of her tribute, and lacking gems in the hilt or similar ornamentation, it looked like just an ordinary if well-made greatsword until someone pulled it from the scabbard. Eshcaz hadn't deigned to take any notice of it where it lay on the floor, enabling a dragonkin to claim it for itself.

Still it was remarkable luck that it had returned to Anton just when he needed it most. Tu'ala'keth, in her daft and arbitrary way, had decided the sword bore Umberlee's blessing, and if she were here, she'd doubtless tell him to thank the goddess or prattle of divine will manifesting itself in pattern and coincidence. He mulled such notions over for an instant then put them from his mind. He had more urgent things to think about.

"You were right," Stedd panted, blood seeping from a graze on his shoulder, "this is worth doing. Let's raid that armory then kill some more of them."

❧ ❧ ❧ ❧ ❧

As Wraxzala wheeled about the sky, casting her few remaining spells, shouting orders to the slaves in a voice worn hoarse and raw, she marveled at how quickly an army's fortunes could shift.

She and her comrades had sneaked up the mountainside, to guard outposts, and small fields and gardens tucked away in pockets in the escarpment. They'd slaughtered dragonkin, cultists, and penned slaves—who might otherwise raise a commotion sufficient to rouse the rest of the enclave—wherever they found them. As long as the ixitxachitls had numbers and surprise on their side, it was relatively easy.

But at some point, one of the enemy, a dragonkin on the wing, perhaps, or a mage shifting himself instantly through space, had evidently escaped to raise the alarm. For in time, wyrms and a horde of their minions exploded from rifts in the rock.

The minions, though they made a reasonable effort to kill invaders, were virtually superfluous. It was the dragons who immediately started slaying their foes by the dozens, like the limitless might and malice of the Demon Ray himself embodied in gigantic snapping wings, roaring jaws, and slashing talons.

The largest wyrm wheeled, vomited flames, and burned ixitxachitls to drifting sparks and wisps of ash. A second dragon, its countenance studded with hornlets, spewed fumes, and a squad of locathahs dropped, skin dissolving, fins riddled with sizzling holes. A third conjured a glowing orb that hurtled down like a crossbow quarrel then exploded into leaping, dazzling arcs of lightning when it hit the ground. Transfixed by one or another of the radiating flares of power, koalinths danced spastically and withered to smoking husks. Perhaps lacking breath weapons and wizardry, the smallest drakes—which were still far bigger than the largest of their foes—ravaged them with fang and claw. Some were content to smash down into a mass of opponents, crushing some in the process, and fight on the ground until they wiped that cluster out. Others swooped, seized an opponent, carried it aloft to tear apart or simply drop from on high, and dived to catch another.

Wraxzala had participated in savage battles before and watched significant numbers of her allies perish. The difference this time was that they scarcely seemed to be inflicting any damage in return. Most of the drakes had crossbow bolts jutting from their scaly hides. Some bore puncture wounds from the slaves' spears and tridents. Now and again, one even faltered or convulsed when a vampire 'chitl swooped in and bit it, or an attack spell pierced its mystical defenses.

Yet nothing balked them for more than a moment. After which they assailed the invaders as fiercely as before.

She realized bitterly that nonetheless, she and her comrades were accomplishing all Yzil expected of them. They were keeping the wyrms busy and enticing them to exhaust their breath weapons and sorcerous capabilities. They were softening them up for the confrontation to come.

In her folly, Wraxzala had dared to hope the diversionary force might somehow accomplish more, might actually defeat the foes counterattacking down the mountain, or failing that, that she might at least outlive the struggle. Now, however, it was clear just how unlikely that was to happen.

In her eyes, the contest became absolutely, incontrovertibly hopeless when the colossal red dragon conjured eight orbs of seething, crackling lightning, which then streaked down to strike and blast every third thrall in a ragged formation of koalinths.

The reptile then oriented on a squad of locathah crossbowmen, ostentatiously sucked in a breath, swelled its throat, and cocked back its head. The warriors discerned that the red's snout was pointing a little to the left, so they madly scrambled right. Most of them escaped the booming flare and kept right on running until the dragon furled its wings, slammed down immediately in front of them with a thud that started loose stone clattering down the mountainside, and roared into their terrified faces. The locathahs blundered about and fled in exactly the opposite direction.

The red was so certain of victory, and so contemptuous of its foes, that it was playing with them.

Enough of this! Wraxzala thought. If she disobeyed her devitan—and he survived to condemn her for it—her rank and life were forfeit, and that was why she'd lingered as long as she had. But it was plain she would surely die if she didn't get away.

Fortunately, she'd had the foresight to save a spell for the purpose. She declaimed the prayer, and darkness swirled and whispered into being all around her. For an instant the touch of it chilled her skin.

By day, a blot of inky shadow would itself be conspicuous against the sky, but by night, it would make Wraxzala effectively invisible. It was inconvenient that she couldn't see through it either, but that wouldn't be necessary just to distance herself from the island. She'd flee until she heard and smelled water below her; then she'd dive for the safety of the depths.

She wheeled, sped away, and a rhythmic flapping sounded somewhere above her. She wondered if she should change course, or dodge, but how, when she couldn't tell exactly where the dragon was in relation to herself? She was still trying to determine its exact position when gigantic claws punched through her body. Dazed with the shock of it, she dully remembered hearing that all a dragon's senses were acute, and the wyrm pulled her apart as if she were no more substantial than a jellyfish.

❖ ❖ ❖ ❖ ❖

It took a lot of killing just to reach the enormous chamber at the top of the mountain. Tu'ala'keth observed that by the time they cleared it of enemies, most of Yzil's thralls were dead. But that was all right. They'd served their purpose.

Weary from fighting, she cast about, making sure the cave was as she remembered it. Then she pointed, noticing as she did so that her hand was spattered and tacky with gore. Fighting on land was a filthy business.

"Eshcaz has to come in either there," she said, "or over there. Those are the only holes big enough to admit him. So we'll set up by that wall, as far as possible from both of them."

Hovering, body rippling, Yzil studied the corner in question. Blood oozed down from a superficial cut above his eyes, and he blinked and swiped it away with a flick of his tail. "We'll be boxed in," he said.

"It does not matter," she replied. "Either we will kill the red, or he will kill us. It is unlikely we could retreat and get away."

"I suppose so." The devitan raised his voice. "Follow me, warriors of Ixzethlin, and be quick about it. We may have very little time in which to prepare."

The other 'chitls, who'd been either gliding about, investigating the chamber, or feeding on dead or crippled cultists and dragonkin, obeyed him. When everyone was in position, Tu'ala'keth opened her satchel and pulled out the book inside.

The heavy volume consisted of plates of horn inlaid with characters of onyx, agate, and obsidian, and perforated on one edge so a chain of worked coral like her silverweave could bind them together. It was plain from the construction that someone other than 'chitls had made it. They were literate, but books of the sort employed by shalarins and sea-elves were awkward for them. For an instant she wondered again where and how her allies had obtained the precious thing then put the irrelevant question aside.

Straining, she snapped the coral chain, gave one page to each 'chitl cleric, and kept the remainder for herself. Perhaps some of 'chitls resented a "slave creature" retaining most of the magic, but it was in accordance with Yzil's orders. He understood that just as she, by virtue of her anatomy, had been best suited to carry the tome, so she, possessed of hands, would be best able to flip from one leaf to another as circumstances required.

She started to read the trigger phrase of one of the preserved spells, and others did likewise, their voices muddling together. The carved stones glittered, flashed, and sometimes crumbled as they delivered themselves of the power stored inside. The gathering magic made everything look somehow too vivid, too real, and therefore frightening, like looming, leering faces in a delirium. The granite groaned beneath her feet.

Eshcaz watched his troops form into squads then tramp forth to scour the island. If any of the invaders had escaped the massacre, the dragonkin and humans would find and kill them. They were competent enough to manage that, anyway.

Once certain his minions were setting about their work with sufficient zeal, he then prowled over the battleground in search of plunder and morsels to eat.

Considering how many had fallen, the latter were surprisingly different to locate because, for the most part, the dragons had sensibly kept to the air, out of reach of the enemies' hand weapons, and annihilated them with spells and breath effects. Which was to say, burned the corpses to charcoal, poisoned them with acids and other malignancies, or blasted and ripped them to such small fragments that it would be awkward and undignified for a creature the size of Eshcaz to bother with the crumbs.

Fortunately, he wasn't actually hungry. It was simply his custom to sample his enemies' flesh after any fight. It made the victory seem complete.

Something flopped feebly on the ground before him. He scrutinized it then grinned. He'd discovered a still-living ixitxachitl, and eating a live enemy was even more satisfying than devouring a dead one.

He scooped the ixitxachitl up in his jaws. It writhed and shrieked for a second as he chewed; then it was too maimed for even that bit of impotent resistance.

He swallowed it whole then turned to the black-robed, skull-masked priest of Velsharoon who'd been trailing him about, awaiting orders. "Tastes like chicken," he said. It was a human joke, and he didn't really understand why it was supposed to be funny, but the cleric laughed dutifully.

Then a ghostly, grayish figure wavered into existence between the two of them. With a twinge of unease, Eshcaz saw that it was Diero, or rather, a conjured semblance that would allow the two of them to speak over a distance. The wearer or purple's snowy hair, which he always kept neatly combed, now dangled over his sweaty brow. He was breathing hard, too, his shrewd features taut with urgency.

"What's wrong?" the dragon asked.

"The warriors you just fought constituted a feint. While they kept you occupied, a larger force climbed up into the mountain from the sea caves, dividing as they progressed to invade every gallery and tunnel. Those of us who stayed inside are trying to fight them, but we're heavily outnumbered. It's difficult to stop them from going wherever they want and holding any position they choose to occupy."

The dragon snarled, angry at the sea creatures for tricking him and at Diero for having been right that it was a poor idea to leave the caverns. Had the magician been physically present, the red might even have clawed him, just to rip away any smugness or sense of superiority that he might be harboring inside.

Eshcaz struggled to calm himself. It was galling that the wyrms would have to fight their way back into their own stronghold, that they'd already expended a measure of their arcane abilities, and that in the confined spaces within the mountain, their wings would prove less of advantage. But even so, surely this fiasco was only a momentary nuisance.

They were, after all, dragons, and he, the most powerful red the Sea of Fallen Stars had ever known. It was insane to imagine that lesser creatures could defeat them under any circumstances whatsoever.

"I'll deal with it," he said, spreading his wings.

"Wait, please!" Diero said. "Listen to me. We don't know why the ixitxachitls attacked us or the full extent of their plans, but if they destroy the work we've been doing, it will set us back by months."

Curse him! He was right again. "What needs protecting most urgently?" Eshcaz asked. "The grand pentacle?"

"Yes. A bit of chiseling at the right point, coupled with the proper counterspell, could ruin it almost beyond repair. I'm trying to head in that direction."

"I will, too." Eshcaz glared at the priest of Velsharoon. "Tell everyone I order them back inside to kill more intruders." He lashed his pinions and sprang into the air.

❖ ❖ ❖ ❖ ❖

Tu'ala'keth trembled as Eshcaz burst into the chamber. She reminded herself that she was a waveservant, and her reflexive dread subsided to a degree.

She glanced from side to side. Hunkered on the floor, crouched over their pages from the compendium of priestly magic, the 'chitls were likely frightened, too. In some cases, their long tails lashed in agitation. But nobody tried to flee.

The red began to charge in eerie silence. That wasn't his doing but theirs. They'd shrouded his side of the chamber in an enchantment that stifled sound to keep him from reciting incantations.

Perhaps Eshcaz realized what they'd done, for he gave them a sneer, as if to scorn the suggestion he needed sorcery to slaughter tiny creatures like themselves. Then he bounded far enough to trigger a second ward.

Whoever had originally crafted the ixitxachitls' book, he must have been a supremely wise and able priest of the sea because he'd stored extraordinary magic in the gemstone lines. A huge wave of saltwater surged up from the dry stone floor and smashed into the dragon. Even his strength, weight, and momentum couldn't withstand the prodigious force. The wave tumbled him all the way backward to slam against the wall before dissipating into nothingness.

The impact didn't even stun him, though. He scrambled to his feet in an instant, cocked his head back, and spat a bright jet of flame. The flare rustled as it left the zone of quiet, then hissed explosively when it met the enchantment the invaders had emplaced to counter fire. Blocked short of its targets, Eshcaz's breath produced a gout of steam at its terminus, as if it had struck an invisible, freestanding wall of water. In a metaphysical sense, that was precisely what had happened.

Tu'ala'keth read the final trigger phrase from one of the pages, and the entire sheet of horn shattered in her grasp. Fortunately, the magic, once unleashed, could strike anyplace, even where silence reigned, and Eshcaz thrashed, stricken.

She'd filled his lungs with water, a bane that ought to kill him, but he mastered his convulsions and retched it forth. Because of the heat in his vitals, most of it burst out in another gout of steam.

By that time, Yzil and another 'chitl had also conjured attacks. A cloud of luminous blue-green wraiths in the form of sharks appeared with the dragon at their center. They whirled around him biting and tearing until he leaped clear of the effect.

Canny enough to know that particular magic couldn't shift to pursue him, he paid it no further heed.

Instead he oriented on Tu'ala'keth and the 'chitls then jerked as the next spell took hold of him. His scaly hide withered, cracking and flaking. But it blurred back to normal a heartbeat later as resilience of soul or body enabled him to withstand the curse.

Enraged, his shark bites bleeding, he hurled himself at his tormentors, and another wave arose and threw him backward. He spat more flame, and it, too, halted short of the mark in a burst of steam.

"By the Five Torments!" cried one of the ixitxachitls. "We're doing it! We're killing a dragon!"

Though she saw no point in contradicting it—it would fight better jubilant than afraid—Tu'ala'keth thought its judgment was, at best, premature. For even the supremely powerful magic sealed in the book of horn hadn't done Eshcaz any serious harm as yet. The second wave, moreover, hadn't flung him backward as far as the first, while his second jet of flame had shot a little closer before their defense balked it. His exertions were eroding the wards, and it was impossible to guess whether they'd manage to kill him before he succeeded in breaking through.

But in essence, this was a clash between fire and water, and there was no flame Umberlee could not drown. She dragged down the sun and devoured it every night without fail, obliging Lathander, god of the dawn, to craft a new one each morning. If Tu'ala'keth could simply reflect the infinite majesty of her patron, then surely she, too, must prevail. She reached and from somewhere—inside herself or Fury's Heart, it was ultimately the same thing—flowed the pure cold malice of the Queen of the Depths to steady and exalt her. She searched through the plates of horn for the spell she wanted next.

Diero peeked around the corner just as Hsala-nasharanx collapsed with so many writhing, flapping ixitxachitls clinging to her that her serpentine shape was almost indistinguishable. Even so, he expected the green to heave herself to her feet again or roll and crush her attackers. She didn't, though, and as they sucked and slurped at the wounds their fangs had inflicted, it became apparent she never would.

The magician cursed under his breath. He hadn't liked Hsalanasharanx any more than he liked—well, any of the wyrms, to be truthful about it—but they were all important to realizing his own ambitions. Besides which, the victorious 'chitls and their gill-men servitors were blocking yet another route to the grand pentacle.

He wondered if he and Olna, supported by the dozen other cultists who were following them around, could fight their way through this particular clump of invaders. Perhaps, but it would be a messy, time-consuming business. Better to go around if they could.

He and his comrades skulked back the way they'd come, through shadowy tunnels echoing with the muddled roar of combat. It was all but impossible to tell precisely where or how close the sounds originated, and he worried he might turn a corner and find himself instantly caught up in a melee. He knew a spell that could have conjured a phantom to scout ahead for him, and wished he'd had the foresight to prepare it at the start of the day. But who could have predicted insanity like this?

He suddenly felt the pressure of another's gaze. He pivoted and cast about, but saw only the passageway and the murky irregular mouths of side tunnels and galleries.

"I don't see anything," Olna said.

"Neither do I," he replied. "But somebody was

watching us. He simply ducked out of sight when I turned around." As both mage and soldier, he'd learned to trust his intuition.

"Do you want to spend time looking for him?" the blond woman asked.

Frowning, he took a heartbeat to consider then said, "No. We have more important matters to concern us. Onward."

In another minute, they came to point where a lava tube squirmed upward, the ascent steep enough that, at his direction, his followers and captives had chiseled stairs. He listened, trying to determine if any of the ambient noise was filtering down from above, and as usual, he couldn't tell.

He led his companions upward and—praise be to the Lady of Mysteries!—encountered nothing lurking on the steps to bar the way. The twisting shaft opened onto one of the ledges overlooking the great chamber; after what had felt like hours of fighting and sneaking, they'd finally reached their destination. He raised a hand, ordering everyone else to hold his position, then prowled to the edge of the platform and peered downward.

The vista below was peculiar enough that it took a moment to make sense of it. Acrid smoke and warm, wet steam mingled in the air. Bloodied and to all appearances berserk with rage, Eshcaz beat his gigantic wings and ascended to the high, domed ceiling. But the pinions didn't rustle and crack or make any sound at all.

Jaws gaping, foreclaws poised to catch and rend, Eshcaz dived at those creatures who were making noise, murmuring ixitxachitls strangely hunkered on the floor, a few terrified gill-men arrayed to guard them, and—Diero blinked. Was that the same demented shalarin who'd intruded here before?

A waterspout whirled up from the stone floor to

intercept the plummeting Eshcaz. It caught him, engulfed him, and whirled him backward before dissipating as suddenly as it had appeared. The red couldn't sort out his wings and the rest of his body quickly enough to resume an attitude of flight, and he fell ingloriously, slamming down on the stone.

At the same instant, other spells assailed him.

Branching and extending like flowing water, a lattice of ice formed on his skin, binding him, searing his scales with its frigidity, until he flailed and shattered it.

A black cloud boiled into the air above the wyrm. Lightning flared in its belly, and thunder would surely have boomed an instant later except for the field of silence. Rain hammered down, mingled with a harsher liquid that blistered the reptile's hide.

Diero scowled. He'd wasted a moment in professional appreciation of the rather neat trap Tu'ala'keth and her allies had lain for Eshcaz, and to be honest, in enjoyment at seeing the arrogant dragon discomfited. But it was time to intervene. If the acidic downpour could burn the red, it was conceivable it could mar granite and deface the grand pentacle as well.

Fortunately, with a wyrm to occupy them, none of the sea folk had noticed him perched on the ledge. So long as he was quiet about it, he should be able to conjure without interference, and better still, his foes had emplaced their defenses in relation to Eshcaz on the other side of the hall. He doubted they had anything oriented to deflect an attack striking down from his angle.

Diero extracted a bit of lace from the pocket of his vestments. Tied up inside were bits of phosphorus and saltpeter. He swept the bundle through the proper pass and whispered the appropriate words of power.

Tu'ala'keth burst into flame. She reeled and dropped a stack of clattering rectangular plates. Gouts of fire leaped from her body to the nearest ixitxachitls and gill-men. They didn't start blazing like torches in their turn. The spell wasn't quite that deadly. But the secondary effect did sear whatever it touched, and the creatures thrashed and floundered at the pain.

The black cloud and its downpour wavered out of existence. It had required the concentration of one of the spellcasters down below to sustain it, and Diero had just disrupted that.

He could see that, in their shock, pain, and confusion, the sea creatures hadn't yet determined where the attack had originated. He should have time to cast another.

It was a burst of glare, and he scrunched his eyes shut so his own magic wouldn't blind him. Afterward, the rays and fish-men crawled or stumbled about helplessly, so bereft of sight they couldn't even avoid Tu'ala'keth, still lurching to and fro like a living bonfire. Tendrils of flame lashed out at them whenever they blundered close to her, or she to them.

Diero waved Olna forward. "You see the water creatures," he said. "They're helpless for the moment. You make sure they stay that way, and I'll dismantle the wards they set." He glanced back at the remainder of his followers. "You fellows, watch for trouble coming up the stairs."

Anton knew it would be stupid to outdistance his comrades, who possessed no supernatural means of enhancing their vigor and suppressing fatigue, or to make any more noise than necessary. Still it took an effort not to run up the steps.

He and the others had given a good accounting of themselves as they prowled through the caves. They'd killed a fair number of cultists and dragonkin, and because of his hatred of these particular foes, reinforced by the greatsword's blood-thirst, he'd enjoyed every second of it.

But such accomplishments paled to insignificance the moment he peeked from one tunnel to the next and sighted Diero, wearer of purple, master wizard, and the whoreson who'd sent him to the rack. Diero *had* to die, to satisfy Anton's need for retribution and, quite possibly, to ensure the defeat of the entire enclave of wyrm worshipers.

Peering upward, trying to penetrate the gloom, Anton skulked around a twist and beheld the uppermost section of the shaft, lit by the wavering glow of a single oil lamp set in a nook halfway up. At the top was an opening, and on other side of it, barely visible in the darkness, two men stood gazing downward. They spotted him and started yelling.

Anton charged as best he could, dashing up a crudely chiseled flight of stairs. The shadows above him shouldered crossbows. He bellowed, "Archers!" and threw himself down on the risers. The quarrels thrummed over him, but one thunked into the body of someone at his back. The fellow made a low sobbing sound.

There was no time to turn and find out who'd taken the wound or how bad it was. The erstwhile prisoners couldn't stay where they were, or the enemy would shoot them all dead. Anton jumped up and scrambled onward.

Figures scurried in the natural doorway above as the crossbowmen, their weapons useless until cocked and loaded once again, yielded their places to two other cultists. The new men pointed spears down at the captives then jabbed with them to bar the way and halt Anton's ascent.

They had the advantage of the high ground and weapons even longer than the greatsword. So long as they maintained their current defensive posture, it would be difficult to get at them, but it would be likewise difficult for them to score on Anton. That, however, didn't matter. Behind them, barely visible between their shifting bodies, a woman with a long blond braid was chanting an intricate rhyme. The spearmen were simply giving her time to complete the spell unmolested.

Anton hacked at a lance. The greatsword sheared through the seasoned ash and chopped the point off. If the spearman knew his business, the remainder of the weapon could still pose a threat but not as deadly a one as before.

Anton paused for an instant, as if he'd overcommitted to the stroke and couldn't come back on guard quickly. The second spearman took the bait and thrust at his exposed flank. The spy pivoted, used the greatsword to bat the lance out of line, and bounded upward, safely past the long steel point. He cut at the cultist he'd just outfoxed, and the dark blade smashed through his ribs and into his vitals.

At the same moment, though, the blond woman finished her incantation and sucked in a deep breath. Knowing he couldn't free and lift the sword in time to threaten her, Anton averted his face and pressed himself against the wall of the lava tube.

The wizard expelled her breath into a searing conical cloud. Anton's skin burned wherever the corrosive vapor brushed it, and on the steps below him, other captives cried out in pain.

He couldn't let the shock of injury balk him, nor allow the witch to cast another attack spell. The greatsword agreed and steadied him with a surge of strength and anger. He jerked it from the first spearman's body and cut down the second one then another cultist who rushed in with a short sword. That cleared a path to the magician.

He sprang out onto what he now perceived was one of the natural balconies overlooking the big cave at the top of the volcano. Smoke and steam swirled through the air, and fire flickered somewhere down below, but he couldn't tell what was burning. Too many people were in the way.

The witch goggled as if astonished he'd survived her initial attack. She started jabbering a second incantation, and the words slurred into a gargling sound as the greatsword crunched into her skull.

Anton stepped deeper into the mass of cultists and cut at another foe. His enemies were all around him now, and even an enchanted sword wouldn't save him from a stab in the back. Only his comrades could do that—assuming any were still alive and fit to fight.

Cries of fury and scrambling footsteps established that they were. They swarmed out onto the platform and ripped into the cultists. Jamark swung a mace. A cultist managed to catch the blow on his shield, but the force sent him stumbling backward to topple off the ledge. Stedd drove a sword into an opponent's chest and laughed crazily. Then the eyes rolled up in his head as the other man, mortally wounded but not dead yet, thrust a blade into his torso. They took a lurching sidestep together, like spastic dancers.

As he fought, Anton looked for Diero but at first couldn't spot him amid the frenzied press. Finally, though, the master of the enclave, with his trim frame, purple vestments, and silvery hair, came into view. To the spy's surprise, Diero was facing outward, away from the battle. His hands slashed through mystic passes, and it looked as if he might be trying to complete a conjuration begun before the escaped slaves intruded on the proceedings.

Anton struggled toward the wizard. If Lady Luck smiled, he might reach him in time to cut him down from behind and spoil the magic, whatever it was.

But he had to kill another cultist first, and it was too late.

A prodigious roar sounded from the floor of the chamber below. Flickering firelight cast a gigantic serpentine shadow on the wall. By the Lanceboard, had there been a wyrm down there all along? Why had the cursed thing kept so quiet until this moment?

There was no time to ponder that, either. Diero was the immediate threat. The wearer of purple called something—Anton couldn't make out the words—to the dragon then turned toward his embattled followers and their assailants. His gaze fell on Anton. He murmured a word and extended his hand, and a bastinado appeared in it. He swept the cane through an occult figure.

Anton rushed in and made a chest cut. Diero hopped back, and the attack fell short. He flicked the bastinado through a final backhanded stroke, as if chastising a thrall.

Agony tore through Anton's body. It was worst in his guts, and he doubled over. Tears blurred his vision.

Diero tossed away the stick to vanish in midair. He took something from a pocket and brandished that instead. Ripples of distortion seethed around his hand.

Anton had little doubt that the follow-up spell, if completed, would mean the end of him. He had to straighten up and strike. Had to. Had to. He sucked in a breath, bellowed it out, and heaved himself upright. The curse inflicted a final spasm, and the torment faded.

But perhaps it had delayed him long enough. Diero lifted the fist clutching the spell focus as if grasping a dagger in an overhand grip. It looked as if it must be the penultimate move in the conjuration. When he stabbed downward, the magic would blaze into existence.

Anton cut as the hand plunged down. The great-sword clipped the extremity off just above the wrist. Blood spurted from the stump. Diero's face paled all at once, and his mouth fell open. Anton pulled the dark blade back for the death stroke.

"The torturer wanted to break you," whimpered Diero, gripping his truncated forearm in a thus-far unsuccessful attempt to stanch the bleeding. "I saved you."

"That was a mistake," Anton replied. He decided to behead Diero, shifted the sword into the proper atti-tude, then hesitated.

Because somehow, in spite of all his hatred and anger, all the terror and excitement of combat, he'd abruptly remembered he was a spy. A gatherer of secrets, and it was certain no one on Tan knew more secrets about the Cult of the Dragon than its resident wearer of purple.

Still he *yearned* to kill Diero, and the greatsword urged him on. His arms trembled with the need to cut. He gave a wordless cry, denying the impulse, and kicked the wizard's feet out from under him instead. Once his foe was down, he booted him in the chin then stamped on the fingers of his remaining hand. Even if Diero escaped death by exsanguination, the fractures should keep him from casting any more spells.

As Anton finished, he heard the wyrm on the cavern floor snarling what sounded like an incanta-tion of its own. He rushed to the drop-off to see what was happening.

To his dismay, the dragon was Eshcaz, the most for-midable of them all. The red bore a number of wounds, but if they'd weakened him, it wasn't apparent from his carriage. Eshcaz declaimed the final syllable of his spell, and a soft, oozing, semitransparent wall appeared midway across the chamber. It looked like water piled up on top of itself, like a tall wave that refused to curl and break.

Rather, the mass simply lost cohesion, shattered, and all the liquid plunged toward the floor. It vanished into nothingness, though, before it could raise a splash. Eshcaz strode toward the opposite end of the cavern and the defenseless creatures gathered there.

Most were ixitxachitls and gill-men, crawling, stumbling, or gliding erratically about in manifest confusion and distress. One, however, was a shalarin shrouded in bright, crackling flame, as if someone had dipped it in oil and set it alight. That one rolled back and forth on the ground.

After her first clash with Kassur, Anton had explained to Tu'ala'keth that if she ever caught fire, dropping and rolling was the way to put it out. Was that her?

Maybe it was, though he couldn't imagine how she could have returned at the head of an ixitxachitl army. As he understood it, the demon rays were hostile to the Nantarn Alliance. Still, what other shalarin could it be?

He reflected grimly that in another moment, it wouldn't much matter who it had been. The shalarin and its allies were helpless, and Eshcaz was about to kill them. Even if Anton had cared to intervene on behalf of a creature who'd given him to the cultists to torture and enslave, he could only delay the inevitable for a moment or two at most, and that at the cost of his own life.

He knew it, jumped off the ledge anyway, and couldn't even say why. He wondered if the sword's irrational, implacable bloodlust had prompted him then decided it didn't matter. Though he was committing suicide, it felt right: pure, in a black and ferocious way.

The final spell in his meager store allowed him

to land softly as a drifting wisp of gossamer, without injury or even a jolt. He charged instantly.

Eshcaz must have been intent on the creatures who'd evidently managed to wound him previously, or else the ambient noise and stinks masked Anton's approach, for despite the dragon's keen senses, he didn't notice the newcomer. Anton cut deep into his flank.

Eshcaz roared and spun around toward his foe, which meant the world shattered into a chaos of sweeping tail and trampling feet. Anton had to duck, dodge, and scramble just to avoid being crushed before the red even oriented on him and made an actual attack.

Eshcaz glared with eyes like hellfire. He opened his fangs, and his wedge-shaped head surged forward and down at the end of the serpentine neck. Anton waited until the final instant—dodge too soon and a foe would simply compensate—then wrenched himself aside. The gigantic jaws clashed shut beside him, and he cut at the dragon's mask.

His sword glanced off the wyrm's scales. Eshcaz flicked his head sideways, and the great bony mass of it smashed into Anton like a battering ram, flinging him through the air and down on the floor. Claws loomed above him and slashed, and he rolled out from underneath. The dragon immediately leaped, trying to smash down on top of him. He scrambled back and just got clear. When Eshcaz slammed down, the cavern shook.

Anton got his feet planted, poised the greatsword to cut, then glimpsed motion at the periphery of his vision. He had to forgo his own attack to jump away from another sweep of Eshcaz's talons.

Well, he thought, at least I managed to cut the bastard once. He feinted left then scuttled right, trying to get back on the red's flank. Eshcaz sneered, and with a quickness incredible in a thing so huge, matched him shift for shift. Wisps of smoke seeped from his nostrils and between his fangs.

Tu'ala'keth rolled and rolled, and still fire clung to her like a horde of leeches. She wondered if Anton—who had, after all, betrayed her in the end—had lied about the way to put out such a conflagration. Perhaps rolling intensified the flames.

But they finally guttered out, either because she'd smothered them or because the curse that had kindled them had run out its time. She tried to lift her head, and even with the fire gone, her entire body cried out in agony.

She slumped back down and might even have stayed that way, too daunted to try again, except that Eshcaz was roaring and snarling, and once she noticed, she remembered how wrong that was. She shouldn't be able to hear the red. Silence was an essential component of the defenses against him.

Despite the torture of charred skin cracking and splitting, she managed to take a look around. The surviving 'chitls and locathahs appeared as helpless as she was. Though she hadn't truly been able to see through her shroud of flame, she'd had a vague impression of a succession of mystical attacks hammering them, and it was evidently so.

Eshcaz was on their side of the cave, and no wave or waterspout was forming to shove him back. Plainly, all the wards were gone. The red would no doubt have finished off his original adversaries already, except that a lone human had appeared from somewhere to challenge him. He had an octopus tattooed on one arm and wielded a huge sword with shadow drifting and twisting inside the steel—impossible as it seemed, it was Anton!

Naturally, he couldn't prevail against Eshcaz. It was miraculous he'd lasted any time at all. But magic had hurt the dragon. If Anton could keep the creature busy a little longer, it was at least remotely possible it might finish the job of killing the red.

Of course, she didn't mean her own personal magic. Even if she were still capable of articulating a complete incantation with the necessary precision, it simply wasn't strong enough. But the remaining spells bound in Yzil's book might serve.

She expected to find the pages lying right beside her. When she didn't, though, she dimly recalled dropping them at the moment she burst into flame then reeling blindly about before she fell. She looked around and spotted them scattered a few feet away. As weak and anguished as she felt, it was like peering through a scrying mirror and observing them on the far side of the world.

She started crawling on her belly. Her silverweave rattled and clinked. Bits of ruined skin broke off and flaked away.

The pain was like a tide trying to sweep her into darkness, and she had to fight the desire to let it take her. Umberlee, she thought, Umberlee, Umberlee, Umberlee. It was as much of a prayer as she could manage.

Finally she reached the sheets of horn. Certain she was on the very brink of losing consciousness, she pawed through them to find the first spell she needed. That was almost as difficult as crawling. Her cooked fingers couldn't bend or grasp.

Here! Here it was, but could she actually use it? Though mercifully short compared to an entire spell, the trigger phrase required accurate enunciation, too, and she wasn't sure she even still had a voice. Maybe the fire had burned that away also.

She sought to steady herself, to hold back the pain

that might otherwise have made stammer and stumble, then tried to whisper. The words came out faintly but clearly.

Magic washed over her like the caress of the sea. Pain faded. Scorched and blistered skin blurred, flowed, and became smooth and soft. Her dorsal fin, which had nearly burned away, extended into the high, scalloped crest it had been before.

She looked at the battle just a few yards away. Somehow, Anton was still on his feet. Perhaps Eshcaz was playing with him. The dragon's chest pumped, and his neck swelled in time. If she'd seen a lesser air-breather doing that, she would have inferred it was winded. But the red's strength seemed inexhaustible, and judging from the smoke streaming from his mouth and nostrils, she suspected he was actually recharging his depleted breath weapon.

Once he accomplished that, his foes would have no hope at all. She hastily returned to the pages of Yzil's book. They were depleted, also, the majority of spells cast already, and most of the remaining ones, duplicates of invocations that had already failed to put the dragon down.

But one potentially crippling spell remained. She would have attempted it already, except that it required the caster to touch the target, and she and her allies had hoped to stay away from him. But now that their defenses had fallen, that was no longer a consideration.

She murmured the trigger phrase, and an aching throbbed deep in her right hand. It was bearable enough—compared to the agony of burning, it was almost laughable—but even so, she could sense the profound malignancy it represented. Fortunately, it was incapable of inflicting its devastation on her.

She cast about, found her trident, snatched it up in her off hand, and ran forward. Though seemingly intent on Anton, Eshcaz must have heard her coming or else felt the bane she harbored in her flesh, for he whirled to face her.

His neck bulged, and his head cocked back. His flame had renewed itself, and he was about to spit it at her, while she was still nowhere near enough to touch him. Nor did she have any realistic hope of dodging the great expanding blaze that was his breath.

But Anton rushed the foe who'd pivoted away from him. Its seething darkness smeared with gore, the greatsword swung high and swept down to bury itself in Eshcaz's side.

It must have found a vulnerable spot, for the dragon convulsed, and the spasm made him spew his flame too high. Tu'ala'keth threw herself to the floor, and the crackling flare passed harmlessly above her. The fierce heat was unpleasant, but did her no harm.

Eshcaz rounded furiously on Anton, which required twisting away from her. She scrambled up and charged. The red lifted a foreleg to rake at the swordsman, and she planted her hand midway along the limb.

She winced at the blistering heat of the reptile's body. Then the power she'd invoked leaped from her flesh into his, and he screeched. His scaly hide split again and again, into a crosshatch of gashes. Between the cuts, sores opened to seep and fester, and knotted tumors bulged. A milky cataract sealed one blazing golden eye.

The dragon shuddered and took a stumbling step. Tu'ala'keth stabbed him repeatedly with her trident. She suspected that, on the other side of the gigantic creature, Anton was attacking just as relentlessly, doing his utmost to take advantage of Eshcaz's vulnerability.

Then, unbelievably, the red regained control of his ravaged body. A wing snapped down out of nowhere to swat Tu'ala'keth to the ground. Eshcaz poised his head to seize her in his fangs. She tried to spring back to her feet, but dazed, could only clamber clumsily. It wasn't going to be quick enough.

But the wyrm's head slammed down beside her. His body listed ponderously to the side then toppled. His limbs flailed, feet clawing, tail lashing, but not at any target. After a few moments, the thrashing subsided. He shivered and lay dead.

Tu'ala'keth surmised that as Eshcaz had prepared to strike at her, Anton must have scored a final, fatal blow. She started around the enormous corpse to find the human.

❧ ❧ ❧ ❧ ❧

Anton slumped over, panting, the end of the greatsword resting on the floor. For the moment, he was too exhausted to hold it up.

Cheering sounded from overhead. He looked up at the ledge. His fellow captives had won the fight against the cultists. Good for them. He didn't blame the survivors for declining to climb down to the cavern floor and fight Eshcaz. The Red Knight knew, it was the craziest, stupidest thing he'd ever done, and the fact that he'd somehow prevailed didn't make it any less idiotic.

Tu'ala'keth stalked around the great mound of Eshcaz's carcass to remind him he hadn't prevailed unaided. As was often the case, he couldn't read her expression. Behind her, some of the afflicted ixitxachitls had finally recovered from whatever magical effect had ailed them. Bodies rippling, they glided forward.

He had no idea what to expect of the comrade he'd attempted to murder, or of her allies either. Until now, he and his band had avoided contact with the ixitxachitls. Partly it was because they were afraid the 'chitls wouldn't be able to distinguish between human captives and human cultists. But it was also because of the 'chitls' reputation as raiders and vampires. Under normal circumstances, they were hostile to mankind.

Still the current situation was far from normal, and he felt an obligation to try to look after his comrades. "My friends," he said, pointing, "fought alongside you, even if you didn't notice. They helped me kill the wearer of purple. I ask that they be allowed to take the cog on the beach and depart in peace."

"The 'chitls," said Tu'ala'keth, "have no use for slaves who cannot live underwater. I expect I can persuade them."

"Thank you." He hesitated. "What about me? Where do I stand?"

"It appears," she said, "that you have resumed your role as Umberlee's champion." A ixitxachitl with blistered hide and a cut above its eyes came flying up beside her. "How, then, can I do anything but accept you as my ally?"

He smiled. "I can think of one or two other things I might do in your place. So thank you again."

"Eshcaz is dead. But it is possible some wyrms and cultists are still holding out. Let us rest for a while then go kill them."

THE **P**RIESTS

Despite the handicap of broken fingers, Diero had managed to fumble the belt from around his waist, loop it around his stump, pull the makeshift tourniquet tight by clenching the end in his teeth, and stanch the bleeding. It had been the most difficult thing he'd ever done, and now he wondered if it had been a waste of effort.

For a quick death might have been preferable to his current circumstances. The victors had locked him in the bare, stony misery of a slave cell. Tu'ala'keth had used her magic to, in effect, cauterize the end of his mutilated arm. But she'd done nothing to mend his fractured jaw and fingers, and all his injuries throbbed in time with the beating of his heart.

He suspected the pain, severe as it was, would pale in comparison to torments to come.

He needed to escape, which meant he needed his magic. He tried to articulate a simple cantrip, but garbled the words. He strained to crook his swollen fingers into an arcane sign, and that was hopeless, too.

"I respect a man," a bass voice drawled, "who doesn't give up easily."

Startled, Diero jerked around. Anton and Tu'ala'keth stood outside the iron grille, looking in at him. He realized he was so weak from blood loss, shock, and dehydration, so sunk in his own wretchedness, that he hadn't even noticed their arrival. He struggled against an unfamiliar impulse to cringe from them.

Anton recited a charm then swung the rasping door open. "I still haven't found the key to this thing. I'm lucky I never needed it."

Tu'ala'keth approached Diero where he slumped on the granite floor. "I am going to heal your jaw," she said. "If you then attempt to conjure, Anton and I will kill you." She recited a prayer, took his chin in her webbed blue fingers, and gave it a little jerk.

A bolt of agony stabbed through his head. But afterward, his jaw didn't ache as it had before. He worked it gingerly, and it clicked. The bone seemed intact and in its proper place.

"We brought you a drink, too," Anton said. He pulled the cork from a waterskin and held it to Diero's lips. The magician gulped the lukewarm liquid. For a moment all he could think of was how wonderful it felt to slake his thirst.

Anton took the sloshing pigskin bag away. "That's enough for now."

"I know," Diero sighed. He'd watched thirsty men guzzle too quickly and make themselves ill.

"Now," said the spy, "let's take a walk."

Diero felt another jab of fear and struggled to mask it. "Where to? What do you want with me?"

"Explanations," said Tu'ala'keth. She hauled him to

his feet, and they marched him out of the cell, catching and steadying him when, in his weakness, he stumbled.

A miscellany of bodies littered the tunnels. Here and there, ixitxachitls glided and fish-men shambled about but not in great profusion. Diero suspected that after the battle, most of them had returned to the sea, thus conserving the magic that enabled them to function above it.

At one intersection lay the shredded carcass of a fire drake, still radiating warmth hours after its demise. "We only killed some of the wyrms," Anton said. "The rest flew away when they realized the outcome of the battle was in doubt. Not very loyal to their devoted worshipers, are they?"

"No," Diero said. He wished the invaders had killed them all. Had Eshcaz only heeded him, none of this would be happening.

His captors conducted him to the upper levels, where the cult's mages, priests, and artisans had labored to produce dracoliches and where their conquerors had heaped amulets, swords, scrolls, battle-axes, quivers of arrows, vials, wands, and books atop a worktable. The pile seemed almost to glow, to radiate a palpable tingle of arcane force.

Diero recognized many of the items but not all. He inferred that in addition to plundering the shrines, libraries, and conjuring chambers, the invaders had located Eshcaz's hoard wherever it lay hidden deep in the mountain. The bastards were clever, he had to give them that.

"Given time," said Tu'ala'keth, "I could study these articles and learn all about them. But I do not have time, so you will help me. You will tell me what they are, how they work, and how they can best be employed to kill dragons."

Despite repeated efforts to muster his courage,

Diero still felt weak and afraid. But if he hoped to help himself, now was the time. "Why should I?" he replied.

"The rack survived the battle," Anton said. "I checked. Maybe you'd like to find out how it feels to be stretched. Or what life is like without any hands at all."

Diero gave him a level stare. "You can certainly torture me. I'll break eventually. Everybody does. But I'll hold out as long as I can. Perhaps long enough to ruin the shalarin's plans. Or maybe the stress will kill me outright. At present, I'm not strong."

"What do you want?" asked Tu'ala'keth.

"Freedom, once I supply what you need."

"No," Anton said. "Even leaving my personal feelings out of it, my chief would flog me if I agreed to that. But I will offer this: When my fellow captives leave the island, you'll go along as their prisoner. They'll hand you over to the Turmian navy and earn themselves a bounty. They deserve some recompense for their suffering, and the 'chitls won't let them carry away any gold.

"From then on," the spy continued, "my superiors will decide what becomes of you, and they just might spare your life if you cooperate. I've heard it said that one Cult of the Dragon coven knows nothing of the others. That way, no matter what calamity befalls it, it can't betray them. But you're a wearer of purple, and reasonably clever. I suspect you possess some information you shouldn't, and in a season when everyone's frantic to ferret out your conspiracy wherever it hides, you may be able to parlay it into soft treatment."

Diero shook his head. "No. I insist you release me."

"To Baator with that," Anton snapped. "You claim you can last under torture? I doubt it. I doubt you can take much pain at all."

Quick as a striking snake, he grabbed Diero's

broken fingers in his own and bore down hard. The
agony dropped the magician to his knees.

"All right!" he sobbed. "All right! We have a bargain."

"Good." Anton shifted his grip to Diero's forearm
and dragged him back to his feet. "Drink some more
water then tell us what we need to know."

Anton found Diero a chair. In his weakened condition, the wizard might have fainted if required to
remain on his feet much longer.

After that, Tu'ala'keth brought him the enchanted
articles one at a time. She didn't permit him to touch
them, and Anton hovered behind him with a dagger in
hand. In his experience, magicians were always dangerous, even when placed at a disadvantage.

It was difficult to remain vigilant, though, when
Diero's explanations were so intriguing, so promis-
ing. Some of the weapons possessed virtues enabling
them to strike dragons with extraordinary force and
precision. Scrolls contained spells to soften their scaly
armor, blind them to the presence of their foes, addle
their minds, or render the caster impervious to their
breath. Shields and coats of mail possessed magics to
fortify them against the bite of a wyrm or a swipe of
its talons.

"Checkmate's edge," Anton exclaimed at length.
"I suppose this is what we were hoping for, but I
don't understand it. I thought you cultists served
the wyrms. Why did you stockpile arms specifically
intended for use against them?"

Diero smiled a crooked smile. "We didn't. Not as
such. At its higher levels, the Cult of the Dragon is
a fellowship of wizards and priests—which is to say,
scholars—who venerate wyrms. When scholars take
an interest in a subject, they want to study it and learn

all about it, and one way to study dragons is to examine artifacts that pertain to them. So, over the decades, our cabal assembled an extensive collection of such things—including dragon banes.

"In addition to those," the mage continued, "you have the items from Eshcaz's horde. Before we mages woke him, he slept for so many human generations that most folk have forgotten him. But prior to that, he was the terror of the Sea of Fallen Stars. Armed with the finest gear desperate princes and hierarchs could provide, heroes used to challenge him on a regular basis. Obviously, after he killed them, he added their swords and staves to his treasure."

Anton shook his head to think he'd helped to slay not just a dragon, but a legendary one. It was the kind of thing a paladin in an epic might have done.

But of course he wasn't a paladin, and Tu'ala'keth and the rest of the sea folk had done the bulk of the slaying. He'd just landed a couple of cuts toward the end. With a snort, he resolved to put such fancies out of his head and focus on the matter at hand.

Which was to say, on a prospect that seemed brighter than he'd imagined possible before. He grinned at Tu'ala'keth. "Well, may the gods bless madmen and dragons both for hoarding because this means you've succeeded. You can use the blades and such to save Serôs."

The shalarin declined to enthuse along with him. The narrow face behind the inky goggles remained as dour as before. "No. They will be useful, but by themselves, insufficient."

"You're joking. I realize some of the items may not work underwater. But many will."

"You have not have seen the dragon flight. Nor have I, but I have heard it described by survivors. There are dozens of wyrms. If my people are no stand against them, we need something more."

Anton returned his attention to Diero. "Well," he said, "you heard her."

"Yes," the wearer of purple replied, "but I don't know what else to tell you. These are the weapons and talismans that were kept here. You found them all, and now know how to use them. I suppose I could give you some pointers on wyrm anatomy and how they tend to move in combat, but that wouldn't be sufficient either."

Anton placed the edge of his knife against the magician's neck. "If you can't help Tu'ala'keth enough for it to matter, you're not going to make it back to Turmish."

The touch of the blade made Diero stiffen, but when he answered, his voice was steady. "Break your word, slit my throat if you want, but I'm not holding back. Haven't you realized I'm not one of the zealots? I joined the cult to further my ambitions, and I'd gladly betray it to save my life. That's exactly what I have been doing."

"All right," Anton said. "In that case you need to tell us all you can about dragons and everything related to them." He was hoping that maybe, just maybe, the magician actually did possess the key to destroying the dragon flight but simply didn't realize it.

"You understand it'll take a while."

"Then you'd better get started."

As Diero had warned, he talked through the rest of the morning and into the afternoon. Anton found parts of the discourse—where to strike to cripple a dragon's wing, for example, or what sort of fortifications were of actual use against a gigantic reptile that could fly— fascinating. But once the cultist ventured into genuine esoterica—such as the link between wyrms and various elemental forces of the cosmos—he simply couldn't follow it. His own petty, intuitive knack for sorcery notwithstanding, he lacked the necessary education.

He could only hope Tu'ala'keth would pluck something useful from all the babble.

In the end his mind drifted. When Diero finally said something that tugged at his attention, he didn't even realize for a while, and wasn't certain what he'd truly heard.

"Go back," he said.

"How far?" Diero replied, hoarse again from so much talking.

"You were explaining how to turn dragons into dracoliches."

"Right. The details vary from one stronghold to the next, depending on which deities the priests serve, the particular strengths and conjuring styles of the wizards, and what have you. But in its essentials, the process is always the same. Artisans craft phylacteries, amulets of precious stones and metals, which the spell-casters enchant in a series of rituals. Even I can't recite all the incantations from memory, but you have the texts in that purple-bound volume on the table. Meanwhile, the alchemists and apothecaries distill a special libation in a process just as magical and complex. When both elements are ready, the wyrm can transform. At the climax of a final ceremony, it drinks the elixir. That frees its soul to leap from its body into the medallion, establishing a mystical bond that will safeguard its existence thereafter. Unless someone destroys the phylactery, the dragon can never truly perish. Then, having ensured its immortality, the spirit returns to its body, which rises as one of the undead."

"So what you're telling us," Anton said slowly, "is that basically, the drink is a poison? It kills the wyrms, and that's what 'frees' their spirits?"

"Well ... yes. Though we don't usually put it that way. It's difficult enough to win and keep the dragons' trust without bandying words like 'poison' and 'kill' about."

"Despite their heartiness, it slays them every time without fail?"

"Yes. A single drop of it would kill almost anything, but the formula was especially devised to stop a dragon's heart."

"What if a wyrm drank some when there was no ritual going on and no amulet for its spirit to inhabit?"

"Why, it would die, pure and simple." Diero smiled like a man who'd begun to believe his captors might permit him to live after all. "Let me anticipate your next questions. Yes, we brewed a supply of the stuff here on Tan, and yes, it's ready for use."

Supervised by the occasional hovering ixitxachitl, lines of koalinths and locathahs trudged through the stronghold, collecting treasure and carrying it down to the sea caves for transport to Exzethlix. Meanwhile, Tu'ala'keth stood watch over her share of the plunder. She didn't think the 'chitls would try to steal it. Puffed up with the glory of killing dragons, Yzil seemed satisfied with his share. But it was never prudent to underestimate the 'chitls' rapacity or fundamental scorn for any species other than their own.

Footsteps sounded outside the magician's sanctum where she'd collected the dragon-killing gear and, later, the clay jugs containing the poison. It was the brisk, sure stride of an air-breather, not the slapping shuffle of a creature with webbed feet, managing out of water as best it could, and for a moment, she smiled.

Beard shaved and hair chopped short again, Anton appeared in the entrance to the chamber. He carried a sea bag slung over his shoulder, and the greatsword in its scabbard in the other hand. "I came back," he said.

"I see that," she replied.

"I seem," he said, "to have picked up the habit of doing stupid things. Now that the cog is gone, I'll have a bitch of a time getting back to Turmish. That is, unless you help me."

"But you do not wish to return to Turmish. Not yet. You have decided to accompany me."

He smiled wryly. "Yes, and judging from your attitude, you're not surprised. Don't you ever tire of being right?"

"Of late, I have often been mistaken. But not about your role in Umberlee's design."

"Just so you know, I still don't see any 'design.' I simply think we've had a lot of luck. I came back because . . . well, I'm not sure why. Except that I tried to kill you, and you wound up freeing me and finishing my mission for me. So maybe I owe you."

"You do not. You helped vanquish the cult, and in so doing, atoned for your apostasy. The goddess forgives you."

"But do you?"

"Of course. You are my comrade in a great and holy endeavor."

"If you say so. I admit, after coming this far, I'm curious to see the end of it."

"Then let us proceed. I found some potions that will allow you to breathe under water and also some netting to fashion into bags. We will carry our plunder down to the water, and I will summon seahorses, those we rode before and others, too. Enough to bear us and our possessions away."

THE PRIESTS

As Anton had initially suspected, all Myth Nantar lay under a benign enchantment enabling visitors from the world above to breathe, withstand the pressure of the depths, and even see clearly despite the hundreds of feet of water filtering out the sun. Thus, he could discern the preparations for war. Mermen strung enormous nets between the luminous spires and equally massive spurs of corals. Sea-elves shot crossbows at targets, and shalarins jabbed in unison with tridents, as the alliance's raw new army, hastily scraped together to replace the superior one the wyrms had already annihilated, doggedly trained for the struggle to come.

It was the loan of Tu'ala'keth's coral ring, however, that permitted Anton to eavesdrop on passersby as he and the waveservant swam through the canyonlike streets. He heard variations of the same fearful conversation repeated again and again: "The dragon flight has turned." "The wyrms are headed straight at us." "I'm taking my family out of the city today."

Tu'ala'keth had been correct about the need for haste. As it was, she'd only barely returned in time.

They swam through a plaza where a fountain miraculously spewed yellow flame, noticeably warming the water. Beyond that lay a blue marble temple, with columns shaped like chains of bubbles, and a frieze of a triton adoring the façade. Adjacent to that stood the imposing five-story keep that was the Council House.

Sentries stood watch before the arched entry. According to Tu'ala'keth, the allied races supplied the honor guard on an alternating basis, and today was evidently the locathahs' turn. Advised to expect the waveservant and her companion, the gill-men ushered them inside with a minimum of fuss. It reminded Anton of his own countrymen, who, as citizens of a republic, often took a sort of pride in eschewing aristocratic airs and elaborate ceremony. But he suspected that in this case, the city's desperation had more to do with it.

The council chamber turned out to be a spacious room with an enormous table made fashioned from a dragon-turtle shell at the center. Around it sat the councilors, one for every allied race, another for each of the three orders of Dukars—a sort of highly regarded wizard who could evidently come from any race—and one for an elven High Mage, for a total of ten. Still, the Serôsians called it a Council of Twelve, and two chairs sat empty, the first representing an extinct order of Dukars and the second reserved for any god who might care to manifest and address the assembly.

The word *chairs* was somewhat misleading. Fashioned in different shapes to accommodate the varying anatomies of the councilors, some resembled cages as much as anything else, and in a realm where everyone floated, each functioned to hold the occupant effortlessly in position at the table at least as much as it did to provide a comfortable resting place for a rump.

A merman functionary announced Anton and Tu'ala'keth. The spy hung back a little as they swam toward the assembly. The councilors were the waveservant's people. Let her do the talking.

The muscular sea-elf representative—Morgan Ildacer, if Anton remembered the name correctly—wore a shirt of sharkskin armor and had brought a barbed lance and crossbow along to the meeting. He was evidently a high-ranking warrior, who, by the look of him, might have just come from drilling the troops under his command. He regarded the newcomers without discernible enthusiasm. "Priestess. Forgive us if we receive you with little courtesy, but we're trying to deal with an emergency. You told our deputies you have a way to help us."

"I do," said Tu'ala'keth. "Umberlee sent me on a mission to find our salvation in the world above the waves and provided a champion to aid me. To put the matter succinctly, we succeeded. If you follow our guidance and use the weapons we procured, you can destroy the dragon flight."

Ri'ola'con, the shalarin councilor, sat up straighter. Gray of skin, with a white mark on his brow and milky stripes on his dorsal fin, he was skinny even for one of Tu'ala'keth's kind, with deep wrinkles etched around his eyes. "Can this be true?" he asked.

"I pray it is." Pharom Ildacer said. Though less overtly athletic, the High Mage bore a familial resemblance to his handsome cousin, but his sympathetic air was in marked contrast to the warrior's brusque and haughty manner. "Please, tell us more."

"In good time," said Tu'ala'keth.

Anton felt a twinge of unease. What did she think she was doing?

"As I explained," said Morgan, "time presses. Speak if you actually have something to say."

"I have a good deal to say," she replied. "Have you wondered why this affliction has come upon us in this season?"

Arina, a youthful-looking mermaid and her people's representative, shrugged bare and comely shoulders. In less serious circumstances, Anton could have spent a stimulating time ogling the upper half of her. "It's just something that happens every couple centuries," she said. "Isn't it?"

"It is," said Tu'ala'keth. "But you would do well to remember that nothing happens without the permission of the gods, and that calamities can embody their displeasure."

Ri'ola'con blinked his round black eyes. "What god have we offended?"

"Do you not know?" Tu'ala'keth said. "Of all those assembled here, you and Tu'ola'sara"—the shalarin Dukar—"are the ones who should. None of the allied peoples honors Umberlee as much as is her due. But some never did, and perhaps considering their lack of reverence beneath her notice, she did not deign to avenge herself. But until recently, the shalarin people did worship her, and now, for the most part, we have turned away. She will not tolerate that affront."

"Nonsense," Morgan snapped. "Any time misfortune strikes, some priest pops up to claim it's because folk failed to heap pearls on his deity's altar. But the world doesn't work like that."

A hideous blend of sailfish, octopus, and crustacean, Vualdia, the morkoth councilor, stirred within her "seat," a lattice of intricately carved bone. "Sometimes it does," she said. Accurately or not, Tu'ala'keth's ring, translating for Anton's benefit, gave the creature the quavering voice of a cranky old lady accustomed to having her way. "History records a number of instances where the gods chastised cities and whole kingdoms that displeased them."

Morgan sneered. "You're a scholar, so I'll take your word for it. But where's the proof it's happening now?"

"Those of you who profess mystical abilities," Tu'ala'keth replied, "should be able to read the signs. If not, I swear on Umberlee's trident that matters are as I say."

"I trust your oath," Pharom said. "I believe you think you're speaking the truth. But that doesn't necessarily mean you're right."

"Had I been wrong, had Umberlee not prompted me to do as I have done, I surely could not have procured the means of saving Myth Nantar."

"Good," said Nalos of Pumanath, the triton councilor, "now we're circling back around to the point. I don't care why the dragons are attacking. We can argue that later. I care about killing them. Do you truly have a way, waveservant, and if so, what's your price?"

"I have the way," said Tu'ala'keth, "and will give it to you in exchange for a pledge. After we destroy the wyrms, Myth Nantar will hold a festival of thanksgiving to Umberlee. The lords and captains of every allied race will offer at her altar."

"Impossible," Morgan said. "Deep Sashelas is the god of the sea-elves, and supreme above all others. I've never prayed to a lesser deity, and I never will."

"Still," Pharom said, "we know he isn't the only god."

Tu'ala'keth continued as if she hadn't heard either of them. "There is more. For the next year, once every tenday, every shalarin in As'arem and Myth Nantar will pay homage in Umberlee's shrines and temples."

Gaunt Ri'ola'con shook his head. His crest, which had a limp and withered look to it compared to Tu'ala'keth's, flopped about. "We can't tell people which god to worship."

"The Rulers Caste can order them to do anything within reason, and this is within reason. I have not stipulated that they forsake the weak, ridiculous powers to whom they have lately pledged allegiance. They may continue praying to them if they wish. But they must give Umberlee their adoration as well."

"This is outrageous!" Arina exploded. "How can you bargain with us when the survival of everyone and everything is at stake? Serôs is your home, too!"

"So it is," said Tu'ala'keth, "and I would grieve to see its people slaughtered and its cities laid to waste. But I have pledged my loyalty to one power, one principle, beside which nothing else matters. I serve Umberlee, and the rest of you who owe her reverence must acknowledge her as well. Or perish beneath the fangs and claws of dragons."

"I know," said Vualdia, tentacles squirming, "some of us are squeamish about torture. But with our survival at issue, perhaps they could put their qualms aside and agree to force this creature to help us."

"If I ask," said Tu'ala'keth, "Umberlee will surely take my soul into her keeping and leave you a lifeless husk to question."

"If I tortured you," said Morgan, "it would be to punish you for impudence, not to extract the secret of Myth Nantar's deliverance. Because you don't have it!" He raked his gaze over his fellow councilors. "Don't you see? It's a trick, a game she can't lose. She'll give us some meaningless blather, and if we wind up defeating the dragons, she'll take the credit. If we lose, and anyone survives to confront her, she'll claim it's because we didn't pray hard enough."

"If you lose," said Tu'ala'keth, "it will be because

Umberlee offered you salvation, and you spurned it."

"If a priest of Deep Sashelas, or any proper, civilized god"—Anton had a hunch that what Morgan actually meant was any patron god of the sea-elves—"made that claim, I *might* take it seriously. But Umberlee is just a spook for human sailors to dread, because she sinks their boats and drowns them. But what influence can she exert over those of us who dwell in the sea?"

"She is the sea," said Tu'ala'keth. "You live your life in her embrace, and at every moment, only by her sufferance. But we need not argue about her majesty. If you accept my help, its worth will prove my contention. If you refuse, perhaps you will achieve greater insight in the afterlife."

"All right," said Jorunhast, frowning, wisps of his hair and beard wafting in the gentle current drifting through the room. Once the Royal Wizard of Cormyr, now, in his exile, a Dukar, he was human, the only such expatriate on the council. "Let me make sure I understand. You'll hand over whatever weapons you collected, advise us how to use them, and we'll decide whether to employ the strategy you recommend. If we do and emerge victorious, it's then and only then that we all need to abase ourselves at Umberlee's altar. Is that the bargain?"

"Yes," said Tu'ala'keth, "but I will reveal nothing until I have the oath of every member of this council."

"You won't get them," Morgan said.

Pharom frowned at him. "That's not for you to say, cousin. Not by yourself. Not before we deliberate." He turned to Tu'ala'keth. "Would you and your companion please withdraw so we can talk among ourselves?"

Tu'ala'keth inclined her head. "As you wish."

The merman functionary conducted them into a waiting area, where dolphins, carved in bas-relief, swam on creamy marble walls. Anton managed to wait until the servant left them in privacy, but then could contain himself no longer.

"What in the name of Baator are you doing?" he demanded.

"You heard the discussion."

"Yes, but you didn't warn me you were planning this . . . extortion. The way you explained it, you'd help your people, and afterward, they'd return to Umberlee out of gratitude."

"Originally," she said, "that was my intent. But I meditated on the journey back from Tan, and the goddess whispered that my simple scheme would not achieve its goal. The common run of folk are blind and heedless. You are a case in point. You are Umberlee's knight and cannot even perceive it. In the aftermath of victory, Serôs would rejoice. People might even think me a hero. But if I proclaimed the credit belonged to Umberlee, would the masses heed me? Would they flock back to her temples? I suspect not, and so I must compel them."

"Doesn't it matter to you that they won't be praying out of honest devotion?"

"Aboard Teldar's sailboat, you yourself observed that most folk pay homage to Umberlee only because they feel they must. They never have and never will comprehend her magnificence, and that is all right. She is well content with their dread."

"So really, you're just trying to put things back the way they used to be. All right. I see that." He lowered his voice. "But I need to know: Are you bluffing? If the council refuses your demands, do you mean to help them anyway?"

"No."

"Damn you!"

"You have sometimes thought me mad, and now you suspect it again. Or at least believe me devoid of feeling. But I am not. I can rejoice to behold Umberlee's face in the burst of blood when predator seizes prey and still not desire to see my entire race slaughtered. If the council denies me, I will withhold the weapons we have found. But otherwise, I will place myself at the disposal of the new army and fight and die with the rest of the soldiers."

He threw up his hands, a gesture that, thanks to the city's pervasive enchantments, he could perform as quickly as if flinging his arms through thin air. "Don't you see how perverse that is?"

"You cannot judge the will of Umberlee by mortal standards."

"They're the only standards I have. I don't hear the Bitch Queen telling me what to do. I've explained that time and again. I'll tell you what I can perceive. Everything in Myth Nantar is strange to me. I see a creature, and I'm not even sure if it's a person or just a fish. I notice workers carrying tools and have no idea what they're for. But I do recognize that this is a splendid city peopled, more or less, with honest folk. Folk as worthy of protection as my own."

"Yes," she said, "they are."

"Well, consider this: I *can* protect them. I know where you cached the poison and the rest of the loot. I listened to that whoreson Diero explain how to use it all. Why shouldn't *I* go back into the council chamber and give the representatives what they want?"

"Do as your spirit prompts you. I will not stop you. It is no longer fitting for one of us to compel or constrain the other. We have come too far and achieved too much together."

"Look, if you know I'd do it anyway, doesn't it make sense for you to do it instead? Wouldn't it be better for your standing among your people, and for your goddess's as well?"

"Umberlee does not wish me to take that course, and in any case, I do not actually know what you will do. Perhaps you do not know yet, either."

With a pang of annoyance, he realized she was right.

He knew he ought to do precisely as he'd threatened. Common sense allowed no other option. Yet he'd come back to Serôs to help Tu'ala'keth, not betray her a second time.

Maybe it wasn't really treachery to thwart an addled mind in pursuit of disastrous folly, and she was right, often enough, she did seem crazy to him. He just couldn't see what she saw or feel what she felt.

But sometimes he wondered what it would be like. How it felt to stalk fearlessly about the world, armored in faith and certainty, to steer one's life by absolutes, not pragmatism and compromise.

It's insane, he thought, but I could do it this one time. I could let go of my own notions and trust hers, if I'm willing to live with the consequences.

"Fine," he growled, "I'll keep my mouth shut. Just don't tell me you knew all along how I was going to decide."

"I did not. Umberlee has called us, but nonetheless, we are always free to swim with the current or struggle against it. Now be of good cheer. The councilors are wise after their fashion. They will see reason."

They didn't have to wait long to find out if she was right. Piscine tail flipping up and down, the merman servant arrived only minutes later to conduct them back to his masters.

For the most part, the councilors—those whose expressions Anton could read, anyway—scowled and glowered as if a physician had forced them to swallow vile-tasting medicine. He felt a sudden urge to grin, and made sure he didn't.

"For the record," Pharom said, "this council regards compelling the worship of any deity as a reprehensible practice. It could easily undermine the mutual tolerance necessary for the six races to live in peace together."

However, Anton thought.

"Yet at the same time," the High Mage continued, "we naturally recognize the existence of all the gods, and understand that over the course of a lifetime, a sensible, pious person may offer to many of them, according to his circumstances. So, waveservant, if you, acting in the name of the Queen of the Depths, can help stave off the dragon flight, then we would deem it appropriate to proclaim a festival of celebration in her honor. As far as obliging the shalarin people to worship her on an ongoing basis, that's an internal matter for As'arem. This council can't command it."

Tu'ala'keth turned to Ri'ola'con. "Then, High Lord," she said, "as eadar, it falls to you to say yes or no on behalf of our folk."

The wrinkled, frail-looking shalarin frowned. "You know very well, Seeker, that As'arem is five realms, not one, and that my authority has its limits."

"Swear to do your utmost to meet Umberlee's requirements, and that will suffice."

In the end, the councilors all vowed in turn, each by his patron god, by one sacred principle or another or simply on his honor, though several offered their oaths with an ill grace. Morgan was the last and surliest of all.

"All right," he said, "enough mummery. Enough stalling. Tell us your secret, and by all the powers we just invoked, it had better be worth the wait."

"Very well." Tu'ala'keth provided a terse account of the weapons they'd seized and what they proposed to do with them. Anton, who rather prided himself on making clear, concise reports to his superiors, appreciated the brevity.

When she finished, the other councilors looked to Morgan. "What do you think, cousin?" Pharom asked.

The warrior scowled and hesitated. Anton could all but see the feelings clashing inside him, resentment of Tu'ala'keth on one side, hope and the need to keep faith with his own martial pride by giving an honest appraisal on the other. "It's ... interesting," he said at length.

Tu'ala'keth responded as if this equivocation settled everything. "I noticed you have started preparations to defend the city. That is good, for even if the army readied itself in time to engage the dragons elsewhere, this is the best place to make our stand. The damage will be significant, but we can turn the architecture and reefs to our advantage. I suggest evacuating all those unfit to fight."

"We haven't yet agreed to your plans," Morgan said.

"That's true," Pharom said. "So should we? You're as able and canny a soldier as anyone here, so speak plainly. Are you in favor, or against?"

"Yes," sighed the other sea-elf. "This plan gives us more hope than anything we've thought of hitherto." The truculence came back into his manner. "But only if her liquids and baubles perform as she claims."

"If they do not," said Tu'ala'keth, "I will be among the first to suffer for my stupidity. As it is my scheme, it is only proper that I play a central role in attempting it."

Anton said. "I'll be in the vanguard, too." Nose to snout with more dragons, may the Red Knight stand beside me.

Tu'ala'keth watched Anton swim experimentally back and forth and up and down. She understood the reason for it. Though they'd passed beyond the field of helpful magic enveloping Myth Nantar, the Arcane

Caste had, at her behest, supplied him with enchantments that should enable him to function just as well in the open sea. A bone half-mask allowed him both to breathe and to see in what he would otherwise regard as impenetrable gloom. A fire-coral ring warmed him, and eel-skin slippers and gloves enabled him to swim with the speed and agility of a shalarin.

Unfortunately, he hadn't had much time to practice with the latter items before Morgan Ildacer led the company forth. He still felt uncertain of their capabilities. It was natural, but though she maintained her composure, as a waveservant should, his fidgeting was making her restless, too. "You will be fine," she said.

Beneath the mask with its amber lens, carved scales, and gill slits, his mouth quirked into a smile. "Can I take that as a guarantee from Umberlee?"

"Umberlee does not deal in guarantees. It is simply that I have found you to be a quick study."

He gazed right, left, up, straight ahead, then down at the dark, silt-covered slopes of Mount Halaath falling away beneath them. Many of their comrades were similarly peering about and making a point to check in every direction. In open water, an enemy could strike from anywhere.

"I don't see the brutes," Anton said. "It would be funny if they just decided to veer off and go somewhere else entirely. They could, you know. A dragon flight can do any crazy thing."

"Not this one," she said.

"Because Umberlee sent it?"

"I have spoken of pattern precipitating from the randomness of life. As it begins to articulate itself, it either breaks against some form of resistance or increases in implicit strength and complexity, until, if it thrives beyond a certain point, it inevitably fulfills itself. You and I have followed such a pattern. Or we created it. One perspective is as valid as the other."

"So now the dragons have to come."

She smiled. "I think that no matter how many times I explain, you will never truly permit yourself to understand. They do not have to. They can do as they like. But they will."

He stiffened then said, in a softer voice, "Yes, I guess so."

She turned and looked upward as he was. At first, she couldn't see forms, just a great burgeoning agitation in the water. That, however, was enough to send a pang of fear stabbing through her, because she comprehended just how many dragons it took to create that seething, onrushing cloudiness.

Many of her comrades were plainly frightened also, staring wide-eyed, shivering, and unconsciously cringing backward. She gripped the drowned man's hand and murmured a prayer. A pulse of clarity and resolution throbbed within her, cleansing much of the anxiety from her mind, and streaming outward to enhance the courage and vigor of every ally within range.

"Steady," she said, "steady. The Queen of the Depths is with us. All our gods are with us." Well, give or take the feeble frauds from the Sea of Corynactis.

Throughout the company, other folk in authority did what they could to maintain morale and order. Priests of every race prayed for good fortune. Magicians—sea-elves, shalarins, and morkoths mostly—prepared to cast spells in as showy a manner as possible, brandishing staves of bone and coral and wands of polished semiprecious stone, leaving fleeting, glimmering trails in the water, tacitly assuring their comrades of their arcane might. Officers talked confidently to common warriors. A squad of tritons lifted their tapals—crystalline weapons with both a point extending beyond the fist and a long blade lying flat against the forearm—and shouted, "Myth

Nantar! Myth Nantar! Myth Nantar!" Other soldiers took up the chant.

Still nothing could take away all the fear. A merman started swimming upward, and his sergeant bellowed at him to get back into position.

"They're above us," the soldier pleaded. "We'll be caught between them and the mountain below."

"They're where we want them!" the sergeant snarled. "Get a grip, and remember the plan!"

A locathah dropped its crossbow, whirled, and started swimming away. Its captain put a quarrel in its spine then rounded on its gaping comrades. "Anybody else want to turn tail?" the leader demanded. If so, the others kept it to themselves.

Now Tu'ala'keth could make out shapes ... or at least the suggestion of them. Prodigious wings beat, hauling wyrms through the water almost as fast as they could fly through the sky. The flippers of the dragon turtles stroked, and the tails of the colossal eels lashed, accomplishing the same purpose. On Tu'ala'keth's right, a shalarin started making a low, moaning sound, probably without realizing he was doing it.

"This is it," came Morgan's cool, clipped voice, magically augmented so everyone in the company could hear. "Start the attacks."

He meant the order for those spellcasters who, either by dint of exceptional innate power or formidable magical weapons, had some hope of smiting the wyrms even at long range. Thanks to a scroll from Eshcaz's hoard, now sealed in a yellowish transparent membrane to keep the sea from ruining it, Tu'ala'keth fell into the latter category.

She read a trigger phrase and felt the magic pounce from the page, supposedly to rip at a cluster of the onrushing wyrms, though at such a distance, she couldn't tell if it was cutting them up to any significant degree. It certainly didn't kill any of them or even slow them down.

Other spells began to strike in the dragons' midst, swirls of darkness and blasts of jagged ice. Those didn't balk them either.

A jittery koalinth discharged its crossbow, and the dart lost momentum and sank only halfway to its targets. Tentacles writhing in agitation, the creature's morkoth master screamed for it and its fellow slave warriors to "Wait, curse you, wait!"

More magical attacks exploded into being among the dragons, close enough now that most of the spellcasters could assail them in one fashion or another. The barrage still didn't slow the reptiles down. Indeed no matter how intently she peered, Tu'ala'keth could see only superficial cuts, punctures, and abrasions marring their scaly hides. It was almost as if the allied priests and mages were merely treating them to a harmless display of flickering light and dancing shadow.

But perhaps they'd done a bit more harm, or at least caused a little more annoyance, than that. For now the wyrms retaliated in kind.

Aquatic dragons commonly lacked the sorcerous talents of their kindred on land. As a rule, it was only the species that thrived in either environment who cast spells beneath the waves. Some such—blacks and at least one topaz—had joined the dragon flight, but Tu'ala'keth had hoped that by now, their madness might have rendered them incapable of using arcane talents.

Alas, that was not the case. Water became acid, searing the flesh of the thrashing sea-elves caught amid the transformation, diffusing outward to blister the skin and sting the eyes of other warriors. Black tentacles writhed from a central point to batter and clutch at a dozen mermen. The morkoth who'd snagged

Tu'ala'keth's attention a moment before wailed, froze into position, and turned into a thing of translucent glass sinking downward toward the mountaintop. Its koalinth thralls exchanged wild-eyed looks as if silently asking one another what to do now.

"Hold!" called Morgan's disembodied voice. "Hold fast. Bowmen, the enemy's in range. Start shooting!"

"About time," Anton muttered. Feet kicking lazily, he'd been floating with his crossbow already shouldered. Now he pulled the trigger, and though he hadn't had much time to practice shooting under water either, the dart streaked forth to pierce the silvery scales of a dragon eel just above its black, deep-set eye. He instantly worked the lever to cock the weapon again.

Countless quarrels hurtled at the oncoming dragons. For their part, the wizards and priests switched to a new set of spells. Tu'ala'keth read another trigger, and a colossal squid coalesced into being in front of the wyrms. Her comrades materialized enormous creatures akin to whales, sharks, octopuses, eels, and jellyfish, counterparts to mundane animals drawn from spirit realms or elementals like those she and Yzil had battled. The conjured servants surged forward to engage the reptiles. Meanwhile, other mages evoked sudden booms among the dragons to stun them and pain their sensitive ears, or sweeping their hands to and fro, wove hanging patterns of multicolored light to arrest a wyrm's gaze and hold the creature stupefied.

The allies hoped this magic, even if it ultimately did little damage, would slow the dragons' advance, giving the crossbowmen time to shoot them repeatedly. It did, for a few heartbeats, and one by one, the reptiles started breaking through whatever barriers, living or inanimate, tangible, phantasmal, or psychic, the spellcasters had placed in their way. A sleek, glimmering, silver-blue water drake caught Tu'ala'keth's squid in its fangs and snapped and raked it to shreds.

A black with a withered, cadaverous countenance snarled a counterspell to thrust an elemental back to its native level of existence. Glittering like the jewel for which it was named, its eyes blank yellow flame as bright as Eshcaz's, the topaz simply stared at a priest of Deep Sashelas who'd attempted to shackle its will. The sea-elf screamed, convulsed, and clutched at his head. Blood billowed from his nostrils.

Abruptly, or so it seemed, on the far left flank of the company, a dragon turtle was much too close. It opened its beak and spewed its breath weapon. Water boiled to steam, and the mermen caught in the effect boiled with it. Furious with bloodlust, not hunger, the huge creature didn't pause to gobble its victims. Rather, flippers lashing, it rushed forward to attack new ones.

Coral-headed spear in hand, other sea-elf warriors swimming frantically to join him, Morgan set himself in the dragon turtle's way. The imminent threat didn't keep him from giving further orders in the same crisp fashion as before.

"It's time to fall back. Remember the route you're supposed to take, and wait for a mage to enchant you before you retreat."

Tu'ala'keth belatedly realized the morkoth wizard had been the nearest conjuror to her and Anton, and it now lay on the slopes of Mount Halaath in the form of a glass statue. She cast about and spied a sea-elf warlock not too far away. She pointed, and Anton followed as she swam in that direction.

Others were racing there as well, sometimes shoving their comrades aside in their haste. The company had held its position as well as anyone could have expected, but now, with the dragons nearly on top of it, many warriors were on the verge of panic.

In fact, in their eagerness to converge on the magician, they threatened to crush him. A shrill edge of fear in his voice, he cried, "Give me some space! I can't conjure if I can't move my arms!"

Tu'ala'keth gripped the drowned man's hand and invoked a surge of Umberlee's majesty. It granted her a moment of mastery over her fellow sea-dwellers, and when she shouted for them to calm themselves, they heeded her.

"Thank you," said the wizard, understanding she'd helped him even if he didn't comprehend precisely how. He swept a scrap of vegetable matter through a mystic pattern and rattled off words of power.

Tu'ala'keth's muscles twitched and jerked. Other folk cried out as the magic jolted them. After the initial shock, she felt no different. But when she looked at those among her allies who were still awaiting enchantment, or at the dragons, they seemed to move sluggishly. In actuality, she knew, the reverse was true. The spell accelerated the reactions of those it touched.

"That's done," Anton said, sliding another quarrel into the groove atop his crossbow. "Now let's get out of here."

"Yes," she said

As if it were the signal for everyone clustered around the warlock, the spherical mass of bodies burst into a ragged, streaming mass. Everyone swam downward and southeast, toward Myth Nantar and the plateau on which it sat, as fast as their magically quickened limbs could speed them along.

The spellcasters still had a responsibility to slow the pursuing drakes. Otherwise, the reptiles might overtake and slaughter everyone, the charm of acceleration notwithstanding.

So Tu'ala'keth turned periodically to release another spell from her parchment, to summon a demon to assault the dragons, or plunge an area into darkness and hinder the reptiles about to pass through it.

Whenever she did, she felt a surge of awe at the spectacle of the onrushing wyrms. They dwarfed the allies as sharks dwarfed minnows, loomed above and extended to either side of the company like a titanic wall of glaring eyes, bared fangs, and curved talons. They were as terrible and beautiful as her vision of the Blood Sea, and she realized that even if this venture cost her her life, it was worth it simply to behold them.

Whenever she wheeled to work magic, Anton turned, shot another bolt from the crossbow, and cursed to see wyrms slaughtering folk who hadn't fled quickly enough. Another burst of dragon-turtle breath—Tu'ala'keth wondered fleetingly if this was the same creature Morgan had engaged, if the councilor was now dead—boiled locathahs so that lumps and strands of flesh slid loose from their bones. A sea dragon spread its gigantic jaws and swallowed two shalarins at once.

Then Anton shouted, "Watch out!"

Tu'ala'keth cast about and couldn't find the threat.

"Below us!" Anton cried.

She looked down. Somehow, a shimmering water drake had been able to swim fast enough to overtake the rearguard but hadn't been content simply to tear into the folk at the very back. Instead, it had dived beneath the fleeing company then ascended in the obvious hope of taking someone entirely by surprise.

It had nearly succeeded. Its jaws spread wide to seize Tu'ala'keth, and she doubted she even had time to evoke more magic from the scroll's ever-dwindling supply. Instead she extended her trident at the creature's head and asked Umberlee for a burst of spiritual force sufficient to cow any sea creature, even a drake.

The power flared, but the wyrm simply failed to heed it. Its essence was too strong. It swiped a forefoot and knocked the trident out of line. She tried to twist out of the way of its jaws and, when it arched its body to compensate, realized that wouldn't help her either.

Anton dived at the drake, the point of Umberlee's greatsword poised to pierce it like a spear. He'd considered trading it for one of the weapons specially designed for slaying wyrms, but in the end, had opted to stick with the blade that had served him well against Eshcaz. Behind the amber lenses, his eyes burned with the contagious fury of the sword. Or perhaps it was simply his own innate determination.

The dark blade plunged deep into the reptile's head. Flailing, it couldn't follow through on its intention to bite, and Tu'ala'keth wrenched herself away from its teeth.

She hoped the drake would die, for surely the greatsword had driven in deep enough to reach the brain. It didn't, though. It roared and whipped around to threaten Anton. Its wing, slightly torn where someone had managed to hurt it a little, swatted her tumbling away.

She refused to let the bruising impact stun her and oriented on the wyrm once more. The greatsword was still sticking out of its mask. Anton had lost his grip on it when the creature turned. Now unarmed except for the pitiful dagger in his hand and the unloaded crossbow dangling from his wrist, he dodged and retreated as the reptile clawed at him. If not for the spell of quickness, it likely would have torn him to shreds already. As it was, it was plain that, bereft of any weapon that could deter the drake from attacking with every iota of its demented aggression, he couldn't survive much longer.

She hastily peered at the scroll. Two spells left. She triggered the first.

Water surged, churned, and spun around the drake. Caught by surprise, engulfed in a miniature maelstrom, even a creature of prodigious strength had difficultly swimming in the direction it intended to go, and as it floundered, Anton kicked and shot beyond its reach.

The drake flailed, trying to break free of the bubble of turbulence. Tu'ala'keth unleashed the final spell. A ragged blot of shadow appeared before her then shattered into flat, flapping shapes like mantas. Untroubled by the violent, erratic currents, the apparitions whirled around the dragon. It was impossible to see how they attacked it, if, in fact, they made physical contact at all. But gashes ripped the reptile's hide, and a hind leg, a foreleg, and half the tail sheared away completely. Head nearly severed, wings shredded, the drake drifted toward the bottom in a billowing cloud of blood.

Anton dived after it, gripped the hilt of the greatsword, planted his feet on the wyrm's head, and pulled the weapon free. By the time he managed that, most of their comrades had fled past, leaving him and Tu'ala'keth at the rear of the throng.

Tail lashing, a dragon eel streaked at them. A vertical plane of azure force abruptly appeared in its way, and it slammed into the obstruction beak-first. Amid the chaos, Tu'ala'keth couldn't tell who'd conjured the effect, but it stopped the creature for a critical moment.

She and Anton raced onward with the great frantic horde of their fellows. People slowed abruptly as their charms of quickness exhausted their power. Time would tell which ones had seized enough of a lead to keep ahead of the wyrms.

It would have been easy for anyone to break away. The officers were too busy trying to save their own lives to interfere with anybody who did, and with scores of potential victims to pursue, the wyrms might well not veer away to pick off a single stray.

But as far as Tu'ala'keth could judge, most of the

company were keeping to the plan. A plan, she realized, that now required her and Anton to bear left. She turned, and others began to do the same, their courses crisscrossing as each headed where he'd been ordered to go.

The soft luminescence of Myth Nantar flowered before and below her. Muscles burning with strain, she put on a final burst of speed, passed among the first of the coral-girded spires, then dared to turn and look back.

Most members of the advance force—or what was left of it—had already entered the city via one of several avenues, and diving lower than the rooftops, the wyrms were splitting up to chase them down the same thoroughfares. It was as the allies had hoped. In normal circumstances, dragons were cunning, but addled by the Rage, infuriated by the harassment they'd already suffered and the frustration of prey fleeing just beyond their reach, the reptiles either didn't realize or didn't care that their foes were luring them into a trap.

Of course, it was possible they didn't need to care. Their power might well prevail against every ruse and tactic Myth Nantar had prepared.

But Tu'ala'keth refused to believe it. Not after she and Anton had come so far and achieved so much. The Bitch Queen had no mercy, nor concern for fairness as mortals understood it, but still the pattern would not complete itself in such a bitter fashion.

She and the human swam onward, past dozens of their exhausted, frightened comrades rushing to get indoors, to the keep that was supposed to be their particular refuge. They hurried through an entry on the third story, an opening blessedly too small for even the least of the wyrms to negotiate, and the shalarin warriors waiting on the other side gaped at them.

"What's happening?" an officer asked.

Somewhere outside a dragon roared.

"That noise pretty much says it," Anton gasped, slumping with exhaustion. "We drew the dragons into town. Now you go kill them."

Anton watched as the shalarins made their last-second preparations for combat. Most were soldiers of the Protectors Caste, with bony spines stiffening their dorsal fins rigid as the crest on a human knight's steel helm. But they had spellcasters to support them.

Across the city other squads drawn from all six allied races were no doubt doing exactly the same thing, and Anton silently wished them luck. It was their fight now. He and his comrades had done their job by luring the dragons down the proper streets in the proper heedless state of mind.

But maybe he didn't want to hold back while others finished the battle. It was strange, really. As a spy, he'd rarely been present when the Turmian fleet or army, acting on intelligence he'd provided, eliminated a threat to the republic, and he'd rarely cared. But this time, for whatever reason, he wanted in at the kill.

The greatsword rejoiced at his witless impulse, at a new opportunity for bloodshed. Calm down, he told it sourly, meanwhile casting about for Tu'ala'keth.

Clasping her skeletal pendant, the waveservant was murmuring a prayer. At the conclusion, she shivered, rolled her narrow shoulders as if working stiffness out, then took a firmer grip on her trident.

He swam to her. "What did you just do?" he asked.

"I suppressed my fatigue," she said, "making myself fit to fight once more."

"Cast the same charm on me, will you? If you've got another."

She flashed him one of her rare smiles. "I do. I expected you would want it."

The spell stung like a hundred hornets, and he grunted at the blaze of pain. It lasted only an instant, though, and afterward, he felt as though he'd rested for a day.

Tu'ala'keth made her way to one of the warriors bearing a satchel. "I will take that," she said, indicating the bag.

The Protector eyed her uncertainly. "I volunteered," he said.

"Your bravery does you credit," she said, "but unless you have experience fighting dragons, I am better suited to the task."

"All right. If you put it that way." He handed her the bag just as a roar from the street outside agitated the water and shook the walls of the keep itself.

Anton hurried to a window. Beyond was a dragon turtle, its spiky shell nearly broad enough to fill the canyonlike avenue. Its beaked head twisted from side to side, and its eyes glared as it sought the elusive prey who'd fled inside the buildings to either side.

Quarrels flew from windows and doorways. Anton shouldered his own crossbow and started shooting. Many of the missiles glanced harmlessly off the reptile's shell or scales, but some lodged in its hide. Meanwhile, the magicians threw darts of light and raked the beast with blasts of shadow. Blood tinged the water around its body.

The reptile pivoted toward one of the larger entryways across the street, a circular opening midway up a marble wall. Anton prayed that everyone inside recognized the danger, that they were already bolting deeper into the structure. But even if so, many wouldn't get clear in time.

With a screech like the wail of a god's teakettle, the dragon turtle vomited its breath weapon, boiling the water in front of it. Framed in the windows to either side of the entryway, shalarins convulsed then floated lifeless.

But other defenders endured elsewhere, to shoot darts and fling attack spells, and it would take the reptile's breath time to replenish itself. Maybe, despite its derangement, it now began to understand it was at a disadvantage. With a stroke of its flippers, it shot a few yards farther down the street then halted as it evidently perceived it couldn't escape in that direction. Myth Nantar was a city half buried in reef, and like many of its byways, this particular street terminated in an upsweep of coral.

The dragon turtle wheeled just as, rippling with rainbows, a curtain of conjured force abruptly blocked the other end of the avenue. The leviathan angled its body upward, preparing to ascend, but a gigantic net, the magically toughened cables thick as a strong man's thigh, now covered the street like a lid on a pot to complete the killing box. A team of warriors had stretched it across while the reptile was looking elsewhere.

Even so, it swam upward. Maybe it had wit enough to realize the net was the least substantial component of its cage. Its prodigious beak could likely nip through, or failing that, its raw strength and immensity could probably tear the mesh loose from its moorings.

Though not entirely unexpected, the dragon turtle's sound judgment was the allies' misfortune. They'd hoped to harry it from the relative safety of the buildings for a while longer, hurt it a little more, anyway, before anyone ventured out into the open. But they couldn't permit it to breach the netting and maneuver freely. So officers shouted the command to go forth, and Anton, Tu'ala'keth, and dozens of others obeyed.

Some of the warriors bellowed war cries to attract the reptile's attention. Anton yelled, "Turmish!" The dragon turtle peered downward then, trailing billows of blood, dived at the foes who had at last dared to come within its reach.

Midway through its plunge, it spat more of its breath. Some of the shalarins recognized the threat, but nobody managed to dodge. Everyone caught in the path of the blast boiled and died amid the burst of bubbles. By pure luck, Anton was safely to the side, but even he had to grit his teeth at a brush of scalding heat.

The dragon turtle hurtled down into the midst of its foes. The crested head at the end of the long neck swiveled left then right, biting a shalarin to fragments at the end of each arc. The elongated flippers bore talons like the feet of a land-born wyrm, and they clawed with equally devastating effect, tearing warriors to tatters and clouds of gore.

How could anything so gigantic maneuver so quickly? The confines of the street were supposed to hamper it!

It spun toward Anton, its beak gaping. He started to dodge, and a jagged block of ice materialized in the creature's open mouth. Finally, one of the wizards had balked the creature in its furious assault. It flailed in shock and pain.

Anton kicked, shot into the distance, and cut at the reptile. The greatsword bit deep into the side of its beak. Maybe a mage had succeeded in cursing it with one of the enchantments devised to soften a wyrm's scales, for other warriors, likewise taking advantage of the behemoth's sudden incapacitation, were also piercing its natural armor.

Unfortunately, its incapacitation lasted only a moment. Then it bit down hard, and the ice jammed in its mouth crunched to pieces. Its head whirled toward Anton, and he wrenched himself out of the way.

More ice! he silently implored—it worked for a second—or, if not that, some other magic to hinder the brute.

But it didn't happen. The warlocks were still trying. Power glimmered on the dragon turtle's shell, and leering, lopsided faces formed and dissolved amid the swirls of blood in the water. Yet now, for whatever reason, the spells simply failed to bite.

So it was up to the warriors. Anton cut, dodged, slashed, feinted low and kicked high. When he'd battled Eshcaz, he'd tried to stay on the red's flank, away from his deadliest natural weapons. But now he couldn't even do that, because it would be futile to hack at the shell. A combatant had to hover within easy reach of a dragon turtle's head and flippers, trusting to his reflexes to save him from its attacks, because there was nowhere else to hit it.

Anton lost another comrade every couple of heartbeats. He wondered how many were left—with his attention fixed on the reptile, it was impossible to count—and if anyone else would have the nerve to come forth to engage the creature once it had torn the first squad to drifting crumbs of fish food. Then he spotted Tu'ala'keth swimming up from below the behemoth's jaws.

He'd lost track of her early on. But he'd known that if she still lived, she was skulking around the periphery of the battle, seeking a chance to slip in close to the dragon turtle's beak while it was concentrating on other foes, because that was what the plan required her to do.

A couple of other shalarins, also carrying satchels, should have been attempting the same thing, but he still saw no sign of them. Maybe they hadn't been quick or stealthy enough to escape the reptile's attention.

If so, then Tu'ala'keth absolutely had to have her chance. He opened himself fully to the greatsword's malice, kicked forward, and attacked furiously.

The dark blade sliced deep, once just missing an eye. The dragon turtle snarled, and the gaping beak shot forward at the end of the long scaly neck.

Tu'ala'keth hurtled up from below it, a crystalline bulb in her hand. Unused to working with liquids requiring containment, the artisans and spellcasters of Myth Nantar had experienced a certain amount of trouble transferring the cult's poison into those silvery, translucent orbs, but had finally managed to devise a method.

Tu'ala'keth lobbed the ball into the dragon turtle's open mouth. Necessitating close proximity, the move was insanely dangerous, but at least it brought the virulent stuff to the target. Had they simply released the poison in a cloud, it might well have diffused to harmlessness without slaying a wyrm, or drifted unpredictably to kill the wrong victim. If they'd dipped an arrowhead or blade in it, the sea would simply have washed it off.

Anton couldn't tell for certain—the angle was wrong—but assumed the ball shattered as soon as it entered the dragon's mouth. That was what Pharom, Jorunhast, and their fellow mages had enchanted the orbs to do. Tu'ala'keth instantly whirled, kicked, and stroked in the opposite direction, less afraid now of attracting the wyrm's notice than of poison reaching her gills or mouth.

Her desperate haste didn't matter. The dragon turtle still didn't notice her, but neither did it react to the poison. Flippers stroking, it kept on lunging and snapping at Anton, twisting its neck to compensate when he zigzagged in a futile effort to shake it off his tail.

He kicked high, cut downward, and finally tore an eye in its socket. He'd have that little victory to cherish in Warrior's Rest, anyway. But he didn't expect it to stop the leviathan, and sure enough, it didn't. The creature's throat swelled, and the water abruptly grew warmer as it prepared to loose another burst of its breath. He had scant hope of evading it when he was right in front of its head.

From the corner of his eye, he glimpsed Tu'ala'keth, trident poised, swimming in to fight beside him. He waved her off, but she kept coming, pig-headed to the last.

Then the dragon turtle shuddered. It tried to spit its breath, but now evidently lacked the strength, for no blast engulfed them. Rather, the heat simply boiled the water around its own head and directly above it; the rising bubbles like flame leaping up from a torch.

In the wake of those, a cloud of blood and slime erupted from the reptile's gullet, as if something had ripped and corrupted its flesh from the inside. Anton shrank from the miasma, not because he feared it would hurt him, but simply repelled by the foulness. Tu'ala'keth did the same.

The dragon turtle drifted toward the bottom. For a moment, the spectacle of such a colossus brought to ruin held everyone awestruck. Then a crossbowman in an upper-story window cheered. An instant later, everyone was doing it.

Tu'ala'keth turned to Anton. "The poison," she said, "simply takes a moment to do its work."

"Evidently," he wheezed. It seemed unfair that he was always the only one gasping and panting. But she had gills instead of lungs; exertion didn't affect her the same way.

"If we swim above the rooftops," she said, "we should be able to see how Myth Nantar as a whole is faring."

"Good idea."

They peered about before completing the ascent, making sure no wyrm was lurking nearby. Once they determined it was safe, it was easy enough to squirm through the interstices of the net. Its weavers had fashioned it to hold dragons, not creatures as small as themselves.

Gazing down on the city from above, they beheld battle raging on every side. The screeching, roaring clamor stung the ears. Drifting blood clouded everything, the taste and smell of it vaguely sickening. Spires had fallen and spurs of reef shattered where dragons had torn them apart in their frenzy. Everywhere, bodies sank slowly, or already lay on the bottom, and as Anton contemplated them, he felt a swell of elation. For while too many of the corpses were mermen, locathahs, allies of one species or another, several were immense.

"It's working," he said. "The poison, the strategy, all of it."

"Praise be to the Queen of the Depths," replied Tu'ala'keth.

A yellow shimmer at the edge of his vision snagged Anton's attention. As he twisted his head, it flickered into two shimmers.

Slender and black, covered with luminous mosaics of purple and golden wyrms winging over a benighted sea, Jorunhast's tower constituted one wall of a dragon trap. In it, he and his comrades had snared the topaz.

Judging by the gouges on the decorations, the topaz had been trying to claw and batter its way into the human magician's spire, either to slaughter those assailing it from within or simply to crash on out the other side. Thus far, the structure had withstood the abuse. Now, however, a pair of identical topazes swam before it, wings beating, yellow eyes burning. By dint of enchantment or some innate ability, the dragon had duplicated itself.

Ignoring the crossbow bolts streaking from neighboring structures and the swimmers swirling about them jabbing with their spears, the twin wyrms launched themselves at the tower and, striking together, tore an enormous hole. The folk inside, many Dukars with the coral bonded to their bones now manifest as ridges of external armor or blades sprouting from their hands, quailed from the oncoming wyrms then flailed and thrashed as some unseen power overwhelmed them.

But one figure floated calm and untroubled. Despite the distance, Anton could just tell that it was Jorunhast, strands of his hair and beard tossing in the agitated water. He held out a crystalline bulb in either hand, as if casually proffering them to friends, and they vanished.

The display made the topazes pause for a heartbeat, maddened though they were. Anton assumed they couldn't understand the purpose of such a petty, pointless conjuring trick.

They found out when pain ripped through them, and they, too, flailed in helpless spasms. The exiled wizard had magically transported the poison into their throats.

Tu'ala'keth nodded. "We are going to win. But there are many dragons left. The sooner they die, the less harm they will cause. Shall we rejoin the battle?"

Anton grinned. "Why not?"

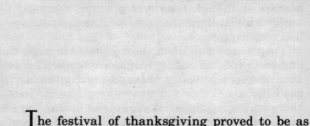

THE PRIESTS

EPILOGUE

The festival of thanksgiving proved to be as solemn an observance as any cleric might have wished, and it seemed to Anton that for the most part, Myth Nantar offered at the Bitch Queen's altars willingly enough. Even Morgan Ildacer wasn't overtly grudging.

After the prayers and sacrifices, however, solemnity gave way to jubilation, and the human enjoyed that a good deal more, especially since he didn't lack for companionship. It turned out that a good many folk regarded him as a hero even if they were vague on precisely how he'd helped Tu'ala'keth procure the poison and other weapons that had saved the city. His well-wishers gave him morsels of spiced shrimp and candied sea urchin as intoxicating as any brandy, and sea-elf ladies and mermaids—the latter coping superbly despite the obvious handicaps—tendered more intimate rewards.

But eventually even such exotic delights lost a bit of their savor. Maybe it was because he craved the sight of the sky and the touch of the sun or heard duty whispering it was past time to report to his superiors, but in any case he felt in his gut it was time to go.

Fortunately, nobody had asked for the bone mask back. He'd mastered the tricks of riding a seahorse, and he knew where Tu'ala'keth kept her animals when not in use. He could leave whenever he liked. He threw himself into a final night of revelry then swam into Umberlee's house early the following morning.

The sanctuary positively glittered with new offerings—so many that the vast majority had to sit on the floor. But that wouldn't do for his purposes. He cleared a space on the largest and most sacred of the altars then laid the greatsword down. Wordless thought surged into his mind, reminding him how brilliantly he fought with the blade in his grasp and what ecstasy it was to kill with it, pleading with him to reconsider. Then he took his hand away, and the psychic voice fell silent.

"Are you sure?" asked Tu'ala'keth.

He turned to see her floating in a doorway. In her own shrine, her own home, she had no need of silverweave or a trident, but the drowned man's hand hung on her breast as always.

"Yes," he said. "I'll never have a better sword, but I'm not myself when I use it. I'm worried that eventually I wouldn't be me even when it was in the scabbard."

"You might be something greater. If you wished, you could remain here, continue to bear the blade in Umberlee's service . . . but I see that is not what you desire."

"No. I'm sorry, but I never felt what you feel. Not once." If it wasn't quite true, it was certainly true enough.

"I know, and you have Umberlee's blessing to depart. But if you are leaving her service, you may not wear her badge. Allow me." She swam to him, murmured a prayer, and stroked his forearm with her fingertip. His all-but-forgotten octopus tattoo, inscribed when they'd first reached Dragon Isle, vanished in a flash of burning pain.

He rubbed his smarting skin. "If you'd asked, I could have erased it, and it wouldn't have stung."

"My apologies," she said, though he almost thought he heard a hint of laughter in her voice. "What will you do now? Will you stop being a spy as you have ceased serving Umberlee? Be your own man in every respect?"

He shrugged. "I'm going to have to think about it. In many ways, I'm sick of spying. But bringing down those whoresons on Tan, helping at least some of the captives to freedom, was ... satisfying. Maybe I'm not finished quite yet.

"I don't need to ask what you'll do," he continued. "Your destiny is clear. You'll go down in the annals as the greatest priestess Serôs has ever seen."

"You speak as if my work is done."

"Well, the hard part. Isn't it?"

"I have won a year, during which the shalarin people must pray at Umberlee's altars and listen to me preach whether they want to or not. It remains to be seen whether they will continue when the time expires. I suppose it depends on my eloquence. On whether I can show them the goddess as I know her to be, or failing that, at least persuade them of her limitless might and appetite for slaughtering those who neglect her worship."

"You'll manage it."

"I pray so. At least I have my chance. No one can ask more."

"Well...." He had the witless feeling, which often

came to him at partings, that he ought to say more but didn't know what. At length he settled for: "We fought well. Better than well. Checkmate's edge, we're dragon slayers! How many folk can claim that?"

She smiled. "All the warriors in Myth Nantar now but perhaps not with as much justification." Then, to his utter astonishment, she opened her long blue spindly arms for a parting embrace. He took care returning it so as not to crush the fin running down her spine.

FORGOTTEN REALMS

The New York Times bestselling author
R.A. Salvatore
brings you a new series!

The Sellswords

SERVANT OF THE SHARD

Book I

Powerful assassin Artemis Entreri tightens his grip on the streets of
Calimport, but his sponsor Jarlaxle grows ever more ambitious. Soon the
power of the malevolent Crystal Shard grows greater than them both,
threatening to draw them into a vast web of treachery from which there
will be no escape.

VOLUME TWO OF THE SELLSWORDS WILL BE AVAILABLE IN 2005!

ALSO BY R.A. SALVATORE

STREAMS OF SILVER

The Legend of Drizzt, Book V

The fifth installment in the deluxe hardcover editions of Salvatore's
classic Dark Elf novels, *Streams of Silver* continues the epic saga of Drizzt
Do'Urden™.

THE HALFLING'S GEM

The Legend of Drizzt, Book VI

The New York Times best-selling classic for the first time in a deluxe
hardcover edition that includes bonus material found nowhere else.

HOMELAND

The Legend of Drizzt, Book I

Now in paperback, the *New York Times* best-selling classic that began the
tale of one of fantasy's most beloved characters. Experience the Legend of
Drizzt from the beginning!

DRAGONS ARE DESCENDING ON THE FORGOTTEN REALMS!

THE RAGE
The Year of Rogue Dragons, Book I
RICHARD LEE BYERS

Renegade dragon hunter Dorn hates dragons with a passion few can believe, let alone match. He has devoted his entire life to killing every dragon he can find, but as a feral madness begins to overtake the dragons of Faerûn, civilization's only hope may lie in the last alliance Dorn would ever accept.

THE RITE
The Year of Rogue Dragons, Book II
RICHARD LEE BYERS

Dragons war with dragons in the cold steppes of the Bloodstone Lands, and the secret of the ancient curse gives a small band of determined heroes hope that the madness might be brought to an end.

REALMS OF THE DRAGONS
Book I
EDITED BY PHILIP ATHANS

This anthology features all-new stories by R.A. Salvatore, Ed Greenwood, Elaine Cunningham, and the authors of the R.A. Salvatore's War of the Spider Queen series. It fleshes out many of the details from the current Year of Rogue Dragons trilogy by Richard Lee Byers and includes a short story by Byers.

REALMS OF THE DRAGONS
Book II
EDITED BY PHILIP ATHANS

A new breed of Forgotten Realms authors bring a fresh approach to new stories of mighty dragons and the unfortunate humans who cross their paths.

FORGOTTEN REALMS

A brand new title from *New York Times* bestselling author Lisa Smedmen, and other great Forgotten Realms tales!

VIPER'S KISS
House of the Serpents, Book II

NEW YORK TIMES BESTSELLING AUTHOR LISA SMEDMAN

Fleeing a yuan-ti princess who has designs on your soul is bad enough, but needing her help to retrieve a dangerous artifact that could enslave the world can really ruin your day.

THE EMERALD SCEPTER
Scions of Arrabar, Book III

THOMAS M. REID

The final installment of the Scions of Arrabar Trilogy brings Vambran back home to settle once and for all the question of who will inherit the power of the great mercenary Houses of Arrabar.

MASTER OF CHAINS
The Fighters, Book I

JESS LEBOW

The first title in a new Forgotten Realms series focusing on the popular Dungeons & Dragons® game character class of Fighters. Each title will feature characters with a different exotic style of fighting. In Master of Chains, the leader of a rebellion is captured by bandits, and his chains of bondage become the only weapons he has with which to escape.

GHOSTWALKER
The Fighters, Book II

ERIK DE BIE

Each novel in The Fighters series is written as a stand-alone adventure, allowing new readers an easy entry point into the Forgotten Realms world. This novel is a classic revenge story that focuses on a man in black with ghostly powers who seeks vengeance upon those who caused his death many years ago.

STARLIGHT AND SHADOWS IS FINALLY GATHERED INTO A CLASSIC GIFT SET!

By Elaine Cunningham

"I have been a fan of Elaine Cunningham's since I read *Elfshadow*, because of her lyrical writing style."
– R.A. Salvatore

DAUGHTER OF THE DROW
Book I

Beautiful and deadly, Liriel Baenre flits through the darkness of Menzoberranzan where treachery and murder are the daily fare. Seeking something beyond the Underdark, she is pursued by enemies as she ventures towards the lands of light.

TANGLED WEBS
Book II

Exiled from Menzoberranzan, the beautiful dark elf Liriel Baenre wanders the surface world with her companion Fyodor. But even as they sail the dangerous seas of the Sword Coast, a drow priestess plots a terrible fate for them.

WINDWALKER
Book III

Liriel and Fyodor travel across the wide realms of Faerun in search of adventure and reach the homeland of Rashemen. But they cannot wander far enough to escape the vengeance of the drow, and from the deep tunnels of the Underdark, glittering eyes are watching their every move.

THE TWILIGHT GIANTS TRILOGY

Written by *New York Times* bestselling author
TROY DENNING

THE OGRE'S PACT
Book I

This attractive new re-release by multiple *New York Times* best-selling author Troy Denning, features all new cover art that will re-introduce Forgotten Realms fans to this excellent series. A thousand years of peace between giants and men is shattered when a human princess is stolen by ogres, and the only man brave enough to go after her is a firbolg, who must first discover the human king's greatest secret.

THE GIANT AMONG US
Book II

A scout's attempts to unmask a spy in his beloved queen's inner circle is her only hope against the forces of evil that rise against her from without and from within.

THE TITAN OF TWILIGHT
Book III

The queen's consort is torn between love for his son and the dark prophesy that predicts his child will unleash a cataclysmic war. But before he can take action, a dark thief steals both the boy and the choice away from him.